NASSER RABADI

THE RAVEN HILL BUTCHER COLLECTED EDITION

BOOKS 1-7 OF THE HIT

SLASHER NOVEL SERIES!

ISBN: 978-1-954931-05-3

Contents

THE CHRISTMAS MORNING MASSACRE

1

ANOTHER GIRL WENT MISSING that year.

They were both from a town called Raven Hill. They both had big brown eyes and long brown hair flowing in waves against cream-colored skin. After a few months their remains were found in scattered pieces. Then after a year the cases were both considered cold as investigators had exhausted all leads. For the new few years, no other women in Raven Hill went missing. But there was no telling if the person who did this would kill again.

Eight years later it was a story to scare children with. Somewhere along the way the mysterious killer got a name: The Raven Hill Butcher. And somewhere else along the way he took form in the minds of children: a tall slender figure with a sense of solid matter. He did not have organs on the insides as humans did. He was solid boogeyman, solid shadow, and nobody could hurt him in any way.

By the next decade most of Raven Hill had forgotten about those two girls. The shock of their deaths lost their luster to time and things in Raven Hill went on.

Both families were haunted by answerless questions. Why had their daughters been killed? Why would someone want to hurt them? Would anybody ever be held responsible?

The families hired private investigators. The families talked and discussed their kids, but neither could ever find closure. They were haunted by those unsolved questions for decades. Maybe there was a silver lining in all of it somewhere. Something good that could come of it. Something good could come from even the most miserable of situations, but it didn't seem there was anything to find.

Kids sat around campfires and recited the legends their friends and older siblings had told them. Now the stories were more imagination than fact. And the more they talked about it, the more real he became. The Raven Hill Butcher. The man who killed two identical teenage girls in Raven Hill and never killed again.

2

Snow fell lightly at first then unpleasantly fast across Raven Hill.

The houses of the gated community were all of a time and style: colonial giants with copper spires that had long since turned green. Although the house was beautiful it was a tad decrepit with windows covered in dust, with Christmas light hanging over them. Red and green bulbs fought against piling snow. The house was different: it almost had a glow.

Christy Morrison whistled, waited for her friends to arrive, and when she saw their car park, she opened the front door. As cold air drenched her, she realized her coat was open, and she zipped it on her run to the car.

Aviana, the driver, slid her glasses off and into a case. She, Julia, Bekah, Katie, and Mary brought down their bags. There was so much luggage she wondered how there was space inside the car for any of the girls.

"Hey how was the trip?" Christy said.

Aviana hugged her. "It was great."

It took two trips to bring everything in.

The big warm living room had Christy's friends in awe. Narrow slanting windows, dark browning carpet, a big television mounted to the wall above the fireplace, and ships in bottles and tiny statues across all the mantle shelves and tables and drawers. Beautiful paintings lined the walls. Some family portraits, some pictures of the sea and some of the desert. The walls were made of smooth stone. In the corner was a record player and two shelves of records. The living room led to three long halls.

Julia wiped snow off her suitcase. "This place is so big each of us could probably get two rooms."

David, Christy's brother, came into the room from the hall next to the fireplace. "There's always room in mine."

Julia gagged.

Christy rolled her eyes. "Don't be a creep. David that's Julia, that's Aviana, Mary, Katie, Bekah. Ladies, this is my brother. Come on, I'll show you to your rooms."

Christy went down the main hall, the main hall that would take them through most of the house, and the girls dragged their bags. David stayed in the living room and put on a record. *Al Hirt's Greatest Hits,* Christy could tell from a mile away.

"Don't blame me if you get lost. My family's territorial as hell about the rooms, so we're a little all over the place."

"Your house is so gorgeous," Katie said. "Like I can't believe how pretty it is."

"Thanks," Christy said, then noticed Julia, ahead of them, straightening out a picture frame and wiping off a little dust with a napkin from her pocket. "Are you cleaning up?"

Julia smiled. "You don't know how much a crooked frame irritates me. I almost stayed behind to straighten up your whole living room."

Christy opened a door to a bedroom. One of the rooms she'd already cleaned for her guests. This room was plain: bunkbeds with white sheets under a window, a dresser with a mirror, and a nightstand.

"There are more rooms upstairs, and one down in the basement. It's not as nice, but you get your own bathroom—"

"I'll take the downstairs room," Mary said.

"Oh, of course you will," Julia said.

"Julia, you take like an hour in there. I'm not dealing with that all weekend."

"So who wants this room? It's the same floor as mine."

"I'll take this one," Aviana said, stepping inside. Then: "Wait, which one's further from your brother?"

"Well he's on this same floor.

"Never mind, I'm going upstairs."

"Yeah, me too," Katie said. "He gives me the creeps."

"I'll just stay here," Julia said. She was straightening out the already made bed.

Bekah shrugged. "I guess I will too."

The girls went down the spiraling stairs to the basement. The steps screamed loudly.

"Christy, I wanted to tell you something," Aviana said.

"Hmmm?"

"You remember that guy I told you about?"

"Which one?"

"Ben."

"Oh, right."

"He finally asked me out."

"Oh no," Katie said. "Not another one."

"Shut up, Katie."

"I'm serious. You cycle through them so fast I can't keep track."

The basement was big, but most of its space was taken up by junk, old dusty boxes and containers, old dressers, and anything else that her family stuffed into it over the past hundred years. Spiderwebs grew over everything, even rusty tools thrown into a corner. A hallway, also filled with junk, gave way to a dark cramped room at the very end with no doors, which was the laundry room.

"Good thing Jules is upstairs," Christy said. "She'd lose her mind down here. She'd probably spend the whole weekend cleaning."

Christy opened the door nearest the laundry room. It would be Mary's room.

"What do you think?"

Mary set her bags down just inside the door.

"It's nice."

Christy pointed to her right. "The bathroom's over there."

Mary laid down on the bed then sighed and closed her eyes. "This trip was only an hour, but can you believe how exhausted I am? I'm gonna nap, let's hope I don't get lost on the way back up."

As they ascended the twisting staircase, Christy said, "Such a workout, isn't it? Getting around in this place."

"It's brutal," Katie said.

"Well it's much needed," Aviana said. "I've been eating like shit all year."

They passed through the main floor then up another flight of stairs to the second floor.

"Being up here probably won't keep you away from David for too long. He'd walk through a bed of flames if he saw ass on the other end."

Katie looked out the window over the back yard, a blanket of untouched snow. "This view is gorgeous. I could watch snow fall all day."

Aviana came across the room to peek out the window but tripped over her duffle bag.

"Ouch. Where did that thing come from?"

"If you had your glasses on you'd have seen."

"Oh shut up."

Christy walked away, and all down the hall she could hear them going back and forth about glasses and car crashes.

A few minutes later, in the kitchen, when Christy looked through the cabinets, she noticed the door to the back yard was gaping open. She was chilled and went to the sliding door and saw that the back yard was now disturbed. A trail of footprints wandered into the house and tracked melting snow around the kitchen to the dining room.

"Huh?"

She shut the door and locked it.

3

Christy went to her room and left the door cracked open. The curtains, bedspread, blankets, and pillow cases were black, her favorite color. Posters of her favorite movies were taped to the walls, she had done that six or seven years ago when she thought it was cool, now it was ugly because the posters had torn and curled and some were yellowed. Next to her door was a bookshelf of romance novels. On one of her massive dressers, she kept a single flower in a pot.

Who had gone outside? she wondered. *Whose footsteps were those?*

But she didn't think about it for long. She looked on her dresser for the new pack of ping pong balls and the pack of red plastic cups she bought for this weekend and took them down to the living room. Then she wheeled in the ping pong table from another room and opened it.

Christy set up the table, minus the beer for now, arranging the cups into triangle formations.

Then there were soft and steady footsteps down the hall.

CREEEAAAK!

Footsteps again, but there was nobody there.

"Hello?" Christy said.

"Hey," David said from the other hallway. "You need any help setting up?"

"Not now, I'm almost done. Did you go outside earlier?"

"Yeah, I had to run to my car. Why?"

"I think you left the door open."

"My bad, sis."

Mary woke up and had to pee.

She yawned and sat up and noticed a set of thin icy tracks leading into her room then leaving. it wasn't all melted yet. Somebody had been in here with her, and had been here recently...

Maybe Christy came back to check on me...

Mary took off her shirt and changed into a pink tank top. It was nice and toasty in the Morrison basement. Mary stretched, yawned again, then heard a noise. She opened the door fully to see Christy coming down the stairs. Her face, even at the distance, was very bright red, like an apple in June. Christy bit her lip, moved hair out of her eyes.

"I was just about to wake you. How'd you sleep?"

"Better than I thought I would. Usually I don't sleep well far from home."

"Well I'm getting beer pong set up."

"Hey, did you come down here earlier to check on me?"

"No... why?"

"Someone did. There's snow on my floor, see? The floor's all wet."

She walked past Mary and looked into the room. "Maybe it was one of the others."

They started to leave the room, then Mary stopped in the doorway. "Oh, Christy, before I forget, I made you something. An early Christmas gift, since I won't be seeing you again until next semester starts."

"Thank you, Mary," Christy said. "You didn't have to do that."

The girls went back into the room, and Mary grabbed her purse. "Now close your eyes."

Christy shut them and smiled.

"Hands."

Christy did so.

Mary put the gift in her hands. "Open your eyes."

Christy examined the baby blue clay cactus in her hands. "Adorable."

"It's a ring holder, but if you don't wear rings you can just put it on your dresser or something."

"I love it." Christy hugged her. "Thank you."

Christy wondered if David had gone down there.

What would he be doing checking on Mary?

Snow was coming down in handfuls. No signs of stopping. In fact, now it was well over a foot, and she wondered how high it would go before it became a problem.

"Do you ever remember it snowing so much?"

"Can't say I have," Mary said. "And I pray Aviana doesn't drive us in snow this bad, she'll kill us all."

They went back to Bekah and Julia's room and knocked on the door.

"Come in," Bekah said.

Christy opened the door.

Bekah was looking through her suitcase while Julia slept. "Hey."

"How long's she been out?"

"Not long. She went over every inch of our room, she almost tried to clean the ceiling but there was no way I was gonna hold her on my shoulders."

"Let's wake her up. It's time to get wasted."

After Julia was up they went to the living room, and Bekah and Julia and Mary waited for Christy while she went off to get Aviana and Katie.

"Could you imagine living in a place like this?" Julia said.

Mary sat down next to Bekah and said, "Does anyone here know how to use a record player?"

"Are you serious?" Julia said. "You just drop the needle."

"Let's put something on."

Julia looked through the boxes. They were mostly jazz until she found *Christmas Hits!* and put it on the turntable, then lowered the needle to the edge of the vinyl.

A moment of static, then music blared through.

Julia winced. “Way too much crackling. These records need to be cleaned.”

Christy came back with Aviana and Katie and David, who was carrying two cases of forty-eight beers.

“Let’s get this started.,” David opened one then poured it into a cup.

He watched them.

He pressed his eye to the hole in the floor and looked at the kids in the living room and tightened his grip on the jagged blade set in aging wood. Excitement filled him. It would be fun—and soon. A wide smile crept across his face. It had been such a long time, maybe he would be rusty, but it would come back to him.

“Is this like, where you grew up, Christy?” the girl with blonde shoulder-length hair asked.

“No, Jules, but it’s just been in my family forever. My uncle owns it and let me borrow it this weekend.” Christy threw a ping pong ball on the table and it landed in a cup. She drank it in one chug.

Christy was beautiful. long coppery hair parted in the middle, freckles splattered on her skin, brown eyes gleaming even from the tiny hole where he watched.

Another girl bounced a ping pong ball and it hit the rim of a cup then fell to the floor. “Ah, screw it,” she said then drank anyways.

“Hey, no cheating,” the only boy among them said.

“You’d make it if you had your glasses on.”

“Fuck you and fuck the glasses.”

He moved away from the hole in the floor then stood up.

It was almost time.

"Mary, don't be a buzzkill," Christy handed her a ping pong ball.

Mary grabbed it. "I don't know, "Last time I tried it, it was…"

"Yeah, yeah, you hated it," Aviana said. "We get it."

"It's one drink," Katie said. "You'll live."

Mary rolled her eyes and gave in. She went to the end of the table and bounced it into a cup. She took one small sip, grimaced, then forced it down. "It tastes awful."

"It's an acquired taste," David said.

Mary kept a disgusted face after a second sip. "God, you guys are the worst."

"Look at her face," Katie said.

"By the ways," Julia said, "Christy, do you have a brush for your records? Do you hear all those crackles? They're not supposed to be doing that."

"A brush?"

"Forget it."

CREAK!

A hollow prolonged creak came from up above.

Christy looked at her friends to see if they heard it too.

"There's no one upstairs, is there?" Mary said.

"No, no, the house just does that sometimes. It's old."

"It's haunted," David said. "I'll tell you all about it tonight."

4

IT WAS HARDLY FOUR o'clock and the ping pong table had already been cleared of its cups.

They sat on the couches directly in front of the fireplace, the record had ended long ago and none of them had bothered to flip it over because they were watching *Rudolph The Red-Nosed Reindeer* on TV and talking.

"We can break out the heavy stuff later," Christy said.

"Oh I don't feel so good," Mary said, clutching her stomach. "I think I'm gonna throw up."

"You barely drank anything."

"And it still hurts. I'm dizzy."

Julia grabbed a can out of the box, leaned over the back of the couch to Mary's shoulder, and cracked it open. "We all had at least one whole can, you need one too."

Mary inched back. "Knock it off, I already had one."

Julia opened it and held it out to Mary, who pushed it away. Julia drank it herself.

"I'm hungry," Christy said. "I'm gonna throw a frozen pizza in the oven."

"Hey David," Julia said, "is it really haunted?"

"Well, I guess I could tell you about it. It happened a long time ago."

Surprisingly, the girls were eager to hear what David had to say, and they all turned to him.

"Now I don't want to scare you girls," he said, "but I'll have to be honest about The Raven Hill Butcher. They never caught him."

"That guy from what?" Mary asked. "Like, the nineteen-forties? If he's even still out there he's ancient."

"Well the truth is that The Butcher isn't human."

“You sound fucking retarded,” Bekah said.

“Let me start at the beginning, then it’ll make sense. The first family to live int his place, back before it belonged to our family, was murdered. Those rooms they died in are bad luck, that’s why my family never uses them and left them for all of you.”

Nobody said anything.

“There was one kid who didn’t die. Somehow he survived his injuries and he became The Butcher.”

A draft passed through the kitchen. Christy felt a cool breeze cutting through the hot air.

She turned into a hall and went upstairs, a little chilled, and found the thermostat. Somehow it was lowered from seventy-five to forty-two.

Hollow footfalls came from down the hall. She turned her head.

The footsteps ended, and for a moment, maybe less, she was terrified. But… *This house is old, it just makes noises sometimes.*

Christy twisted it back to seventy-five, then went to her bedroom for a sweater. It was red and green with reindeer lifting Santa’s sleigh through the air in the dead of night, surrounded by dozens of snowflakes.

CREEEEEAK!

Christy turned her attention abruptly to the door. Chills crawled under her skin. There was somebody out there. She was sure of it.

In the hall, she looked right then left then right again. Christy was all alone in the hall. For all she knew, she was the only person in the entire house. She looked over her shoulder every few steps in the hallway.

Christy looked through one of the windows. It was the most snow she had ever seen. At three or four feet tall it was a barricade. A blockade sealing them into the house. And it was only growing bigger. She wondered what her guests would do if it were ten feet tall, which it would certainly hit at this pace, when it came time to leave after the weekend was over. But it was only Friday and it was not time to think about leaving yet.

"Should I cook a third pizza?" Christy said.

"Ugh, this is all gonna go straight to my thighs. Do not let me eat so much, do not let me have more if you make a third," Julia said. She wiped crumbs from the table onto a napkin and tossed it in the trash.

"Don't worry about it," David said. "I can help you work it off."

"Yuck. I wouldn't touch you with a thirty-nine-and-a-half-foot-pole."

"Even if my heart grows three sizes?"

"Sorry," Christy said. "If I knew my brother would be this weird I wouldn't have let him stay this weekend."

David left awkwardly. "Geez."

"He reminds me of this guy I was seeing last year," Aviana said. "I stopped taking his calls, then he keeps calling. Then at school I'd always catch him looking at me. It was so gross."

5

DAVID WENT TO HIS bedroom, which was on the main floor and down the hall which passed by the fireplace. He shut the door, turned on the radio, then laid down in bed. His room was rather void since he didn't keep as many things here as his sister did. Most of his things were back home and not here in the mansion. His room only had a bed, a dresser, and a desk with a radio.

His eyes shut. He thought he heard somebody moving around in the hall. *Christy, what do you want?* David wondered and almost asked, but decided not to. The footsteps eventually passed.

Carol of the Bells came through the radio.

He yawned, turned on his side, thought about grabbing another beer or maybe another slice of pizza if there was any left, but his bed was cool and comfortable and sleep was washing over him, so he stayed and listened to the pretty music that put him to sleep.

Hark how the bells sweet silver bells all seem to say throw cares away.

He yawned again. A dream was forming.

Christmas is here, bringing good cheer to young and old, meek and the bold.

Hours later, in the living room, with the lights dimmed, they watched *It's a Wonderful Life* and drank some warm beers.

Cold was finding its way into the house from the four-foot obstruction of snow, sneaking through the cracks in the Morrison house's old walls. Although the temperature was on seventy-five, the girls were still chilled.

"Christy?" Mary said.

"Yeah?"

"Were people really, um, killed in here?"

"What? Of course not. It was just a thing our dad made up to scare him. Nobody was killed here."

"Okay. Good. I hate stuff like that."

"Mary you're so gullible."

"Yeah, but The Raven Hill Butcher was real," Julia said. "A couple girls did die around here. And their murders weren't solved."

"Mary," Bekah said, "are you five years old? I mean you'd have to be stupid to be scared of fucking ghost story."

"Come on, there's no reason to be rude," Katie said. "Bekah..."

"What?"

"So what if she's scared?"

Bekah shrugged. "It's funny, it's dumb."

"Bekah, your mom should've bent a coat hanger in the bathroom at 3 a.m. and scraped you out. You are such a rude bitch and I am so fucking tired of you. You should just go kill yourself."

Bekah ran out of the room without saying another word.

"Bekah." Christy yelled, then looked at Mary. "What the fuck is wrong with you?"

"She's been a bitch to me this entire trip. All semester, even. You should've seen her in the car, she just..."

"That was the first time I saw her be rude to you."

"Well in the car—"

"I don't care about the car. You don't say something like that."

"Whatever."

"I'll check on her," Julia said. "I'll be right back."

"I think I'm getting tired," Katie said. "I'm going to bed."

"Same here," Aviana said.

"Well, okay then," Christy said. "Goodnight, girls."

Christy and Mary were the only ones left in the living room. Christy watched her friends go down the hall and disappear. Somehow, less than a minute had passed when she heard their footsteps on the second floor... shouldn't they have been on the staircase still?

It's a Wonderful Life finished thirty minutes later. After the credits rolled, they both stood up and stretched and yawned and looked at the window. Chills crawled up their spines.

"Woah." Mary traced her hand on the window.

Mary said goodnight to Christy then double checked that she was going the right way to get to the stairs.

In a distant part of her mind, she thought, *Such a storm, might it be Krampus? I wonder which of us is the naughty child he came to punish. Maybe it's me. Maybe it's all of us.*

She imagined the horns from Krampus's goat head emerging from the endless crypt of darkness and jamming into her abdomen. She imagined him waiting for her in her bedroom across the basement, hooves covered in melting snow, shedding fur on her blankets, red sack for him to stuff her in.

Quit it. There is no Krampus.

But you've been very bad, you all have. And he's gonna punish you.

It was so dark in the basement that she crossed her fingers and hoped she didn't stub a toe or knock into anything as she made her way to that soft, gentle light barely emerging from that one inch space beneath the bedroom door.

When she was inside the bedroom, Mary opened her suitcase, then stripped to her bra and underwear. As she took off one sock, she paused

CREEEAAAK!

Somebody was coming down the stairs. Heavy steps, much heavier than her friends.

She waited.

Whoever was coming across the basement did so quickly, as if familiar with it and the surroundings.

"Christy? Um, David? That you David?"

Somebody opened the door.

A man dressed in an old dusty Santa Claus costume that must have been stored away in the attic for years came into the light. He held a foot-long candy cane which he then extended to her.

"Awe, David, thank you. You know, *I* don't think you're creepy like the others. And I like your costume. It's cute but a little dirty. Want me to help you clean it up?"

Silence.

The black mask over his face hid him completely except for sunken eyes.

"I know you're trying to scare me but it isn't gonna work."

No reply.

"Nothing to say, huh?" She turned the candy cane around in her hands then sucked on the end of it. "I love having sweets before bed. Want some?"

He shook his head.

"Why don't you take that costume off and come over here?"

He sat down, put his hands on her legs, then grabbed the cane and jammed it down her throat so far that she couldn't scream. Her fists beat weakly against his chest. Her eyes shut as she tried to process the pain and think of a way to fight back.

His hands clamped around her throat. She wished for air—any air at all, even if it was the frozen winds separated from her by the thin walls. The room spun. Her eyes twitched then closed, stuttered open, then fluttered closed. The last thing she saw was the long blade with a faded wooden handle. She mouthed words that did not reach the air, then she was gone.

6

THE HOUSE WAS CALM with stillness through the halls. wind beat against the windows and screamed over the rooftop that pointed against the sky full of dark clouds massed together. Cold set in past the fading heat.

In the bottom bunk, Julia turned her pillow over to the cool side and then turned onto her left. She was drifting away, when—

"Are you awake?" Bekah asked, looking down from the top bunk.

Julia's eyes creaked open. She looked up to see her with thin moonlight filtering through the window; Bekah brushed her curly brown hair from her eyes. "Yeah. You all right?"

"I can't sleep."

For a moment the girls were silent because there was the sound of footsteps in the hallway and they thought somebody was going to enter the room, but the person did not. Whoever it was went straight past their door, through the hall, and, as they imagined, up the stairs.

"Who else is up?" Bekah said.

"I don't know."

"I know I'm a bitch," Bekah said. "I know it. And honestly I *have* thought about killing myself before. I'm not saying that for sympathy. I just. I don't know. I think about it sometimes."

They talked about it for a few more minutes then Bekah rolled back over and said she was gonna try and sleep, thanks, Jules, for letting me get it off my chest.

Julia laid on her back and stared at the white bars supporting the mattress. The room was quiet except for Bekah's tiny snores.

Julia shut her eyes, tossed and turned, but she could not return to the very edge of sleep she had previously been climbing over when Bekah had started talking to her. She had been so close to falling over the edge, but now she was wide awake.

I wish I could sleep.

She tried to fall into the blackness behind her eyes, tried to dream, tried to tell herself what to dream. It never worked, but sometimes daydreaming knocked her right out. She was comfortable, very comfortable, but sleep was avoiding her.

"Bekah?"

No response.

Some weekend this is turning out to be. Day one has majorly sucked ass. There's gotta be something fun around here.

Julia sat up, slipped out of bed, and went to the door.

After one last glance to Bekah, she went back to her bottom bunk and fixed the covers. It would irritate her so much to know that there was an unmade bed. She fixed the covers, straightened out any wrinkles, then went back to the door.

Julia stepped into the pitch black hall. There was one single light on. The lights in the hallways were divided into sections, and there were multiple switches to light up one hallway. She thought she remembered them being all the way down at the other end, and instead went the opposite way to the living room. The living room was a mess, with all the cups and beer cans scattered, and some beer spilled out on the ping pong table and dripping onto the floor. She would have made too much noise if she cleaned up everything right now.

In the morning, she thought, *I'll help clean.*

She found switches on one of the walls, but didn't turn them on. She didn't know exactly where she wanted to go or what she expected to do. She still hadn't explored the place yet, still didn't know where everyone's rooms were at. Then, as she turned around, something crunched under her foot.

An empty chocolate bar wrapper. There was another one a few feet down too.

You know, it's not that hard to find a garbage can people. But what do I expect from people who can't even clean their vinyl?

Julia laid on her stomach on the couch. *Let's see if I can sleep here.*

Minutes ticked away; she was more awake here than in her bunk. She did all she could, moved into every different position she could find, daydreamed, cleared her mind, counted sheep, but nothing could bring her sleep. So she stood up and walked around, looking at the little statues of penguins, snow globes, ships in bottles, and other little trinkets and knickknacks. Then she went to the window and looked out at the world. The snow was calming down. Instead of fistfuls of snow falling, it was now a soft trickle. But the snow was about five feet high and untouched. The streets were not cleaned and it would be impossible to go through it. Their ride was completely covered.

I wonder when they'll clean the streets. Can they clean the streets when it's like this? I've never seen anything like this. I hope we aren't here that long.

But she had to admit that the unblemished sea of white was beautiful. It *was* a White Christmas, which she had hoped for. It hadn't snowed yet a week into December, and it only started to come down once she and the others left campus for the Morrison house, an idea that had been Christy's. And it had been a fun idea, but now being here she realized it wasn't so great.

Julia yawned; maybe sleep would come now. Maybe.

She turned away from the winter wonderland and stepped on another wrapper.

"Seriously?"

Then footsteps upstairs. Somebody else was up.

"Hello?" Julia said. Then: "You idiot, they can't hear you from here."

A breeze crept up her back. She thought she heard another step being taken directly above her, and wondered what Aviana or Katie was up to.

Through a hall she had not been through yet, the one next to the fireplace, she made a left past two beautiful paintings of the ocean. A door far down on her right was cracked open and there was dull light flowing water-like into the hallway. The hallway was different in the raven darkness, even with that small smudge of light shining at the end. In total darkness it seemed like something out of *Dracula.* It seemed like a hallway in a castle, and soon Dracula's coffin would open, and he'd creep into town at night to suck blood from unsuspecting people.

Listen to them, Julia thought, *the children of the night. What music they make!*

She came to the door slowly, peeked inside, and saw David laying on his bed, looking at the ceiling, listening to Christmas music coming through the radio. *I Saw Mommy Kissing Santa Claus.*

He turned to see her as she opened the door wide.

"Julia?"

"Unless I have a twin." Julia closed his door behind herself. "I couldn't sleep."

"Me either. I napped earlier and now I'm wide awake. And bored out of my mind."

"I've been wandering around the house." Julia sat next to him on his bed. "Have you seen the snow outside?"

"It's insane how hard it's coming down. Looks like you're stuck here with us."

"That might not be a bad thing."

"Why couldn't you sleep?"

"Oh who knows. Just one of those nights."

"So out of all the places to be, you visit me?"

"Yeah, well, you were the only one awake," she said.

David stood up, went to his dresser, and grabbed a candy bar out of a box. "Want one?"

"Were you the one who threw those wrappers on the floor?"

"Wasn't me."

"Well no thanks," she said. "Maybe if you tell me another one of your stories it'll put me to sleep."

He returned to his bed and sat next to her. "What, you want me to bore you?"

Her hands were interlocked under her chin. She sat cross legged on the bed, looking at David with her pretty blue eyes. David was red. He fidgeted with a loose thread on the covers.

Julia leaned back on her hands. "What did you ask Santa for Christmas this year?"

"Nothing until about a minute ago when I wished we were standing outside the house."

"Outside the house?"

"Yep."

"Standing in snow up to here?" Julia said, raising her arm up as high as it could go.

"Of course."

"What for?"

"Because there's a mistletoe out there."

Julia rolled her eyes.

"I should've hung one in here."

Julia pulled him in with both hands for a kiss. It lasted for half a minute then she let go of him. "There you go. We didn't have to die in the snow for it. Merry Christmas." Then she took her shirt off and he climbed on top of her.

7

IT WAS A DARK morning.

The snow had picked up again despite slowing down in the night, and the sun was completely shielded behind thick black clouds. There was no sunlight or warmth to melt the snow.

Christy Morrison woke up, turned over, then slept again. She slept dreamlessly.

After a while, she was awake again and thirsty. When she stood up, colors flashed in front of her eyes. She caught herself on the bedpost, rubbed her eyes, then she was fine. Footsteps upstairs squeaked above her. Somebody must have been up already.

It was Saturday morning, they only had each other until Monday morning, or perhaps longer now, being that the snow was insane outside and it did not look as if anybody was coming to clear the streets any time soon, and she wanted to make the most of it.

Christy went downstairs. She found a candy bar wrapper in the kitchen, picked it up, threw it away. *Must've been David,* she thought.

Christy looked through the glass kitchen doors that led to the open back yard. It made her feel small, made her feel like a child again, when even four inches of snow seemed like four feet to her. She remembered when she'd crave the snow so there'd be the possibility of a snow day. That was the complete opposite of when she learned to drive, because when that time came, she despised even the smallest snowfall. But this morning it took her back to being a child. Christy missed when it was winter break and she'd play in the snow with David, have snowball fights with the neighbor kids, watch Christmas movies and specials all the time without thinking or worrying about an upcoming semester of college, and seeing Christmas decorations on every building and in every store just felt so different when she was younger compared to now.

Most of all, she had loved the feeling of not knowing what day it was, back when she hadn't known winter break would ever end, it felt like that would always be life. It felt as if she'd be a little girl forever. Without even the slightest notice, those days stopped abruptly. She hadn't a clue what year that actually was, but at some point, she and David stopped playing in the snow, and the neighbor kids stopped having snowball fights, and eventually she came to realize what the dates were.

Christy thought to wake Mary first, wanting to talk to her about yesterday and feeling bad for her being the only girl in the basement. She descended the stairs; she came to the dark basement and searched her hand blindly on the left wall for the light switch. Lights stuttered on with static noise. Christy went to Mary's door, making a mental note to bring up the laundry.

KNOCK! KNOCK! KNOCK!

Quietness.

"Mary? You awake yet?"

When Mary did not reply, Christy opened the door. What she saw was a neatly kept room outside of the candy wrapper on the bed. The suitcase was open, untouched, with the outfits she had been wearing yesterday tossed lazily to the ground. There was one little pink sock on top of the pile. The other pink sock was missing. The bed was still made. The sheets were tucked into the sides. It hadn't been slept in.

"Mary? Where are you?"

She looked around the room, but there was nowhere for her to be… the place was empty, expect for a candy wrapper on the floor.

A sweater and jacket were on the bed, on the floor were pants, a shirt, and one single sock turned inside out. Her belongings in the suitcase were definitely not touched, the clothes were all folded neatly, and her bed was definitely not slept in.

Maybe she's showering, Christy thought then left the room, but as she approached the bathroom she realized two things: there was no light coming from under the door, and there was no sound at all of water coming from the shower. Then she wondered if the pipes were too frozen to shower if she even tried.

"Mary are you down here?"

Maybe she went to sleep in someone else's room, maybe she was too scared down here or lonely.

Christy went back upstairs, back to the kitchen. *"Mary? Mary?"*

She half expected Mary to suddenly pop up from out of nowhere and say, "Here I am!" but that didn't happen.

"Mary?" she called again, going down a hall.

Silence. Only silence.

She went to check on her friends. Bekah and Julia were closest, so Christy headed for them. She came to their room just in time to catch Julia straightening a picture on the wall before opening the door.

"Jules, good morning."

"Oh, hey, morning."

"Were you with Mary?"

"No, why? Were you looking for her?"

"Yeah, she's probably upstairs, she wasn't in her room. Her bed didn't even look slept in."

"It didn't? Well, me and Bekah heard footsteps last night in the hall, so yeah, she probably went upstairs to Aviana or Katie and was too tired to walk *alllll* the way back."

"Is Bekah up yet?"

"No I don't think so. What're you up to?"

"I dunno, was about to make breakfast and put on some records or something."

"I'll wake her up."

Julia went into the room and shut the door; Christy turned towards the stairway and walked up. On the second floor, she looked through the window that started the hall. For a moment she wondered if Mary had gone outside, but the snow in the back was undisturbed and now towered, oh God, how high was that now? She was positive that even if Mary tried, she wouldn't have been able to open any of the doors into that outrageous mountain of snow.

The clouds were beginning to part and that was a great thing. Christy couldn't feel the warmth of the sun just yet, but it was going to come soon, she was sure.

He watched through a cracked open door. He hid in the shadows of the room and pressed his face to the edge and watched her. Christy, he had come to know her name was, opened the door on her right, and a few minutes later she went into the room on her left. He couldn't hear her conversations but knew what—who—she was after.

"What do you mean you haven't seen her?" Christy asked. "If you haven't then where is she?"

Aviana looked at her with curious eyes. "Are you joking with me?"

"No, really. I don't know where she is. Her bed hasn't been slept in, Julia hasn't seen her, Katie hasn't, Bekah was asleep but I'm pretty sure she hadn't seen her either."

"Did you ask David?"

"No… come on, what would Mary be doing with my brother?"

"I don't know, but you still can't find her and we haven't seen her."

Katie came into the doorway next to Christy. "How can she be missing in a snowed-in house?"

"This place is huge," Aviana stood up. "Come on, let's find her."

"*Mary? Mary?*" Christy said as they came off the stairs.

In the kitchen, Julia was looking through the fridge. "Hey ladies, good morning."

"Is Bekah up yet?"

"Nope, the sleepyhead is snoring away."

Aviana and Katie followed Christy past Julia. They went to Bekah and Julia's room, turned the knob, and went in. Bekah was asleep on her stomach, mouth open and dripping out drool. The room was as tidy as Christy expected from Julia. The only mess was Bekah herself.

"Bekah? Wake up," Christy said. She climbed halfway up the ladder to her bunk then shook her. *"Bekah, come on."*

Bekah shut her eyes tighter without opening them, then turned away. "Huh? What?"

"Wake up. Have you seen Mary?"

"Mary?"

"Yes, Mary. Did you see her last night?"

Bekah finally opened her eyes, stretched, wiped her drool with the back of her hand. "What do you want now?"

"Did you see her last night?"

Bekah yawned again, looked from Christy to Aviana and Katie then back to Christy. She stretched again. "What do you mean did I see her last night?"

"We can't find her."

"She's not in her room?"

"Her bed doesn't even look slept in."

"Where's Julia?"

"In the kitchen."

"None of you saw her this morning?"

"No."

"Oh. Well I don't know."

"Let's ask David," Christy said, coming off the ladder.

In the hall the girls bumped into Julia.

"Did you find her?" Julia asked.

"No, we're going to ask David."

"Well I don't think he'd know."

"Why's that?"

"He just wouldn't."

The girls went to the living room and from there the hallway on the left took them to his room. His door was shut. Christy knocked, waited for an answer, and was a little worried that he wasn't up yet. Was he missing too? Were David and Mary both gone? Christy's heart beat as loud as a hammer against a brick wall.

She knocked again. "David? I'm coming in."

Christy turned the knob. David was asleep, his arm outstretched over half of his mattress as if an invisible woman was there with him. Then she noticed a pink sock on the floor, picked it up, and turned to her friends. "Um… this is her sock…"

"How do you know?" Aviana asked.

"There was only one pink sock in her room. Here's the other one."

"So she *was* with him?" Katie asked.

"Explains the footsteps we heard last night Julia, doesn't it?"

Christy shook her brother awake. "Where is she, David? Where is she?"

David woke up, looking around the room of girls, then stared at his sister. "Where's who? What?"

"Mary's sock is in your room." Christy tossed it to him. "Why is it in your room?"

"I don't know what you're talking about."

"Whatever you did was bad enough that we can't find her now."

"I don't know what you're talking about, I didn't even see *Mary* last night. I don't think I even remembered her name."

"About this tall." Christy raised her hand to her shoulder. "Black hair, dimples, slept in the basement. Pink sock that's also in your room."

"Come on, Christy, what the hell do you think is going on?"

"I don't know but it had to be you."

"Why'd it have to be me?"

Christy rolled her eyes. "Oh God I didn't want to have to say this…"

"Say what?"

"I know you went to her room when she was asleep. After you went to your car and you tracked snow all over the kitchen then her room, she asked me who did it. I told her I didn't know, but that was to make you look like less of a pervert. Why did you go to her room? You left tracks, I know you did it."

"Christy, are you insane or what? You know damn well where I went. I went out the front door, grabbed my wallet from my car, and went back to my room. That's when I found you setting up beer pong. I never went downstairs."

"You went out the front…" Christy trailed off. *Then who was in the back yard?*

"Yes, I went out the front," David said, then looked at Christy's friends. "I really don't know what she's talking about."

"Then who tracked snow in her room?" Christy turned to her friends and asked. "Did any of you go back outside since you got here?"

Her friends all said no.

Suddenly, Christy had a very bad feeling in her stomach.

She looked back at David. "So you really didn't see her last night?"

"No he didn't," Julia said. "I know he didn't. I was with him last night."

"What do you mean you were *with* him?"

"I… was wandering the house, I couldn't sleep, he was up, and we—I fell asleep in his room."

"Oh gosh, I can't believe this," Christy said. Then, when Christy saw the pile of candy wrappers on his dresser: "And the candy wrappers? There was one in her room, a little piece of plastic on the floor."

"Does nobody else eat candy in this house?" David asked. "Why don't you just leave me alone?"

"Because I have no idea where my friend is."

"Then go find her. If she isn't in her room, there are a million other places to look."

Christy, Aviana, Katie, and Bekah left to find her. Julia stayed behind to talk to David. She shut the door then said, "You really don't know anything, right?"

"Oh come on, you were in here with me. You don't believe me?"

"I know, I know, it's just the sock…"

"That could've been anybody's. I don't know. I really don't."

"It would be funny if this whole time she's just taking a hot shower."

"And you haven't seen her either?"

"As far as I know, none of us have seen her since the argument last night."

"There was an argument?"

"Eh, kinda sorta. Just Bekah and Mary at each other's throats again. You should've seen them on the car ride. It's a whole thing with those two."

"Oh geez."

"I just hope Mary doesn't ruin the whole weekend. Yesterday was lame and today is already starting off awful."

"Eh, she'll come out of her hiding spot eventually. Mary can't hide forever."

8

"I'LL GO CHECK THE basement again," Christy said, "maybe she was in the bathroom. I didn't go inside there but I thought the light was off… maybe one of you can double check this floor and another one of you can go upstairs?"

Katie and Aviana looked at each other. "Nope," they said together.

"What?"

"This place totally gives me the creeps."

"Fine, then both of you go upstairs together."

Christy watched them go up, then she went downstairs.

There's nothing to be scared of. She just wants to prank us all. That's her idea of payback for… for whatever. I should've known that with so many friends over, there was bound to be an argument and ruin everything. Now look at us, what kind of weekend is this? I hope Mary knows that all she's doing is being a pain in my—

"Mary?"

The lights were still on in the basement, but were off in the bathroom. She pushed the door open and called for Mary. No answer. The curtains were pulled back on the tub and it was completely empty, not even a drop of water underneath the shower-head. It hadn't been used in a while.

"Mary, where are you?"

Christy was growing hot with worry.

"This isn't fun. It's not funny."

She shut the bathroom door, then went across the basement to Mary's room. Where was she hiding? Was she down the hall? Was she in one of the other rooms?

In Mary's room, not a thing had been touched. The clothes and sock still lay in their spot, the wrapper was still near the bed, and the bag wasn't touched. She tried to figure out how the other sock ended up in David's room if Julia had been with him. Julia could have been lying, but why would she? No, that couldn't have been it. Maybe Mary was in there before Julia. But then where did she go? Christy couldn't think of how it fit together. If Mary hadn't slept here then where had she been all night?

Now she wasn't just worried, but terrified. It didn't feel like a game or a trick or a prank anymore, it felt like something much worse than that.

She checked the laundry room. She hurried to find the thread hanging from the lightbulb, pulled it, then quickly looked at her feet to make sure there were no bugs nearby. She had once stepped on a roach down here and was terrified of the laundry room ever since. But there were no bugs, and there was no Mary. She hoped she could've found Mary here hiding, or somehow asleep, maybe she came to wash something and suddenly slept. But that was not just silly but stupid, she had one whole outfit that needed to be washed.

Christy left the laundry room.

She must be in one of these rooms.

"This is the worst game of hide and seek ever," Christy said, hoping Mary would hear. "I hope you know there're bugs in there. In each of those rooms. Lots of spiders, roaches, and... dammit Mary, come out *now.* Come on, stop hiding."

Christy sighed.

No response.

Her stomach twisted in a knot. She was scared that something bad had happened to Mary. The footprints in the back yard and the open door flashed in her mind. Then she remembered what David said, *I went out the front door.*

Dammit then who came in from the back? Who tracked their footprints and snow down to Mary?

She twisted the handle of the nearest basement room, looked into the dark abyss, and went inside to look for her friend. The room was dusty; there was one light, similar to the laundry room, and when she yanked on the chain the light came on, and she saw a roach on the ceiling and jumped back and screamed.

She backed away slowly, not wanting to take her eyes off the monster on the ceiling, and did a quick glance into the room to be sure Mary wasn't hiding or asleep in the room. Nope. No Mary. Only a treadmill with webs over it and some dusty weights and exercise mats that nobody had touched in a decade. Mary definitely wasn't sleeping with the bugs and empty old water bottles.

Christy was sure as hell not turning the light back off and risking getting near the bug. Once she was out of the room she slammed the door shut.

She looked down at the other rooms she needed to look in. "You've got to be here somewhere."

"I'm getting a beer from the fridge," David said, "do you want one?"

"Please. And don't take too long." Julia winked.

"I'll be right back."

David left his bedroom. The door closed on its own behind him.

Dude how did you get so lucky? David wondered, turning the corner of the hallway. *Don't even question it just go with it. This is the best thing to ever happen to you. Snowed in for the day and she's spending all her time with you instead of her friends. This will definitely speed things up—spending a holiday together accelerates a relationship, it's like the effect of twelve months condensed into one.*

In the kitchen, David looked out the tall sliding glass doors. The snow seemed to calm down now. It was no longer falling and the sun was out and blazing. He wondered how long it would take for the ungodly amount of snow to melt; how long it would take for the cleaners to come through and make the streets drivable again.

David whistled *Carol of the Bells* as he opened the fridge, looking inside for beers, pushed past the plate of leftover pizza, and grabbed two cold ones. When he shut the fridge, the black gloved hand jammed a fork through his nose.

David did not feel pain at first; first it was the sensation of pouring blood like a nosebleed. Then the fork went deeper. David opened his mouth to scream but only a gasp escaped from behind his lips. The scream was too deep and too big to find its way out.

David shot his hands to the counter for support. Tried to push himself away from the man, tried to tell his body to run, and feeling a damn painful searing pain going through his face and reaching his brain.

David then desperately reached his hand towards the knife set on the counter, taking his eyes momentarily off the man dressed as Santa who raised the long blade of his knife set in aging wood and brought it down on David's fingers before he could reach the knife set. As the scream finally began leaving David's throat, the man brought the knife across David's throat and dragged it from end to end, silencing him for good.

Julia laid on David's bed smiling.

It was going to be a great weekend after all. She could feel it.

It really is. It really is going to be a great weekend. Maybe it'll be more than a fling.

Ah, his bed is so warm and cozy. What's taking him so long with these drinks? I hope Christy isn't still lecturing him about Mary. But how exactly did her sock get in here? It could be Christy's sock. What, Mary is the only one who wears pink socks? I think I even have a pair of them myself in one of my bags. Looks like I wasn't so crazy for packing extra, since it looks like we'll be here at least another couple days.

Julia took her shirt off. She stood in front of his mirror and applied lipstick and made kissing faces.

The doorknob turned and the door opened an inch. Julia turned around, expecting David to open it and walk through, but he didn't. Nobody did. The door hinges squeaked loudly. There was definitely someone standing behind the door, she could hear the floorboards screeching below his feet as he took a step back.

"David?"

The door creaked again.

"David, you there? Are you trying to scare me? Oh I am *so* scared."

The door shifted on its hinges; it came back to almost close, but the latch didn't catch. Julia listened to the heavy breathing.

“Oh no, Mr. Butcher, don’t kill me.” Julia laughed. “If only David were here to protect me from the evil maniac.”

Everything was still.

“Okay you can come out now. I want my drink.”

The door creaked open another inch.

Julia crossed the room.

“You could do something funnier than this,” Julia said, but when she pushed the door open and looked down the hall in either direction, she did not see David or anybody. “Hello? Who’s there?”

The door slammed shut on its own and Julia jumped back. She nearly had a heart attack. “Shit.”

If David wasn’t here, where could he be?

“Christy? Katie? Bekah? Aviana? *Mary?”*

Nobody.

I wonder if this is Prank/Annoy Julia Day. This was their plan for today: this stupid shit. Creaking doors, supposedly disappearing. Yep. This must all be a prank. Did any of them even go with Christy to Mary’s room? I bet she’s down there and they’re all in on it. I was stupid to believe Christy for that. Mary can’t be missing, even in a giant place like this. How lost can someone get?

“Nice try guys.”

Julia listened quietly for giggles but all she heard were footsteps coming from upstairs. The house was noisy, and Julia knew that if Mary had wandered off somewhere, they would’ve at the very least *heard* her. And she laughed at herself for being so gullible. It all had to be a very dumb prank.

“Come on out, David, Mary, everybody. I know it was all a joke. Ya got me. Now let us get this weekend started. We can put on some records, drink until we pass out, you know, the stuff we had *planned* to do instead of stupid pranks on Julia.”

Then, after waiting several long moments for a response: “Guys?”

Julia sighed. “This is the lamest game ever, okay?”

She walked down the hallway and headed for the kitchen.

Christy was still shaking from the roach—how she despised them!—and finished checking the basement rooms. They had mostly been storage rooms with nothing of importance to her. She was scared to death of looking through them for her friend, unsure of if she'd find her. It was tough not to assume something bad. Christy burned with nervousness, half from Mary, half from the bug.

Then Christy was still as she heard a terrifying scream.

It was so intense it put her every thought and movement on hold. Somebody, and she couldn't tell who, was screaming endlessly.

Christy moved carefully to the stairway. She trembled on her ascent.

Mary? Is it Mary? Oh my God what is happening?

The screaming didn't stop, it blended into cries. Then she heard stampeding footsteps coming from the second floor. Suddenly she was running, slamming one foot in front of the other.

A hush came over the house. The others entered the kitchen first, she could hear them from the stairway. Christy stood motionless, heart thumping loudly, sweat billowing down her skin, knees shaking. Christy had an obscure compulsion to scream.

Whispers: audible but wordless.

She sprinted, then went to the kitchen.

Christy screamed, backed into the glass doors, then covered her eyes and wailed and sniveled. Only once did she peek through her fingers just to be certain she was seeing things correctly.

And she was.

David was sprawled on the kitchen floor in front of the refrigerator, blood mixing with exploded beer cans, and his hand chopped in half and resting on the countertop. His throat was torn open from end to end and… oh God, who put that fork in his face? It must have gone far enough inside of him to reach his brain.

Julia was at the other end of the room crying. Katie and Bekah and Aviana were stunned and sickened and came over to console Christy. Aviana put her arms around her and tried to hug her, but Christy hit her away.

"Don't touch me."

"Christy I'm—"

"Ohmigod ohmigod ohmigod."

"Christy—"

"Shut up shut up shut up!"

Aviana, Katie, and Bekah looked back at Julia.

"Was it—was it Mary?" Bekah asked.

"I think—I think Mary's lost her mind," Julia said.

"Ohmigod," Katie said, looking out the glass door. "I want to go home."

Christy screamed and cried. *"Mary I'm gonna kill you I'm gonna kill you you maniac!"*

"Oh God oh God oh God," Julia shrunk into her corner. "Oh God oh God."

Aviana went to the counter, breathing heavily, staying as far away from David and the severed hand as possible, and reached for the set of knives.

"Wuh-what are you doing?" Katie asked.

"That girl is insane. If she comes near me..."

Katie cried. *"This is not what I had in mind for winter break."*

Aviana handed her a knife. "Just. Fucking. Take it."

Katie did. Then Aviana handed one to Bekah and grabbed another for Julia and another for Christy.

Katie took Julia by the hand and helped her up. Aviana came back to Christy, who was watching them with sunken watery eyes, and hugged her. Christy didn't hit her away this time, she needed it.

The girls walked closely together through the kitchen and through the hallway to the living room where they were huddled together, each raising a knife. Christy set hers down on the arm of the couch and collapsed onto her seat. She couldn't bring herself to grab it in such a *nasty* situation. Coldness reasserted itself in her flesh, even if it was bright outside the windows.

Katie joined Christy and put an arm around her while Julia and Bekah stood in front of them. Christy felt like they were all sitting ducks. Aviana stood in front of the fireplace and faced them. She looked as if she had something important to say, and her mouth opened then shut. Christy studied her with weary eyes. She couldn't believe David was dead.

Just like that.

Waking up not knowing it was his last day... and how could Christy live with herself, accusing him of possibly doing something to Mary, when it had been Mary all along who was going to do something to him?

Then the memories came back: she was a kid again and David was alive again. They were playing in the snow back home, their real home, not this place, and he was on the top of the deck in the back yard and she was below it, and they were in a standoff, snowballs raised in each of their hands threatening to fire. David stepped to his left and she stepped to her right. He tossed one and she tried to duck but fell face-first into the heavy layer of snow covering the brown deck. And David *still* threw snowballs at the back of her head. She almost laughed here thinking about it.

"How will I explain this to Mom and Dad?"

Tears streamed like a waterfall. Katie hugged her tighter. Everything seemed like a grey-black blur. She wiped the tears away but every single tear was replaced by another two or three or four. No matter which way she tried to process it, she just couldn't believe it. Her brother dead, by a killer she had invited into her own home. Mary made the tracks that had led into her room, that was it. She made them, she asked about them to make everyone think it was David, but it was her, it was Mary.

She killed him and I'm gonna kill her.

"Listen, Ladies," Aviana said, "we've got to stick together. Let's all stick together. Nothing could happen to us if we're together. There's strength in numbers."

Santa Claus came around the corner of the hallway only two feet away from Aviana. His bloody knife was raised and he grabbed Aviana by the collar of her shirt then jammed his blade into her side and dug it across her stomach. The ball of Aviana's intestines swung against her body. She grunted. Blood spilled from her mouth. Then the man shoved her head into the fireplace and held her down while she squirmed and burned.

Christy screamed. She hadn't realized that the others had already run away. When she ran, she didn't remember to grab her knife from the couch's armrest.

Footsteps echoed through the house. Doors slammed and bolted shut. At the end of the hallway, Christy turned around and saw the man standing near the living room, staring at her through the dirty Santa Claus mask he wore.

Abruptly he raised the knife from his side and came for her.

Christy knocked over a little table in the hall, as if that would somehow slow him down, then turned a corner and rushed downstairs. As best she could tell he was moving at a calm pace, not running, but he had still seen where she had gone and not the others and he would surely be after her.

He would undeniably hear her footsteps. And suddenly a thought came to her as the darkness of the stairwell overtook her and she came nearer to the must basement: *He's the one who killed David. Oh God, he must've killed Mary too. Who is he? Dammit, he was the footsteps, the back yard, the glass door. Ohmigod.*

She tried to calmly open one of the basement room doors but the rusty hinges squealed as the door unlatched and opened but she didn't think he heard it. His footsteps were still above her, he wasn't anywhere near the stairway yet, there was no way he heard her… was there?

Hopelessness filled her. She felt nothing but desolation when she shut the door and entered the raven-black storage room of old boxes.

A nervousness in her gut. The door didn't have a lock. None of them save for the bedroom and bathroom did in the basement. She hid behind the door, her body flush against the wall, and wondered how she could get to a phone. There was a landline in the living room, there was a line upstairs, but there was no line down here. Her best chance was to make a run for the living room. Could she do it? Could she get back there? There was the poker, he hadn't taken it. She could defend herself with that. But would the police ever get here in time? Were the streets cleaned at all? She tried to remember but when she tried to shut her eyes and think, all she saw was David's severed hand. In her mind, it witched.

Tears fell.

She needed to be brave.

Suddenly his footsteps came down the stairs after a period of silence.

Christy threw her hands over her mouth and tried not to scream. She listened to his knife being dragged against the walls.

The scream almost escaped. Almost. She pressed her hands tighter and reminded herself to shut up or she'd end up like the others. Just then, image of Aviana's guts came back to her. Christy could almost feel blood dripping from her own mouth as it had fallen from Aviana's.

Her stomach clenched at the thought of grabbing the poker and dialing the police, because she realized that the smell of Aviana's melting flesh must've filled the room.

All at once the footsteps stopped and she couldn't tell which part of the basement he was in. For all she knew, he had somehow phased through the walls and was in here with her. For all she knew, he was about to strangle her in darkness without any warning. Just a mass of evil. A mass of wickedness ready to slither his hands around her like snakes and choke her. The thought was so real she could almost feel it. Christy searched the room with her eyes.

CREAAAK!

The steps came back, and they were coming her way.

He tried the door of the room next to her. Her heart sank. He was the reaper, and he would be here soon. Christy listened carefully. The boogeyman went into the room and stood there for about a minute before shutting the door. She hoped and prayed that he'd go the other way, or go back upstairs and not open the door to the room she was in.

Go away, go away.

The knob turned. Christy almost lost it. She held her breath. Light from the hall illuminated the room. He stood in the doorway and studied the room. He did not bother going inside. There was no need to. The way the boxes were laid on the floor, there wouldn't be a single place for her to hide, unless she was the world's most flexible woman and could hide in one of those small brown boxes.

He closed the door and moved away but was still in the basement.

THUD!

A roach landed on Christy's head. She was frozen in terror. A nasty chill raced up her spine. She cringed as its gross little legs pattered in her hair; it was stuck on its side and trying to move. Shivering, Christy hit it and almost yelled. Then she gasped silently. Her foot banged into the wall and made a noise. The roach was still in her hair.

The butcher suddenly stopped moving, and she knew she blew it. She knew he was going to come back and push the door open so far that it would crush her. She could see the obituary now, and the embarrassing headlines of the newspapers: *College Student Christy Morrison Impaled by Doorknob.*

She knew he was listening.

She waited.

The final seconds of her life ticked by.

Footsteps. She almost screamed. It was on the edge of her lips, until the footsteps moved farther away and back to Mary's former room. She wondered how long she could hide here. Wondered how long he'd be spending in the basement. Would he ever leave? Were the others okay? Was anybody else dead? Did they know where the phone was? Had they tried to make a call? Were they worried for her? Would any of them come to help her?

Her mind couldn't stop flooding with questions.

She listened to him pace around the basement, drag his knife across the walls. Eventually—thankfully—he left with heavy footsteps over screaming stairs. A bit of calmness came back to her but it wasn't much. Her heavy breathing now almost masked his footsteps. He went up to the main floor, his footsteps disappearing above her.

As she cried in the dark, finally hitting away the roach in her hair, Christy wondered what she should do next.

9

Bekah and Julia shut themselves into one room. Katie had been ahead of them and ran into a room all by herself.

"We should grab the phone," Julia said, ear pressed tightly to the door. "I don't care if it's impossible to drive in these streets. We can't just sit around. We have to get help." Then she moved away from the door. "I haven't heard him come anywhere near here. I can make a run for it."

"Oh no you fucking won't."

"So we just sit here until he gets us, Bekah? Is that what you want?"

"If we open that door, we die."

"Listen to me, Bekah, listen to me. We're not gonna die. Not if we get the phone. Not if we call the police. I'll dial it and run back in here with it, okay? The cord can fit under the door."

Bekah cried uncontrollably. "That's a stupid plan and we're all gonna die."

"Calm down, it'll all be okay, it'll all be okay, calm down." Julia said. "I'm gonna dial it, okay? We're gonna call them and they'll come and everything will be okay. You and me and Katie and Christy, we're getting out of here, okay?"

Through tears, Bekah agreed.

Julia stood up, pressed her ear to the door one more time, then unlocked it. She crept into the hallway. The phone was right outside the room. Bekah kept watching from the door and gripped the knob so tightly it would eventually hurt to let go. After dialing, Julia hurried back to the room with the phone; Bekah was in such a hurry that she slammed the door loudly before locking it.

"That was so loud oh God oh no oh God oh—"

"Hurry, he's coming for us," Julia told the person on the other end of the line, then told them some of her friends were dead and that the man was still here and after them.

Bekah hugged her. Tears still streamed down her face.

Then, as she gave the address, Julia's face went blank and the words stopped coming.

"Julia?"

"Bekah… the line went dead."

"But they—but they heard you, right? Right?"

"I don't know."

"You don't know?"

"We have to try dialing again."

"Ohmigod Jules are we really going to try—"

"We had to put it back sometime or he'd see the cord under the door and come for us."

"I don't like this."

"Neither do I, Bekah, you moron. Either we get the police here or we die here. Come on."

Julia unlocked the door again, paced to the dial, and listened to Bekah telling her to hurry from the doorway.

Julia hit the buttons but it wouldn't dial. It wouldn't ring.

"Come on, come back. There's no use."

"Hold on," Julia whispered. "Be quiet."

"Oh Julia…"

Bekah tiptoed to her, put her arms around her, and tried to pull her away.

"Let's go before he gets us."

Footsteps came up the stairway.

"Christy?" Bekah whispered.

Julia backed away slowly.

Santa Claus stood at the end of the hall then charged. Julia and Bekah sprinted down the hall. Julia's heart nearly leapt out of her chest. Her mind rushed. This couldn't be real, this couldn't be happening, this couldn't—

Julia glanced over her shoulder. The Raven Hill Butcher was so close to Bekah, who was so much slower than Julia was.

Oh no.

The Raven Hill Butcher wrapped his hands around Bekah and pulled her into his arms. Bekah's single hand stretched out to Julia. *"Help me."*

"I'm sorry Bekah. I'm sorry."

At the end of the hall, a new hall, one Julia had not been through before, formed on the right. Julia turned the corner.

"Julia you bitch, you motherfuckin—"

The Butcher grabbed Bekah's hair and dragged her. He pulled and her hair slowly tore from her scalp. He took her to the end of the hall, raised her face to the big glass window at the intersection of the halls. Julia saw it all happen as she watched in the new hall: The Raven Hill Butcher smashed Bekah's face through the window, then brought her throat down on the jagged glass.

The Butcher cocked his head sideways then went after Julia.

Now or never.

The darkness seemed to choke her. Or maybe it was just the crying.

Christy built up the courage to leave the room and discretely headed for the stairs, walking with extra care and hoping not to make noise. But that was impossible. The whole house was old and jittery and each movement would almost surely make sounds.

Christy took her first step, putting as little weight as possible on the step, but it was no use, it made noise. As she took her fourth and fifth steps up, she heard commotion coming from a great distance, it must've been coming from the second floor, and hurried up the stairs, unafraid now of making noise if the killer was… *distracted.*

She forgot David's body was in the kitchen, and screamed again when she saw it. A bolt of terror ripped into her heart.

Be strong he'd want you to be strong just go get the poker and go to the phone. Just go get the poker and go to the phone. Just go get—

A heart-stopping shriek came from upstairs. She had to hurry.

She kept repeating to herself to get the poker and go to the phone.

She tiptoed, moved quietly, then altogether gave up on any attempt to be quiet. Forget being quiet. She ran the rest of the way to the living room, preparing herself to see Aviana's body...

That smell. That damn smell.

Aviana had been pulled from the fire and was on her stomach in front of the fireplace. Christy was glad she couldn't completely see her friend's charred face or her spilled guts.

She grabbed the poker, fumbled with it, then raced to grab the phone. She pressed it to her ear, it was cold enough to send a chill through her, then she realized it was dead. It wouldn't dial. There wasn't any way for her to call for help. She was trapped with a monster.

Julia couldn't keep running, she was so tired, but she had to force herself, or else she'd die. There was much distance between her and The Raven Hill Butcher—so much space, but it was never going to be enough.

Chills rolled up and down her spine. She had stared death in the face. She wished she had her knife still but she had forgotten it in the room she and Bekah—the mere thought of Bekah made her shudder—had hidden in, and now she was defenseless with him on her tail.

He breathed heavily and never ran, only walked, but managed to keep up with her. She was shaking, tremors ran through her entire body, and Julia raced down the stairway two steps at a time, nearly slipping to her death on occasion.

When she was halfway down, she glimpsed up. He was coming down with his bloody knife raised. Her stomach clenched and her head ached. Everything was hot. Adrenaline pumped through her body.

"Ohmigod."

Christy heard her friend screaming, clutched the poker tighter, and ran towards the noise. Two sets of footsteps were coming the other way. From the hallway leading into the kitchen she locked eyes with Julia, and Julia ran towards her with her arms flailing and telling Christy to run for her life.

Julia tugged on Christy's arm. She was suspended in place for a moment at the sight of The Raven Hill Butcher behind her friend. She snapped out of it and the girls ran back through the living room to the hallway where he had come from when he killed Aviana, the hallway that led back to David's room.

"I know where we can go."

"Where?"

"The—"

He appeared at the end of the hall as if by teleportation.

The girls screamed and went back through the living room. The Butcher gave chase with his knife extended and ready for the girls.

Christy and Julia beat him to the kitchen, then pushed the table into the doorway. But as they went to the stairs they realized he wasn't with them anymore. They couldn't even hear him. All was still. All was silent. But they wouldn't wait there for him forever.

"Come on," Christy said, "up here."

Christy kept the poker raised and Julia kept close to her, constantly looking behind themselves for The Raven Hill Butcher.

"Do you… do you really think we'll be safe?"

Christy said nothing.

Julia cried.

"Who is he?" Christy said. "Is he—"

"Oh I don't know."

On the second floor, Julia shielded Christy's eyes from Bekah's corpse. In a hallway that Christy had not taken Julia or the others to yet, Christy stopped at its center.

"I-I ran through here when he… when Bekah…"

"Let's hurry," Christy said, then raised the poker to the latch on the ceiling.

Christy tugged. The latch didn't want to come loose on the drop down stairs.

Hollow footfalls sounded distantly in an adjacent hallway.

"Oh no," Julia said. *"He's coming. We need to hide."*

"Just shut up."

The stairs finally unlatched. A blue ladder came down effortlessly and with it fell Mary's body on top of Christy, knocking her to the floor and knocking the poker out of her hand. She pushed Mary's body abruptly off herself and screamed painfully.

Mary's throat was slashed horizontally, and the end of a giant candy cane stuck through. The candy cane's hook dangled in her mouth with her dried tongue glued to it. A sort of Columbian necktie with a candy cane.

Julia glanced at the body. Christy picked up the poker then she pulled on Julia's arm, and the girls went up.

Inside the attic was a small and dusty space with Christmas decorations flooding several shelves. A lot of the room couldn't be seen because it was drenched in darkness. Their only light source came from the hallway below them. Christy began pulling the stairs up when The Butcher grabbed hold of the steps and climbed.

There was no closing it. He was too strong.

Christy's grip tightened around her poker and she hit it in his direction but couldn't land a hit on him. He dodged them then grabbed the poker in one hand and jerked her forward then pushed it back. Christy moved away from the entrance. She and Julia held each other and moved back into a wall and cried.

The room was warm when they entered it but his presence made it colder. Christy was chilled to the roots of her hair. She gulped. Her grip tightened around not only the poker but around Julia too.

Then she let go of her.

Christy stretched the poker out and jabbed him in the stomach.

The Butcher smacked it away with little effort. It fell from her hands and she was defenseless as he towered over her, becoming one with the shadows. She saw her own face between globs of blood on his knife as he winded it back, brought it forward...

She was the ground. Julia pulled her down.

The girls were crawling away to the stairs, then he yanked Julia up by her hair and sank his knife in her chest.

"Julia."

Christy climbed to her feet, took the poker, and jumped through the entrance without climbing down. She landed on her elbow, looked up, and saw The Raven Hill Butcher standing there. Blood dripped from his knife down the entrance.

Christy hurried to her feet and ran.

Katie heard muffled screams and running and was hesitant to leave the room, but remembered there was a phone in one of the halls on the top floor, and one in the living room. She desperately wanted to know what was happening. There was commotion every few minutes, but she couldn't make heads or tails of it. Katie was under a bed and burying her face and tears and screams into a pillow.

If I could just get to the phone.

She wiggled out from under the bed then stood and listened. There had been a loud thud a few minutes ago, followed by a scream, but nothing since then.

Katie opened the door an inch, peeking through the opening, and saw the empty hall. Her knife was held tight in a white-knuckled grip. If anybody came for her, she was prepared.

She cautiously snuck out of her room. Everything was still, everything was quiet, the only sound was her footsteps.

You've got this.

Katie went down her right, turned to the next hall, found the telephone, then screamed. Bekah's throat was buried in jagged glass in the window at the other end, and blood ran over in freezing streaks. Katie felt gusts of coldness trace her body.

Then somebody was behind her.

She felt them but didn't turn. She was suspended in place. The phone was lifted then the cord was rolled around her throat like a ball of yarn. Her fingers dug into it the cord, attempted to separate it from her body, and she gasped for air—begged for breath—but her attacker only made it tighter and her throat smaller. Black wires shot across her vision as pressure behind her eyes swelled. She was dizzy and scared and desperate to breathe.

Her tongue rolled out of her mouth and she panted. She couldn't go much longer without air.

Then the person she couldn't see took the receiver and shoved it through her throat.

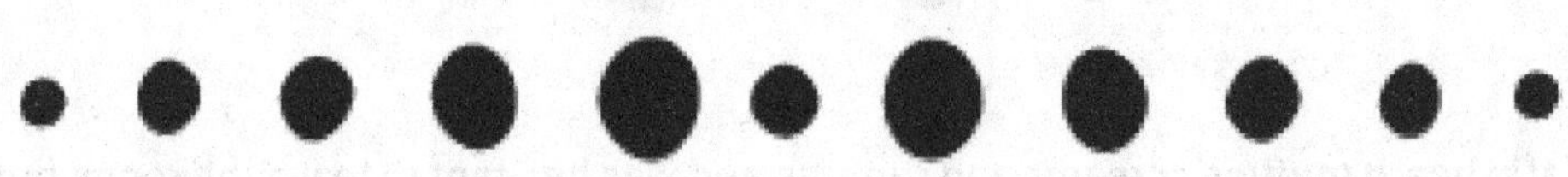

He could've been anywhere.

Christy waited beneath the stairway, hunched over, body pressed tightly against the wall. She was waiting for him and she was ready. He'd come down the stairs and she'd stab him in the legs, she saw it in her mind. He'd come down the stairs, she'd stab his calf, and he'd fall down and break his neck, but she'd still stab him anyways. She'd kill him.

She wondered, *Where are you? In a house full of dead people, where could you be?*

She had heard Katie scream two short minutes ago and knew she must've met her end. There was no surviving the monster. She wanted to give up and cry and die where she stood, but she kept it together. She'd kill him for David. She'd kill him for her friends.

Tears came at the same time as footsteps.

He was approaching.

Just put it through the posts, put it through the posts as hard as you can, sever his Achilles, let's do some damage.

She couldn't see his feet yet but knew from the steps it had to be him. They were heavy. Not only that, but they were the only two still living.

Christy tried not to cry again. Let out the breath she didn't realize she had been holding in. Raised the poker and readied herself.

His footsteps were a steady thumping. He reached the halfway point and came into view. She started her countdown.

Seven…

THUD!

Six…

THUD!

Five…

THUD!

Four…

THUD!

Three…

THUD!

Two…

THUD!

Now.

His legs were within reach.

Christy pushed the poker with desperation and it did not stab him but it did trip him. She watched him fall on his stomach and smack into the floor and watched his knife slip away from his hand. She stood over him just as he had towered over her in the attic, raised the poker with both hands, then brought it down—but he moved.

He moved out of the way. The poker banged against linoleum.

BANG! BANG!

Fists pounding on the front door.

"Police! Open up."

She was momentarily filled with hope until his hand coiled around her ankle and twisted.

BAM!

They were breaking down the front door.

But oh God what if they don't get to me in time the table's in the way and what if he kills me like he killed the others.

"I'm in here." Christy screamed, but they couldn't hear her yet. The door wasn't fully broken open and her voice must've died somewhere in the distance between the stairs and the front door.

He pulled Christy to the ground and she fell on her back. She hit his hand away with the poker. He recoiled, and then she lodged it in his throat and pushed it deep—then to be sure she slammed on it with her fist and sent it further. His body convulsed then he laid still.

That's when she heard the door come off its hinges.

Her ankle still hurt from his grip, but after she crawled under the table in front of the doorway, she ran to the living room and collapsed in front of what must've been a dozen officers.

"He killed them all! He's in there! Bottom of the stairs in the kitchen. I killed him with the poker."

Most officers moved forward. Three stayed behind with her.

The minutes ticked by and she didn't hear much. Maybe because The Butcher was dead there would be nothing more for them to do but find the bodies.

Soon, one officer came back and said, "There was nobody at the stairs."

Christy wailed. She screamed so violently that her blood ran cold. She screamed until she passed out.

"All of them are dead," Z said to Red as they stood outside the Morrison house. "All of them except the crazy girl that they took to the hospital, and the other one that's up in the attic barely clinging to life."

"Poor kids," Red said. "And the guy who did it?"

"There is no guy who did it."

"Whatcha mean, Z?"

"They didn't find no one, Red. That's what I mean. He's gone."

"Oh no."

"She said she stabbed him in the throat with the poker, but…"

"But…?"

"Red, the poker had no blood on it."

RETURN TO CAMP SOLGOHACHIA

1

Raven Hill has always been an unlucky town.

The moon looks so out of place in daylight, Wesley Lawrence thought, looking through the bus window to the sky. He was reluctant to go back to Camp Solgohachia but all his friends were going so he figured why not. And now, as the bus went down the familiar bumpy road, he still regretted it. Wesley thought about all the things he'd rather be doing at home, like playing a video game or setting up glass bottles in the alley behind his house and seeing how far he could hit them with his slingshot.

His friend Bill sat next to him, and his friend Darren was alone in the seat behind them. Darren was so fat he took up enough room for two campers. He'd been trying to get Darren on a diet for about a year now, but Darren wouldn't listen.

It's probably going to be a fun two weeks, he thought. It always was. He was seventeen, and it was his fourth and final time at Camp Solgohachia, but camping was something he had outgrown. But at least there'd still be pranks and mayhem. He had his slingshot in his pocket and would surely launch rocks at the younger campers and first timers.

WELCOME TO CAMP SOLGOHACHIA, the banner over the tall wooden entrance read.

The driver parked in a big gravel parking lot, opened the door, and wished the kids fun times. Most of the luggage was piled into mountains in the back of the bus, and kids tackled each other to find their things so that they could get off and find a cabin. Wesley, Bill, and Darren each kept their single bags at their feet so that they were the first ones off. Wesley was glad to finally stretch his legs. The ride was four hours with no stops and he had to pee from the two cans of Jolt Cola he downed within the first hour.

"Hurry up," Wesley said as Darren wobbled through the bus.

"I'm coming I'm coming."

Bill whistled and looked around, wiping sweat from his face with his shirt. "It feels like it's a hundred degrees out."

When Darren was out of the bus, the boys sped to a path on the right that went to the boys' cabins at the edge of the woods that hemmed around camp. The cabins stood on a slight rise. The girls' cabins were on the other side of camp.

The boys' cabins were named: Grizzly, Polar, Kodiak, Sun, and Panda. Grizzly was the first cabin, the most desirable one, and not technically a cabin. It was the only one with air conditioning and had nice tile floors and newly installed bathrooms.

"It must be taken already," Wesley said. "No way we made it in time."

"Definitely is." Bill pointed his thumb. "Somebody already put a garbage can outside. Look."

Putting a garbage can outside the door was tradition amongst the boys at Camp Solgohachia to let the later arrivals know a cabin was full.

"Well kill me if we've gotta be stuck in Panda."

"Panda isn't so bad," Darren said. "It may be ugly and falling apart but it's not so bad."

"The toilets in Panda don't even flush! And look how the trees almost grow *into* it, I bet it's swarming with bugs."

Polar was next on the path of cabins and was the next most desirable, but that too had a garbage can in front of it. So did Brown, Kodiak, and Sun.

The boys stopped in front of Panda. Its name was painted in wobbly red letters, and the green paintjob on the cabin was chipping away. The branches of giant trees covered it and almost formed a second roof. Somewhere in the distance bees hummed. Then a powerful wind came.

"Panda it is, I guess," Wesley reached for the knob. "I had Grizzly my first year, right after they fixed it up. Man I wish all cabins were like that. I had all sorts of bragging rights that first year…"

"I remember when you showed me inside," Bill said. "Sure was nice."

"Maybe Panda won't be terrible this year," Darren pushed his crooked glasses up.

Nobody else was in Panda. They had the cabin all to themselves.

The cabin stunk but it was unclear where the stench was coming from. The bunkbeds were high off the ground, and were old and rickety, as if they hadn't been replaced since the place opened in the 1930s. At least the blue covers over the musty grey mattresses were new, but they didn't have bedsheets, and there was no way Wesley was touching that with his body. Tall dressers were set between the bunks, and there were some other dressers at one end. The floor creaked with every step.

Wesley tossed his bag atop the high bunk in the far left corner with the window facing camp. "Dibs."

He climbed the ladder then studied the beams that raced across the ceiling. Often times the boys had races with these, seeing who could climb to the other end and back first. Wesley thought that if anyone tried that in Panda, that the roof would surely collapse. Wesley put his hands to it anyways and searched around the beams for treasure but only found dust. He had been lucky once and found a silver dollar on a beam, but he hadn't been lucky since.

Bill tossed his bag on the bunk below Wesley's, and Darren took the bottom bunk next to Bill.

A whisper of cold came when Wesley opened the door to leave the cabin. He looked up to see the clouds covering the sun, then turned back to his friends who were still loading their clothes into dresser drawers.

"Come on, retards."

Clouds moved away from the sun and the temperature rose. The boys went to the flagpole at the center of camp. All the boys and girls of Camp Solgohachia were heading there for morning announcements.

The flagpole was probably twenty feet high and danced in the wind. A man stood on the bricks that ran in circles around the pole and the flowers that grew around it.

"Goooooood morning campers! I'm your camp director Charlie and welcome to Camp Solgohachia. I know a lot of you have been here before and know the spiel but listen up! It's time to go over some camp rules before we get things started! Now let's see a show of hands, who has *never* been camping before?"

Plenty of campers, mostly the younger kids, raised their hands.

"And who's been camping before but never been to Camp Solgohachia before?"

Some others raised their hands.

"Well it's a pleasure to have you all here! This is going to be the best summer yet! I'll need you kids to pay attention and save all questions for the end. We have five very special rules we ask you all to follow at Camp Solgohachia. The first is to be a happy camper! Be kind to everyone. No name calling, bullying, or fighting. The second rule is to listen to your counselor. Every cabin will soon be assigned their own counselor. Camp counselors are there to make sure that all campers have the best time possible while also looking out for every camper's safety. Listen to them. Third is to keep the camp and cabins clean! Four is to have fun! Make new friends and try new things. You'll make friendships here that can last lifetimes. Now, the fifth and final rule is the absolute most important. *Do. Not. Go. Out. After. Curfew.* Once we hit the twilight period, the period before our evening events, there is absolutely *no* wandering alone, always accompany a friend. After that is curfew, and there is absolutely no sneaking out. Every year we have kids who try to break into the boarded cabin through the east end of the woods. This is absolutely frowned upon, and that area of the woods is off limits. Any camper found going there will have to clean the latrine and have privileges taken away. Is that understood?"

Wesley pulled his buddies to the side. "Guys?"

"Yeah?"

"It's our last year here. What if we went to that cabin?"

"Go to the cabin?" Darren gulped. *"Why the fuck would we go to the abandoned cabin?"*

"Shut up, not so loud," Wesley said. "Yes, go to the cabin. It sounds like fun. What're they gonna do? Send me home? I didn't wanna come this year anyways. Look, nothing's gonna happen, it's just an old cabin."

"You're not gonna do it," Bill said. "You're a pussy."

"Fuck you, Bill."

"Let's make a bet." Bill stuck out his hand.

Wesley shook it. "It's a deal."

2

When Charlie was done speaking, the campers were free to wander around and do as they pleased.

There was plenty to do: baseball, basketball, human foosball, golf, water balloon volleyball, and carpetball. Carpetball was played on long, narrow tables set under a ramada. A pit ended each side of the long tables. Each player lined up their pool balls in whatever formation they wanted, then took turns rolling another ball straight down the middle, trying to knock the other side clean into the pit, arguing over the rules that seemed to be made up on the fly, changing depending on who was playing who.

The tables stood near the vending machines, where campers sometimes tried to break open the latches. Wesley remembered his second year at camp, how he'd pried one open and slipped away just before anyone could catch him.

Now he sat at a picnic table under the ramada, his eyes fixed on a blondie in a denim skirt and pink shirt who was watching one of the carpetball games.

He crouched over the edge of the table with his hands and slingshot underneath, and a stack of pebbles hidden at his side. He slipped one into the leather pad on the rubber and winded it back. It hit a boy of thirteen or fourteen in the calf. Wesley laughed watching the boy grab his leg on the brink of tears. The way he acted it was as though somebody hit him with a real bullet.

Wesley looked away, and when nobody fessed up, the boy tried to go back to carpetball. Wesley hit him again. Everyone laughed at his painful reaction. Nobody saw who had shot him. Nobody, of course, except the blonde girl.

After the third time he hit the boy, Blondie came over and said, "You're a real jerk."

"What?"

"I saw you throwing rocks at that boy."

“So what?”

“Forget it.”

“I’m Wesley, what’s your name?”

“You wish.” Blondie upturned her nose then left the ramada and went off into camp.

Wesley stood up from the bench and tripped onto the cement floor. He got to his feet and hurried after her. *“Hey wait up.”*

She turned around confused. “You gonna shoot me with that thing too?”

“What?” He looked down at his hands then stuffed the slingshot into his pocket. “I was just joking around. We do that all the time.”

She turned and walked away.

“What’s your name?”

Blondie stopped. “Wendy.”

“Have you been here before?”

“No,” she said.

“I’ll show you around then.”

“As long as you don’t hit me with any rocks.”

“I won’t, Wendy. Just as long as you behave yourself.”

He took her off the path and through the grass as a shortcut.

Next to the carpetball armada was the open space behind the cafeteria and before the start of the golf fields. It was on a rise, an area not typically traveled since there was nothing beyond it. The back of the cafeteria had a porch that nobody actually used, and below it was an open hiding space that, as far as Wesley knew, no one else knew about.

“You can hide here.”

“Hide here?”

“You know, if you ever want to skip out on activities.”

“Uh, okay?”

He led her back to the path. It curved into the camp. “Back around here are the basketball courts. That building right next to it has postcards and candy and stuff you can buy. And a payphone in the back.”

Wendy turned towards the basketball hoops and watched some girls play.

“Are those your friends?”

“No,” Wendy said in a low voice. Her face turned red. “Some of them are in my cabin, but, I don’t know anybody here. I just moved to Raven Hill.”

They walked around a little bit more.

“Well down that way’s the swim hole, past the boys’ cabins. I’m down in the last one.”

“Thanks for showing me around,” Wendy said then walked away. “I think I’m gonna use that payphone.”

“See you around?”

“I think so. This place isn’t *that* big.”

Wesley found one of the coolers of ice water that were placed around camp, and filled a paper cup. It was refreshing. A few minutes later Wesley took his slingshot out and went back to the armada, grabbed handfuls of pebbles, and sat back alone at the bench.

He looked around for the boy he had hit last time. It would be hilarious to see him squirm again. But Wesley didn’t see him. Instead, he launched his rocks at a new target: another boy in shorts watching an intense game of carpetball, cheering every time the guy in the green shirt knocked over the pool balls of the guy in the *Led Zeppelin* shirt.

Wesley fired a pebble at the boy’s shoulder. The boy nearly jumped over the table when he felt it hit him. The boy turned around. His face white under freckles, and turning to anger. Wesley secretly launched another from under the table and it hit the boy in the stomach. Wesley looked away quickly, bursting out in laughter, and the boy looked around the crowded armada wondering who the hell could’ve been firing rocks at him.

Camp is gonna be just fine after all, Wesley thought.

3

Wesley, Bill, and Darren were some of the first ones to line up for dinner in front of the cafeteria.

"Could you believe it?" Darren said. "Really, could you guys believe it? Playing baseball in this weather? I almost fainted, I tell you. *Fainted.* They laughed at me when I asked to pause for a water break."

"Calm it, tits," Wesley said. "You didn't even get on base. You struck out every time."

"I got on base once."

"Because the pitcher hit you," Bill said.

The cafeteria doors opened and the line got to moving.

The camp served pizza today as they always did on the first and last days. Technically not camp food, and it was delicious. One of the only two or three days when the food they served was tolerable. Wesley was not looking forward to "Bean Surprise" for lunch tomorrow or "Mystery Meat" the day after.

Wesley and his friends sat at the end of a crowded table near a window.

Welsey drank some lemonade then said, "I met this girl today named Wendy. I'm gonna ask her to the bonfire tonight."

"Oh yeah?" Darren said. "What if she already has a date?"

"That's the thing. She doesn't know anybody here. She's new."

"And she's pretty?" Bill said, leaning in.

"Yeah."

"A pretty girl with no friends?"

"Yeah, that's right."

Darren and Bill looked at each other, then back to Wesley and laughed.

"What? What are you pricks laughing at?"

"Well, Wes," Bill said, "don't you know it? If a pretty girl has no friends it's usually because she's a bitch. Everyone wants to be friends with a pretty girl."

"She's not a bitch, she's nice."

"That's the Tic Tac between your legs talking," Darren said. "You've barely met her. She *has* to be a bitch."

"You'll see tonight. Just don't embarrass me."

"We won't embarrass you," Bill said. "Maybe you should try taking her to the abandoned cabin."

"Oh yeah, are still up for our little bet, Bill?"

"Definitely. Are you? Maybe after the bonfire?"

"Yeah dude."

Darren took a bite of his pizza then spit it out. *"Too hot! Too hot!"*

Darren picked up the piece he spat out and ate it.

"Gross," Wesley said. "You're gonna make me sick."

A little while later, it was time to swim, so the boys walked back to the cabin for their trunks.

The weather cooled. Soft breezes whistled through the trees and fell over Camp Solgohachia. The clouds were low and thick.

Hair clung to Wesley's face. He moved it away but it only fell back in place and became stuck again with hot sweat trickling down his face.

When they entered Panda, there were three other campers filling up dresser drawers and changing into trunks, and a counselor who sat on a bottom bunk closest to the door and was all ready to go to the swim hole.

"Hello," the counselor said in an overly happy voice, a voice that Wesley thought the counselors were all forced into faking. "I'm Vince. Have you guys been having a great first day?"

"Yeah," Wesley said. Then he added: "I'm Wesley. This is Bill and Darren."

The boy in blue trunks and a blue shirt said, “I’m Al.”

“Chester,” the redhead said.

“Ralph,” the short one mumbled.

“I’m heading to the swim hole now,” Vince said. “See you guys there.”

Vince shut the door behind himself.

“Man, what a faggot,” Wesley said.

“For sure,” Bill said.

Al laughed. “Yeah you’re probably right.”

“Hey, let me ask you new guys a question,” Wesley said. “You meet a pretty girl, she’s new here, she’s got no friends. What’s it mean?”

“Easy,” Chester said, “she’s a bitch. Every hot girl without friends must be one or she’d have friends. Everyone wants to be friends with a hot girl.”

“Even if she’s new?”

“Especially if she’s new,” Al said. “You kidding? She wouldn’t be alone unless she’s a bitch.”

“Well she didn’t seem like a bitch.”

“Who is she?” Al said.

“Wendy. But she isn’t a bitch."

“Wendy… Wendy…” Chester said. “Doesn’t ring a bell.”

“Heh, we tried to tell him,” Darren said. “We *tried* to tell him. But ole Wes here doesn’t listen. Oh boy, he wants to learn the hard way.”

“You assholes haven’t even met her.”

The swim hole was a giant in-ground circle of murky green-blue water divided in half by a yellow fence.

On one side, the shallow side, which anybody could use, was a volleyball net, a small slide, and two low basketball hoops with green and white striped basketballs.

On the other end, the deep end, which you'd have to pass a swimming test to use, was a bigger slide, a wooden deck, and *the blob.*

The blob was a giant yellow and blue inflatable structure that required two people to use. One person, usually the smaller of the two, would jump from the deck to the blob and sit on the far end of it. The other person, the bigger of the two, would then jump straight down from the deck, causing the smaller person to go flying through the air then landing in the water.

Wesley kicked off his flipflops and ran down to the far end, where he waited in one of two lines for his turn to take the swim test. The test was simple, and he passed every year: swimming down to the other end and back.

When his turn came he jumped in and swam. The water was lukewarm, a little on the cold side, but he hit a warm pocket and went to the other end as fast as he could. When he made it there, he touched the concrete edge, glanced quickly around to see if Wendy was there, didn't see her, turned around and swam back. Down at the end he was returning to, he saw Bill and Al and Chester in line.

Now it was time for the blob.

He raced up the wooden steps. Wesley's turn came and he jumped off the platform, which must've been about ten feet high if he had to guess, then crawled to the edge. He prepared himself for liftoff, turned around, then gave the tubby dude on the platform a thumbs up.

"Ready."

Wesley turned back and by the time he was looking forward he was already in the air. There was a loud *SMACK!* of the guy slamming into the blob then everything became a blur: the world rushed by and he had that thrill of falling, limbs flailing, mouth agape but shutting as he realized he was coming down face-first into water. He splashed under the green-blue chilly surface then rose with his hair plastered to his face and big smile running across his thin lips.

Wesley looked over and saw that the tubby man who blobbed him was about to be blobbed by an even bigger man. Wesley put his arms around the yellow fence then watched the fatty climb into the sky, panic on his face—he must not have been blobbed often—and come crashing like a cannonball not far from Wesley.

Wesley swam back to the wooden deck and went back up the dripping wet stairs, grabbing the railing tight, went back in line—longer now than it had been the first time—and waited in line behind a girl. From his place up top on the deck he could see most of the swim hole, although most people on the shallow end were just dots from up here, and tried to find Wendy.

The line moved fast and when it was Wesley's turn again he was blobbed by an even bigger guy than the first time, and was flung so far he almost became the second person in history to hit the fence that divided the deep end and the shallow end. For a moment he was suspended in air, and all he saw was yellow. Even as he shut his eyes he saw the bar coming closer and closer, tried to somehow push his body away from it, and landed on his back in the water just a foot away from the fence. When he resurfaced he heard many people laughing.

After that, he decided it was time to head over to the shallow end and see what was going on. Darren and Ralph were chilling against the fence, hardly waist-deep in the swim hole. Bill, Al, Chester, and some other boys were playing basketball on one hoop while some girls were playing basketball on the other.

Wesley snuck through the game of basketball, put Bill in a choke hold, which was difficult since Bill was much taller, then dragged him under the water and let go. Bill resurfaced, grabbed Wesley, lifted him up, then dropped him in the water with a big splash.

The game of basketball abruptly ended and suddenly everybody was dunking everybody. Chester dunked Al, Al dunked a random baldheaded boy, somebody Wesley couldn't see dunked him. When Wesley came back up he saw that Darren and Ralph hadn't seen the dunking party going on because they were watching people get blobbed.

"Hey, over there." Wesley pointed. "Let's get 'em."

Wesley and Al crept over to their unsuspecting friends, then Wesley put his arm around Darren, and Al helped grab him too.

"Oh what is this what are you guys doing don't dunk me don't dunk me please."

"Everybody gets at least one," Wesley said.

Al turned back to Ralph. "What he said. You're next, Ralphie."

Ralph was frozen with terror.

Darren tried to wiggle free. *"But I can't swim I don't know what to do what do I do? Please—"*

"Just plug your nose," Al said.

Darren slipped an arm free from Wesley. He started to ask, as he raised his hand to his face, "Like this—" but before he could reach his nose, they let go of him and he went under three feet of water. A moment later he came to the surface thrashing his arms around as if the shark from *Jaws* were after him.

"I'm drowning I'm drowning oh God this is the end! Goodbye cruel world!"

Bill grabbed him by the shoulders. "Get ahold of yourself, you're standing up dude."

"Huh? I am?"

Darren looked down and wrinkled his nose. "I swallowed some of it! Some of it went in my nose! It hurts! Oh God, you know what kind of diseases could be in this water?"

"None of us have aids," Wesley said.

Al looked back at Ralph who was climbing out of the water. "Your turn Ralphie."

"Come on, Al, no."

That was the most Wesley had heard Ralph speak yet. He was a quiet boy, short and thin. He looked like a small frightened child the way he backed away from Al. There were almost tears in his eyes.

"I hate the water. Come on please no."

Wesley laughed. He was like Darren's skinny twin.

He watched Al pull Ralph back into the water and toss him down. Ralph jerked and squirmed and reached for something to grab onto as he sank. It was funny to watch, but Wesley felt bad for him and reached down to help him up. Back on the surface, Ralph spat out a mouthful of water and coughed uncontrollably. Al walloped his hand on Ralph's back to help him spit the water up, but very little came out.

"Sorry, buddy."

One of the basketballs drifted near Wesley. He grabbed it, looked at all the guys who had been playing a few minutes ago, then asked, "Can one of you guys show me how to throw this thing?"

Bill grabbed it from his hands then demonstrated. "Like this, Wes, rest it on the tips of your right fingers like this. Left hand on the side. Just flick your wrist."

Bill took a shot for example. It hit the backboard and went in. A stranger grabbed it from under the hoop and tossed it back to Bill. Bill handed it to Wesley, then Wesley tried to shoot. It clanged off the front of the rim and splashed five feet away.

"It'll be easier on land," Bill said.

Wesley grabbed the ball again and took a shot from the left of the hoop. Backboard. Far right rim. Then down to the end of the swim hole by the concrete edge.

“You’ll get the hang of it,” Chester said, grabbed it, then waddled to the hoop for a dunk. “Must be what Kareem Abdul-Jabbar feels like.”

Chester reached for the ball, then Darren of all people grabbed hold of him and dunked him under water. Chester resurfaced and splashed handfuls of water at Darren. Darren flinched, turned away, and flopped face-first into the water and squirmed. The boys laughed then Ralph helped him out.

Clouds ripped away from the sun and it was bright again. The water was heating up and the occasional breeze swung by. Somebody dunked Wesley again, then Wesley dunked Al, and there was another round of dunking everybody before a shootaround on the hoops. A few shots later, Wesley finally made one. It was probably one make out of fifteen tries, but at least he made it.

Time was flying by, and he went to the blob one last time before some of the counselors announced swim time was over.

4

THE SUN WAS SINKING.

Tints of orange mixed with shades of red and tones of purple across the wide fading hues of rich blue sky over Camp Solgohachia. Everyone was leaving the swim hole. Cool breezes swept over them.

Wesley yawned and dried himself with his towel and went back to Panda.

Back in the cabin, the boys showered. There were three separate showers, and Wesley, Bill, and Darren were first since they had arrived at the cabin first today and therefore had dibs on first showers. The water was hot and relaxing, and Wesley didn't want to leave.

From the stall next to him: *"Ahhhhhh!"*

"Darren?" Wesley said.

Darren screamed. *"Give me back my clothes oh God my towel too! They took my towel too! Come on guys how will I get out of here?"*

Their bunkmates were laughing, and Wesley couldn't help but join in. Bill too. When Wesley was done, he dried off in the stall then dressed up, and leaving the shower, Darren was still screaming for his clothes.

"Come on guys," Wesley said. "Let's give him back his things."

Chester grabbed his can of shaving cream from the counter. "We're just getting started. Watch this."

"Take it easy on him."

Chester didn't listen. He crept up to the stall, put his hand over the railing, then sprayed shaving cream all over Darren.

"Oh my God." Darren screamed as if he were being stabbed.

"It's just shaving cream is all," Bill said. "Chill out, man. We'll get you your clothes now."

Al tossed the towel over the railing. "Here dude."

"Thank you," Darren said on the brink of tears. "My clothes? Where are my clothes?"

Chester rolled them up then tossed them into the shower like a basketball. "*Three-eee pointerrrr.*"

"They're wet! They're all wet! How am I supposed to dress in these? You ever dress in wet clothes? They don't fit right!"

Wesley brushed his teeth, then laid down on his bunk and shut his eyes for a minute.

"Don't fall asleep," Bill said.

"Just shutting my eyes until we head out. Besides, it's kinda hard to sleep with Darren over there sniffling in the corner."

"I'm not crying."

It had been a tiring and fun day.

Wesley did almost sleep. He was on the brink of passing out when Al, Ralph, and Chester were all done showering then changing into new outfits.

Bill shook him. "Wake up. Bonfire time."

Darren was complaining again: *"These guys took my towel they threw my clothes into the water, what's next? They're gonna throw me into the bonfire?"*

"Oh quit it," Al said then whipped him with a towel. "Loosen up."

"Ouch."

Wesley hopped down from his bunk and put on his shoes, then all the boys from Panda headed out for the bonfires and food, if it could even be called that. The food that camp served at the bonfires was crud. But the campers would eat it anyways. Doughboys, which was dough roasted over fire on a stick, without any sauce or cheese to dip it in, smores made of chemical bomb marshmallows and generic gram crackers with Hersey bars that are already half melted, and sometimes unsalted sunflower seeds.

Several small fires set around camp. Logs burned surrounded by even bigger logs used as seats. And now that it had gotten even darker outside while the boys had showered, the lights of the distant fires were the only things to guide them off the path from Panda and the other cabins down into camp.

"How do they expect us to see without lights?" Darren said. "I could fall here and twist my ankle! This is—this is insane! Do they think I have night vision? Oh this is dangerous! Very dangerous!"

"Do you ever shut the fuck up?" Chester said.

The boys went around the camp looking for an empty fire, and found one just off the basketball courts. There were boxes of smores ingredients, dough, green sticks, packs of unsalted seeds.

"Where's that chick of yours?" Al asked.

"I don't know," Wesley said. "I haven't seen her since earlier."

"Maybe Wes made her up," Bill said.

Wesley walked away from the groups. "I'll go find her."

Wesley found her by the basketball courts then took a few shots with her in darkness, barely able to see the rim, then they threw the ball into a bin and went to the bonfire.

"So you didn't make her up?" Bill said. "I thought Wes meeting a girl was too good to be true."

"Guys this is Wendy. Wendy, this is everybody."

"Nice to meet you all," she said.

Wendy and Wesley sat next to each other in the last open spots.

Under the dark sky devoid of any clouds, and scattered with stars many lightyears away, they passed around the sticks and marshmallows and dough. Wesley roasted a doughboy while everyone else went for marshmallows.

Flames flickered and shadows moved along Al's face as he suddenly said, "The murders weren't very far from camp. I'm gonna give it to you straight: he's still out there, The Raven Hill Butcher was never found. Raven Hill is jinxed."

"Yeah right," Wendy said.

"Some folks have claimed to see him in this very camp."

"None of that is true," Wendy said.

“Didn’t you know why he killed them?”

Wendy leaned forward. “You mean those girls who died like… a million years ago? And the guy dressed up like Santa Claus?”

“Right. My older brother told me all about it. You know that boarded up cabin the counselors tell you to stay away from? There’s a reason it’s boarded up. It belonged to that guy who killed those girls, and legend has it if you go to the cabin, he’ll find you.”

“Then why isn’t it demolished?” Wendy asked.

“Like that would stop him,” Al said. “He’d come for the campers anyways.”

Everyone went silent. Embers rose from the fire then fizzled out.

Al said, “If he catches you… it’s not worth thinkin about. The Butcher… he’s not human. Not anymore.”

“You’re—you’re scaring me man,” Darren said.

“Shut up, Darren,” Bill said.

Darren stuffed his face with a smore.

“If you think those girls were random targets, think again,” Al said. “You know why he killed them?”

“I’d be much more scared,” Wendy said, “if I knew it was something *real*. Not boogeymen.”

“My brother told me about a girl who died here when he was a camper. Do you wanna hear it?”

“Someone died here?” Ralph said.

“Does he only kill girls? Am I safe?” Darren said.

“No,” Al said. “Nobody’s safe.”

“I wanna hear, Al,” Chester said.

“Tell us,” Bill said.

Al cleared his throat. “There was a girl one night who was dared to sneak out to the cabin, so she left after the counselor fell asleep. Now her bunkmates all watched her from the windows until she was out of sight. Then after a couple minutes they heard her screaming for help. It was so loud when it woke up their counselor, the girls all acted like they didn’t know what was going on… and their counselor ran outside with a flashlight. You know what she found?”

Everybody was still.

“Her head. The rest of her body was never found.”

"Hey Wes," Bill said, "you ready for the thing?"

"Oh yeah."

"What thing?" Wendy said.

"We're going to the cabin, that one off in the woods somewhere," Wesley said. "Last one back gets butchered."

5

THINGS CHANGE IN THE dark.

The fires were put out and the group walked away. What were once prolific tree branches now seemed like twisted contorted arms ready to grab them.

"You guys know where the cabin is, right?" Al pointed deep towards the woods on the right. "Over there. Down past the flagpole, just off of the girls' cabins."

"Now Wesley," Bill said, "we gotta make this interesting. What's the winner get?"

"Nothing. It's just a competition. Who can get there first then back. Friendly race."

"Well good luck you two," Wendy said, "but I need to get back to my cabin. Uh, bye, Wes. And it was nice meeting you all."

"Bye, Wendy," Wesley said.

Wesley and Wendy looked at each other for a brief second before she left.

She went through the grass and over to the path that led to the girls' cabins. Soon she disappeared into the night.

"You didn't kiss her?" Al asked.

"What? We've just met."

Bill put his arm around Wesley. "Now don't blow this. This cabin thing might impress her."

"How would that impress her?"

"So she knows you're not a wimp."

"I tell you what, Wes," Al said, "if you don't make a move I think I will."

"I can't make a move this early."

"You see how close she sat next to you dude? She was practically on your lap. She was practically asking for it."

They came to cabin Panda.

Ralph opened the door and everybody flooded in, exhausted.

"Where's Vince?" Darren said.

Everyone ignored his question. They went for their bunks and collapsed.

"I'm exhausted." Wesley kicked off his shoes then threw them off his bunk. It was nice and cool in the cabin.

A bit later, Wesley grabbed onto one of the rafters and did a pullup. "Al, Ralph, Chester, you guys ever raced on these things? See who can get to that end and back like monkey bars?"

"That looks dangerous," Ralph said.

"It's harmless. If your arms start to give you can jump to a bunk."

"Jump? And what if I miss? And fall? Split my head open? And down by the door there're no beds."

"Geez, it's like having two Darrens."

"I'll race you," Al said. "We'll get you warmed up for your race with Bill tonight."

Al climbed the ladder to the top bunk across from Wesley's and grabbed the rafter. He found his balance, then said, "Whenever you're ready."

"Ready," Wesley said. *"Go."*

Wesley pulled himself across the bar, glanced at Al, and saw he was on pace with him.

"When you get to that end you have to smack the wall," Wesley said. "And winner gets Chester's mom."

Chester ran below the race and tried to jump at Wesley's feet but missed.

"Come on Chester we're racing here." Al said. "Knock it off."

Wesley was temporarily distracted and Al took the lead. He kicked into high gear, forgetting to breathe and using all his strength to get to the end as if his life depended on it, but he was too late. Al smacked the wall first.

Wesley focused on getting to the wall and didn't pay attention to what he was hearing behind him. It sounded like an argument was brewing.

Wesley smacked the wall then turned around. Chester was on the beam.

"Really Chester? During the beam race?"

"I'm gonna get you, you faggot."

Chester raced down the beam. His face turned red, he was out of breath—for a skinny guy, he wasn't very in shape—and Wesley laughed at him.

Chester came within three feet of Wesley and kicked. Wesley realized his arms were tired but he was still near the door and there was no bed to jump to, just hardwood floors.

"Move it," Wesley said.

Chester kicked Wesley again so Wesley kicked back.

"Fight! Fight! Fight!" everyone else in the cabin chanted.

Wesley wound his legs back, jumped forward a couple inches, then went for the gut. His foot landed in Chester's stomach. Chester lost his grip momentarily around the beam then regained it. Then he climbed forward as close as he could get to Wesley and tried to hit him with his elbow, then kneed him.

At the same time, the door opened and Vince came in confused at the chanting.

"What's with all the yelling and the—" Vince looked up. "Why are you two fighting?"

Wesley said, "Well—"

"I don't wanna hear it. Get down from there immediately."

Chester climbed backwards to the nearby bunk, got off first, then Wesley.

"Now shake hands and apologize. Come on guys, that's a rule. No fighting, and if you do fight, we apologize."

Wesley and Chester sat on the edge of the bunk and shook hands.

"Sorry," Wesley said.

"I'm sorry too."

"Great," Vince said. "I hope that's the end of all our fighting in cabin Panda. I've got zero tolerance for it. Let's all focus on having a great time here. Now it's time for lights out."

6

Hypnotizing coldness slipped through the rusty hinges of the door and through hidden cracks in the structure of the cabin and twisted through Wesley's flesh like wire.

"Wes? You up? Guys?" Bill whispered from the bunk below and startled him.

Wesley turned over. "Yeah. Anyone else up?"

Wesley climbed down from his bunk. He stood frozen between bunks momentarily, double checking Vince was asleep, then Wesley made his way to the door and looked outside. Something strange about the darkness tonight, he thought.

The others crept over careful not to make noise, careful not to wake Vince, but the floorboards were creaky and they made loud noises.

Thankfully, Vince did not wake up.

The boys all looked out of the windows together, then Wesley went back towards the bunks.

"Chickening out?" Bill whispered.

"Good! Let's not do this! No good can come of this!" Darren said.

"Shut up before you wake Vince," Chester whispered.

Wesley came back with his flashlight. "You got one too?"

Bill nodded, went to his bag, and pulled out a flashlight.

Al turned the knob slowly. The hinges squealed as he pulled it open a few inches. Al then stopped, turning back to Vince. Vince turned in bed but did not wake up. Al turned his attention back to the door and opened it wider; everybody piled out, then he gently closed it behind them.

"Let's go over the rules," Al said.

"Yeah we should," Bill said. "First one there and back wins. No tripping, hitting, or any other interference."

"How'll we know who actually got there first?" Ralph asked.

"I don't like this one bit," Darren said. "You'll die out there! You're crazy for this! The Butcher will get you!"

Al rolled his eyes. "Listen, Darren, it's all made up."

"How about a splinter of wood?" Wesley said. "To prove we actually got there first."

"Sounds fair," Bill said. "And if we aren't back in ten minutes then come looking for us."

"Just don't let Butch getcha guys," Chester said. "I hear he's dying to add new heads to his collection."

Al walked from the door down to the gravel path spanning next to the cabins. "Wes, Bill, come on down here. Get ready, on the count of three…"

Wesley and Bill went down in front of Al, stood in running position, and looked straight ahead. The boys wished each other luck.

"One… *three.*"

The boys were off.

Wesley took the lead with a sudden burst of speed, barefoot feet pounding against grass and soft earth as they went off the gravel path. The night smelled like bark and pine needles. Wind blew hard and knocked his hair into his eyes. Wesley brushed his hair away and looked at Bill on his left, who was catching up to him and about to pass him. All at once, Wesley's legs felt stiff. The ground was getting hard and it was hurting to run.

The boys raced across open grass to the center of Camp Solgohachia. Wesley and Bill passed the flagpole at the same time. Wesley was losing speed and Bill was ahead of him by only a step or two or three.

His lungs burned for gasps of air. He breathed through his nose as hard as he could and kept pushing. He desperately wanted to win to impress Wendy. His heart pounded so hard he felt it in his throat. Wesley moved his heavy legs with all the strength in his body, feeling chilly air beating against him. All the day's activities had worn him out. He wondered if Bill was as exhausted as he was.

Bill's heavy breathing came from behind Wesley. A smile came across Wesley's face. He was in the lead.

His feet pulsed. *Why had we done this barefoot?* Wesley wondered. They were about to enter the woods.

There was a long stretch of grass before the forest, but soon they'd be stepping over twigs and rocks. Wesley prepared himself for the pain of the hidden forest floor and for the intensity of the run back. And the flashlight wouldn't do him much good. He couldn't figure out what was on the ground in the brief seconds they were illuminated while he ran furiously.

He and Bill weaved past remains of fires from earlier, and the ground was littered with green sticks and remnants of doughboys and smores and sunflower seeds that were in the process of being devoured by ants and flies.

As they came into the woods, Wesley took the lead. The race was neck and neck. Back and forth. It would be a tight one.

Fifteen feet into the woods, the boys came upon the cabin.

Jagged and faulty, as if constructed by blind men. Splintery planks were sprawled across the windows and doors with rusty nails, nails that seemed they'd turn to dust if touched. It was nothing more than a ghostly silhouette. It shuddered in the wind, creaking in the night, home to clusters of spiders. Dust lay over the cabin like a layer of dirty snow. Nasty weeds twisted up from the ground and worked their way upon the sides of the cabin as if attracted like magnets.

Wesley and Bill looked at each other. The boys had come to a halt.

"Woah." Wesley whispered, then ran the final five feet to its front door.

"Dang it." Bill bolted after him.

Wesley fastened his hands around a loose section of wood at the very end, a splinter that was almost falling off around the nail, as if it had been crafted and waiting there for Wesley Lawrence to come and pick it off.

He ripped it free then looked at Bill, who even through the veil of night looked pale. His hand was frozen on the plank across the broken glass of the front window. His eyes stared holes through Wesley.

"Bill? Are you okay?"

Bill stared silently.

"Out with it. What's going on?"

A gust of cold wind swept through the trees as Bill said, "Is that a snake?"

Wesley followed Bill's eyes down at the small three- or four-foot space between each other. There, creeping along the ground up the front wall of the building, was a snake at least four feet long, possibly even longer.

Together they screamed.

Wesley clutched the splinter so hard it was buried in his palm and probably left smaller splinters in his skin.

Wesley took off. Behind him he heard Bill still screaming. When he turned around, he saw Bill had fallen, and the snake was staring at him with its head upside down from the wall of the cabin.

Wesley turned back and helped Bill up.

The snake writhed down.

The boys backed away from the woods, not daring to take their eyes off the serpent, but soon lost track of it while it slithered through tall grass and vanished. It could have been anywhere.

"Where'd it go?" Bill said.

"I'll be damned if I know."

Together they inched backwards, gasping, and Wesley figured they'd walk slowly backwards until they came back to Panda. Now that would be a sight. He already imagined the guys laughing at them. Wendy would probably laugh too if she were there... Wesley turned red thinking about it.

But after a minute more of walking backwards the boys turned around and screamed again when they ran into their friends. Al, Darren, Ralph, and Chester.

"Fellas, what's the matter with you?" Al asked.

"Was there something out there?"

"I want to go home," Ralph cried.

Chester was the only one laughing. "What a bunch of pansies."

Then, in the distance, footfalls.

Chester squealed. "Who's there?"

Al hit him on the shoulder. "Quiet, moron."

A shape emerged from the darkness. The boys stared at it.

As it came closer, it took form and they saw it was Wendy.

"Are you guys okay?" Wendy said. "I heard screaming."

"Wendy?" Wesley said. "What are you doing here?"

Wendy came closer before answering. "I couldn't sleep and was thinking about your race. I was coming by to see if you guys were awake when I heard screaming. Did something happen?"

"There was a big snake."

"About four feet long, maybe more, maybe five," Bill said. "I couldn't even grab my splinter of wood."

"Oh yeah." Wesley held up his splinter nice and high. "Guess that means I won."

"I guess it does." Al yawned. "I'm tired."

"Let's get going," Wesley said. "I don't wanna stick around for that thing to come back."

"Hey," Wendy said, "at least it wasn't The Butcher."

Things *do* change in the dark. More so than any of them knew...

Something had been awakened. Something brewed underground, deep within the earth. The ground of the woods trembled. Leaves drifted from the dirt next to the old cabin as if trying to run away. Chilling winds drilled past the grass and sank into the dirt. The crescent moon shone its light down on the cabin and winked off the broken remnants of what had once been windows.

The ground shook abruptly, and its loose soil opened.

One filthy black hand broke the surface of the earth and clawed. It dug its other hand free and dredged away handfuls of dirt until its decaying head was pulled through.

It dragged itself out of its tomb, coming up from one black abyss to another, and listened to the laughter of children, the children who awoke him.

He stepped forward. It was more a wobble than a walk. He'd have to get used to walking again now that he had escaped his crypt. From far away he watched. Six boys in one direction, and a girl in another.

It was hard to smile, but his sore muscles found a way.

After the kids disappeared, he turned back to the cabin he had once lived in and broke the board off the door. It was easy to remove. Rusty nails crumbled and he tossed the wood towards the swaying trees.

Inside the cabin it was as black as a cat but he didn't need to see. He remembered how it looked in the light and he knew where he had hidden it.

At his right, he found the bathroom, and felt along the wall behind the rotting old door for the loose panel of wood. It fell to the ground as soon as he touched it.

Sure enough, it was where he had left it all those years ago.

His knife had done so much damage. The long blade set in aging wood felt so natural in his hands, as if they hadn't been apart a day.

He was only missing his mask.

It's around here somewhere.

Then he found it. The mask. The big white beard. The Santa Claus costume he wore each year during the Winter Camp season.

Al opened the cabin door slowly, and it squeaked.

Inside, the boys found Vince snoring very loudly. The floor creaked under their footsteps, but they found their ways back into their beds without waking Vince. He must've been a heavy sleeper, and Wesley thought about inventing a game where they could see who could make the most noise without waking him up. He thought how funny it would be to light a firecracker and see Vince waking up from the sounds thinking they were gunshots.

Wesley curled the covers over himself. Yawned then shut his eyes. He kept the wood from the abandoned cabin on the windowsill next to his bunk.

7

"Rise and shine campers!"

It was first thing in the morning and Vince was already speaking at the top of his lungs, waking everybody up. There were a few groans, some of the guys were turning back over to sleep, but Vince kept on marching around the cabin nearly yelling.

"Good morning fellas, good morning. Up, up, up, come on guys. Ralphie, wake on up. You up there—Wesley—come on, wake up."

Wesley rubbed his eyes, looked around, and saw Chester sliding out of bed, and Bill and Darren and Al already fixing their sheets with glazed over eyes. He and Ralph were the last two awake.

He yawned, shut his eyes for a moment and sat up a little, then almost fell asleep again while sitting up.

"Up, up, up, Mr. Wesley. Time for breakfast then to get the day started!"

Leave me alone, Wesley thought.

He groaned, slipped out from the covers, then fixed his bed. Then he climbed down the ladder and went to the bathroom to relieve himself then brush his teeth. After that, when he came back to change into a new shirt and pants and to throw on his shoes, most of the cabin had left besides Bill and Darren who decided to stay behind to wait for him.

"What's the point of a counselor?" Wesley sat on Bill's bunk to slide his socks on. "Is he just here to be our personal alarm clock? Dude doesn't even know when six kids sneak out of the cabin at night."

"I think so," Bill said. "Vince is annoying but it's his job."

When Bill was ready the boys left Panda and headed for the cafeteria. The line was short. Most kids were already served.

“Hold up,” Darren said. “Oh man, I left my retainer case in the cabin. I’ll be right back you guys.”

“Suit yourself,” Wesley said.

Darren sprinted away.

“Fastest I’ve ever seen him run, Bill.”

“He doesn’t know he could wrap it in napkins, does he?”

“Probably scared he might throw them out by accident again. Remember that time?”

The wait in line was six or seven minutes, then they were served little cartons of milk, single serve plastic containers of cereal, and their choice of either an apple, pear, or banana.

Wesley and Bill sat by one of the windows. They didn’t see their cabinmates or Wendy anywhere. Wesley tried to look through the window up the path to Panda but it was a little too obscure at his angle in the back of the cafeteria and he could only see the first half of the path.

“You see Darren anywhere? What’s taking him?” Wesley said. It had been about ten minutes since Darren left.

“No clue. He might’ve had a heart attack on the way there or back. Might’ve ran out of breath. Might take him a year to catch it.”

“Yeah, maybe. He runs out of breath lifting a spoon to his mouth.”

“As soon as we get back, we’re putting him on a diet. No chocolate no sugar no nothing. No ifs ands or buts about it.”

“We’ll make him walk a mile a day.”

“Let’s start small. Half a mile a day.”

“Nah dude, he can walk a mile. I think.”

“Three or four laps around the block, Wes?”

“We’ll just put him on the treadmill, doesn’t his family have a treadmill in the basement?”

“Yeah. Yeah I think they do. And I don’t think any of them have ever used it.”

“It’s probably for show.”

“What’s on the agenda for today?”

“Think they’re gonna put us into teams, after breakfast. They’ll probably start the competitions soon. I think I’m gonna ditch ‘em all this year.”

Bill shrugged. "Don't do that. Have some fun. It's our last year here."

"I'll consider it. Let's all try and get on the same team again."

Darren huffed on his walk back to Panda.

It was a hot cloudless day and that made it worse. Sweat dripped into his eyes and burned. He stopped, leaned against a tree, and rubbed his eyes with his shirt collar. A moment later he continued up the slope to the cabins. It was a pain walking uphill. After three steps up he was out of breath.

The inside of Panda was refreshingly cool. Darren sat on the edge of his bed and found his retainer case on the windowsill. He laid down to catch his breath.

"God I'm out of shape," Darren said. Then when he was ready to rejoin Bill and Wesley, he left his bed and went across the cabin. "When I get home, no more Twinkies. Or Jolt Cola. Or Tootsie Rolls. Or..."

Darren was blinded by the sheet that was wrapped around his face and choked him.

Powerful arms pulled him against his attacker's body. Darren strained to hit the menace away but he couldn't move. He was paralyzed under the monster's grip.

He had never been more scared in his life.

His struggle to breathe worsened when the rope was set around his throat. It pulled tighter by the second. Suddenly he knew that this was it. He was going to die.

After Wesley and Bill finished eating, they still hadn't seen Darren, so they walked back to Panda. Along the way they kept an eye out for Vince, Al, Chester, or Ralph. Maybe one of them had seen Darren, or maybe he was hanging out with them. But the boys didn't see any of their bunkmates.

"Not like him to miss breakfast," Wesley said halfway through the gravel path.

"I thought he'd only be a minute," Bill said. "We better not walk in on him jerking off."

"Yeah, Bill. Wouldn't be the first time."

"I know."

Wesley opened the door then walked in first. Bill followed closely.

"Darren?" Bill called out, then they were both chilled and suspended in place.

However badly they had screamed last night, their screams after walking into Panda were worse. Wesley's throat strained. He couldn't believe it. He just couldn't believe it.

His eyes darted away then darted back. He was too disturbed to keep looking at it, but his eyes rolled back to Darren.

He ran.

The rope weas tense and strained under Darren's massive weight.

"Darren ohmigod ohmigod what the hell what the—"

A thin sheet was fastened over his head under the noose and covered part of his body. They couldn't see his face but they knew it was him.

Wesley and Bill climbed up the nearest bunkbed and reached to bring him down. Bill wrapped his arms around Darren's torso, attempted to lift him to try and stop any choking. Wesley loosened the rope from the rafters and helped Bill to bring him down to the bed.

Darren's body was slack. Loose and malleable under their grips. Almost rubbery. Almost as if it weren't a real person.

Wesley struggled to rip the sheet and the noose off of him. After a minute of struggles it slipped right off, without a single movement from the boy underneath them.

"Darren? My God Darren—"

His eyes were sunken, his skin was turning purple and waxy. His neck was snapped.

"He's dead he's dead!" Bill screamed. *"Why would he do that?"*

Wesley jumped off the bed, fell on his knees on the floor and heaved. His stomach clenched. Heat ran through him. Everything was blurry. *"He didn't do it. He couldn't."*

"The hell do you mean he couldn't, Wes? Do you—do you see him? He did it."

"How's a lard like Darren gonna pull himself onto the rafters? He's never been able to climb—"

"I don't know Wes! But he's dead, look at him."

"Ohmigod Bill, he can't be dead. He was fine on the way to breakfast."

"If he didn't… what—what does this mean?"

"The Butcher."

Bill came down from the top bunk and joined Wesley on the floor. Bill sat with his legs crossed, wiping away tears. He opened his mouth to speak then shut it.

Wesley gulped. "You remember what Al said about The Butcher?"

"It's not the time for a stupid fucking story."

Wesley went on anyways. "I've… I've… oh God, forgive me, Bill. This is all my fault."

"Your fault?"

"What if it had to do with taking something from the cabin? What if I woke him up?"

Bill didn't say anything.

Wesley cried. *"What if I woke him?"*

8

Charlie the camp director held a camp-wide meeting to discuss the situation, but Wesley could hardly pay attention.

"We have some awful news. Some terrible news—"

He didn't kill himself.

"—found dead—"

I woke The Butcher…

"Camp will proceed as normal, however—"

If we hadn't done the stupid race if we hadn't gone to the cabin he'd still be alive I just know it. I don't know how I can prove it, but I know it.

"—always talk to someone—"

Wesley was angry hearing Charlie talk about Darren as if he knew what he was talking about. *Always talk to someone. Darren didn't need someone to talk to, he was murdered. And… and all of us were there. Me. Bill. Darren. Al. Chester. Ralph.* Wendy. *One down, six to go.*

"If any of you have any questions—"

How do we stop this thing? How do we stop The Raven Hill Butcher? I know—I just know—it was him. Someone had to do it. It wasn't Darren. He could hardly lift a ten-pound barbell, there was no way he lifted himself up to the rafter.

Vince talked to the boys from Panda after the camp-wide meeting in a cabin-wide meeting.

The boys all sat on their bunks and Vince stood in front of them, but Wesley zoned out during this meeting as well. He wasn't sure how much he could take of it. Stories about The Raven Hill Butcher flooded his mind. He wanted to yell at Vince to shut the fuck up but held his tongue.

All he could think about was the touch of Darren's dead body. He wondered what happened to it now, if it were on its way back to town, how they broke the news to Darren's parents. Wesley wondered if the news had spread to his family yet. He planned to call them eventually. But for now he was too stunned to talk to them or anyone.

I will kill him. I will kill whoever did this to you. I will kill him myself. That's a promise, buddy. I'll kill him I'll kill him I'll fuckin kill him.

After the meeting, the scheduled activities were starting. Wesley guessed they missed getting their wristbands that indicated what team they'd be on for the duration of camp, since they were here in the cabin, but the boys from Panda ditched anyways, and gathered in the woods behind their cabin and sat down to have a real meeting about Darren for once. The previous two were utter bullshit.

Wesley stood before his friends. "Darren didn't do it. Outside of me 'n Bill, you guys didn't know him, but I think you understand he—he couldn't have killed himself like the counselors think. He couldn't have lifted himself up there to that rafter. He wasn't strong enough to hang himself."

"This is fucked up," Al said.

Bill ran his hands over his face speechlessly.

"We need to stick together," Wesley said. Then, after a pause, added: "It was The Butcher."

"He ain't real," Chester said. "Have you lost your mind?"

"Listen to me for one minute, don't you remember what Al said? That's his cabin. That's why people said they've seen him in this camp, that's why he's killed people who weren't far from here. If it's his cabin, if we disturbed it, if we brought him back—"

"Listen, Wes," Al said, "I know this is a really tough time, isn't it? But think straight for a minute, okay? If we brought him back now, how did he kill those girls a few years ago?"

“Then maybe it was someone else or maybe he was already back. I don’t have all the answers. And maybe he saw us last night. Maybe he’s coming for us all who were there. Darren, you, me, all of us, and Wendy.”

“Then why’s he come for Darren first?”

“I don’t know.”

Activities between battling camp teams—Apache, Navajo, Cherokee, Shawnee, depending on which color wristband you pulled from a bucket—were scattered throughout the day, leaving campers with a lot of free time to do whatever they want. Some went canoeing, some were playing basketball, some were playing carpetball, some sat around and walked, but as for Wesley, he slumped in his hiding spot beneath the deck of the cafeteria.

He needed to be alone. Bill had believed him, but just barely. The others not at all, although he suspected Ralph might have believed him just a little bit. Right now he didn’t even know where Bill was. Last he saw him, Bill was trying to play golf. He almost hated Bill for trying to move on so quickly, but what was Bill supposed to do? Maybe Bill was just trying to take his mind off of it…

So Wesley hid in darkness, twisting a twig between his fingers, wiping away sweat with the collar of his white t-shirt, feeling small beams of hot sun sneak through cracks and warm his body.

He wanted to leave. There’d be no leaving for about twelve more days. The road wasn’t very far from camp. And he knew a shortcut. If he had to go back through the entrance near the parking lot, it would take at least two hours on foot to reach the main road. But going through the woods, he could reach the road in ten minutes. He learned of the shortcut his first year when exploring with Bill and Darren and still remembered where in the woods it was and how to get there.

Footsteps came from his left. He snapped the twig in half. He knew who it was. He could tell by her steps.

"Wesley?"

Then a few seconds later, she came into view.

"Yeah."

"Is there space for me in there?"

Wesley didn't say anything. She crawled under there with him without waiting for an answer.

They sat silently for a moment until Wendy said, "Sorry. I'm so sorry."

Wesley wanted to say thanks but said nothing instead.

"I ran into some of your friends, they're all worried about you. They didn't know where you were, but I told them I knew where I'd find you."

"The others wouldn't listen to me, Wendy. But I need you to listen to me. I really need you to. Because unless we do something… he's coming for us too."

"What do you mean?"

"It's true. I don't know which parts are true but fear brought The Raven Hill Butcher back, that's what happened last night at our race. Darren didn't hang himself. He was too fat to reach the rafters and to do all of that… he'd never have succeeded. What we did last night awoke The Butcher. All seven of us who were there… he's coming to get us now Wendy. Any of us could be next."

Wendy was silent for a while. Then she said, "Wes…"

"Yeah?"

"Do you really believe he's out there?"

"I do. I don't know how I do or why I do, but I do. I can feel it. Something wrong is going on here. Something seriously wrong."

9

Wesley and Bill sat on one of the metal benches next to the basketball courts, sun beating on them heavily, and Wesley launched pebbles at unsuspecting passersby.

Normally he'd have fun with that, but after a few minutes and hitting two campers, he gave up. He put the slingshot at his side, stared off into camp, watched people move in a blur. Watched people move happily, watched people going from place to place with friends, watched people play games.

None of them cared about Darren. It was as if he had never died, or had never existed in the first place. None of them cared. All of them went on with life. Was that what was gonna happen after Wesley died? Was everybody going to be happy and live their life as if he were still there, or had never existed at all?

Wesley grabbed a pebble and fidgeted with it. "I want to go home."

"Yeah. Me too."

It was probably twenty minutes later when they heard the first scream. It was followed by a second, much louder one, then it became a sea of screams.

Everybody froze. Wesley looked around but couldn't tell what he was supposed to be seeing. The screams were coming from far away but everything was still. Even the screams quieted down for a moment, but that didn't last long. Soon campers were running away from the left end of the camp and towards the far right where Wesley and Bill were.

Counselors ran around telling kids to calm down.

Wesley turned to Bill. "You don't think…"

Bill was pale.

"Oh God, who did he…"

Wesley stood up. It was so silent now he could've heard a blade of grass grow. He noticed some kids look at him then look away. Wesley rushed off the bench, and Bill followed. The two pushed past clusters of people while counselors yelled at them to stay put, but they didn't listen. They sprinted toward the small crowd around the flagpole, and the counselors didn't stop them.

At the head of the crowd were Al and Ralph.

Al ran his hands through his hair angrily, and Ralph cried uncontrollably and tried to mutter something incoherent. There were other campers—all girls—crying as they attempted to explain something to some counselors. They must've been the ones who discovered the body.

The body was nearly impossible to find through the crowd of kids and the counselors trying to shield the body away from curious observers, but Wesley saw a wrist on the ground, slashed open half an inch deep and nearly severing it totally from its arm.

Wesley grabbed his stomach then looked away. *"Oh hell."*

Bill stared blankly at it. Wesley helped him turn away. Al and Ralph moved closer to them.

"He got him," Al whispered. "He got him. He got Chester."

Charlie and Vince were in the private counselors-only room on the other side of the cafeteria building where campers were never allowed to enter. Vince pulled on the collar of his purple Camp Solgohachia shirt that all the counselors had to wear. It was burning hot in here.

"Vince, this is the second kid from your cabin…"

Vince nervously tapped his fingers on the table. "I'm aware."

"Parents are going to ask questions. We're going to be ruined. Is there anything you can think of, anything that might clue us in on why these boys have done this? Some sort of pact? Some sort of… some sort of…"

"I don't know. I really don't know."

"Two kids from the same cabin don't kill themselves for no reason."

Vince nodded, then tapped his fingers more frequently on the table. "You saw that kid's wrists, Charlie. They were too deep. He didn't do that on his own. And I don't think the other kid hung himself either."

"Did any of the kids fight with each other? Did any of them not get along?"

"This boy that… slit his wrists. Chester. He had a problem with another boy named Wesley."

"Keep an eye on this 'Wesley.'"

It was ruled suicide.

There was a second camp-wide meeting. Al, Ralph, Wesley, Bill, and Wendy sat together in the back. This time it wasn't at the flagpole but in the cafeteria. Everybody was seated, and camp director Charlie paced up and down the middle aisle.

Al had told Wesley what happened: some girls stumbled upon Chester's body at the flagpole. Al and Ralph thought Chester had gone to play baseball and they hadn't seen him for a while, but there he was. Dead. *Both* wrists slit so deep they weren't sure how he could physically do that with the knife they found near the trail to the cabins.

Why slit his wrists then run to the flagpole?

Wesley didn't believe Chester had done it at all. He knew it had to be The Raven Hill Butcher, and Al and Ralph and Wendy finally believed Wesley and Bill. Wesley couldn't say he was happy about the circumstances.

He trembled. He worried who would be next. And he could only think of one way to escape it: to run away. To find a way back home. It would be dangerous and would take hours but it was the only way out of this madhouse.

Wesley thought, *I'll give Mom and Dad a call. And if they can't bring me home I'm leaving. The Butcher might find his way out of the camp but he doesn't know where I live, he can't just find me. I'll be long gone from here.*

Wesley didn't realize Charlie had already begun his speech. "We've had another unfortunate... accident—"

Wesley's hands formed into fists. *Accident?*

He thought it was bullshit how Charlie was acting. As if this were normal. As if this were standard procedure. In all four of Wesley's years here, the most he had seen was a sprained ankle or a broken pinky finger, and that was rare. This was two murders in a row. Why wouldn't Charlie just say what it was and send them all home? Did they want this to continue? Wesley was confused.

"Please," Charlie said a few moments later when Wesley started paying attention again, "if any of you are remotely thinking about it, don't do it. There's help. There's always someone here to help you. Find an adult. Any of our counselors or staff or even myself. Please. Things get better."

No matter what Charlie said, Wesley knew it was endless piles of bullshit.

After it was over, Wesley felt sick. After the meeting, he went to the bathroom then washed his hands. Strangely, after he left the bathroom, he noticed Vince eyeing him, and noticed that as he went towards the door to leave the cafeteria, Vince stood up and followed him out, trying to trail a few feet away and remain hidden, but he could feel him watching.

Wesley didn't say a word to him. He just kept on going through the camp. Wesley wondered why Vince was following him, and how long was he going to do it for? What did he want? What did he think he was gonna find?

So instead of going straight for the phone like he had planned, he circled back around the flagpole—the blood wasn't all cleaned yet off of it—then went from there through camp and back to the cafeteria to use the water fountain on the inside. Still, he noticed, Vince following him discretely. Except he didn't follow him into the cafeteria this time, he waited around the outside for Wesley to come back. At least he was *trying* to be sneaky, but not succeeding.

Wesley left from another exit. He went to the little giftshop building, and went to the back of the shop where there was a payphone and little bit of privacy. He searched his pockets for change, put a quarter through the slot, then dialed home.

"Mom, it's me, I'm calling from camp. I really need you to pick me up."

"Pick you up? Is it... oh honey, this is about Darren, isn't it? I am so sorry honey."

"Well yes Mom, but another kid... did something similar and I want to go home."

"Another? Oh my..."

"So can you come and get me?"

"I'm afraid I can't do that, your father needs the car for work. I can't just borrow it for *such* a long trip. I'm sorry about Darren honey. And sorry about the other kid. I hope you understand."

"But Mom—"

"I'm sorry, but I can't drop everything we're doing to pick you up. It's only a few more days."

"Mom, two kids are dead."

"I'm sorry Wesley. Be careful, okay? We'll be seeing you soon. You always have a good time at camp. Just stick close to Bill and make some new friends."

"Mom, goddammit, but I need to leave. You don't underst—"

"Don't use that language with me, young man."

He hung up the phone aware that it could have been the last time he ever talked to his mother.

Wesley went into Panda and shut the door.

He stood for a moment under the spot where they had found Darren.

I'm so sorry, Darren.

Then he went to the back and washed his face in one of the sinks when the door to Panda opened. Wesley called out, "Hello? Who's there?"

There was no answer, only fast footfalls coming through the cabin towards him. Wesley looked up from the sink, and Vince turned the corner.

"Why are you following me? What is this?"

Vince raised a fist. "I know you had a problem with Chester. You tell me now if you had anything to do with it."

Wesley stared at him.

Vince grabbed Wesley by the collar and pulled him closer. "You tell me right this minute, kid."

"You're fucking crazy man. You're sick."

Vince threw him to the floor.

"Maybe I did do it," Welsey said. "And I'll kill you next."

Vince turned around and left.

If Wesley suddenly decided to become a serial killer, Vince would be where he would start.

Vince left the cabin and thought, *Charlie's right, it's him.*

Two black gloved hands came around the corner of the cabin and pressed so tightly to his throat that not even his squeals could escape. Vince was pulled behind Panda into the woods. The person dragged him far until the cabins were just a memory.

The figure pushed Vince into a tree and held him with one hand by a throat.

Vince tried to scream but it was locked inside of him. He looked into the eyes of a madman behind a Santa Claus mask.

The man lifted his blade. In that moment Vince remembered all the stories, but he couldn't reminisce about them for long.

The Raven Hill Butcher brought the knife halfway through Vince's skull and watched him squirm and writhe.

Vince's eyes twitched, pleaded, begged. They fluttered shut then creaked open again, and his body convulsed. The Butcher removed the blade—Vince wiggled like a torn worm—then sank it into Vince's pelvis and dragged it downward.

He raised the blade up above his head and slammed it into Vince's shoulder. His arm came off in one clean swoop.

10

Tonight was not a normal night.

The moon was full and its light came brightly upon the camp.

Wesley sat with the others at a bonfire. To his left was Wendy, to his right was Al, and across from him were Bill and Ralph.

And then there were five.

"I can't believe a counselor would do that to you," Wendy said. "We've got to tell someone."

"No, it doesn't matter. It wouldn't matter at all. I don't know if any of you phoned home. Well, I did. Nobody can come pick me up, so I'm leaving. The four of you are welcome to join. Seven's already become five. I can't stick around to see it become four, then three, then two, then one, then zero. We're all bound to die if we stay. The adults are useless, they can't help us."

"I'm in," Bill said.

The others agreed too.

"We'll all go tonight. What time is it?"

Al looked at his watch. "Nearing nine."

"Light's out is ten. Eleven on the dot, let's all meet over there." Wes pointed down towards trees on the far end of camp, somewhere after the boys' cabins. "One year I went exploring there and found a shortcut to a road. Bill you were there, you might remember. You me and Darren."

In panda, the boys packed their bags. Wesley slipped the woodchip in his pocket then said, “Anyone seen Vince?”

Nobody had.

“Maybe you really did kill him,” Ralph said. “You didn’t kill him did you?”

Wesley laughed. It felt strange to laugh in a time like this, strange but good. “No I didn’t. Nothing to worry about, Ralph.”

“I’ve got a knife, anyone else have one?” Al said.

He was the only one.

After they were done, Wesley turned on his flashlight, and the boys left the dark cabin and set out into the night. It was ten-fifty. Wesley figured Wendy would be heading out now too unless she fell asleep or chickened out. Then he wondered what if something bad happened to her all the way over there? Something bad, and he wouldn’t be there to help her.

She’ll come, she’ll make it, don’t worry, she’s okay, she’s fine.

They crept along the final remnants of the path until it merged into grass and a bit of undergrowth.

Wesley led the way with his flashlight. He almost started to whistle then he held his tongue. Even the slightest things might risk the plan. It was tricky, but it would work: they’d cut through here to the road, then travel uphill. Al had a map and they’d follow it to the bus station a few miles ahead. They’d take the bus with what little money they had and get home, and by the time the counselors discovered that the kids were nowhere to be found, each of them would be explaining it to their parents.

On paper, it was perfect.

But things never go as planned.

Wendy showed up around eleven-ten and apologized for being late. She didn’t have a single bag with her besides her purse, and said it would’ve been impossible to pack two suitcases with all those other girls around.

Wesley led them through the dark tangled woods. Every shadow became The Raven Hill Butcher. Every shadow was his arm, every shadow was his knife, and every shadow threatened to pull them into their death and demise.

"Is—is it far?" Ralph said.

"No, not very far," Wesley said. "We'll be there soon."

From the right came footsteps. The group stopped.

Through the night, they all looked at each other, eyes darting, wondering who the stranger with them was. The distant person was silent for a while—frozen—then the footsteps started up again. It was coming from the direction they intended to travel in.

"Who—who's there?"

"Shush." Wendy whispered.

The noises stopped again.

"Must've been an animal," Al said.

"I hope you're right," Wesley said.

The group moved past low branches and swatted mosquitos. Night thickened. Night consumed them. The darkness was claustrophobic.

"Now through here," Wesley said, lower than a whisper, "towards the right a little ways we'll find a path. A clearing. We—"

Ralph tripped on something, bumped into Wesley's back, and both boys crashed into a tree. Pain raced up Wesley's body. He was so angry at Ralph he could've smacked him.

"Sorry," Ralph said after catching his breath. "I slipped on something."

Wendy lent Wesley a hand. "You okay?"

"Yeah, thanks."

Al and Bill offered hands to Ralph but he didn't take them. He was staring at something between his feet.

"Ralph?" Al said. "Come on dammit let's go."

Wesley shined his light on Ralph's body then lowered it between his legs and to his feet to reveal the severed foot of a man being picked at by bugs. Veins hung over the sides and the jagged edges of bone tore through a layer of flesh.

Wesley moved the light away quickly. Ralph screamed at the top of his lungs, so Al put his hands around his mouth to mask it.

"Shut up."

"Oh God," Wendy said. "Whose could that be?"

The boys gave each other a look as if they knew. Then, at the same time, Wesley, Al, and Bill whispered, "Vince?"

It was no longer footsteps from the distance to their right, but full-fledged running. Someone was rushing to get them.

The kids scrambled away from the sound.

Wesley didn't know what waited in the other side of these woods. Everybody had gone their own direction, completely avoiding whoever was running at them from their intended destination.

Wesley was all alone and pressed his body against a tree. Down below him he heard footsteps. People running and hiding in every direction.

He peeked around the tree to see Santa Claus ten or twelve feet down the slope towering over Ralph.

Ralph cried, threw his hands over his face, staggered backwards, then the figure—The Raven Hill Butcher—put his hands around Ralph and raised him into the air. He knocked Ralph back and forth and Ralph screamed.

The Raven Hill Butcher raised Ralph and slammed his neck into a six-inch thick tree branch. Ralph's head split off his body.

Wesley couldn't control his own screams and dropped his flashlight in shock.

The light was still on and signaled The Raven Hill Butcher to his location.

Wesley reached to pick it up then changed his mind. The Butcher was after him.

Wesley ran.

Al shrieked somewhere far away. He screamed when he found Ralph. Wesley could hear it even over the crunching leaves below his feet and the killer's.

It took him a while to realize the killer's footsteps had stopped. Wesley flinched when he turned around to see darkness. He wondered if the killer was hidden in pure darkness, becoming one with it, and was ready to grab him and decapitate him too. He wondered if The Butcher could move through shadows, teleporting from one shadow to the next, and was going to come up from the ground and slash his legs open.

Footsteps suddenly came from behind Wesley. He turned around, ready to fight somehow.

But it wasn't The Butcher. It was Wendy.

"We're gonna die," she whispered then hugged him, her face full of tears. "I don't wanna die."

He hugged her back and ran a hand through her hair. "No, no, we are not dying. Come on. We need to find Bill and Al. We need to get out of here."

"He's gonna kill us."

"Shush. No he's not. Come on, Wendy."

He held her hand and they cautiously tiptoed back the way he was originally running from, the way that they were originally meant to go. He took deep breaths, bravely leading her, and looked furtively for the others or for The Butcher.

They hid behind a tree, looked in every direction, then paced to another one.

Al's cries started again, and with the cries came footsteps.

The Raven Hill Butcher came forward down the slope and raised his knife, then cocked his head to the side.

Wesley and Wendy held each other, looking down at him slithering closer to Al. Wesley wanted to yell, but that'd be a dead giveaway. He prayed Bill was safe somewhere, maybe he had made it back to the road, maybe he was running and running and going to make it home.

Again he felt the urge to yell. He didn't know what they could do, but they had to do something, didn't they?

"Let's run," Wendy whispered. "Let's go—ohmigod."

Wesley was fixated on Al and The Butcher. The Butcher came within five feet of Al, and Wesley finally screamed, *"Al watch out."*

Wesley was ready to run with Wendy but couldn't leave without Bill—it might've been too late for Al, but Bill was his best friend, he couldn't leave him alone in the forest to die. Maybe Bill had made it to the road already and wasn't still here, but Wesley needed to know for sure.

Al faced The Raven Hill Butcher. *"I'm gonna kill you."*

Then Al raised his knife and charged, aiming for the throat, and came within inches of it; The Butcher grabbed him at the wrist and twisted it around all the way backwards; Wesley heard it snap through Al's screams of pain. With his other hand, he tried to punch The Butcher—tried to do something, anything—then The Butcher brought his blade up from his side and severed Al's other hand.

The Butcher grabbed Al by the hair, then split his head open on a tree. Brains oozed from the crack. Blood gushed like a fountain.

Immediately, he turned straight around to face Wesley and Wendy. The pair looked at each other and screamed. Hand in hand they ran, and The Raven Hill Butcher chased. He moved with an elegance, with a knowledge of where every branch and root in the woods was. Where everything in the woods was. And when Wesley and Wendy ran, they had to dodge many crooked branches and winding roots and it slowed them down. Wesley glanced over his shoulder...

...The Butcher was near.

Wendy was tired and slowing them down, their hands were slipping away from each other.

She was two feet behind Wesley, and he tried to pull her forward when The Raven Hill Butcher grabbed her first. He yanked on her hair and pulled her body into his arms. He set his dirty blade to her throat and she wailed uncontrollably.

The first incision was small, and as he started to pull it across her squirming body, he collapsed.

Bill grabbed onto the killer's torso, brough him to the ground clutching Al's knife—Wesley couldn't imagine prying that from a dead man's hands—and buried it in The Butcher's neck. The Butcher let go of Wendy and reached for Bill.

"Go." Bill screamed. *"Go now."*

"We can't leave you."

Wendy pulled on Wesley, trying to pull him with her into the woods.

"Go."

Wesley listened to Bill. He ran away with Wendy.

They ran to the road and never stopped, even when they heard his footsteps behind them.

From the road, they ran for miles to the bus stop, and even when they arrived back to their homes...

…they still heard him running behind them.

NOEL HELL

1

The world became a snow globe.

Snow drifted through Raven Hill and carried rumors with it.

Whispers slipped from the lips of locals, wondering if the horrors from the previous winter would return, or if they had wandered somewhere else on earth.

Christmas decorations covered Raven Hill from head to toe, but it did not feel like Christmas. It did not feel peaceful. It did not feel merry and bright. No matter how much snow fell, it couldn't return that joy that had been stripped from the town.

It snowed, and snowed, and snowed.

Last year was the only other time it had snowed this generously.

One whispered to the other, "Do you think it's really over?"

And the other whispered back, watching the snowflakes tumble blindly, "I hope so."

But both of them knew it was not over.

2

THE VAN SKIDDED A little, but Jill had it under control.

The roads had been cleared a little while ago, but as snowfall resumed, the once empty streets were full again.

Jill and her sister Emma were ready for their getaway at the Asylum Resort. It looked beautiful in all the pictures Jill had seen. There'd be a pool, a nice bar, comfy beds. Who could ask for more? She smiled thinking about it, turned off the highway exit, and continued straight down the road where acres of farmland surrounded either side. It was a different part of Raven Hill, a quieter part, a part that Jill had picked because it was far away from where that massacre happened a year ago, and she was terrified of it.

Massacre. Thinking of the word made her shudder.

Jill glanced at her sister. Emma was staring through the window, watching the snowflakes, tapping her fingers against the glass. *Have Yourself A Merry Little Christmas* came through the radio, and Jill sang along. Next came *White Christmas.*

When they were thirty minutes away, black clouds covered the sun, and snow gushed from the sky. The brightness that had previously filled the morning evaporated, and they were left with a hollow shell of how cheerful the day had looked. It was as if someone had placed a black and white filter over earth. Loud gusts of wind banged against the car as it passed over the winding road. Jill wondered how much snow they could possibly be buried in before they reached the hotel.

The hotel looked nothing like it did in its photos, which must've been taken at a more pleasant time than now.

The hotel's bricks were discolored. The big glass doors were smudged. The Asylum Resort looked miserable. It had been converted out of an old warehouse and seemed to still resemble one.

"This is the place you picked out?"

"Trust me, it looked better in the pictures."

The sisters walked awkwardly through the piling snow, and checked in with the receptionist. The tables in the lobby had ashtrays instead of flowers. The carpeting was old and ugly. The place was atrocious.

After checking in and getting the keys for room 429, they went on the elevator and Jill pushed the button for the fourth floor.

"What a trash place this is," Emma said. "There's not even a cart for our bags."

"I'm sorry," Jill said. "Hotels are *always* nicer in the pictures aren't they?"

"I guess we'll be fine as long as they have a pool and a hot tub. At this point I'd settle for just *one* of those two."

The elevator made a *PING!* when it came to the fourth floor and the metal doors slid open and let them into the hallway. It was long, blue, and formed into a plus sign at the intersection. In all there were four hallways on the fourth floor. It seemed nicer up here—so far, at least—than in the lobby.

The rooms outside of the elevator started with 400 on the right and 401 on the left. In the middle of the hallway, where it turned into a plus sign, they made a right. The numbers continued to increase, starting with 420 on the right and 421 on the left. Each segment of the long hallways had about twenty rooms. Halfway down they came to room 429 and slipped in the key.

The door sealed behind them on its own.

Coldness crept against their bodies. The curtains fluttered on the wall opposite of them and just for a moment, maybe less, Jill could have sworn she saw legs behind them. But that couldn't have been.

She rubbed her eyes, went forward across the brown carpeted floor, and shut the windows. It was a miracle there was no snow in the room, and she wondered how that could be. It was almost as if... *It hadn't been open until now.*

"Should we say something to management?" Emma said.

"No," Jill said. "Let's just crank the heat up."

Jill turned the dial on the thermostat and put the temperature to eighty degrees. It had been on seventy beforehand.

The room was cozy. Two twin beds cramped on either side of a nightstand, a television on a dresser across from them, and a mini fridge and a coffee maker next to the sink outside of the bathroom near the entrance. There was no balcony, but the windows provided a view of the street and the parking lot.

Snow came down reminiscent of last year's winter. The girls stood together and watched it. With it came dreadful feelings for Jill, whose lips had pulled into a grimace. It had never snowed this much in Raven Hill until last year and she wondered why it was doing it again now. She thought about those girls who were snowed in last year… snowed in and killed.

"We should check out that pool," Jill said, then opened her suitcase and moved things around until she found her bathing suit.

Nobody else was here, or anywhere in the Asylum Resort, except for the staff behind the front counter. So that meant they had both the twenty-foot-long pool and the hot tub all to themselves.

Large windows lined the walls and snow brimmed to their bases and was still coming down hard. There was a hot tub in the corner, and Emma ran straight towards it and jumped in despite the sign that said diving was not allowed. Jill was one step onto the hot tub stairs when Emma pulled her in.

He watched them.

He peered through the window. The girls splashed each other in the hot tub.

He was ready for them.

Oh, was he ready for them.

His hand wrapped tightly around the blade set in aging wood.

Then he disappeared.

3

Although she was in the hot tub, Emma felt the chill of a premonition.

Gusts of cold traced her spine softly.

For a moment, all she saw was blackness. Something was here, something was with them. Doom was present.

Emma emerged from under water and dried herself off, then looked out the windows lining the pool area. Snow was piled up as high as her waist.

"Where are you going?" Jill said, floating on her back, enjoying a beam of sunlight that filtered in through the windows and caressed her.

"Back to our room," Emma said. "I want to lay down."

The bad feeling in her guts, that strange premotion, became stronger. It drilled into the back of her head. She glimpsed behind her shoulder but saw nothing. Without realizing it, she was sprinting now to the end of the long hall once she was out of sight of her sister, and when she arrived at the elevator she smashed the 'up' button.

The elevator doors opened instantly and she stepped inside. She slammed a hand on the fourth floor button, and the feeling burrowed deeper inside of her. She felt two dark black eyes watching her...

The eyes weren't only watching her, but scanning her, *touching her.* Bottomless pools of darkness...

The elevator doors would not shut, and the lights inside of it flickered.

She left the elevator and turned the corner, and at the end of the hall she found a door that led to a stairway.

The heavy door barely opened. The grey walls were black in the gloom, gently curving upward out of sight. It was a long way up.

Emma glimpsed over her shoulder and did not see anybody but felt a lurking presence.

The lights flickered as they had done in the elevator.

At the fourth floor the door squeaked open and she walked the empty halls.

Once inside room 429, she collapsed on the bed.

Then she noticed the cold.

The window was open and the curtains fluttered.

She sat up and wondered how that could be. Then she stood up and shut the windows. Then there were the footsteps.

She was not alone in the room.

Two hands with narrow crooked fingers reached from behind her and gripped her throat. He pushed her onto her belly, his weight restricting her movements. She writhed and shook and tried to fight back but she was too weak to hurt him.

Then the man loosened one hand away from her throat, holding her tight with his other one. Suddenly she heard a swift tearing noise, a knife being dragged through the covers and tearing them. He set the knife in front of her eyes, the shine of the dull lightbulbs on the ceiling reflected off of it and Emma saw her terrified reflection in its rusty surface. She also glimpsed the man. Santa Claus.

It was the last thing she ever saw.

Santa Claus pushed the knife onto her scalp and sawed it through her flesh.

Emma let out a heart-stopping shriek, and the man pulled up a handful of her hair, separating her skin away from her skull. Threads of flesh tore hideously, and one final stab of terror pumped through her heart before she was gone.

The Raven Hill Butcher cocked his head sideways, then wiped the blood from his blade onto the bedsheets.

4

Jill swam.

For another twenty or thirty minutes she enjoyed herself.

Suddenly the lights went out then flickered back on, flickered wildly without completely returning to normalcy, then Jill left the pool. She wrapped a towel around herself and wondered what Emma was up to.

She went to the elevator and hit the fourth floor button.

The elevator lifted slowly and the lights fluttered rapidly just as they did in the pool. It made a ticking noise as they passed the second floor. When Jill arrived on the third floor the doors opened partly and were stuck. As she tried to pry it open with her hands, she heard a scream.

A woman ran up to the elevator doors. She shoved her hands through the small opening and forced herself inside. Her screams hadn't stopped even after the doors were shutting again and she crawled into the corner, burying herself into the metal walls and crying uncontrollably.

"He killed everybody. Now he's gonna kill us."

The elevator was moving again, and Jill said, "What the fuck?"

The frantic woman wouldn't answer.

The elevator ticked again as they reached the fourth floor

Jill ran out of the elevator, and behind her, she heard the woman's cries one last time: *"You're going to die."*

Jill fumbled with her key as she reached room 429.

The door hissed open to Jill and Emma's room. hat hit her first was that godawful smell, that acrid smell.

Everything was dark. The lights were off. Jill traced a hand blindly over the wall while holding the door open with her other hand. She felt the switch and turned it. The lights flickered on.

Emma's covers were torn and soaked with blood.

"Oh no—God no. *Emma.*"

Jill's hand slipped away from the door. It slammed loudly. She flinched and turned around. There, on the coat hook on the back of the door, was Emma's bloody scalp, completely severed from her body.

The Raven Hill Butcher walked the main floor of the Asylum Resort.

Many of the lights were broken and very little of the halls were illuminated. He opened the doors and let in the chilling winds. He stabbed his knife into the chipped paint of the wall then dragged it with him to the elevator at the end of the hall. The elevator, as he could tell by the dial above it, was on its way down from the fourth floor. He cocked his head. Whoever was inside would never see it coming.

Eager anticipation built inside of him as the elevator passed the second floor, and within moments it was opening on the ground floor. He saw hands reach through the partly opened doors and attempt to open them. It was too easy.

He slammed his knife over the fingers that gripped the cold metal door. They dropped to the ground like raindrops. As the woman screamed, The Butcher pressed his knife into her throat and listened to the pleasant sounds of guttural chokes mixed with an agonizing roar. She raised her hands in fists as if to beg him to stop. Tears cascaded down her face rapidly. With her eyes she pleaded, but he would show no mercy.

The Raven Hill Butcher grabbed her by the back of her head then slammed her face into the metal. Chunks of skull broke away in grotesque unrecognizable shapes and showers of fragments littered the floor. He tossed her into the corner, then pressed his knife deep into her sternum and tore in a contorted line through bone to her pelvis.

His fingers wiggled into the gaping hole and he peeled away flesh and cocked his head again. The Butcher dipped his fingers into the flow of blood, then on the back wall of the elevator, spelled out in misshapen letters:

MERRY CHRISTMAS!

The woman was dead. There was only one more person still alive…

He wiped the blood from his knife into one long streak inside the elevator, hit the fourth floor button, then left to take the stairway up.

The woman upstairs would have a pleasant surprise. He was not leaving behind a single survivor like last time.

Jill's heart thumped loudly in her chest, her head throbbed, and her stomach clenched. She wanted to vomit, wanted to find her sister, and wondered where her sister… where her sister's *body* could be, and how somebody could do this to her.

The phone cords were cut up. There was no way to phone for help.

Jill thought about the windows being opened, how she had seen them before. Somebody had a key to the room, somebody had a way in. Somebody… somebody wanted them dead.

The tears came furiously again after ceasing for a couple short moments, and her body trembled. She stumbled over the bloody carpet, kicked off her flipflops, then dropped her towel. She searched for new clothes to change into. Heavy winter clothes. She'd be leaving everything that didn't fit into her pockets behind.

She bundled up nice and tight in a jacket and jeans and grabbed her purse and clutched her keys tightly. She decided she wouldn't even take the time to clean off the snow from her car. There'd be plenty of time to do that once she got nice and far away from here.

She twisted the knob then went into the hallway.

She looked both ways before leaving the room as if crossing a street. Jill paced quietly. So softly that the floors did not make a peep under her shoes.

She hit the down button on the elevator, and instantly its doors spread open to reveal the bloody message of ***MERRY CHRISTMAS!*** written on the back wall in blood, and the bloody piece of meat that had once been a woman.

Jill shrieked and looked behind her shoulders where the man now stood at the other end of the hall.

He was dressed as Santa Claus. And as he stepped forward into dimming light he raised his knife and cocked his head.

Jill had nowhere left to run. She had to go into the elevator. As she went inside, he stepped forward slowly, calmly. She hit the ground floor button.

The elevator sunk down and her stomach filled with that terrible feeling of descending. An air of finality wrapped around her.

It felt like forever before the doors opened again and she was on the ground floor.

She hurried out of the elevator and all that was on Jill's mind, aside from escape, was Emma. She hadn't seen her body. For all she knew, her sister was still alive, and she kept repeating those very hopeful thoughts. Emma was missing a chunk of her scalp but she could've been alive. There could be a way to save her. Those girls had been saved last year, why couldn't Emma be saved too? But police weren't on their way now like they had been back then...

The whole first floor was ridden with frosty winds and Jill was running to the cross section of hallways which led to the doors. Jill shielded her face from on-coming blasts of winds, momentarily blinded, then heard him dragging his knife across a wall.

Her arms fell to her sides and Santa Claus towered over her. Even from the distance he was terrifying.

She ran.

Jill went down a hall with no specific destination in mind.

Oh no oh no oh no.

Jill came to a door with a glass window and through them she saw the winding stairs, and pushed the door open then ran up the curving steps and gripped onto the metal railing. The second floor platform came and she headed for the door.

A room marked *EMPLOYEE LOUNGE* was on her right, and Jill knew it had to have a phone, so she went running in.

The light was off, she ran her hands blindly along the walls. She was full of hope, picturing a phone in here, already going over what she'd tell the police, already imagining them rescuing her and Emma, and preventing her other friends from showing up.

The others... where are they? Oh God...

She found the switch.

She flicked it on and the room was illuminated: slaughtered bodies of the hotel employees thrown into a pile in the corner. It was a bloody mess and she couldn't tell what exactly was done to them because she looked away in horror.

Oh God all that blood.

A lake of blood under hacked up bodies flowed under her feet. She wanted to wipe it from her mind but there wasn't any doing so. Then she remembered the phone. She put a hand up to shield the bodies from her sight, and slowly scanned the other side of the room, starting with the couches around a circular wooden table that these dead people once ate lunch around. A fridge in the corner, followed by a counter with a microwave and sink. Then, on the wall, she saw it: the phone. An old rotary phone.

She ran to it, lifted it from the receiver, and in the corner of her eye she saw her. Emma. Lying next to the mountain of guts. She was missing her scalp, and blood was plastered over her face, but she still recognized her sister, who was still in her bathing suit.

Jill's screams melted into the room. Hands of a stranger reached from behind her and pulled her closer to the stranger's body.

The Butcher slammed her into one of the tables and pain jolted through her body and reverberated in her sides. She breathed shallowly through her nose. Her head pounded and her body tensed. She put her hands up between them and begged him to stop.

"Why are you doing this?"

He cocked his head and lifted the knife.

"Please stop please don't—"

His slice across her throat was so swift she didn't feel it at first. Then blood gushed like a fire hydrant and her hands shakily found their way to it, but there was nothing Jill could do now. Her heart raced for the last time. Soon, she knew, it would stop.

He picked her up and threw her on top of Emma.

5

MADISON, ARABELLA, AND BRYNN arrived at the Asylum Resort.

The parking lot was so buried that they couldn't fit the car into a parking spot, let alone seen the lines. The world was worse than a snow globe, it could have been the north pole for all they knew. For all they knew this was Santa's workshop in the middle of endless snow in any direction, and Santa was inside preparing toys for all the good little girls and boys. Maybe they'd soon see the reindeer, or maybe soon they'd see elves. Perhaps they'd bake cookies with Mrs. Claus and sit around the fire with her and Santa. It was a winter wonderland.

But they needed to park somewhere, so Madison parked crookedly next to a heap of snow. She turned the car off, unbuckled, and yawned.

Brynn said, "In all those Christmas movies where Santa is real but the parents don't believe it, don't the parents ever question where all the gifts, you know, where all the gifts come from?"

"There's no logic in movies," Arabella said. "Maybe they just think the other parent bought it or something."

"No, that wouldn't make sense."

"Well it's only a movie."

The girls left the car and carried their bags past hills of snow up to the Asylum Resort. The back of a van was revealed below piles of white, and the 97.9 sticker on the back was a dead giveaway that it was Jill's.

"Look, Jill and Emma are here," Madison said. "They must've been waiting a long time, look at all that snow."

Arabella shrugged. "Well look how much snow is already on your car, and you've been parked here all of two minutes."

Madison looked back at her car. "Yeah, maybe they haven't been waiting for us that long. Could you believe the detour? And getting stuck by a train, gosh, I hate trains, who puts them right in the center of traffic? And when they break down nobody can go nowhere."

Madison was excited to see them. It had been a while, with her and Jill having very different work and college schedules they seldom had time to see each other, and when they did have time to see each other, it was brief. But she was glad for today. It was going to be a good day, she could feel it. Her and Jill and Brynn and Arabella and Emma, this was exactly what she needed. A stress-free girls trip. Just thinking about college and her dumb job gave her a headache.

Briefly, Madison thought she saw something move in a window in her peripheral. She quickly looked up the disgusting brick wall, stared through the window, and saw that it was open. The curtains billowed inward with the heavy gusts of freezing air. Who would leave a window open in this weather? Oh well, maybe they forgot to shut it and it was a room that hadn't been used in months. Judging by the looks of this place, Madison didn't think many people ever stayed here.

Icy air traced her lungs. These winds were uncomfortably cold. Her legs felt like stilts, and she pushed as fast as she could over the parking lot of ice to get into the Asylum Resort. Madison passed through the front doors. The others followed closely behind.

What struck her first, even before the silence, was how chilling it was. How it was just as cold in here as it was out there.

The girls looked around. It was about four o'clock and already the sun was dimming outside, and in the Asylum Resort it was already a little dark. Most of the lights were on, but some were off.

"Hello?" Madison said, then shouted: *"Hello? Anyone home? Helllllooooo?"*

No answer.

"Where are all the workers?" Madison said. "Jill's car is here, she and Emma must be here. This is too weird. What's with the lights?"

Then, as the words left her lips, some of the lights flickered back on.

Madison leaned over the front desk. "Come on, where is everyone? No workers at the front desk? That's silly. Why, anyone can just walk up and take a key. What room did we have again, four-thirty?"

"Yep, four-thirty," Arabella said. "Jill and Emma are in four-twenty-nine."

Madison looked at the long rows behind where the receptionist should have been standing. She found 429, and the slot was empty. Both keys were gone. The girls definitely were in their room all right, or somewhere in this hotel. Maybe swimming, or maybe at the bar. She glanced at 430, and saw both keys were still there.

"Should we grab them?" Brynn said. "We already paid… and if nobody's around…"

Madison noticed a bell on the counter and rang it four times. Still, nobody came. She shuddered. "Are we in *The Twilight Zone?"*

Arabella looked down the halls again then slowly walked past the counter. She grabbed the keys from the room 430 slot then tossed one to Madison. "Let's go."

Madison twirled the key around her finger then turned towards the elevator and walked down the hall. The lights flickered. "Does something smell bad to you two?"

"Wait," Arabella said abruptly. "Madison come back here."

"What's up?"

"I'm afraid of elevators," she said. "We have to take the stairs."

"With all these bags? Is there a cart?"

"I don't see a cart."

"Can't you just go up the stairs alone?" Brynn said.

"No," Arabella said angrily. "This place is cold and gives me the creeps. I don't want to be alone. None of us are splitting up. Can we please just take the stairs."

Madison didn't feel like arguing. "Fine. Stairs it is."

Madison slipped her key into the lock, turned it, then opened the door, while the others knocked on Jill and Emma's door.

But neither Jill nor Emma answered.

Madison dropped her bags into the corner of the room. The girls took their jackets off and changed into more comfortable outfits. Then they left room 430 and went across the hall to 429.

The hallway was quiet. Too quiet.

Madison knocked. Then Brynn knocked.

No answer.

"Are you two awake?" Brynn rested her hand on the door, then gave it another knock. "Jill? Emma? Are you two awake? They must be sleeping. Hello? Jiiiiiilll Em-mmmmmaaaa!"

Then Arabella knocked. *"Jill. Emma. Wake up sleepyheads. Come on."*

"Maybe they're not in there," Madison said.

"Maybe not," Arabella said. "Did they go to the store or something?"

"No, their car's here, remember?" Brynn said. "They wouldn't walk anywhere in this weather, right?"

"Something strange is going on here," Madison said. "Let's go back downstairs and see if we can find an employee."

They went down the stairs again, and on the second floor landing, the girls heard footsteps coming from the hall.

Madison opened the door, peeked into the bright hallway, then stepped inside. Her friends followed.

Madison felt relieved.

There was a cleaning woman's cart outside of a door only halfway down the hall. There were workers here, of course the place wasn't empty, of course everything was fine, there was a cleaning lady going around from room to room. The receptionist must have been on break or something when the girls arrived a few minutes ago. And maybe Jill and Emma were around here somewhere, maybe they met some boys or something...

Brynn walked up to the door next to the cleaning lady's cart and knocked a couple times and said hello. Then she put her ear to the door after knocking again.

"I don't hear anything."

She knocked one more time. "Anybody in there?"

If there was a cleaning lady in there, she did not reply, and that only made Madison more worried. She said, "Maybe she's not allowed to say anything while she's cleaning."

Brynn rolled her eyes.

"Oh I want to get out of here." Arabella frowned. "Can we go?"

“Go where?” Madison said. “We just drove all the way here to turn around?”

“Let’s just go back downstairs. Let’s see if we can find them. Maybe if the receptionist is back, they might know.”

The girls passed through the door again. It let out a hiss as all the doors in the Asylum Resort seemed to do when they were opened or closed, then there was the abrupt sound of footsteps again when they went down the stairs.

Madison turned back to the door. She studied it, wondering if it would open.

“Jill? Is this a joke?” Madison walked back to it.

She opened the door, stepped back into the hall, half expecting the cart to be moved now, but it wasn’t. There wasn’t a soul there. Who had she heard then? Who moved that swiftly that they could be gone already? Where was the unseen person going to and coming from?

Madison noticed there was a door marked *EMPLOYEE LOUNGE* with an ‘employees only’ sign below it, and wondered if maybe that’s what they heard. Maybe it was an employee going in there.

But Madison didn’t check. It was, after all, employees only, and Madison was not an employee.

Her friends finally decided to walk back up the stairs after her.

The lights flickered again in the stairwell and this time it was more rapid. The lights hadn’t flickered anymore on the second floor. It was darker outside and that darkness flowed fluidlike into the hotel halls and filled them. Madison thought she was going to see something or someone pop up whenever the lights went out then on.

The Asylum Resort became colder. So cold that the girls could see their breath.

Back at the front desk, there was still no receptionist.

Madison walked to the front doors and looked outside.

Snow fell chaotically. Her car was covered in such a large pile that she could barely see the bumper. It would take all three of them to clean it off and leave. And while leaving sounded like a good idea, all their bags were still upstairs.

“Let’s try Jill’s room one more time,” Madison said. “If she doesn’t answer, let’s just get out of here.”

So the girls walked back down the hall to the stairs, calling out for Jill or Emma or anybody that might be hearing them.

But, as they approached the fourth floor, they noticed something that had certainly not been there before.

Another key.

The key to room 429.

Jill and Emma's room.

6

IT WAS ONLY ONE of the two keys, and it was now on the ground where they had passed through twice but hadn't seen it until now.

Because it wasn't there until minutes ago.

Because someone, Madison thought, knew that they'd be coming back through here and would see it.

And that someone had to be Jill and Emma.

"Are they pranking us?" Madison said.

"Maybe the staff is in on it too," Brynn said.

"You think a hotel would prank its customers?" Arabella said. "I don't think they'd do that."

"I don't know," Brynn said. "That's the only explanation I can see. Why else would nobody be around?"

"I don't like this," Madison said.

The girls were all at a loss, and all they could do now was go back upstairs… and try the key to Jill and Emma's room.

Madison pictured, as stupid as it was, Jill and Emma and the whole hotel staff jumping out and yelling surprise as if it were someone's birthday. The more she thought of it, the stupider it was, but she would give anything for it to happen. Keys don't just appear from nowhere. It had to have been put there by someone, which meant the girls were not alone in the hotel by any means. And that gave her hope, because it meant things might just be fine after all.

The walk to the fourth floor felt as if it would take another decade, but they finally arrived.

Brynn knocked on Jill's door.

There was no answer.

"Should we?"

Madison leaned against the wall with her arms crossed. "I don't think so."

"Then why'd they leave us the key?"

"I think I'm gonna be sick," Madison said suddenly holding her stomach, then searched for the key for room 430, slipped it in the lock, then opened the door. Before she shut it, she reached into her pocket and tossed Brynn the key for 429.

"Are you okay?" Arabella asked, then followed her into the room.

"I think I will be."

Madison kneeled at the toilet, heaved, but did not puke.

"It's the weather. I always get so fucking sick in wintertime."

Brynn stood alone in the hall.

She was about to put the key into the knob when she heard footsteps coming from around the corner.

She slowly turned around, looked around the corner, but did not see anybody. The hall was empty, the lights flickered, and she wondered if they were in some crazy escape-room instead of an actual hotel.

PING!

It was the elevator.

Brynn walked towards it, eager to see who had just arrived. She crossed her fingers in hope that it was Jill and Emma. Where the fuck were they and what the fuck was going on in here?

A bad feeling in her stomach grew as she approached the elevator...

The elevator doors were stuck just an inch apart.

She couldn't see inside yet but was hit with that godawful smell, and slipped her nose into the collar of her shirt.

Brynn nervously reached her hands through the one inch space and pulled them apart.

Jesus fucking Christ.

The scream was lodged deep in her throat and was beginning to emerge when two smarmy arms stretched out and pulled her deep into its grimy body.

The hands clamped around her neck and she couldn't breathe.

She saw the dead woman in the bloody elevator, and the ***MERRY CHRISTMAS!*** message smeared on the back wall and knew that this was her fate. She wanted to scream, warn the others, but not even a gasp could find its way through her ever-compressing throat. Perpetual pain flowed through her body, and he slammed her into one of the elevator walls then hit the second floor button.

As the doors closed she stretched out her hands as if she'd open the doors again with her mind, but alas, Brynn was not a telekinetic.

Her heart banged fiercely. She knew there was no escape. Nobody was coming to rescue her. Nobody could save her.

And her final thoughts she'd ever have were about her friends upstairs in room 430. *Get the fuck out of here right now!*

The heart sank, and the smallest cries fled from her mouth.

The doors opened and he dragged her by her hair out of the elevator, across the second floor, and into the employee lounge.

The blazing lights on the ceiling almost blinded her.

The Raven Hill Butcher, she realized this was who the man was, tossed her onto the pile of corpses in the corner, and that's when her scream finally left her lips and she saw the mutilated bodies of Jill and Emma.

One more time, the knife found its way into her chest, then across her throat, and up and down her stomach.

7

Madison slept.

Arabella used the coffee maker then after finishing her drink went to check on Brynn. Brynn had the key to Jill's room and was not back yet, so they must have answered.

Before leaving the room she looked out the window.

Snow had finally stopped coming, but it was the worse she had ever seen it out there. The streets were being cleared, but besides the men operating those machines, there was not a single other soul in sight.

Arabella glanced over to where Madison's car was parked. Besides a thickness of black indicating a tire, the whole thing was consumed in ice.

She shivered, turned back around, and went to room 429 and knocked.

Silence.

Maybe they really were pulling a prank…

"Brynn? Jill? Emma? Hello? Quit it ladies. Let me in."

Nothingness.

As if nobody was on the other end.

As if whoever stepped through the threshold to room 429 was greeted with instant death.

Her fists pounded on the door. "Open *the door you idiots.*"

KNOCK! KNOCK! KNOCK!

NOTHING! NOTHING! NOTHING!

It was pointless, so Arabella decided to let them have their little games.

She took a few steps back toward room 430 then her hand stopped just shy of the knob. Her head turned back to the door and she listened real hard, listened real close for any sign of movement, a whisper, a bedspring, maybe even a soft footstep on the carpet, but there was not a peep, and she doubted that anyone on earth let alone three girls in a hotel room could be that quiet.

She peeked over the corner and looked down each hall.

Nobody.

Nothing.

But she did not feel alone. She felt watched. Someone was in here with her. Someone somehow watching from each direction imaginable. Somebody was in front of her behind her next to her on either side, above her and below her.

Arabella twisted open the door to room 430 and went back inside.

She was about to wake Madison up and ask her if they could leave now when suddenly—

KNOCK! KNOCK!

A knock on her room's door.

"Yes?"

Nobody said anything.

Arabella moved a step closer toward the door.

A soft knock came again. A gentle knock, like from the fist of a young woman.

"Who's there?"

No reply.

"Ladies, this is stupid. Enough is enough, okay?"

Arabella looked through the peephole but the hall was empty.

And when she turned away, the knock came again, louder.

"Brynn is this you?"

Her hand fell to the knob. It was icy. Somehow, even in the hot room, the knob was icy.

KNOCK! KNOCK! KNOCK!

"Be quiet, you'll wake Madison."

She held her breath, the knocking stopped, and she twisted the knob and opened the door.

It opened wide and she looked straight ahead. Nobody. And nobody was on either end of the hall when she turned her head.

She knocked on the door of room 429.

"Ladies I'm tired of this game. Give it up."

She turned around to get back to her room and bumped into a man.

Santa Claus.

The man cocked his head, lifted his knife, and Arabella ran to the nearest door: the stairway.

She slammed the door shut behind herself, glanced for a lock but did not see one, and wasted no time going down the steps.

Arabella raced like she had never done before.

She looked over her shoulder but did not see the man or anybody. It was as if she were only racing against herself, against her own wild imagination, against a figment of her thoughts. Something that wasn't real.

She wondered what she'd do when she reached the bottom. Her jacket and belongings were in room 430. She'd die from the coldness outside.

Maybe I could hide somewhere.

As Arabella went down to the third floor platform, her feet slipped on the final two steps and she faceplanted onto the cold hard metal ground.

Her body was wet.

She looked up to see the steps painted with blood. It was all over her clothes and hands and face.

Then, turning slowly to the corner of the platform, Brynn's severed head watched her.

8

Madison was deep in sleep.

She dreamed of Christmas, that she was watching Santa Claus hand her a gift, then Santa opened his mouth and screamed, screamed like a frightened twenty-year-old girl would scream, then Madison awoke and realizing where the screams were coming from.

The lights were on in the hotel room. Madison's eyes needed some moments to adjust. Then she scanned the room for her friends and listened closely for the scream that echoed in her ears but now it was gone…

She was alone.

And she was a little scared.

"Hello?" she said softly, then a little louder: *"Hello?"*

Oh, they're over in Jill's room, she thought. *But what was that scream? Was I just dreaming?*

Madison put on her shoes, found her room key, then decided to look out the window and see if it was still snowing.

It wasn't, but her car was totally buried. She couldn't find one inch of it under the snow.

Dammit.

Madison left the room, looking around the hall for any sign of her friends, then knocked on 429.

There was no answer.

Then the scream came again. The one from her dream.

Madison ran towards the noise, turned the corner, and arrived at the stairwell. She heard somebody running and shouting.

"Who's there?"

"Madison!" The voice shouted back from far away. It was unmistakably Arabella. *"He's gonna kill you."*

Madison went down the stairs.

At the upcoming landing her feet slipped and she almost fell off, but gripped the railing so tightly that she didn't fall off the steps. Holding the railing strained her arms and pain ripped through them as her body jerked.

Blood.

Buckets of blood.

More blood than she had ever seen in her life

More blood than she wished to ever see again.

And when she caught sight of the severed head in the corner, her screams bellowed so loudly that if every room in the Asylum Resort had been filled, every soul would have heard her clearly.

It was hard to stomach walking over blood, it was hard to force herself to do that, and she did not want to look away from the gruesome sight of the head, but there came a point where the stairs curved and she had to stop looking. She tried as best she could to wipe the blood from her shoes onto the stairs and keep going, but it was hard to keep pace.

Arabella's footsteps were farther and farther ahead of her.

"Don't leave me." Madison cried. *"Arabella!"*

"Oh God!" Arabella screamed back. *"I'm here Madison I'm here."*

Madison ran with a fury, and Arabella went back up a couple steps, and the two met then burst through the doors of the second floor landing.

"Oh God oh God we need a phone," Arabella said. "The lounge—"

We're gonna find the phone, Madison thought. It was hard to think straight, but she could piece together the basics.

Madison and Arabella stood closely together as they entered the employee lounge, but they were not prepared for what they stumbled into.

9

THE STENCH HIT THEM first before they saw the pile of dead employees torn open with their insides decorating the walls.

They were thrown lazily into a pile, like how one would toss out garbage into an alleyway.

Lackluster dead eyes from a face looked at her. Their last moments of sorrow plastered into them. Then she realized she knew the face. Jill.

Emma was next to her sister, missing her scalp.

A decapitated body was there too. She recognized the outfit as Brynn's.

It couldn't have been real.

It did not feel real.

Suddenly Brynn was crying on the phone dialing 9-1-1.

Madison collapsed in the corner, hugging herself as she cried. She couldn't process what Arabella was saying. Her head pounded and her eyes shut tightly.

Madison did not know how long had gone by until Arabella was off the phone. She seemed to hang up in a hurry.

When Arabella came and put her arms around Madison, Madison cried, "Did you tell them? Did you get through to them?"

"Yes," she said through an ocean of tears. They were coming even worse than Madison's, and Madison wondered if Arabella could even see her clearly.

"They didn't want you to stay on the line?"

"They did but we can't stay here," Arabella said. "He might come back to this room."

Madison looked around for a weapon, or something that could be used as one. There were chairs, tables, a fridge, and severed heads. What could she possibly fight him with? Nothing. She just had to hope she'd live long enough for the police to arrive and bring them home safely.

"I don't want to die," Madison said. "I don't want to die."

Wiping her tears away, Arabella said, "Let's go."

"Where?"

"Anywhere. Anywhere that's not here."

10

They came to the hallway intersection and looked around the corners.

There was nobody, and they discovered that the back hallway gave way to one more hallway, so they went that way to see where they might hide.

So far they couldn't find a single door that was unlocked. They panicked and whispered to each other to try and figure out what to do.

Then the girls were abruptly hushed at the sound of distant footfalls. And the sound of a knife dragging along a wall.

The girls looked at each other with fright, then Madison gave one last attempt to a door—a storage closet—whose handle opened to her surprise. It was the one room that wasn't locked.

They hurried inside and didn't make a peep as they closed the door gently.

They held each other in darkness, trying not to squeal, listening to the horrible tapping of the knife coming so close it was almost on top of them.

The footfalls came closer with every fading second, every second counting down to the end, coming into the very hallway the girls were in.

Madison reached for the doorknob but realized it didn't have a lock. Nothing could stop him from finding them.

Madison was full of terror. The air of finality gripped her tight.

The sounds stopped for a little while, as if the person, The Butcher, had been erased from existence.

Then after a silent minute the doorknob turned ever so slowly, and Madison and Arabella cried.

The door flung open and diminishing light glimpsed into the supply closet.

The Raven Hill Butcher raised his knife and the door slammed shut behind him. They were in pitch blackness, and he could've been anywhere or anything. For a split second, Madison thought she heard something like music in the distance, but didn't have time to think about it.

The girls squirmed and backed away from the monster, but the closet was tight and there wasn't any space to hide in. Something poked Madison in the back, and she realized it was the light switch. Her back flicked it on by accident and she saw more clearly now Santa Claus towering above the both of them.

The Butcher slammed his knife down as Madison and Arabella broke away from each other, each girl going in either direction, and the knife was struck into the drywall. He pulled it out, and Madison was frozen.

Arabella was closer. The Butcher grabbed her by the throat and pinned her to the wall. Arabella yelled for Madison to run but she couldn't, she was suspended with shock.

The Butcher slammed his knife in one fatal swoop through Arabella's face and pinned her into the wall. Her body convulsed and her hands twitched, then her feet straightened out and she was gone.

He turned to Madison.

Madison opened the door and ran.

The music was more pronounced in the hallway. It wasn't music but sirens.

Oh Arabella I'm so sorry I'm sorry Arabella I'm sorry.

He was behind her. She heard his heavy breathing, peeked over her shoulder as she went across the fading carpet towards the stairwell, and saw him with the bloody knife still dripping Arabella's blood.

She ran, flung open the door, and rushed down the stairs. He had been so far away from her but now he was on the topmost step, as if he possessed incredible speed unlike anything known to mankind.

Her heart beat so loudly that she felt it pumping in her throat, threatening to escape.

Madison raced with every ounce of her spirit to the first floor landing and beat him there. Somehow he had gotten to the stairs quickly, but couldn't use that same speed to grab her.

On the first floor, running for her life to the open doors that brought in the coldest air she had ever touched, the doors seemed ten—no, twenty miles away. Her feet pushed hard on the ground and she felt as if her heart would explode from all the force she was putting her body through. She needed to breathe, needed water, needed a break, but she kept pushing.

Then she heard noises at the distant front doors.

11

RED AND Z PUSHED through the mountains of snow.

Some other officers were following, others had the building surrounded. The police of Raven Hill were eager to put the guy away who was behind this and the massacre one year ago tomorrow.

There was a girl running from a man. The man was dressed in the same Santa Claus costume that the killer from one year ago at the mansion was described as wearing.

Z put two bullets in his chest.

When the man fell to the ground, Red added five or six of his own.

Madison fainted, and the men knelt at her side.

When Z looked back to their suspect, he was gone without a trail of blood. Bullet casings scattered on the floor.

The other officers came through the doors and asked where the man was.

"He's gone."

The entire hotel was searched head to toe over and over again, but The Raven Hill Butcher was not found.

Jill, Emma, Brynn, Arabella, and other guests and employees were all dead.

Hours later, as Madison cried in her bed in the hospital, the clock struck midnight.

Her hospital room's door open, and a dark figure crept in…

THE CURSE OF RAVEN HILL

1

IT WAS A GRAY bleak summer day, with now and then a hint of rain.

Stunted sickly trees formed the border between Raven Hill and its sister town of Carpentersville, where Wesley and Wendy lived.

Since the seasons of horror, there hadn't been many visitors in Raven Hill. Most people kept their distance, and so did Wesley and Wendy.

For now.

***

It had been years since the killings abruptly stopped, but not a day passed where Wesley hadn't been trying to solve them.

"It's starting again," Wesley said. "He's not gonna stop unless..."

"Wes, you have to forget about it."

"How many more people have to die? It's something I can put a stop to."

Wendy frowned. "Is there anything I can say that would make you forget about all this?"

"No," he said.

There was no way he could forget about it. There was no way he could give it up. Not when he knew the truth.

Not when he knew who The Raven Hill Butcher really was.

2

Understanding who The Raven Hill Butcher was, was complicated.

Wesley's two separate theories had both twisted together. He took pieces from the legends, rearranged them, and cut whatever he thought might have been bullshit. The results were…

Strange.

The probable: he was just a man.

The unlikely: he was a camp worker that supposedly died decades ago.

The even more unlikely: Raven Hill had talked about The Butcher for so long that maybe someone finally believed in him enough to become him. Maybe the stories themselves built him. Maybe the town had been feeding the legend for years until one day it just became reality.

And the absolute most unlikely possibility: all of the above.

Through lengthy research into the history of Camp Solgohachia, which had more urban legends than he originally knew of, he found the story of a man named Bob. A man whose cabin, when it was new, looked strikingly similar to the one he and Bill raced to, the one that was boarded up, falling apart, and looked as if it were constructed by a crew of blind men.

Bob was an orphan, very poor, and went around from awful job to awful job until he settled on being the camp's groundskeeper. That was, until he mysteriously disappeared...

It wasn't easy to find information about a man who worked at a small camp in a small town, but Wesley found a newspaper article from the year when Bob had gone missing.

It wasn't much, just had his date of birth, a crummy picture, and said he worked at the camp.

But there was just something Wesley didn't like about the man's sudden disappearance...

There was only one person that Wesley could find in his years of researched who knew the old groundskeeper, and who Wesley could legitimately confirm had actually attended Camp Solgohachia during that time...

"You said you knew the groundskeeper."

"Yeah, I did. We killed him. It was all an accident."

"What can you tell me about this accident?"

"Hard to remember. It was so long ago. We broke into his cabin that night. Somebody had a thing about Bob, some grudge. Something Bob did to him, I don't remember. It was all Dale's idea. Can you hand me that water, boy?"

"Here," Wesley said. "What happened after you broke in?"

"Where was I? Let's see. We burned him up. He was on fire. It was a nasty thing, a real nasty thing. He was screaming and crying..."

"Wait, so after you broke in, how did you light him on fire?"

"No. No. We didn't break in. I don't know why I said that. We were outside, we never went inside. Dale had the bag and we were outside and he threw a firework through the window just to scare him. It was Dale's idea. Dale's dead now so you can't ask him about it. Which is convenient for Dale."

"I don't think I understand what happened here."

"He died. We buried him. I think it was Jimmy that found the shovels and we dug real deep and we put the body in. He's in the ground somewhere on that property near the old cabin."

"Did anyone ever find out? Did you ever get in trouble? I mean, what happens after something like that?"

"Nobody found out nothing. We went to breakfast the next morning and nobody said a word. I think Jimmy told Bethany. Or maybe it was Dale told Bethany. She wanted to see the body because she didn't believe us so we dug him up a little and showed her his face and she swore not to say nothing. Nobody ever asked us about Bob or any of it."

"But why didn't you go to the police?"

"Tell them yourself. Tell the sheriff, the mayor, the president, whoever you want."

3

THE BOOK HAD BEEN buried in the back of a mom-and-pop bookshop.

Its surface was bumpy red leather, and a black cloth bookmark stuck out from the binding.

Wesley bought it for fifty cents. It turned out to be worth more than anything else he'd found.

The pages were filled with old reports collected from newspapers, journals, and private letters. Most of them described the same sort of story appearing again and again in different places.

A town begins repeating the same story long enough and the story starts to settle into the place like dust. People argue about it, and some deny it, while others swear they've seen proof of it. And eventually it's no longer a rumor but something real.

The writer suggested that these stories didn't stay just stories for very long.

But belief was not enough. In every account something physical had been waiting for it. A body or a place or some item waiting to take on its form.

The book wandered through strange examples. Small cult meetings in the woods, and groups who believed they could give shape to spirits by spilling blood.

The unsetting part, Wesley noticed, was how often the same idea appeared in different cultures. People who had never met, living on opposite sides of the world, had written almost identical warnings…

So was he foolish for wanting to go back?

To find The Raven Hill Butcher? To finish it?

The book had offered little comfort. Several pages near the back had been torn out long ago. Whatever they once contained was gone, and Wesley had never found another copy complete enough to replace them.

Only one passage from the ending survived. It described a container.

The shape varied in the sketches. Sometimes an urn with a narrow neck, sometimes a heavy box with a lid that sealed tight, but the purpose was the same: to trap its spirit.

The instructions were written carefully, almost reluctantly:

Destroy the body first

As it dies, open the urn and place it over the dying body.

If done correctly, the thing inside would have nowhere else to go.

And the more people who trapped it in the urn, the stronger its seal.

The urn needed certain symbols carved into it, and Wesley did this the day after the drizzles. It was hot out. Bright. Cloudless. Wendy had gone with her friends for a swim, and he sat in his room and carved. The box was a basic wooden piece a friend put together for him on short request. His friend's dad built things from wood as hobby and built it for Wesley no problem.

He hunched over his desk, moved his knife carefully, engraving the symbols to the perfectly square beech tree box.

The first symbol, which went on top where the lid was connected by a small, simple hinge, was a giant cat's eye.

There were other shapes—hieroglyphics—in the book, and Wesley shuddered as his hands traced their patterns. He didn't dare look any longer than he needed to, for he could sense these symbols came from a dark, evil time. A time of cults, witchcraft, and Satanism. A dreadful time.

He was going to kill The Raven Hill Butcher. He didn't know how he'd find him, but he would. He swore he would.

4

CHRISTY MORRISON NEEDED HAPPY thoughts on a gloomy summer day.

She laid in her bed—her real bed in her real home, not the family's *mansion*, she'd never set foot in there again—and felt horrible. She was sick. Her nose was stuffy and every four or five seconds she had the urge to cough or clear her throat.

A funny memory, perhaps her favorite with her best friend Julia, came to her. It was the best memory in the past year and a half since…

She and Julia had been walking around the college campus one day when she had carelessly run her hands over a bench and couldn't possibly have seen the WET PAINT sign.

Christy looked at her hands. *"They're blue."*

"And they don't even match your outfit."

Whenever one of them brought it up again, they still laughed as if it *just* happened moments ago.

The thoughts always came when she was home alone.

Mom and Dad were each at work, and the door to David's old room across the hall would taunt her if she glimpsed it. She missed him, and she felt guilty about it all, about living.

Christy cried again. She didn't want to but did a little anyways. It was almost always on her mind, and severe guilt always pounded in her heart. Even during all the happy moments in her life in the year and a half since that night, she still couldn't shake that awful feeling. That filthy feeling. That feeling she desperately wished and prayed to go away but it never wavered. It bogged down every happy moment of her life.

Christy went to the kitchen and found the plastic bottle of vitamin C tablets. She took one, coughed again, then poured a cup of water.

She was refilling the cup, leaning on the kitchen sink for support, when the phone rang and startled her and the cup slipped out of her hand. Christy stared at the phone and her guts twisted like wire through flesh.

She did not have a good feeling about it.

She looked back into the sink to discover a trail of red spinning down the drain with the water. Some of the glass had sliced her thumb open. Scarlet pumped. It was so thick she could see her reflection in it.

She looked at the phone one more time, ignored it, then ran her hand under water. Pain ebbed from her thumb into her palm.

By the time she was done putting on a Band-Aid, the phone rang again.

She nervously answered. "Hello?"

"My name's Wesley Lawrence, is this Christy Morrison?"

She was silent for a moment. "What do you want?"

5

MADISON'S LIFE HAD BEEN changed forever.

The funerals had come and gone. The town moved on. She avoided hotels now, and elevators, and sometimes she avoided leaving the house altogether. Her therapist said that was normal, but she didn't feel normal at all.

Her life changed again when the phone call came.

Madison stood up, cleared her throat, then answered.

"Hello?"

Julia came home from the grocery store and set down her bags.

She was about to call Christy to check up on her, and to see if she should come by, when the phone rang.

Julia wasn't expecting anyone, and assuming it was Christy, she answered the phone.

"Hey, are you feeling any better?"

"Hi, is this Julia?"

"Oh, I'm sorry. Who is this?"

Later in the day, when Wesley and Wendy were having dinner, she asked, "How did it go?"

He didn't have the heart to tell her they all said no. "They agreed."

"They did?"

"Yeah. You surprised?"

"Well, it certainly is a strange offer."

Wesley shrugged. "Well they did."

"You're not sure if it'll work, are you?"

"I'm not."

"I never thought our lives would come to this, coming back to Raven Hill. It's been years. Oh, I don't like this one bit. I don't want to go back."

"Once it's over we'll never have to return."

"Are you gonna chuck it into the ocean?"

"What?"

"The box. The urn. When we.... Are you going to, you know, hide it in the bottom of the ocean?"

"No. I'd be scared a diver might find it. I'm going to seal it with cement then hide it someplace nobody would ever find it."

"Somewhere more unsearched than the ocean floor?"

"Yes."

"Where? Pluto?"

"My lips are sealed. I'm not telling a soul."

"Not even me?"

"Sorry. I'm taking this to my grave."

6

THE NEXT MORNING WAS a beautiful day in Raven Hill.

The pain in Christy's thumb was still throbbing. It throbbed almost in rhythm, as if trying to send her a message.

Christy, this is your thumb, you're in danger.

She wondered about what that Wesley guy said on the phone. He sounded so strange. And he said that there was more. What more was there that he couldn't tell her unless they met face to face?

No way was she ever meeting him, so she'd never know what he had to say.

But she had to admit, he sounded genuine. Not necessarily convincing, but genuine. As if he really could stop the monster from striking again.

The nerves in her stomach twisted. She hated to think about the monster.

At Julia's house, she knocked then waited. Julia let her in and they went to her room. Her curtains were closed and the lights were off. They sat on her bed, and Julia turned on the TV without saying a word.

"Did some creep call you too?" Julia said.

"Yeah," Christy said. "Something about meeting up at the library?"

"Yeah. Can you believe it? How long do we have to put up with these prank phone calls?"

"I dunno, but I changed my number three times in the last six months alone and somehow every weirdo in the country seems to get their hands on it. I wonder if some person at the phone company is selling it."

"Yeah, they probably auction it off at Weirdos Anonymous."

7

THE DARK CARPENTERSVILLE SKY changed abruptly to clear and blue at the forest border of the two cities, where demented twisted trees grew and where leafless branches clutched the air.

A breeze blew into the cracked open windows of Wesley's van.

His worry was stronger now. As soon as they passed the border, it became real again.

Wesley hoped he knew what he was doing. The other survivors had all told him no but he and Wendy couldn't do it alone. The more people that trapped the creature in the urn, the stronger their hold. And could he possibly stand a chance against The Raven Hill Butcher face to face? When the time came, could he do it?

He almost felt like a coward hiding behind a bunch of girls. What if they got hurt because of him?

Maybe he should forget about them and do it on his own. Leave Wendy alone in a motel room somewhere and fight the monster alone.

Wendy tapped her fingers on the box in her lap. Wesley peeked at it then looked back to the road.

Fear came over him in fistfuls. A black cloud hovered over his mind and masked his thoughts. He had his doubts now more than ever, wondering if he had made the correct decision or if this was the work of a madman.

"Sorry, I just had to see it."

"I thought so," Wendy said, holding his hand tightly as he drove.

Wesley pulled in front of his childhood home. It was a humble house, and looked a lot worse than it had when he lived here. The sidewalk had cracked sometime in the past five or six years, the paintjob somebody had given the place was horrendous, it looked like some group of kids were hired to paint it instead of actual painters.

Memories flooded back. Dozens of them.

The first one was from just days before leaving for Camp Solgohachia: the boys set up glass bottles in the alleyway and had a slingshot competition. Wesley won, of course. He always did against Bill and Darren. Bill kept it close, but Darren was a loser every time and never came in higher than last.

They checked into their motel room.

He didn't take his eye of the box all afternoon.

They kept it at the little table in the motel while they ate. Wesley kept his eyes more on that box than he did his food or on Wendy. He was really going to go through with it. They came all the way here. He was going to kill him, going to imprison him…

…but how?

"What time are we meeting the others?"

"We're not."

"Huh?"

"Wendy… none of them wanted to meet with us. All three girls said no."

Maybe, Wesley thought, all he needed to do was face The Raven Hill Butcher like a man. Face to face.

Him and him alone.

8

IT WAS ALMOST TIME to meet her, so Scott sneaked out of his house and disappeared under the shadows of night.

They were supposed to meet at the park.

He waited for her on the bench, cracking his knuckles, checking his watch, wondering if Jenny remembered or if she had fallen asleep yet again. It wouldn't be the first time she overslept and missed their little rendezvous.

Scott yawned, leaned back, and tried not to fall asleep. His bed was nice and comfortable, and when he left his bed, he had almost regretted it. It would've been worth it if she were here already, but now he wished he was back in bed.

What the fuck is taking so long?

He waited a little longer.

Usually she was the first one here.

I should get going. She's probably asleep. There's always tomorrow night…

He looked at his watch. Only a quarter past two.

I'll give her until two-thirty. If she isn't here by then, then I'll go home.

After a couple more minutes of sitting on the bench, he needed to stretch his legs. He walked from the end of the bench to the other end, back again, yawning, watching a distant star shine. A beautiful night like this should never be spent alone.

Scott checked his watch again. Two-twenty. It was clear she wasn't gonna show up, but he'd give her ten more minutes anyways. It was possible Jenny woke up a little late, and she just needed a few more minutes. And Scott didn't wanna miss out on spending a little time with her, when this was their only chance to get together.

So he kept waiting, kept pacing back and forth.

Scott stretched, then, looking into the bushes behind the fence, Jenny's eyes looked back at him.

As the scream escaped his throat, hands grabbed the back of his head and slammed his mouth onto the metal armrest. Hot pain sank into his gums. A tooth was knocked out of its socket by the force and several others cracked. Then the person worked Scott's lower jaw around the bench and forced his face upwards until the jaw was stretched as far as it could go.

His lips tore. The unbearable pain in his mouth spread to the rest of his body. His jaw cracked. The force didn't stop until it was ripped from his face.

The person threw Scott on top of Jenny as blood pumped from his wounds. His eyes shut. This was the end.

The monster jammed Scott's jaw through his throat.

In the morning, two boys walking their dogs found the bodies.

"Hey, look at that. Two dead bodies. Right here in the park. And the festival's tonight. What good timing."

"Oh yeah," the second boy said, getting on his hands and knees for a closer look at the bodies. "That's the Butcher all right."

"You think?"

"Look at the work. You can tell. Early Butcher stuff was sloppy. Just your standard stab-and-go, nothing memorable. But over the years he's really sharpened things up. More brutality, more presentation. People are gonna love this one."

"Yeah, I can see that."

"This is easily the best pre-festival sacrifice we've ever had."

9

Five o'clock arrived slowly.

The festival was underway.

There was music, a three-piece band on stage with people gathering around. Somebody in the crowd picked their nose and wiped it on their cup. A photographer neared the stage and took pictures. Everybody was happy.

Vendors set up folding tables and their tents and laid out their merchandise.

Others grilled meat and fried onions.

It seemed like just about everybody in Raven Hill was here today.

Kids darted between the booths. A group of them ran past wearing plastic Santa Claus masks. Each one carried a rubber knife from one of the novelty booths. They chased each other in circles, swinging their fake blades and shouting curse words at each other.

"Watch out, I'm the motherfucking Butcher!!"

"You're dead meat, bitch!!"

"I'm gonna stab you in the ass!!"

One of the boys tripped and fell in the grass and laughed so hard he couldn't get back up.

And the most popular item at a festival: t-shirts.

BEWARE THE RAVEN HILL BUTCHER

I SURVIVED RAVEN HILL

SANTA'S GOT A KNIFE

WELCOME TO BUTCHER COUNTRY

People paid fifty dollars per shirt, and some bought all four of them for a slight discount.

At the end of a rack a fat man with a red beard stood on top of a carton and shouted over the music, *"BEWARE THE RAVEN HILL BUTCHER! LIMITED RUN! GET 'EM BEFORE THEY'RE GONE!"*

A couple pimply faced teenagers bought two and pulled them on right there in the street, laughing as they posed for a picture with their arms around each other.

Near the edge of the square, a row of portable toilets stood baking in the heat. The door of one swung open and a man stepped out licking chili off his thumb. He held a cardboard tray of chili cheese fries in one hand and kept eating as he walked away.

The next man in line said, "You were eating in there?"

The first man kept walking. "Mind your damn business."

The second man stepped inside and covered his nose.

Across the street, another vendor had set up a folding table covered in stacks of glossy comic books. The cover showed a muscular figure in a red Santa coat standing in a hallway soaked with blood. Bodies lay scattered around his boots while the title stretched across the top in jagged letters: THE RAVEN HILL BUTCHER: SLEIGH BELLS AND SLAUGHTER!!!

The man behind the table was blonde with a big crooked nose and a smug smile on his face.

When the young woman walked up to his table he said, "It's all based on the real murders right here in Raven Hill. I drew this myself. This is the glossy variant cover and it's a limited print run." He shoved the book into her hands. "It's pretty gnarly. The way those girls got fucked up in that mansion. I studied all the crime scene photos. I have never seen anything like it in my life. There was blood everywhere and on everything. I almost wish I could've been there. I know that sounds crazy but I almost wish I could've seen it in person. I have all the photos printed out at home. I look at them all the time. I think about it every single day. Anyways, that'll be twenty-five bucks."

Christy Morrison tore the comic book clean in half.

The rip of paper was loud enough that a few people nearby turned their heads.

"What the fuck is wrong with you, you bitch?"

Christy dropped the two halves back onto the table and walked away.

Somewhere up ahead she finally saw Julia and Madison arriving with the signs. They gave Christy one that read, **THEY WERE REAL PEOPLE!**

NO MERCH FOR MURDER!

THE BUTCHER KILLED MY FRIENDS!

THIS TOWN SHOULDN'T CELEBRATE A KILLER!

A group of teenagers in Santa Claus masks ran past the girls and their small group of protesters.

"I'M THE BUTCHER!"

"I KILLED YOUR FRIENDS!"

"STOP TRYING TO CANCEL THE BUTCHER!"

"YOUR FRIENDS HAD IT COMING!"

"YOU'RE ON THE WRONG SIDE OF CHRISTMAS!"

"FAKE NEWS! FAKE VICTIMS!"

"GET OVER IT! STOP LIVING IN THE PAST!"

Madison rolled her eyes. "Deplorable."

A man and a woman a few years older than they were approached them, and the man said, "You don't happen to have any extra signs, do you?"

JUSTICE FOR THE DEAD!

ENOUGH BLOOD FOR YOUR PARTY?

"My name is Wesley," he said. "I'm the one who called the other day."

10

A FEW HOURS LATER they met again at a bar a few blocks from the festival.

It was empty in here because the festival was still going on down the street.

They pushed two tables together and Wesley paid for a round of drinks.

It all sounded fictitious, but he gave it his best shot. "There's a way to stop him," Wesley said then pushed the nameless book forward. "The Butcher, he isn't human. But you already know that, don't you?"

The girls looked at him strangely.

"Well, this is what I know," Wesley said, then explained it all from the very beginning.

He started with the book he found at the mom and pop bookshop, and flipped through the pages. He read them definitions and passages and explained the different beasts throughout history and folklore that were similar.

Wesley spoke of the dimension from which certain ancient spirits came, and the cults and covens that prayed to them and sacrificed to them. He told them about rituals and certain mutilations, and all the things that helped bring demons through to our world. And how they sometimes inhabited corpses.

Wesley went into the story of the teenagers killing Bob, the groundskeeper at Camp Solgohachia, and the body that was buried somewhere at the camp.

He tried to convey the story clearly, and never did they ask him any questions about any of it.

"But we could all stop it," Wesley said, "if we form a bond and trap him in this box. Then I could hide it forever, and nobody could summon The Butcher again."

Everybody was quiet.

"Yeah it's… I know how it sounds. I feel crazy just saying it out loud"

“But how does any of this work?” Christy said. It was the first time someone other than Wesley spoke. “What do we do?”

Wesley had not prepared for how he’d say this next part. It was more outrageous than all the other elements of the convoluted story combined.

“Tomorrow is the anniversary of the Camp Solgohachia murder. So I’m going down to the camp. It’s abandoned now, and I’ve got weapons in my van. Once he’s hurt… we’d need to all hold the urn over his body.”

“You expect us to get near enough to *The Butcher?”* Julia said. *“That’s fucking retarded.”*

“Sorry, but that’s the way it has to be done.”

She rubbed her chest, touching the scar where The Butcher stabbed her.

“I stabbed him before,” Christy said. “And Madison saw the police shoot him. Nothing worked. Why would it work now?”

“Because you’re not strong enough alone.”

“Do you really believe we could really kill him?” Madison said.

“Well, no. The pages about how to kill one of these things were ripped out. All it can tell us now is how to imprison him. How to trap his spirit.”

The rest of the talk was lengthy.

Wesley didn’t receive a direct answer from any of the girls, but wrote down the directions for them anyways.

He’d be leaving in one hour, he said. Then he and Wendy would be on their way to Camp Solgohachia again.

Everyone went their separate ways.

11

Pain boar like maggots into Christy's stomach.

She and Julia sat in her car, debating what to do. There was a sharp nervousness in her guts. It was hard for them to make a decision. Things like this shouldn't be decided in minutes, but that was all she and Julia had. Wesley had given them an hour.

She wondered what The Raven Hill Butcher would be doing until then. *Buying bread, milk, and eggs from the grocery store then needing to set it all down to go to camp to kill us all? What's he do during the rest of the year? Twiddle his thumbs? Whittle wood until it's time to cut off someone's head?*

Christy never thought she'd find decapitation funny, but it was funny for a moment. Because what did he do during the rest of the year? What were the movie monsters doing between all the sequels? She assumed it was the same thing serial killers did in real life. Between kills, Ted Bundy must've lived a normal life. Must've woken up, used the bathroom, brushed his teeth just like any other person would've done.

"I think I want to help him, Jules."

"You must be fuckin crazy, Christy."

The roads were clear today, as if everyone knew what was to happen and had gone out of their way to let Madison travel quickly.

The sun was setting early, much earlier than it was supposed to, as if even the sun did not want to see what was going to happen, as if the sun did not want to shed light upon the horrific acts Madison could feel approaching her.

It then clicked in her mind that she hadn't talked to her mother or father before leaving. She hadn't told a single soul where she would be. She hadn't told a single person that she would be at Camp Solgohachia that night.

"Camp? You're suddenly going to camp?" Madison could hear her mother say. "You're too old for camp. You never even went as a kid."

"No, Mom, Camp Solgohachia. It's closed down."

"Closed down? What do you mean?"

"I'm going to a closed down camp with four strangers. We're gonna kill a crazy murderer. The guy who almost killed me, remember?"

"Oh *him?* You're gonna see *him?* Okay sweetie, have a good time."

If her mom knew where she was going she'd have slashed her car tires to keep her from leaving. Her mother would've tied her up with rope and bubble wrap and locked her in a closet had she told her about Camp Solgohachia and Wesley and Wendy and the others.

Madison wanted revenge.

Tears welled in her eyes. She wiped them away, focusing on the road.

She tried to imagine what it was like for Jill and Emma.

She tried to imagine what it would have been like stuck in that hotel waiting for her and Brynn and Arabella. She hoped it was painless. That would be comforting to know. But she hadn't the slightest idea, and every time they resurfaced even remotely, she felt guilty.

Gorgeous trees and open land lined both sides of the road. It was a pretty sight.

When Madison arrived at the entrance to Camp Solgohachia, she wondered if she had made a mistake.

She was all alone, and the sky was dark, and her stomach turned over time and again. Eerie winds rattled her car, and coldness crept over her body.

What could be taking the others so long? Had they really needed that much more time to catch up with her? Madison didn't like it one bit.

The lot was big, empty, and the sign was smeared with faded black paint, but it was still possible to read the camp's name clearly. Slurs and insults were written in sharpie on the sign and its poles, thing such as "Camp Death" and "Camp Headless."

She shivered.

Madison reached for the heat and turned it up. She looked back down at the directions. They were simple, she had made only three turns or so to get down here, it was mostly a straight shot. She retraced them in her mind, going over where to turn first if she left here right now. It would've been a waste of her whole night, but it was better than being here alone. Why didn't they all just leave together?

She wished she had a phone in her car. She pictured the conversation with her mother:

"Him Mom. I'm on my way home."

"Where are you? I was getting worried."

"A stranger told me to meet up with him at this camp. You know, the one where kids got beheaded? We're gonna kill the killer."

"You're what?!?!"

"Oh no, don't worry, nobody showed up, so I'm on my way home."

"Oh okay. Supper will be in the fridge."

"Great, I'm starving."

From her car, all Madison could see of the camp was an open strip of land leading inwards towards cabin, and the grass was short and dead. In her mind she had expected the grass to be so high it would reach her waist. Who would be cutting the camp grass all these years later? But the grass had probably been dead a long time. The ground was barren, nothing would grow in it now. Even the trees she could see from her car looked rotten and sickly, their branches devoid of the leaves that should have sprouted for summer.

She wondered where everyone was as she turned her head around to look at the empty parking lot.

I'm sure they'll arrive at any minute... any minute now... come on guys.

When she looked back ahead to the sign, she thought she saw something move in her peripheral. A split second. Something subliminal.

Madison gulped.

She eyed the rearview and for the second time, was sure something had moved. This time it seemed to come from *inside* her car. Nervously, slowly, she turned her head. She clutched her seat with white-knuckled fists.

No one was there.

She looked ahead.

Her headlights illuminated the area in front of her, but the darkness was thickening, coiling around the lights, fighting back and attempting to mask them. The rain had ended briefly but a drizzle returned.

Her hands loosened from her grip on the seats and her foot pressed down on the break. She changed gears to reverse.

She turned her steering wheel to the right, put it in drive, then started to leave when another car came in first.

Their bright lights blinded her. Madison slammed on the breaks furiously and her body went flying inches off the seat. She was pulled back by her seatbelt.

"Ouch."

Pain squirmed through her body and she rubbed her left elbow which had gotten hit the worst as it flung into the door.

After a minute the pain was receding.

Then, finally, she looked at the other car. They were an afterthought to the pain.

Christy and Julia. No sign of Wesley and Wendy yet.

Madison wondered what to do now. Leave or stay?

Suddenly a thought came to her: why were the others so lucky to have friends that survived with them, when she was the only one to survive her night? Suddenly she was jealous. She wished just one of her friends could be here with her right now.

12

Even in the night and through the rain, all these years later the trees and road still looked the same, as if Wesley had traveled them to camp just yesterday.

Wesley parked, turned to Wendy, then kissed her. "I love you."

"I know." Wendy rolled her eyes and smiled.

Wesley turned the car off, then he opened the trunk and found the suitcase.

Inside were cleavers and bowie knives. As he opened it, Wendy brought the girls over. The rain stopped, and a stillness came over the land. Wesley glanced towards the trees and did not see them moving, which only made the thread of disquiet running through him twist tighter.

When the girls came to him, they asked what the plan was.

Wesley made it up on the spot: "We'll start a fire. Just like we used to."

"Is he a moth that's gonna fly into the light?" Madison said. "Or do you have a real plan?"

"This—this is a real plan."

"Is it?" Julia said.

"It is."

"I still don't understand how you know he'll be here," Christy said.

"Because we're all here. He has to come. He wants us dead. The time for all these questions was at the bar. Are you all gonna back out now that we're here?"

It must've been a good enough answer for her because she didn't reply, but Wesley saw deep fright in her eyes.

Wesley shut the trunk.

They each had a weapon now. Death by knives. Fitting.

Under the strongly pouring moonlight, and through Wesley's flashlight, he saw that the grass was all dead, and the trees were dying. Somehow, the cabins and buildings left at Camp Solgohachia all seemed to be in great condition, as if somebody had still been taking care of the cabins.

The camp had been sued by the families of his deceased friends, and was forced to close. If it weren't for the slurs written with markers on the entrance to camp, he'd have assumed nobody besides him and the girls had come here since that horrible night.

He remembered it all again, all their deaths playing on repeat in his mind.

Tonight seemed almost an exact replica of that night, from the rich darkness gripping the earth, to the all too familiar sounds his shoes made against the ground. It brought back memories of the race to the cabin, and now his heart was beating furiously. Wesley remembered pushing himself, running barefoot, pain poking up from his feet, being cautious not to step in glass when they approached the cabin and he noticed broken windows.

He heard Ralph's cries again, then Al's. Wesley halted. He stared towards the woods where it had happened. He could still hear it all, all their screams. Then, as vividly as the night it happened, he saw Wendy's hair being yanked by The Raven Hill Butcher before Bill came to the rescue.

Wesley wondered if any small pieces of his friends were left behind in those woods, decomposing for all those years.

They gathered wood and lit a fire.

Embers sparked brightly against a dense charcoal sky, and its warmth made the night pleasant and bearable. There were no logs left to sit on, for the ones left behind were rotten.

Approximately two minutes after the fire was started, it rained heavily. It came down like bullets.

"Dammit," Wesley said. "Let's wait it out in the van."

"Wait it out?" Julia crossed her arms. "How long do you plan to keep us here?"

"This is useless," Wendy said.

"Well," Wesley said, "let's go back to the van and talk it out."

The girls said nothing. Regret was all over their faces.

Wesley watched the diminishing fire. All his hopes went with it. This was an utter disaster. It was all going wrong. He was foolish to think this would've been successful.

The girls ran through the rain as if that would prevent them from getting soaked. Wesley took one more look at the fire which was entirely put out, and for the briefest of moments something passed through the camp.

Were his eyes playing tricks on him?

He turned back to the ladies, opened his mouth to say something, then shut it. Was he right all along? He glanced back again and saw nothing.

The girls were far ahead of him now, and he reached into his pocket for his keys, smashed his fingertip into the unlock button, and Wendy went into the van.

The others went their separate ways.

Wesley grabbed the handle, but looked back towards where the fire had been and tried to look deeper into the camp.

Just your mind playing a trick…

Suddenly, Wendy was yelling at him to get into the car.

He climbed in and shut the door. His thoughts were scattered.

13

MADISON DROPPED HER BOWIE knife then went into her car.

She had enough of this. This pointless wild goose chase and these crazy people. She was going back home and she'd never see these people again, and that was comforting.

How could I be so stupid to get dragged into this?

She unlocked the door, sat down, turned the key in the ignition, then pressed her hands on the wheel. For a moment, maybe less, she thought about staying, but her head was pounding so loudly it was difficult to hear her own thoughts.

Madison was about to put her car into reverse when the knife was thrust through the window, and shattered glass tore her skin.

Her hands patted against the seat for her own knife, then she remembered the thing wasn't in her car.

She was helpless.

He reached through the window for her. Her screams sank into darkness. She wondered where the others were. Hadn't they heard? Hadn't they seen?

The Raven Hill Butcher drilled his knife into her leg then rammed it upwards into her pelvis.

At last, Madison heard car doors opening—but would they make it in time?

She prayed she could get to a hospital in time. Tried to convince herself she hadn't lost much blood but her body looked as if someone spilled a bucket of red paint over her.

He removed the knife, slammed it into her chest, pulled it out, then disappeared.

Through the corners of her pale blue lips, blood trickled.

It felt as if it took the others a million years to come to her side.

By now her eyes were shutting. Her eyes felt as if strings were looped through them and some fairy was winding them shut.

Madison heard them say something. Specifically what they were saying, she couldn't tell. Words were slipping in and out of her ears. Nothing was making sense anymore. Nothing felt real. Her sense slipped away from her.

Suddenly Wesley was at her side. With her last remaining strength she grabbed his hand. He was apologizing furiously, rapidly, but her lips wouldn't give words. She wanted to say it was okay. Somehow she was fine with it, her anger was drifting out of her body with her blood. She wanted to whisper *It's okay,* but her lips pulled apart then slumped onto each other.

14

Wesley had cost a woman her life.

He should've come here by himself, lured The Butcher out on his own, faced him man to man... but instead he decided to hide behind four women.

Wesley turned back to the others. "She's dead."

They were silent in the rain.

Suddenly, Wesley heard his friends—Bill, Al, Ralph—screaming again. He heard their pain and torture. It was all too real, as if he were being transmitted back.

He ran.

He ran towards the voices. He pushed past Wendy and almost dropped the urn.

Their cries were broken for a minute as Wendy called from behind him asking where the hell he was going.

He heard the women chasing after him. That only made him run harder. This was something he needed to do alone. Without Wendy. Without anyone. This was a battle he had to fight alone. How it always should have been.

After a minute or two, the cries of his friends were uninterrupted, and he glanced over his shoulder to see the girls watching from far behind. They had stopped a little ways back, watching him go past the cabins. He still remembered the names of all of them from Grizzly, the best cabin, to Panda, the godawful cabin he stayed in when his friends were killed.

The screams of his friends were louder here than anywhere else. Rain came down as fast as an ocean turned upside down, and Wesley stood on the path where he and Bill had taken off to get to the cabin. The spot where it technically all began.

"What are you waiting for? Come and get me."

Silence.

"Where are you?"

Then, abruptly, Wendy screamed at the top of her lungs: *"Behind you!"*

Even through the harsh screen of night and amazing downpour, he saw the outline of the man. His knife in aged wood was raised, its previous stains of Madison's blood had been washed away by rain and were probably sinking fast into the ground and would later be absorbed by the roots of weeds.

The Raven Hill Butcher swung. The knife twisted through air. It came down on Wesley's shoulder and met soft flesh just as Wesley jerked out of the way. Wesley dropped the urn, took his cleaver in both hands, raised it, and The Butcher swung again before Wesley could. Wesley backed away down the little slope, accidentally giving The Butcher the advantage.

Pain screamed through his body, strong winds blew across Camp Solgohachia, and Wesley threw his clever at The Butcher's face. It sank into his flesh.

The girls were running. Wesley screamed stop, but they did not listen.

Wesley was no longer scared. He grabbed The Butcher's arm—the one with the knife—and tried to pry it out of his hand.

Fright never wavered from the faces of the girls. They knew this was it. Help Wesley or they all died.

Wesley struggled with The Butcher. Julia and Wendy were digging their knives into his back and reaching for his neck, but he was a tall man and their blades wouldn't reach. Christy slammed her cleaver into The Butcher's hand, but it did not penetrate his flesh. Wesley's cleaver had penetrated The Butcher, and it was still stuck in his face, but there was no blood.

As best any of them could detect, he had no real injuries. It was like trying to hurt a shadow. The Butcher *should* have been hurt, his body *should* have torn.

The book—that stupid book—had said that the spirits were still bound to the properties of the body they inhabited, so why couldn't they kill him now? Was he really not a demon? Was he something more? Something else? Something worse?

"Stop being afraid of him," Wesley said. *"That's the only way."*

Their blades dug violently into the creature but it seemed to have no use. Christy ripped the cleaver from his face and tried to jam both knives into his belly.

The Raven Hill Butcher squirmed his arm away from Wesley then pushed him on his back. The Butcher gripped his knife tightly and held it close to his chest. Christy backed away and so did the others.

Suddenly Julia was running away, and The Butcher locked his eyes on her.

She shouldn't have done that.

The Butcher ran after her.

Wesley jumped to his feet. Christy and Wendy were already after them.

Wendy held the box. Space built between Wesley, Wendy, Christy, and Julia and The Butcher. They were heading towards the swim hole.

Wesley and the girls were roughly twenty feet from The Butcher and Julia and the swim hole when The Butcher tackled Julia into its dark waters and pressed his knife to her neck. Julia wrapped both hands around him and forced it away. She held him away as long as she could.

Wesley made it into the waters, and while Julia had The Raven Hill Butcher distracted, Wesley sank the cleaver into his back.

For the first time, there was blood.

"There's blood Wendy get the urn I made him bleed get me the urn Wendy. *Now.*"

The knife dropped from The Butcher's hands.

As Julia backed away from him, Wendy brought the urn with her into the water, and stabbed her bowie knife into The Butcher's chest.

It was Christy who delivered the final blow to his throat.

Everybody held his body under the nasty water filed with dead ants and a variety of leaves. Under the circumstances, the extremely cold and grimy water was beautiful.

His head split three-quarters of the way off his throat, hanging on by small threads of skin. His body convulsed violently with unnatural movements that a human who was nearly decapitated could not possibly make.

His Santa Claus mask fell to reveal the face of Bob. The old man looked exactly as Wesley had seen in the missing persons picture. Bob's hands tightly gripped Wesley's arm, then Bob let out a gasp and let go. His body continued shaking violently.

"Hands on the urn," Wesley said.

Wendy's hands shook as she opened it, and everyone touched their hands to it.

It wasn't black as Wesley had suspected, but red. The mist left Bob's corpse, twisted through the air, then came down in swift zigzagging motions into the box.

Wendy shut it immediately and refused to remove her hands from holding it down. The body drifted away into the waters.

Wesley hugged Wendy then he gasped. She pushed him away to see what he was looking at.

Bob's body rapidly decayed from that of an old man into a skeleton with very little remains left on him being picked away by bugs.

15

Wesley and Wesley stayed for Madison's funeral.

That was the last time they saw Christy and Julia. After that, they parted ways.

They stopped at a little diner halfway between Raven Hill and Carpentersville called Nicky's.

The walls were plastered with pictures of musicians from the 50s. Neon lights surrounded the menus on the wall, the booths were red, and the floor was checkered. The daily specials were written with chalk on a blackboard, and behind it hung giant posters of milkshakes.

Wesley still felt guilt—old guilt and new guilt—but things would be good now, they could be happy now. All Wesley had to do was get rid of the urn. He knew exactly where he was going to hide it. Some place where nobody would ever find it. Some place nobody would ever look in a million years.

After they started eating, Wesley said, "Wendy?"

"Yeah?"

"Do you have the urn?"

"I think I left it on the passenger seat."

Wesley and Wendy ran back to the van in a hurry.

Their windows were bashed in.

When they opened the door, the urn was gone.

It was the only thing missing.

THE FINAL CHAPTER

1

THE PETALS OF PLUCKED flowers curled at the edges from summer heat.

Rays of sunlight licked Ingrid's sunburned shoulders. It must've been past ninety degrees out, and the air conditioning on full blast in her car did not help her one bit.

It also didn't help that she might have been lost.

She looked down at her map. She should've been passing the crossroads of Thompson and Westlake, but ahead of her was Thompson and Stark. Everything else seemed right, but she wanted to be sure, so she stopped for directions.

The only store she had seen for miles in any direction was a little restaurant called Valenzuela's, and a little candy store next to it called Gumdrops. Ingrid parked in front of Valenzuela's, brought the map down with her, and laid it out before the lady at the counter.

"Hello, I was wondering if you could tell me if I'm at the right place, I'm supposed to be at Thompson and Westlake…"

"We get people confused about that all the time," the lady said. "Don't worry, they renamed it Stark two years ago. Where you heading?"

"To the old camp. They're reopening it."

"The camp?"

Ingrid took her map from the counter. "Yes, ma'am. The camp."

A lanky old man at the nearest table stood up, staggered towards her, putting the cap back on his pint of Smirnoff. *"You're doomed if you go up there. Doomed."*

Ingrid staggered a step backwards.

"You're going to Camp Death, aint ya? You'll never come back!"

Ingrid left Valenzuela's. The old man followed her out to her car.

"Stay away from me."

"It's cursed. You're gonna die up there."

Ingrid opened her door, slammed it shut, and locked it just in time. She pulled away as the man banged his fists on her window.

"You're gonna die. Turn around and go back home or you're gonna die."

The restaurant and candy shop faded from view, and soon she was a couple miles away from the old man, but that did not stop her heart from beating so fast and loud. Nervously Ingrid bit her lip.

You're going to Camp Death, ain't ya? You'll never come back!

She didn't believe him, and she didn't believe the others. She didn't believe the rumors, the legends, the stories that spread. A place couldn't be cursed, a place couldn't be haunted. Besides, all that stuff happened ten years ago...

What could possibly go wrong now?

This was what Raven Hill needed. A fresh start. It was time to fix up the cabins, fix up the facilities, get everything up and running again. It would be great for the community, and it would pay well. Very well.

Ingrid glanced at the map again. So she was going the right way. And she was almost there, taking a right turn. A minute later, the path became a dirt road. Trees spanned for miles on her sides. It was such a pretty place.

A little while later, the Camp Solgohachia sign entered her view.

Ingrid was the first person to arrive.

She parked her car in the spot closest to the camp, hopped out of her car, and stretched her legs.

Her two big suitcases were packed with so many things that they nearly did not close. Ingrid dragged them from her car to the very first cabin, the nicest cabin, she was told, and under the immense heat of the Raven Hill sun, found the key under the doormat just as she was told.

She took one more look at the camp before opening the door. The grass was tall, but it had been cut a few weeks ago, she was told, in preparation for her and the others to come and fix up the camp. Now it needed to be cut again.

The place really didn't look half bad, and would look so much better when it was nice and cleaned and ready to be reopened. She turned her attention back to the door, slid the key into the knob, then felt a chill slither on her back.

Ingrid turned. She was not alone. Eyes were watching her. She felt them.

Quit it, she thought, *don't let that weirdo's words get to you.*

The cabin had nice tile floors, new bunkbeds with new sheets, air conditioning—a luxury all the other cabins did not have—showers with locking doors instead of thin stalls with thin curtains, and fistfuls of dust in the corners.

Ingrid set her bags on the first bottom bunk, unzipped them, then spent the next few minutes putting her clothes into dresser drawers.

Ingrid slid her empty bags under her bed, then set out to explore Camp Solgohachia. She had seen pictures but had never been here herself. She passed the flagpole then walked up the path to the boys' cabins. She wondered if any of them had left anything that had been resting undisturbed in a drawer or under a bed, something waiting years and years for its owner to return. A little part of someone that was left in Camp Solgohachia this whole time.

She ran a hand along the cabins, then went down from there to the swim hole. The water was filthy with leaves, ants, and gunk. She hadn't the slightest idea how they'd even begin to tackle cleaning that thing.

Ingrid loved swimming, it was one of her favorite things in the world, and looking at the blob made her excited, she couldn't wait to try it out once the swim hole was good to go.

Next she went to the center of camp to the mess hall. Behind it was wide open stretches of land, before going down to the golf area and eventually a little stream of water for canoeing. The canoes were attached still to the same poles they had been a decade ago, and she thought about trying one out soon.

She thought that maybe the others would be here by now, as she checked her watch, but she was still the only one. At the parking lot, her car was still the only one there. Maybe she should call someone. Maybe she could call and find out where everyone was.

Maybe all the others were just running late…

She was partway back to her cabin when she saw a fawn standing in the woods. Beautiful red fur with white spots shining in sunlight. It looked at her then looked away, nibbled on grass, then moved further into the woods.

She went back into the cabin, found her polaroid camera in her purse, then came back outside to take a picture of it. She could hear it moving deeper into the woods but didn't see it.

“Awe, come back.” Ingrid took a step into the woods. “Where’d you go?”

A few steps later, she saw it again. It was fifteen feet down from her at a clearing with another fawn that was even smaller. The big one licked the smaller one, then they took a few steps together to the right. Ingrid discretely followed, keeping her distance, careful not to scare them.

The fawns came to a little stream and drank. Ingrid crouched, took her picture, then her body jerked forward with pain. She looked down and saw the point of the knife rip through her stomach.

Panful screams left her lips.

The knife was pulled out of her, then raised again and brought down into soft flesh. The blade rotated inside of her. Ingrid’s screams rose past the clouds, but there was nobody around to hear her or help her.

The blade sank half an inch into Ingrid’s guts, just enough to make her writhe.

A smile crept across the killer’s face.

Even after Ingrid was dead, the knife was thrust back into the corpse and turned, making satisfying squishes.

2

Meredith's blonde hair looked as if it was spun from pure sunshine. It tumbled down her shoulders and was plastered to her olive skin with sweat. Burning sunlight blinded her momentarily as she drove, and she lifted her hand up to cover the sun.

It was a hot day, and not only did they have the AC up, but the windows cracked. Meredith thought that that would let all the cool air out, but Angie was convinced that this would somehow make it cooler.

Empty road for miles and miles. Dirt, open fields, no sign of human life whatsoever. It were as if they had driven right into *The Twilight Zone,* into the fifth dimension, a place beyond that which is known to man.

They stopped so Meredith could get them coffee from the little restaurant while Angie went into Gumdrops.

Meredith asked the woman behind the counter if they were headed the right way, and a shadow of worry came across the woman's face.

"Yes, you're going the right way," the woman said. "But be careful out there."

After getting two coffees, she went up the path to Gumdrops, and neared the door when Angie came out with a bag of marshmallows and red gummy fish. Meredith handed her sister a coffee.

"He's gonna kill you up there. Don't go to the camp."

An old man drinking a pint of vodka stood a few feet away from them. He kept telling them they were gonna die and not to go to the camp. Meredith and Angie hurried into the car, and Meredith pulled away before Angie finished shutting her door.

"The one time I needed to use my pepper spray," Meredith said, "and I left my purse in the car."

3

Meredith parked a space down from the only other car that was here, then she and her sister took their bags out of the back.

Between them both, there were six bags, three for each of them. It was a tough decision what to bring and what to leave back home, so they brought it all.

They each dragged two bags up to the path that led to the girls' cabins.

"This place is so pretty," Angie said.

At the door, Meredith knocked, expecting whoever was here first to open the door for them. Then Angie turned the knob and pushed the door open. The other counselor's bag stuck out from under the first bed, and one of her shirts was sticking out from the corner of a dresser drawer.

"Hello?" Meredith said. "Anybody in here?"

"Maybe she's looking around. She probably got bored waiting for us."

Meredith chose the first bottom bunk on the right side of the cabin, set her bags down, then went back to her car to get her final bag. Angie chose a bed then quickly followed her twin. They made their second trip to bring all their bags inside.

Meredith shut the door behind her and her sister then looked out at the camp.

She came off the doorstep and down onto the path again, looking in every direction of the camp. She had seen pictures of it when it had been a much nicer place. It was withered by time now, but everything in here could be salvaged with just a little paint, cleaning, time, and care.

Meredith led the way to the big mess hall. She stood outside of it, hand on the door, pausing to watch the little beehive at the far end of the building. After a minute, she and her sister went inside. The bright sun leaked enough through the windows so that the place was illuminated, but Meredith reached for the light switches anyways and turned them on.

"Hello? Anybody home?" Angie said.

"Hellllooo," Meredith said.

"She's not in here, let's go." Angie pushed the door open and left, and her sister followed her.

As the door shut, Meredith heard a floorboard creak from within the building. She turned around, opened the door again, and stared into the empty lunchroom, staring down at a dark doorway that she couldn't see the other side of.

"Hello? Is anybody in there?"

When there was no answer, she left.

"Did she vanish?" Angie said.

"Maybe we should've listened to the old man," Meredith said. "She's probably dead and we'll be next."

"Maybe we should just stab each other now, Meri, and get it over with."

"Let's stab the others first then we can stab ourselves."

Upon returning to the cabin, they did not find the other counselor. Meredith walked to the back of the cabin to the stalls and showers, knocked, opened the doors, but did not find anybody.

Angie was staring out the front door. "Meri, look. A baby deer."

Meredith joined her sister at the door.

The baby deer chewed on a stem, dropped it, picked it up, then made a frightened noise when he saw the girls.

"Did we scare it?" Angie said.

Meredith pinched Angie's arm. "Shush."

The baby deer suddenly ran as fast as it could behind the cabin into the forest.

"See what you did? You scared it away."

Angie rubbed her arm. "You didn't have to hurt me. How did I scare it?"

"Have you looked in a mirror?" Meredith said. Then, "Hey look, the others just pulled up."

Two additional cars were parked. Three boys came out of one, and two girls from the other.

They left their cabin then went across to the parking lot to greet everybody and introduce themselves. The boys were Jimmy, Rick, and Eddie, and the girls were Bianca and Allison.

4

Meredith and Angie stared at the dirty countertops in the kitchen.

Globs of dust, about eighty thousand three hundred and fifty-one dead flies, and all sorts of gunk stained them. It would take days or possibly weeks to clean up the kitchen. Meredith's stomach turned as she pushed an endless mountain of dead flies into a garbage bag and a strange, stinky green liquid leaked out of pile.

Angie inched towards the door. "I think I'm gonna go help Jimmy with the canoes."

"You're not going anywhere. This kitchen is so disgusting and I need your help."

"You're doing great without me."

"It's just a canoe, Angie. Besides, you don't even know how to paint, and our job is fixing up the kitchen."

"Our job is fixing up the whole camp. And the canoe is part of the camp." Angie pulled out a quarter from her pocket. "I call heads."

"It can land on your ass for all I care, Angie."

Angie caught the quarter. It was on heads.

"You clean this up, I'll be painting."

"What? No, no, you're supposed to flip it when you catch it. You know, you catch it then flip it over. You only caught it but you didn't flip it. You have to redo it."

"We're not getting a redo," Angie said. "Have fun in here, sis."

Meredith rolled her eyes, opened the fresh bag of rags, and sprayed down the counters. She must have cleaned them off ten times and that still wasn't enough to fight all the grime. And it seemed that everywhere she looked, there were new piles of flies and even some roaches and spiders materializing out of thin air. For every dead bug she threw away, two more came to take its place.

Angie smiled under the sun.

The air was so warm, so lovely.

She went around the mess hall to the open stretch of land. Far down, Jimmy was painting the canoes green and white.

She snuck up behind him.

He was so focused on his work that he must not have heard her. She covered his eyes and said, "Guess who?"

Jimmy turned around and wiped fresh white paint from his hand on her. "Hey. How's kitchen duty?"

Angie smiled, looking at the canoes that were all centerline-side up. "Mmm… my sister's taking care of that all on her own. I had other things I wanted to do."

Jimmy pulled her to the ground next to him.

Angie jumped on top of him, grabbed the paintbrush and dipped it quickly in fresh green paint. "I think you'd look better painted."

Jimmy grabbed it from her hand and tapped the ends of the bristles on her left cheek. "So do you. Look at you, pretty as a picture."

Jimmy set one of the newly painted canoes into the water.

They climbed in, then he rowed them out a little bit.

"You better not tip this thing over, Jimmy. I can't swim worth a damn."

"I think drowning girls are sexy. I always wanted to fuck a girl who was drowning."

"Shut up and take your pants off."

Jimmy took his pants off and Angie wrapped her legs around him…

Meredith gagged.

She was making progress, filling up trashcan after trashcan with garbage. The kitchen was shaping up, and she was moving along a little bit quicker than she thought she would. Of course, she could've made even more progress if her sister wasn't such a bitch and went out to chase some boy instead of helping her.

The front door of the mess hall opened, and Rick entered the kitchen.

Curly chestnut hair and a beautiful face. He wore a loose white shirt that was already drenched in sweat. He wiped his forehead with his palm.

"How's it going?" Rick said.

Meredith looked at the floor then back to his eyes. "Good, except my sister abandoned me."

"That's too bad," he said. "Anything I could help you with in here?"

Meredith pointed at a cabinet. "I can't reach inside that cabinet."

Rick helped her empty it and throw away the old moldy boxes. "Did you ever go to camp here before?"

"No," she said. "Did you?"

"Yeah I did. In fact I was here that year it happened."

"Oh God, you were?" Meredith stopped scrubbing. "You knew those boys?"

"Didn't know them exactly, but they were a few cabins down. I played basketball at the pool with them before it happened."

"Does it bother you? Coming back here?"

Rick shook his head. "We've got to move on sometime. That's life."

"They never found that guy, right?" Meredith said. "The guy who did it?"

"Never."

5

Eddie finished screwing in the door hinges then swung the door. Good as new. Bianca, who was not any help whatsoever, wiped the sweat from her forehead then sat down on the steps they planned to replace soon. Allison was on her way to grab the nails that they forgot in the supply closet.

"Woo, I'm exhausted."

"You just stood there."

"I helped."

"You leaned against the wall."

"I was standing there looking pretty. That takes effort."

"Maybe you can scrape the chipped paint off the walls."

"Do I have to?"

"You've gotta do something."

"I did something. I supervised."

"That's not supervising."

"Fine. I'll help with the next door. Or something."

Allison came back with the box of nails. "Nice work, Eddie. Bianca, excellent job just standing there."

Eddie raised a hand to his eyes to block out the sun, jumped down from the mess hall's porch, then his eyes wandered to one of the cabins on the girls side whose door was partway open. Something moved swiftly in one of the windows.

"Did either of you ladies see that?"

"See what?" Bianca said.

"I didn't see anything," Allison said.

He pointed his thumb. "Either of you in that cabin? The one with the open door?"

“No, we’re all in the first one.”

“I’m gonna check it out. I’ll be right back.”

“What if it’s a bear?” Bianca said.

“Then you have nothing to worry about, bears don’t fuck with whores. Now start scraping up the paint.”

At the cabin, Eddie turned back to look at the girls. They waved. He slowly went up the stairs.

All was quiet.

“Anybody in here?”

Nothing.

The door creaked open.

Eddie’s hand slid on the wall for a light switch.

The bulbs stuttered on and illuminated the dusty room. It looked almost exactly like the interior of the cabins on the boys side did, with old ugly beds, walls that needed to be scrubbed, old dressers that were falling apart.

He went to the window and looked out of it. It gave no clear view of the mess hall because it was obscured by a tree and the angle. Then he went to the back of the cabin, peeked through the bathroom, but couldn’t find anybody or anything.

Had he really seen anything at all?

Probably not, probably a trick of the light. That was it. Nothing was in here. He left the cabin and went back to the girls. Allison was slamming nails into boards, and Bianca was scraping up paint that came off in very long white strips that were easy to peel off.

“Did you see anything?” Allison said.

“Nothing.”

“Too bad it wasn’t a bear,” Bianca said.

Eddie joined her in tearing off the old paint.

“What did you think of that one in the kitchen?” Bianca said.

“I think I’m in love with her,” Eddie laughed. “She’s so fucking hot.”

“Rick must *love* her too. He’s been in there an awful long time.”

Allison raised a nail and hammer. “If I caught him cheating I’d put one of these through his balls.”

Meredith scrubbed her hands in the bathroom sink.

She went back to the kitchen and cleaned with Rick. Minutes later, Rick went outside when Eddie called him. Alone in the kitchen again, she whistled, grabbed the mop, and cleaned the floors.

She felt so filthy that she couldn't wait to shower. Angie was off doing who knows what with Jimmy, and Eddie and Bianca were in charge of doors, Allison was fixing steps, and Rick was sort of in charge of everything and everybody. None of the other counselors were probably getting as slimy and nasty as she was.

In the big pantry, she found an old radio. She plugged it in, turned the dial, moved the antenna, and it worked. Music filled the mess hall. Awesome. That would help pass the time while continuing the daunting task of cleaning the kitchen.

Watching, tapping the knife on cabin's wall, the figure moved through the shadows. It was almost time.

Most of them were outside of the mess hall. All were happy, all were smiling, all were unsuspecting. That made it even better. The thrill, the chase, the unknown. None of them were fearful yet, but they would be.

Fingers slid against the edge of the blade. It was ready to sink into another one.

How great it felt when the first one died. How great it felt watching her eyes turn from innocent to confusion to fear.

Their time was coming.

6

Meredith opened the door and stepped outside.

Eddie and Bianca peeled huge strands of old dry paint while Rick was popping open the lid of a paint can, and Allison was painting the new steps she put in.

"Watch where you step, Bianca accidentally knocked over a can of paint," Allison said.

Eddie jumped off the mess hall's porch then grabbed Bianca by the waist and helped her down. "We've got a few more doors to put in. See you guys around."

"So did you go here before?" Allison said to Meredith.

"No I didn't."

"Thought so. I would've remembered you."

Angie and Jimmy put their clothes back on, then he rowed the canoe.

She kissed his neck. "Which cabin are you in?"

"We're all in the first one."

"We should grab one for ourselves tonight."

"We better move fast before everyone else gets the same idea."

"I'm curious, who's fucking who?"

"Allison's fucking Rick, Bianca wants to fuck Eddie but he's too retarded to figure it out. So your sister might be out of luck. Unless you girls like to share."

Back at the dock, Jimmy hooked the canoe to a rope on the post.

“I’ll be in the third cabin.” Jimmy slid an arm around her waist, pulled her against his body, then kissed her.

Rick went to buy dinner while everybody else freshened up.

“The day’s passing so quickly,” Meredith said to her sister on the way back to the cabin, “and I feel like we’ve got nothing done.”

“I don’t know about you but I’ve been very productive.”

“Yeah, yeah, you’re looser than all these doors falling off their hinges.”

“We need to get you laid. I think Eddie’s single.”

“Ew.”

“What’s wrong with Eddie?”

“That schnoz.”

“Alrighty then. We’re not sharing Jimmy.”

“That’s ever worse.”

“Relax. I’m not offering.”

Meredith opened the cabin door.

“Rick’s your only other option but he’s fucking Allison.”

“That’s unfortunate.”

“I dunno, maybe they’ll break up.”

“We’re not stranded on an island, Angie. There’s more to do around here than just fuck around.”

“What else are you gonna do for the next couple weeks?”

“I have a book in my bag. I can read.”

“Read? Really? Read? Who reads anymore?”

There were three showers in the back of the cabin. Meredith turned the knob on the first one. The pipes groaned but no water came out. She tried the second one. Same result. Angie tried the third one and it worked just fine.

"Oh come on, that's not fair. I did all the work today and I'm covered in dirt. Let me go first, you're gonna be in there for three hours."

"I'll be quick this time."

"Yeah, right."

"Meri, come on. Not my fault those other two are busted. Just keep messing with them, I'm sure one of 'em might start working."

There was no winning an argument with your little sister.

Angie was probably going to take five hours in there, not a few minutes like she said. So Meredith grabbed her things, then left the cabin and headed for another one. When she was almost at the adjacent cabin, she heard her name called from behind her.

She turned. Angie was waving from the window.

"Meri. I told you I wouldn't be that long."

Meredith went back into the cabin and pointed at the first bed. "I completely forgot about her. Did the others say anything about it?"

"Nothing," Angie said. "Where do you think she is?"

"I have no clue."

Meredith went to the shower, turned on the water, then felt it with her hand before going in. All she could think about now was that other counselor, the one who had showed up then somehow vanished. As the minutes passed, she wondered what could've happened. Her car was here. Why leave everything behind? Where could she have gone?

Her shower was quick and hot. She felt reborn cleaning away the filth. The bottom of the shower was black with dirty water, and she watched it become clear as there was less and less gunk to mix with it.

She dried off, dressed in jeans and a t-shirt, then rejoined her sister at the beds.

"Should we go through her stuff?" Angie said.

"No, what if the others think we're thieves?"

"I just think that we need to see if we can find anything."

"Well, I don't like going through people's things."

"Meri, she's missing, let's just see what we can find."

"Okay, Angie. Go ahead."

Angie pulled out a suitcase from under the bed, then noticed a purse. She opened the purse instead.

Angie rummaged through it and pulled out a few old receipts and lipstick, then found a small wallet.

She opened it, then showed it to Meredith. There was an ID in there for a woman named Ingrid. She was gorgeous.

Behind the mess hall, they had a fire going. On a little table somebody brought out from inside, the food from Valenzuela's was spread out. On another table next to them, there were the ingredients for smores. There was a cooler next to both tables with water bottles and beers in them.

The fire roared.

After she was done with her meal, Meredith put a marshmallow on a stick and roasted it to make a smore. When she was done, she reached the tip of her stick into the fire, then pulled it abruptly back and held it close.

The flame moved slowly.

Angie was sitting on Jimmy's lap, telling him how all the candy she had bought from Gumdrops was melted because she forgot it in the car. Rick and Allison sat across the fire kissing each other. The way the flames roared between her and them, it looked as if they were lovers frying in the depths of hell.

Down at the water, Eddie was rowing himself and Bianca in a canoe. She heard them laughing, turned to watch them, then turned back to look at the flames. Her stick was halfway burned.

Meredith discretely glanced at Rick and Allison again. Allison looked a little sick. She buried her face into Rick's shoulder. Rick ran his hand along hers, kissed her head, then momentarily looked at Meredith and smiled.

"I don't feel so good," Allison said. She pulled away from him and rubbed her stomach. "I think it was something I ate."

"Do you need anything?"

"No. I think I just need to lay down…"

"I think we've got Ginger Ale." Rick went to the cooler and grabbed an ice cold can. When he turned around, Allison was gone.

7

Allison turned the corner of the mess hall, leaving everybody out of sight.

She walked alone in darkness, chills slithering up her back. It had gone from extremely hot to chilly out seemingly with no transition whatsoever.

Her stomach heaved. she felt as if she were about to puke. She rushed across the dark camp, pain bubbling inside her stomach, and made it to the path along the cabins when she was yanked backwards into darkness.

A hand slid under her jaw and clamped her mouth shut.

Both hands wrapped around her head, she was dragged backwards into the very last cabin. She couldn't see anything through darkness as her eyes desperately scanned the room. Nothing but shadows moving within shadows, nothing but a small extension of blackness shutting her jaw.

The person tugged on her scalp. Shockwaves exploded through her body. She couldn't breathe. She needed to scream, needed to breathe, needed to run, needed to fight back, but her body was frozen.

The fingertips of the unseen hands pressed deep into her body, and Allison desperately reached behind herself to hit her attacker, but her hand could never reach. The person must've been standing a mile away. There was nothing to grab onto.

A sharp pain stung her neck as her head was twisted to the right. The person moved her head fast at first, then slowly, as if to savor it, as if to enjoy her pain, as if to watch the helplessness gloss over her eyes.

The face she saw in her peripheral was not human. Floating eyes in a thick cloud of darkness. Eyes devoid of any human emotion.

Her attacker's blade caressed her cheek, then cut carefully down the left side of her face next to her eye. One drop of burning blood trickled over her lashes. She blinked, staining what little vision she had. The person twisted her neck further. The pain was unbearable. Her neck was turned farther than a neck was supposed to go.

The monster moved her head back, giving her slight relief, then turned it back abruptly. It stuck the tip of its knife under her neck, caressing her, enjoying her terror, savoring her fear. Her body convulsed. She needed to break away, needed air desperately.

Allison choked.

The hand clenching her throat moved away but she didn't dare scream, didn't dare do anything that might cause her attacker to hurt her.

She stood completely still. She was alone in darkness. The person—a living shadow—disappeared. They could've been anywhere in the room, they could've been on the ceiling, or could've been outside the cabin. They were one with darkness, one with night.

Allison took one small step, then her hair was yanked back again, and the sharp blade was dragged across her forehead. Her attacker ripped her scalp away from her body. Allison fell on the freezing floor engulfed in pain.

"Just kill me," she whispered. *Put me out of my misery.*

But that was only the start.

8

Rick sat next to Meredith, and Meredith smiled, fidgeted her fingers over the burning stick that she held partway into the fire, then inched as close to him as she could get.

His hand brushed against hers when he rested it between them on the log seat. His eyes held hers.

"It's a pretty night," he said.

Meredith slid the stick from her left hand to her right. "If every night is like this, I'll be happy here. Rick?"

"Yeah?"

"What makes someone want to reopen a place like this? After what happened? Why did you decide to sign up for this job?"

"Well it sounded like something that could be good for the community. And I had so many memories here. It wasn't until I came back recently that I realized I was happy here. I don't think you know this, but my family owns this property. During the year when there wasn't any camp, I'd come up here with my family and it was so… weird to go to the pool or go hiking and not have the other people around. It was fun but it wasn't the same. A place like this is meant to be shared. And if I don't share it, you know, eventually we'd have to sell it. What's the joy in this place becoming a parking lot for some giant corporation?"

"Feeling alone, I know what that's like."

"You do?"

"I do," Meredith said. "And I don't want to be alone tonight."

Eddie and Bianca came back from their little canoe trip. **"You know, Bianca's practically throwing herself at Eddie and he has no clue."**

"He really doesn't know?"

"No, and don't tell him, don't say anything, it's funny that way," Rick said and looked passed her to Jimmy, who was kissing Angie. *"Right Jimmy?"*

Jimmy gave a thumbs up, not daring to break away from Angie's embrace.

Eddie and Bianca sat in Rick and Allison's old spots. Lovers burned in the bonfire's flames again.

"Where'd Allison go?" Bianca said.

"She was sick," Rick said. "She's asleep back at the cabin."

"Wasn't there supposed to be one more of us?" Eddie said. He pointed a finger at everyone and counted, making sure to point off towards the cabins to count Allison. "Seven, Wasn't there supposed to be eight?"

"That's six of us," Bianca said.

"Allison makes seven."

"Does she?"

"Aren't we missing someone? Wasn't there supposed to be another chick here?"

"You're right," Rick said. "Ingrid, I think her name was."

"Guess she didn't show," Bianca said. "Guess it's just the six of us."

"Seven," Eddie said.

"Whatever."

It drizzled, so everybody went inside the mess hall. Angie sat with Jimmy, across from them were Eddie and Bianca, then Rick sat across from Meredith. Eddie went back to one of the counters and came back with two decks of cards.

"We're gonna play a game of bullshit," he said.

Eddie pulled out the jokers and set them aside. He riffled the deck a time or two, then set it down. "It's a pretty simple game and pretty simple to catch on and get the hang of it. Usually me and the guys go by oldest picks first, all the way down to youngest, but I know, I know, never ask a lady her age. We'll start with Bianca then go around the table. There's six of us, fifty-two divided by six isn't even, so somebody's gonna end up with nine."

Bianca drew eight cards, then passed it down to Jimmy.

"Actually," Eddie said, "I'll take a ninth. That's forty-nine. Three more of you take another card… know what, I'll have ten since I'm instructing. Jimmy and Rick, you each take nine, let's give the girls a fair chance."

"Hey, I could win with ten cards," Meredith said. "Give me ten, you take eight."

"No, that wouldn't make me a gentleman."

"So? Just give me ten."

When the cards came around, Meredith had ten, Jimmy and Rick each had nine, Angie and Bianca and Eddie had eight.

"Tell me who's got the two of clubs."

"I do," Jimmy said. He set down three cards. "Three twos."

"Meredith, Angie," Eddie said, "we start with the two of clubs, then he's supposed to put down any 'two' cards he has. He could be lying, and you'd know it now if you had two or more twos in your hand, or if you're feeling lucky, then you could call him out on it. Just scream *bullshit.*"

"Angie, you're next," Jimmy said.

"So I put down a two? Or a three?"

"Threes," Eddie said. "We go through in order. So after that, Meredith puts down however many fours she claims to have. When we get up to king, next person's gotta put down a two or an ace."

"What did you say happens if we call bullshit?" Meredith said.

"It's a game of bluff, and if you call *bullshit.* the cards are flipped over, and say it's a lie and you did a good job you called their bluff, then they're in deep trouble now because that bluffer takes the whole discard pile. If you called out wrong, you must take the whole pile yourself."

"One three," Angie said.

"Bullshit." Meredith said. "Turn it over, I don't believe you."

Angie shamefully turned the card over to reveal a five. "I just didn't have a three."

"How'd you know?" Rick said.

"I can tell when my sister's lying."

"Did you read her mind?" Eddie said. "Is it twin telepathy?"

"I think me and my sister have that," Bianca said.

"You and your sister aren't twins."

"But we still can have twin telepathy."

"No, we don't have it," Angie said.

"Well we used to, but when we were kids they dropped Angie her head and our twin telepathy hasn't worked since," Meredith said, and put down two cards, two fours she actually had. "Two fours."

"Bullshit." Bianca said.

Meredith flipped them over. "Nope."

"Two fives." Rick put down.

"One six." Eddie played his first move.

"One seven," Bianca said.

Everyone was pretty much playing it safe.

By the time the game ended, the rain had gone from a drizzle to a storm. Eddie won, started a second round, this time betting a five dollar bill on the game. Nobody else cared to put down any money.

He won the second game too. He started up a third round, but Meredith didn't want to play anymore. She was bored with it midway through game two.

Meredith walked away to the room by the back door of the mess hall that they had all come in from when they left the bonfire. Rain streaked the glass pane of the door and raced to the bottom. Just like when she was a kid and rain streaked the car windows, she took bets on which of two specific drops would win the race.

She wondered about Ingrid, where she was, what could have happened. If she was around here somewhere they would've found her by now. So what happened? Why were her bags here? Where could she have gone?

Meredith opened the door. A hand grabbed her shoulder. She gasped and turned.

"Woah, it's only me," Rick said. "What's got you all jumpy?"

"Can we talk outside?"

"In the rain?"

"It's stopping."

The rain was settling down, and the edge of the roof would keep them dry on the back balcony, so they went out.

"What's going on?" Rick said, holding both her hands in his. She didn't realize for a second that he was holding them, but she didn't want to pull them away.

"Ingrid. The other counselor that's supposed to be here. Her things were here when me and my sister came, and a little while ago I found her wallet in the cabin so I know it belongs to her. So… where is she?"

"I don't know. I tried to call somebody about it but the line's dead. If something happened we'll find her."

"What if she's hurt?"

"She's not hurt. We would have seen her or something."

"Then where might she be?"

"Hey, come on, you're shaking. Maybe we should get you back to your cabin."

"Yeah. Yeah that sounds good. Allison probably feels all alone in there."

"Surely she's asleep by now. Hey, I'm just gonna tell the others I'm walking you over, I'll be right back."

"Okay."

Rick went inside and left her all alone. She looked around. This place was so creepy in the dark, so different than in day. In day it was friendly and inviting. At night, it was frightening and mysterious, as if anything could be around any corner.

Rick was back a second later and put his arm around her. "I'll call again in the morning, I'll drive to Valenzuela's again if I have to use their phone. We'll get this figured out. I'm sure there's a logical explanation. She could've, I don't know, she could've…"

Meredith waited for Rick to finish his sentence, but he didn't. She was very curious to hear what he thought Ingrid might've done.

Halfway to the cabin, Meredith saw something move out the corner of her eye in the window of the final cabin all the way at the right, the complete opposite of where they were going. She looked at Rick, and their eyes met.

"Did you see that too?"

"Somebody was in there."

"Maybe it's Ingrid."

"Look like a squirrel to me."

They hurried to the last cabin, went up the quiet steps, and found that the door was cracked open. Rick grabbed the handle, led the way inside, then shut it behind her.

All was quiet and still. He found the light switch, turned it on, but saw nothing out of place.

They looked around from where they stood.

“You were right,” she said. “Maybe it was just a squirrel.”

Rain was pouring hard again.

“I’m dreading going back out there,” Meredith said.

“We don’t really have to,” Rick said.

Meredith moved closer to him. He put his arms around her and pulled her in. She knew it was wrong—she couldn’t stop thinking of Allison—but she kissed him anyways. She had been craving this the entire day, and she didn’t think it would happen.

After a minute, she pulled away. “I feel guilty. What about your girlfriend? What if she finds—"

He kissed her again midsentence, but she didn’t care. It felt good. Who cared about Allison?

Without moving away from him, her hand slid on the wall, gliding up and down until she found the light switch. Shouldn’t bring any attention to themselves, should they? Together they moved to the back of the cabin, to the bottom bunk in the right corner, and he laid on top of her.

She struggled to pull off her clothes since she was drenched, but she managed. The warmth of the cabin was soothing on her cold skin. She traced him with her hands, and he traced her.

She had no thoughts, no focus, only desire.

9

Rick was bewitched the moment he first saw Meredith, and now he couldn't believe what was happening. It had moved so fast, happened so suddenly, that he was clueless how they ended up here together. The last time he cheated on Allison it took a month before anything happened. The time before that, almost three months.

This time, less than a day.

Meredith was soft, her skin was cold from the rain, but now she was warm. She was so responsive to his touch. She kissed his neck while his hands became tangled in her hair. Neither of them wanted this to end.

When they were done, he noticed the rain had stopped.

He hugged her tight, not wanting to let go, even when she told him he was pulling her hair. She shifted, wrapped herself around him under the blanket, and her body heat warmed him. It had never been that passionate with Allison.

"We should be careful," she said. "If anybody found out, well, it would make for an awkward couple weeks."

"Allison's not gonna find out. God, we could do it back here every night."

She kissed him, then kissed his neck. "I would love that," she said, then Meredith squeezed out from his arms.

"Where are you going?" Rick said, his eyes flowing up and down her body.

"Can't be gone too long or they'll ask questions. They'll probably ask where you've been for so long, you told them you were only walking me."

"Who cares?"

Meredith shrugged.

Rick yawned. "This bed is so comfortable. I don't want to get up."

"Stay there a while."

"No, I should be getting back to them all like you said."

"I could do it again right now."

"Then let's do it."

She put her shirt on then kissed his cheek. "Really I have to get going. Goodnight."

"Goodnight."

He watched her leave the cabin, listened to her footsteps fade away.

Oh, she was wonderful.

Rick sat up, put his pants back on, then his socks. He had to get down on his knees to find his shoes, and found them under the adjacent bed.

A droplet fell on his head. Was there a leak? Oh—he'd fix it tomorrow. He sat back on the bunk, fixing his shoes, then grabbed his shirt when another droplet fell on his head. He went to the back of the cabin to pee.

He flicked on the light, opened the first stall, and Allison's *skin* looked back at him.

Rick was so shocked he shouldn't scream.

He stumbled backwards, tripped over somebody, and landed on his back, his head smacking into the cold hard ground.

Rick was not alone. He turned his head to see who else was with him. The rest of Allison was under the bed he and Meredith had slept together on—that was when his first scream finally escaped. He started to stand up, but the invisible person, the person who moved like a shadow, pushed him back to the ground.

The figure pinned him, slid a rope around his neck, then tied him to the post of a bed. With another rope, the creature bound his hands then bound his feet. The long knife was more visible than any other part of the person, save for the eyes.

Those awful eyes that would never leave his mind.

The knife cut his through his shirt, then small incisions were made an inch at a time, starting near his bellybutton. The attacker paused for minutes in between incisions, watching him writhe, watching the pain come over him, savoring it, enjoying it.

For a brief moment, Rick thought he saw a smile, but the rest of the features were impossible to find on the monster.

The monster cut until Rick's stomach was fully opened, then pressed the knife inside, moving it past organs, seeing how deep it could go. The attacker wasn't cutting anymore, more like placing it within him, seeing how uncomfortable a foreign object in his stomach could make him.

Blood pumped out of him and spilled over his sides. He was lightheaded. He wondered if the killer had been torturing him for five minutes or five hours. The passage of time was something that Rick could no longer understand. He was too cold, too weak, too scared.

Rick shut his eyes, and never opened them again.

10

Meredith was hesitant to turn on the lights so that she wouldn't wake Allison, but when she stepped through her cabin, she saw that Allison was not there.

She double checked the beds, then turned on the light, then went to the back of the cabin. Allison wasn't in any of the stalls or anywhere.

Maybe she went back to the mess hall while me and Rick…

That would be the worst possible thing, if Allison went back to the mess hall, then heard that Rick was taking her back to the cabin… then Allison would know how long they were gone, she'd know they didn't go back to this cabin, that they slept together in another one.

She prepared her story: part truth, part lie. She'd tell her what she told Rick about Ingrid, then she'd tell Allison that they thought they saw somebody in a cabin window, and she'd tell her they went around looking for Ingrid…

Oh, it sounds so fake.

Now she was so nervous that she didn't think she could sleep.

Meredith sat on her bed. She felt so filthy for what she had done. Meredith wondered what was going on now in the mess hall. Rick was surely back by now, and if that's where Allison was, Meredith was sure she was asking questions. She could see it now:

"Where were you?"

"I was—"

"You were with that tramp."

"No, Allison, listen—"

"No, you listen. You slept with—"

"No I didn't. Look, I only walked her back to the cab—"

"Yeah, yeah, back to the cabin. Which one? Which one did you fuck her in?"

"Allison why are you being like this?"

"Because you slept with her. You cheated on me."

"No, look, if you'd let me talk for just one sec—"

"Then talk."

"Look, she told me about this other counselor Ingrid, and her stuff's here but she's missing. We went to look for her, and—"

"Yeah, right."

It was going to be an awful time if she found out. Meredith would probably have to leave the cabin and sleep in another one all by herself.

"Rick and Meredith have been gone a long time, huh?" Jimmy said. "Maybe it's time to call it quits for the night."

"I want to keep it going," Eddie said. "I'm on a winning streak."

Jimmy's hand slid up Angie's leg. She smiled at him, winked, then put down two cards into the pile in the middle.

"Two sevens," she said.

"Bullshit," Eddie said.

The pile had been building for a while, and she took at least fifteen cards and added them to her hand. She was never going to win. Good part was that with so many cards, it was a little easier to tell when somebody was fibbing, so that way if she had 'three eights' and somebody said 'two eights,' it was clearly a lie.

She just wanted the game to be over with so she could be with Jimmy. It had been so, so long since they had left the canoe, and the she was craving him now.

Angie put her whole hand in the middle of the table during Bianca's turn. "Twenty-something whatevers." Then she grabbed Jimmy's cards and put them in the middle. "And a few more."

"Come on," Bianca said, "I was totally gonna win."

"Totally," Angie said, getting up from the table. "Good job."

Jimmy followed her. He put his hands on her sides and walked behind her.

"Now what are we supposed to do?" Eddie said.

"Eddie, you idiot," Angie said, "she wants to fuck you. What do you think you're supposed to do?"

"What?"

Angie blew them a kiss, then she and Jimmy left. The rain had stopped, and the night felt cool and gorgeous.

"I wonder what's been keeping Rick and your sister."

"Light in the cabin's off. Either they're having a three-way or Rick's back in your cabin."

"Yeah, let's go somewhere more private."

Angie kissed his cheek.

He led the way to the third cabin on the boys' side of Camp Solgohachia.

"Hey, Jimmy?"

"Yeah?"

"I need to tell you something."

"You're don't have a disease, do you?"

"Excuse me? Why would I have a disease?"

"It's a joke, Angie."

"Do you think I'm some kind of whore?"

"I told you I'm kidding. What is it?"

"There was another counselor's things in my cabin when we got here. That other counselor that was supposed to show, well, she did show. But where is she?"

"What do you mean she showed but where is she?"

"Her things are here, but we haven't seen her."

"You sure about that?"

"We looked through her purse," Angie rubbed her cheek, "and found her ID, it's her, but she isn't here."

"Well I don't know. What if she had an emergency? Maybe she hurt herself and had to leave?"

"Didn't you see her car in the parking lot, Jimmy?"

He turned to look at the lot. "I dunno, it's dark, I can't really—"

"It's there. Trust me, it's there. Very first car, it's hers. It was there when we arrived."

"Then she has to be here somewhere."

"Exactly. So it's been bugging me all day. Why isn't she..."

Angie was worried. She caught her breath as they entered the cabin. She found a bed and Jimmy turned on the light. He sat next to her, kissed her, then pulled away when he saw her sullen eyes. Jimmy ran his hands through her hair.

"You all right?"

"A little nervous is all."

"About Ingrid?"

"Yes. About everything."

"We'll find her. I'm sure there's some explanation."

"I'm nervous. I kept thinking about, you know, what happened here before. You sure Rick's okay? And my sister? Wouldn't Rick come back to say goodnight?"

"I don't know, should we be worried someone's not saying goodnight? He was tired, he did a lot today, maybe he just wanted to crash."

"Okay. Okay I guess that's..."

"Relax." Jimmy kissed her again. "Just relax."

She kissed him back. "I just have a bad feeling about this."

"It's nothing."

"A girl's missing. I think you're thinking with something other than your brain."

"Can you blame me?" He kissed her neck.

"No," Angie said, and gave in.

Eddie and Bianca walked away from the table, arms all over each other.

"Why didn't you ever say anything?" Eddie said.

"Well why didn't you?"

"I—I don't know, I didn't think you—"

"I gave you every single hint. I basically threw myself at you. I don't know what else I was supposed to do, show up naked at your door? Get on my knees and beg for it?"

"That would've helped."

"Maybe you're the dumb blonde."

"My hair's black."

"Oh well," she said, "you're still a dumb blonde to me."

Eddie opened the door then tripped over Rick's severed head. The porch was stained with blood. He screamed loudly, inching away from it, then hopped to his feet and shielded Bianca away from their dead friend's mutilated face. She backed into the wall and he held her tight while she wailed.

"It's okay, it's okay, it's ok—"

"What the hell what the hell—"

"It'll be okay Bianca, it'll be ok—"

"What the hell."

Eddie didn't know what to say or what to do.

"He's dead! Rick's dead! Who could've—Meredith! She was with him! Meredith! Did she—Allison! Where's Allison?"

Eddie led her off the mess hall's porch, still shielding her face, and they ran. She looked back once at Rick's head sitting on the porch. It watched them with unblinking eyes.

He let out another scream, then Bianca screamed too.

Bianca grabbed his arm. "Let's go back—let's go to the car."

"My keys are in my cabin."

"Allison."

"What? Where?" Eddie turned, scanning the open camp. He didn't see her.

"That window! Look!"

Eddie scanned the windows, and saw a glimpse of somebody moving in the last cabin. They disappeared instantly.

"In the last one? Are you sure?"

"Sure I'm sure—what's she doing over there?"

Eddie shivered. "Let's go get her."

They ran across Camp Solgohachia. Chills crept up his spine. A thick wind rattled the trees furiously. Eddie wanted to get out of here, Rick was dead, and he had to be sure Allison wasn't hurt either.

"What could she be doing..." Eddie opened the door with Bianca grabbing his arm so tightly that it was about to snap off.

He turned on the light. In a corner in the back of the room, Allison was crying next to Rick's corpse. She draped herself with a bloodstained blanket.

"Allison?" Eddie said. "Allison oh God what happened Allison?"

No answer, only cries.

Bianca turned away and screamed, hands gripping the doorknob.

"Was—was it Meredith? We've got to get out of here, we've got to get to my car, Allison. Whatever happened it's okay, it's okay."

She screamed with pain and sorrow.

Eddie nervously stepped closer to her, putting a hand on her shoulder then pulling it immediately back. Blood thick and warm slid between his fingers. He wiped it on his pants, then put his hand on her again.

"Allison?"

Empty eyes looked at him through sockets that had once been Allison's. From behind her mask of flesh, a wide smile formed. The thing wearing Allison's skin rose. As it lifted its knife, the lights turned off on their own.

Bianca was already out of the cabin by the time he took his first step back. He bolted out the door, running desperately to get to Bianca, and the monster behind him was running furiously. All he could hear were the sounds of its loud footfalls, and Bianca's screams.

Cabin—gotta get to the cabin, gotta get the keys, gotta get the hell out of here oh God. Oh God what the hell is happening?

He caught up with Bianca and grabbed her hand and forced her to run even faster than she already was. Then, when her screams ceased, he realized the footfalls were gone too. He gave one momentary furtive look over his shoulder, and the hideous monstrosity behind them had vanished.

Bianca stopped running for just a second, and he tugged hard on her arm. "No—no stopping, come on, need keys—need the keys, come on."

"It killed them it's killing us it's gonna kill us!"

"Don't think like that, just—" Eddie swallowed a deep breath.

His body trembled. At the cabin, he slammed his hands on the knob, pushed Bianca in, then locked it. He was so glad that there were no bodies in here. He grabbed his keys off the dresser, his body still aching and shaking, his mind rushing with all the possibilities. His body pulsed with fear.

When Bianca turned the lights on, he screamed then shut them off.

"You idiot. Do you want that *thing* to see where we—"

"Don't call me an idiot, you—"

He shook her. "Stop it let's try and find our way out of this. Are you okay? Are you hurt? Can you run with me to the car?"

"How—how far?"

"Just a few steps the lot isn't far, we will get out of here, we aren't dy—we aren't getting hurt."

She stepped to the window, pulled the curtain back to glance, then screamed. A hand burst through the window and reached for her. Its fingertips brushed against her hair, and Bianca staggered backwards.

"Eddie help me."

He grabbed her and they inched back from the window to the center of the cold, cold cabin.

"There must be a back way," he whispered in her ear, "to get out of the cabin, get around—"

"Oh there's no—"

"Shush," Eddie still whispered, tempted to yell at her for yelling. "Let's find another—"

The window burst open, and the thing in Allison's skin stepped forward slowly, smile never wavering, enjoying their fears, enjoying the moment. Its knife was raised, ready to penetrate their flesh. It cocked its head to the side.

Eddie pushed Bianca behind him, then stood between her and the monster.

"Get out Bianca get out."

"I can't."

"Get the hell out."

The monster took another step forward, then Eddie charged at it, knocking it to the ground. He wrapped his hands tight around its head then slammed it into the ground.

The knife fell from its hand. In the corner of his eye, Bianca opened the door and left without shutting it.

"Die already." Eddie slammed it's head again.

He slid off the creature, its eyes through Allison's sockets drilling holes through him. He reached for the knife, held it with both hands, raised it, and the creature punched him in the gut so deep it almost tore through him.

The knife accidentally slipped and Eddie choked. The wind was knocked out of him. The creature picked up the knife, towered over him, then slashed slowly on Eddie's arms. Pain raced through his body uncontrollably. Warm blood drenched him.

There was no fighting it.

It sank the knife into his chest.

Eddie knew he was going to die.

Everything felt too hot. His eyes felt as if stones hung from the ends of them. It was getting hard to keep them open.

When the creature brought the knife back down, Eddie grabbed its hands, trying to hold it away, but he was too weak, his hands fell away, and it brought down its knife again into his chest then twisted it sideways.

From the doorway, he heard Bianca calling his name, coming back to see what happened.

He wished he could open his mouth. He wished he could warn her, he wished he could have made her stay away.

And above all else, he wished he had given her the keys.

11

BIANCA HID BY A bush by the cabin.

When the monster left, she wanted to scream again, but slid her hands over her mouth to prevent her from doing so. The creature looked in either direction for her, and nearly looked right at her.

The creature became one with the night. It passed through the shadowy camp and vanished almost instantly, and Bianca had no clue where it went, but she had to get to Eddie. She gulped. She slowly moved away from her hiding spot, knowing it was life or death.

She prepared herself. Eddie… Eddie could have been dead.

None of it made sense—none of it ever would. Rick, Allison, Eddie. Why did they have to die?

She moved slowly to the cabin, afraid that if she moved quickly, the thing would have an easier time finding her. The small steps leading up to the cabin creaked under her feet; she slid in through the partly open door without touching it.

"Eddie…. Oh Eddie…"

She knelt over his body and hugged him then kissed his cheek.

He died so she could get away. She'd never forget that.

She reached into his pocket and grabbed the keys. Her eyes swelled with tears. She wiped them away, went through the cabin, then walked calmly towards the parking lot as if she hadn't just taken the keys from the body of a dead man, and as if at least two of her other friends weren't dead.

She slid the key into the door, unlocked it, pulled it open. She glanced up at the camp. Nothing moved.

She was free.

She was going to get away.

She was going to survive.

She'd get help, she'd get to the police and—

Bianca looked down slowly at the knife that had gone through her back and out her stomach. She was so shocked she didn't feel the cold pain, not at first.

The creature in Allison's skinsuit turned her around, looked deep into her eyes with those hideous dark eyes in Allison's sockets, then she felt it explode through her body all at once. All she knew was pain.

The knife sank into her again and again, even after she was dead.

12

MEREDITH WAS ON THE brink of sleep when she heard screams.

Terrible screams following one after the other, then they stopped abruptly. She wondered if it were a dream as she floated along the dense black sphere of sleepiness, wondered if the screams were coming from within.

When she heard them again, she realized they were coming from somewhere else, coming from outside her window.

At first she didn't move. She looked around her cabin from where she laid. Was anybody else in here with her? She felt the presence of somebody near, but through the darkness she saw nobody. Every bunk was empty. If somebody was in here with her, they were hidden, and that thought made her uncomfortable.

She slid out of bed and had an obscure compulsion that something was gonna grab her from under her bed and pull her under, never to be seen again. Meredith shivered, rubbed her arms to warm herself up, then looked out the window.

At first she didn't see it, then she did a double take.

Bianca hung from the flagpole. Blood dripped from a dozen incisions.

Meredith wanted to scream. She put on her shoes without putting on her socks, then ran out of the cabin. She didn't want to look at the body, but was morbidly curious, and it filled her eyes. She cried. It was even worse up close. Bianca's face was mutilated and her eyes dangled from their sockets. Her scalp was half removed from her head.

Meredith couldn't help but scream at that point. It strained her throat.

Footsteps at a distance. Meredith still screamed, even when she saw it was only Angie and Jimmy. Then they screamed too.

She hugged her sister and cried.

"Where are the others?" Meredith said when they calmed. "Where's..."

"I don't know," Angie said.

"Oh God." Jimmy shielded them from looking at Bianca's body. "We need to get out of here."

"My keys are still in the cabin," Meredith said. Then, when she broke away from her sister, she saw something hideous looking at them from the mess hall. She took another step forward then collapsed.

It was Rick's severed head.

Meredith flailed her arms and wailed. Jimmy and Angie picked her up.

"I'm sorry, I'm sorry," Jimmy said.

Angie hugged her tight again. "Oh Meri..."

"Meredith," Jimmy said, "we need to get those keys, we need to get out of here. I'll drive, let's—let's get out of here."

"Okay," she wiped her tears, but they flooded back twice as bad. Her vision was so blurry that she only *guessed* that she was walking the right way. Everything became a black and green swirl under the heavy moonlight.

The moon was full. It illuminated the camp through the veil of night.

At the cabin, she wiped her tears again, then her eyes filled once more. Would the crying ever stop? She wanted to stop but she just couldn't, she just couldn't.

"Is—is there anyone else left?" Meredith said.

"I don't know," Angie said.

"I haven't seen Allison or Eddie," Jimmy said.

They didn't grab their things, only their purses, and Meredith gripped her keys so tightly in her trembling hand that they painfully made impressions in her skin. The crests of her nails sunk into her palm too.

When they left the cabin, they ran to the parking lot. Meredith took deep, sad breaths. She couldn't process it. All dead. They were all just alive playing cards, she goes to her cabin, then they were all dead.

"Oh no," Meredith said. "Oh no, no, no."

All the tires were slashed. The cars were useless. They couldn't drive with all flats.

"What do we do?" Angie said.

"Goddammit," Jimmy said, "there must be some way—could we get out of here on foot? Could we—"

Meredith hadn't seen the creature move, as if it had traveled through shadows and appeared at Jimmy's side through a hidden doorway or by teleportation. Its knife flashed under the thick moonlight then was thrust through his throat. Blood squirted in every direction, then he fell over dead.

The twins held each other. A hideous monster wearing Allison's skin chased them.

They turned back to run towards camp, ran into the mess hall, and into the kitchen. They each grabbed two knives, each waited with their backs pressed tight to the counters, wanting to keep as much distance between them and that *maniac* as possible, while also being prepared to do anything they needed to survive.

There was silence, only silence.

Angie stared at Meredith, took one tiny step forward. The floorboard creaked. She cried.

"Listen," Meredith said, "it's just you and me, just you and me, we can get out of this. It's just you and me."

"Huh-how will we..." she was crying too much to finish what she was saying.

They locked arms then moved through the mess hall, carefully approaching the doorway, when the thing in Allison's skin jumped in front of them.

Angie screamed and broke away from her, dropping her knives. Meredith still had both in her grasp; Meredith moved her right hand to stab the monster, then it suddenly sliced Meredith's fingers open with one small swoop of its knife set in aging wood. Her hand shook and dropped the knife.

Angie grabbed its hand that held the knife.

"Stab it now Meri stab it now."

Meredith thrust the knife forward with all the force in her arm, but the creature moved out of the way. Then it knocked Angie off of her, and cut open part of Angie's arm. Angie grimaced, ran back, and Meredith knocked the monster to the ground. It banged its head on the wall sickeningly, then slumped over.

There was blood all over it, Meredith didn't know how much belonged to the creature, and how much belong to Allison or the others...

The twins bolted out the door. The monster never chased after them.

She prayed it was dead.

Hand in hand, Meredith and Angie ran away from Camp Solgohachia.

[illegible] watched as the creature moved, as it had traveled through [illegible] appeared at Jimmy's side through [illegible] gray, [illegible] apart from the [illegible] that was [illegible] mouth [illegible] in [illegible] fell over dead.

The women held each other. Angie's [illegible] Anne's skin [illegible] them. They tucked beneath [illegible] into the kitchen, they [illegible] with their backs pressed right to the counter. Wanting to keep as much distance between them and that thing as possible, while also being prepared to do anything they needed to survive.

There's [illegible].

Angie stared at Meredith, took one tiny step forward. The floorboard creaked. She [illegible].

"Okay," Meredith said. "It's just you and me. Just you and me. We can get out of this. Just you and me."

"[illegible] all we [illegible] too much to think that she was saying.

Their linked arms [illegible] moved through the [illegible], carefully approaching the doorway, when [illegible] in [illegible].

Angie screamed and [illegible] away from her [illegible] themselves. [illegible] had both [illegible]. Meredith moved [illegible] right hand [illegible] suddenly [illegible] with one small [illegible] knife [illegible] her hand [illegible] and dropped the knife.

Angie grabbed its hand that held the knife.

"Stab it now, [illegible]."

Meredith thrust the knife forward with all the force [illegible], but the creature moved out of the way. Then it [illegible] Angie off of her and [illegible] part of Angie's arm. Angie [illegible] and Meredith [illegible] the [illegible] on the wall [illegible].

There was blood all over it. Meredith didn't know how much belonged to the creature and how much [illegible].

[illegible]

She prayed it was dead.

Hand in hand, Meredith and Angie ran away from [illegible].

13

THEY RAN FOR TWENTY minutes before they were so tired they had to stop.

The road was empty. It was the middle of the night and they were in the middle of nowhere. It was by sheer luck that headlights approached. It must've been the only day in a million that this road had seen a driver so late at night.

They waved it down. A woman with sleepiness glossing over her eyes stopped for them.

"Other way," Meredith said, "can we go the other way?"

The lady didn't turn her car around. "My God, we need to get your girls to a hospital—what happened to you? Oh God, oh God."

"Cuh-Camp Solgohachia," Meredith said. "They're—they're dead, they're all dead. We need the—the police, oh God, they're dead."

"My son Bill went to camp here, you know," the woman said. "He died there too."

She stopped her car then pulled out a knife.

A long knife set in aging wood.

When the twins were dead, she smiled so happily. That would show them. That would show those monsters. Reopening the camp when her precious child—her only child—had died there. Those monsters.

She took the bodies back to the camp and dumped them in the center of it, right by the flagpole. What a shock people would get when they came by the camp and saw the decomposing bodies, she thought, the bodies eaten up by maggots and wildlife.

She smiled. It was wonderful.

She was halfway back to her car when she heard footsteps. Had she missed one? She turned around, watching the empty camp carefully. Nobody moved, nobody else was with her. She was all alone…

She twirled the knife in her hand. Somebody ripped it away from her. The man dressed as Santa Claus held her in a painful grip.

“Who—”

The Raven Hill Butcher raised the knife.

A NEW BEGINNING

1

KARINA LEFT HER CABIN at midnight after the last of her bunkmates fell asleep because she was going to meet a boy.

The boy waited for her at the flagpole. He checked his watch. Fifteen minutes after midnight. He was sure she had fallen asleep, but he waited a little bit longer. By twelve-thirty he went back to his cabin and went to sleep.

None of Karina's bunkmates could find her the next morning. And she never showed up throughout the day. And even after the extensive searches that were conducted in Camp Solgohachia's woods that year, she was still never found.

2

One year later...

The horrors that befell Camp Solgohachia all began on the first day of camp when David Morrison and his friends decided that they would go to the forbidden cabin deep in the woods that coiled tightly around the campgrounds.

The sun was setting, and all the little campfires were burning, casting formless shadows. New friendships were being made, laughs were being shared, secrets were being whispered. There was something about this feeling that David hoped would never go away.

He was sitting with Jennifer, Betsy, and Dean. They were passing around dough-boys. He grabbed one from Dean, told him thanks, then held it into the fire.

"What's he look like?" Betsy said to Jennifer.

"Tall with blonde hair," Jennifer said. "I don't see him anywhere. Just my luck. I meet this *great* guy and then he forgets about me."

"What are you girls talking about?" David turned over his doughboy.

"Jenny met a guy, but he stood her up."

"Cut the guy a break," Dean said, "it's the first day of camp."

"Jenny told me she already picked out baby names."

"Oh God," Dean said. "Maybe that's why he stood you up."

"I only told that to Betsy, and she can't keep her mouth shut. Just like her legs."

"Well," David said, tracing her body with his eyes, "if he doesn't show up, my cabin door's always open."

"Oh, there you are." A guy exactly like the one Jennifer described sat next to her on the log. He put his arm around her. "Sorry I missed you. I got in a little trouble."

"What trouble?"

“I was in a fight.”

“Seriously? Are you okay?”

“It was two on one I kicked both their asses.”

David laughed. “They must have been kids left over from Junior Camp last week.”

“Okay fat ass you would’ve just tried to eat them.”

“Russel,” Jennifer said, *“don’t be mean to David.”*

“I’m not being mean, I’m just saying he couldn’t have handled it. You want to talk about who could’ve handled two guys, David? Put your elbow down. Right now. Arm wrestle me. That’s the only honest test of a man there is. You can’t talk your way out of it. I’ve never lost an arm wrestle in my life. Not once. Ten bucks says I put you down in three seconds, maybe two.”

“You’re on.” David tossed his uneaten doughboy into the pit then grabbed Russel’s hand.

“Awe David,” Dean said, “you don’t know what you got yourself into. I’m not gonna help you out when he beats your ass.”

David’s arm strained under Russel’s strength. Russel seemed to effortlessly overpower David, and while David held on as best he could, Russel pinned David in about four seconds. David wiped away sweat from his forehead then challenged him to a rematch.

“Two outta three.”

“Then you’ll say three outta five.”

“You backing out?”

“Just promise me you aren’t gonna take a bite out of my hand.”

“No guarantees.”

David tried again to hold on for longer than a few seconds but it was no use. He wasn’t strong enough. Russel pinned him almost instantly.

Afterwards the boys shook hands.

“You’re all right, Russel. Jenny, I like this guy.”

“You’re a good sport, David.”

“Thanks. But you know, I still don’t think you’re so tough.”

Russel laughed, rejoining Jennifer and grabbing a doughboy of his own from their little box to roast over the fire.

"Anyone could beat up a couple Junior Campers or win a couple arm wrestling matches against a guy like me. I wanna make another bet with you." David grabbed his wallet from his pocket. "Ten bucks, how about it?"

"Ten bucks for what?"

"I bet you ten bucks you won't spend a whole minute in the cabin. That one way out there, the one that the counselors always tell us is off limits."

"Ten bucks for one minute? That's it? Hell for ten bucks I'd stay in there for ten minutes." Russel pulled out his own wallet for two five dollar bills. "You're on."

"You guys can't do that," Jennifer said. Everyone ignored her.

"Witness?" Dean said.

"Sure."

They each gave Dean their money.

"Do I keep a percentage?"

"No," both Russel and David said at the same time.

"You guys, this is a bad idea," Betsy said. "I really don't think we should get kicked out of camp on the first day."

"Oh, they're not kicking us out," David said.

"Let's quit wasting time," Russel said, pulling his doughboy from the fire. It had just finished. "Let's head there now."

3

Thin contorted branches reached with crooked fingers for the group of campers as they were swallowed up by the cavernous darkness of the woods.

The last remnants of the firepit's lingering warmth on their skin was quickly fading, and the chill of night washed over them.

Betsy had a flashlight in her purse that she used to light the way. "It's not too late to turn back you guys."

Jennifer put her arm around Betsy. "I really want to go back to the fire too. I have a bad feeling about this."

"We can't do that, sweet cheeks. Me and your friend have twenty bucks riding on this. It's easy money."

"You guys ever hear the story of the forbidden cabin?" Dean said.

"I don't wanna hear it," Jennifer said.

"Supposedly it was the headquarters of a local serial killer for about ten years. I heard a rumor that the girl who went missing last year was meeting her boyfriend there, but the boy overslept and—"

"Enough," Jennifer and Betsy said at the same time.

"So Russel, I think we need to set up some rules."

"Ah ha, here we go with the rules. You wouldn't be trying to find a way to back out, would you?"

"What? No. Of course not."

Jennifer let go of Betsy and stepped between the guys, pulling on Russel's arm and pouting. "Please can we go back to the fire? I'm cold."

"I'll buy you a sweater from the gift shop with the twenty bucks."

“But I don’t want a Camp Solgohachia sweater. I want a Fleetwood Mac sweater instead.”

“Sure, whatever baby.”

The group had momentarily paused while Jennifer was begging to go back, then they went forward again.

Betsy’s light passed over the cabin.

Jagged and faulty, as if constructed by blind men. Splintery planks were sprawled across the windows and doors with rusty nails, nails that seemed they’d turn to dust if touched. It was nothing more than a ghostly silhouette. It shuddered in the wind, creaking in the night, home to clusters of spiders. Dust lay over the cabin like a layer of dirty snow. Nasty weeds twisted up from the ground and worked their way upon the sides of the cabin as if attracted like magnets.

Russel broke away from the group and went all alone to the front door. He grabbed the board that had been nailed into the door, and it came away easily in his hands. He looked the thing over.

“Hey, somebody’s already been here.”

“Get away from there.” Jennifer moved a pleading step forward and extended her hands. “Russel come on.”

“This wasn’t even nailed in. Look.” He opened the door. “I think somebody was already here before us.” Then he tossed the board down. “You got your watch ready, David?”

“Yeah. One minute.”

Russel shut the door behind himself.

Jennifer punched David. “I can’t believe you made him do this.”

“What? I didn’t make him do anything.”

“Chicks, man,” Dean said, “you can’t argue with them.”

“Oh what’s that supposed to mean?” Jennifer put her hands on her hips.

Betsy flashed her light against the broken windows. “I don’t see him in there.”

“Of course not,” Dean said, “those windows are all covered up.”

“Oh, I think it’s already been a minute. Where is he?”

“No, not yet. It’s only been thirty-eight seconds.”

“I’m going after him. I can’t believe I met the most *perfect* guy, he’s so adorable and kind, and you force him to go into the haunted cabin. What if he gets killed?”

David laughed. "What? He's not gonna get killed. And yeah, 'great guy' didn't he beat up a couple kids?"

"It wasn't a couple of kids and I'm sure he had a good reason. I'm gonna check on him."

"No, you wait here. This was my bet, I'll go in. I'm sure he's just trying to scare us."

The cabin door shut on its own behind David, cutting him off from the glow of Betsy's flashlight and trapping him in an indistinct crypt. His eyes were adjusting to the darkness as he moved careful steps forward.

"Russel? Where you at?"

No response.

David was about to rejoin his friends when a powerful scream tore through the silence that had been draped over the cabin. It was coming from the cabin's cellar, the echoes spilling into the room from some area that was completely buried by darkness that even the faint traces of moonlight that penetrated the back window couldn't uncover.

He was halfway through the filthy cabin when the cabin door opened and a beam of light struck against him. It was Dean entering by himself with Betsy's flashlight.

"What happened? Where's Russel?"

"I don't know."

"God you made the girls cry with that scream."

"It wasn't me."

CREEEEEEEEEEAK!

In another room there was the screeching of a rusty hinge and then the thudding footsteps of somebody frantically running their way. His pocketknife was gripped tightly in his hand.

"She's dead."

"Who's dead?"

"What are you talking about?"

"In the cellar. She's dead."

4

David borrowed the flashlight to go down with Russel and check it out while Dean waited outside with the girls. David carried a pocketknife of his own, and he pressed the button that released the blade. They descended into darkness, Russel first, then David right behind him.

There were no windows down here, so the darkness wasn't only heavy but it was *strong,* as if it were fighting back against the flashlight's feeble touch.

The cellar was freezing, but David didn't think much about that when he saw the remains of the girl. They were on a stained dog bed. Nothing but a skeleton. Nothing but a skeleton in a blue dress with a blue bow on top of her skull.

"Holy fuck."

"What's happening in there?"

"Where are they?"

"I told you this was a bad idea. Why does nobody ever listen to me?"

"You were right, we should have turned around. I can't believe we went through with this."

Dean didn't know what to tell them, so he said, "They'll be out soon."

SNAP!

Something stepped over a tree branch at a distance in the expanse of woods ahead of them. The three of them looked for the source of the sound, and the girls gasped when they saw a man dragging a shovel. He hadn't noticed them yet.

The girls were running into the cabin while Dean was momentarily frozen, then he chased in behind them and went through the short hallway to the back room where Russel and David had gone down into the cellar from.

"They went this way."

David and Russel were heading back up when the entrance to the cellar opened and the others were coming down in a frantic hurry. The girls were talking over each other simultaneously so the explanation was indecipherable.

"One at a time."

Jennifer shut up while Betsy said, *"We saw somebody."*

"Who? Who's out there?"

"A guy."

"What guy?"

"I don't know. Quit yelling."

"I'm not—"

CREEEEEEEEEAK! CREAAAAAAAAAAAK! CREEEEEEEEEEEEAAAAK!

Somebody moving above them. The man that they had just seen in the woods.

Jennifer fell into Russel's arms. "Hold me."

"Okay," he said.

"We all need to hide," David said.

"Why did you two come down here?" Jennifer whispered.

Russel patted Jennifer's back. "I thought I saw something."

"What?"

"Nothing. It's nothing. Just… don't worry about it."

"Darling? You in here?" The booming voice of the man upstairs.

His footsteps were going the other way. That was good. But not good enough.

"We need to hide," David whispered again.

He strategically aimed his flashlight not to reveal the bones in the corner of the narrow cellar. The cellar's floor was earthen, and against the two long walls were many shelves containing jars and tools. There were also boxes of various sizes here and there. The options for hiding were very limited.

Dean was taking Betsy to hide behind the stairs when they both tripped over a dog bowl and fell hard. Betsy let out a scream until Dean put his hand over her jaw and shut her up.

CRRREEEAAAKKK!

He was coming this way.

Russel pushed Jennifer far into the cellar. "I won't let him hurt you."

"What's happening?"

"We gotta tell them," Russel said, then ripped the flashlight from David's hands.

"Russel. Don't."

He shined the light upon the remains. "I think it's the girl who went missing last year."

"Oh my God." Jennifer let out a sharp scream.

Russel tried to console her, and Dean was trying to calm down Betsy who was also crying, but there was no stopping the inevitable. The man opened the cellar door and the light of his lantern squirmed down.

"Who's down here?"

The girls both tucked into the far corner opposite the bones. Russel and David were ready with their pocketknives. Dean picked up a plank of wood that was leaning against one of the walls. A fight with a murderer was the last thing any of them wanted to be in, but they had to be prepared.

The man was halfway down and had a view of the boys. *"You shouldn't've come here."*

The boys stepped backwards, each adjusting their grip on their weapons.

When the man was off the final step, David recognized him as the groundskeeper. A man roughly in his sixties. A grey beard. Bushy eyebrows. Many wrinkles.

"Where is she?" He said. *"What have you boys done to her?"*

"She's dead," Russel said. *"She's been dead for a long time."*

"What? What are you talking about?"

"You killed her you maniac."

The groundskeeper raised his lantern and was going to bring it down on Russel's head when the girls screamed from the back of the cellar and the groundskeeper was distracted. In that split second Dean raced two or three steps and whacked the groundskeeper in the back of the head with the plank.

The groundskeeper dropped to the ground and his lantern shattered.

He didn't move again.

5

AMONG THE TOOLS IN the basement there was rope. While Russel cut it up, the girls were sent upstairs for a chair that they then passed to David on the cellar stairway. Dean helped him put the man into the chair while Russel bound the man's hands and feet.

Upstairs the girls had found lanterns that they brought down for the guys. The guys set them up around the cellar.

Dean found duct tape and cut a thick piece that he stuck over the man's mouth.

"We should get the girls back to their cabin," David said.

Dean paced the cellar back and forth. "This place is probably littered with dead bodies. How come they didn't look in here when that girl went missing?"

"I think we can get the answers out of him when he wakes up," Russel said. "Let's go check on the ladies."

The boys went back upstairs. The girls were waiting outside the cabin in the cold night air wiping away tears. David couldn't believe that one harmless bet had led to all this, and he wondered what more it was going to lead to. They were in deep. They had a man tied up in a cellar. They found the remains of a missing girl. And what now?

Now they should have been telling the police, but none of them said it. Nobody mentioned the police, perhaps they didn't want to. Perhaps they had all wanted to do something about this themselves.

"How are you ladies feeling?"

The girls frowned, neither one answering Russel's question.

They all stood around in silence, listening to the hum of the night. It was eerily silent, and although the man was tied up, David couldn't help but feel watched. Couldn't help but feel a pair of hidden eyes keeping track of his every move.

Furtively he looked over his shoulder. Nobody was there, of course, because everybody in camp was asleep and completely unaware of what was happening here at the forbidden cabin.

It was a nightmare that had come to life.

6

A LITTLE WHILE LATER the guys returned to the cellar to check on the groundskeeper. Upon their descent they heard his muffled pleas from behind the duct tape.

Each boy handled his own weapon again: David and Russel with pocketknives, and Dean with the same plank that had knocked the man out.

Russel pulled the tape back. "Why did you kill her?"

The man said nothing.

"We know what you did, dude," David aimed Betsy's flashlight at the corner of the cellar, while Dean grabbed the groundskeeper's head and turned it for him to see the pile of bones.

"I didn't kill her."

"Put that tape back, Russel. Maybe we can get him to talk another way."

"I like the way you think, Dave." Russel stepped behind the groundskeeper and put the knife against one of his fingertips. "For every question you avoid, you're losing one of these."

The man struggled against his restraints as Russel came away with a little piece of his finger, holding it up like a trophy.

"Gnarly," Dean said. "Now old man if you don't answer my next question I'm gonna whack you again. How did you get away with stashing the body down here? Didn't they search the whole forest when the girl went missing?"

Russel again was the one to peel the tape back, but the old man didn't answer. He coughed and gasped for breath.

"We're giving you the chance to explain yourself. Tell us the truth."

"Please don't hurt me. I'm just an old man."

Dean swung the plank and stopped it just an inch shy of the man's nose. He recoiled with terror plastered on his face. The guys patted each other on the back and laughed at the groundskeeper's misery.

"All right maybe we shouldn't hurt him too bad you guys," David said. "He murdered that girl. We should turn him in to the police."

"What are the police gonna do about it, Dave?" Russel put the tape back in place once more. "I saw on the news one time this guy killed a bunch of kids, but the officer didn't read him his rights so he was let go on a technicality or something. None of it held up in court I think."

"Yeah well when the officer gets here we can remind him about that sorta thing."

"Nah. I wanna have a little more fun with him. Plus, how are we gonna explain the fingertip?"

"Self defense?"

"Eh, I don't think they're gonna buy it. But look at the facts, that's her bones right there." Russel pointed. "Do you remember her picture in the newspaper and the missing posters that were plastered everywhere? Blue dress. Blue bow in her hair. That's her. There ain't no two ways about it."

David nodded. "I remember the picture."

"Yeah me too."

"He gets what he deserves. We could be heroes."

"Hold on a second, even if he is a murderer nobody's gonna praise us as heroes for this." David shook his head. "If we're gonna do this we make a pact right now to keep silent about this forever. We're never telling no one."

"What did you think I meant? We were gonna hang big neon signs over our heads saying what we did?"

David shrugged. "Let's ask him another question. Enough about the girl, maybe we can start him off with some basics. How old are you? Can you tell us that?"

Russel had sort of become the groundskeeper's attendant, and pulled the tape back for him to speak. Once more he took a deep breath when the tape was removed from his lips. "Six… sixty."

"There we go. See guys? We're getting somewhere. He knows how to speak after all. Now tell us, how long have you been working here?"

"I—I don't know."

“You don’t know? Some employee you are.” David laughed. “What were you doing last summer, the third week of camp, when that poor girl Karina went missing?”

It took the man a while to spit out his answer: “I don’t remember.”

“You don’t remember? How come?”

The man didn’t answer.

“It was the middle of the night,” Dean said. “Were you asleep that night, or were you sneaking around spying on girls?”

The man shook his head. *“I didn’t do it. I didn’t do it.”*

“Buddy,” Russel said, “we’ve got you in this cabin with her remains. It wasn’t no camper that did that to her. You must have come in and out of this cabin a million times between then and now, and you didn’t know her corpse was down here?”

“No.”

“All right, I guess I’ll have to take another fingertip.” Russel put the duct tape back in place.

The old man was screaming before Russel even did anything, but his screams died out behind that thin layer of tape so that it sounded more like a panting rather than the pure terror that was now pulsing in his veins. He squirmed back and forth, so Dean grabbed him to be sure he stayed straight for Russel, who sized up another finger. Blood squirted up with it and stained his shirt.

“Damn, I liked this shirt too. It was a gift.”

“I don’t feel bad for the guy anymore,” David said. “What kind of man kills a poor little girl and won’t even admit it? Piece of shit.”

“Maybe we won’t get the truth out of him, but we’ll at least get a bit of revenge.” Russel wiped his blade clean on the man’s shirt. “So now I want to ask you the sixty-four dollar question. Why did you do it?”

But the man wouldn’t answer that either.

7

Jennifer and Betsy kept their arms around each other while they sat below a nearby tree. Night was becoming much colder and clouds gathered in front of the full moon to completely blind them. Betsy searched through her purse until she found her lighter and her pack of Super King Size Winstons.

"Want one?"

"*Need one.*" Jennifer pulled one from the pack. "Thanks a bunch."

"Did you ever meet her, Jen? The missing girl?"

"Meet her, no. But I saw her before. She was in the cabin next to mine. God that could have been any of us. I feel so sick thinking about it."

"Me too. I wonder what's on TV right now."

"Did you bring a TV guide with you?"

"Yeah it's with my other magazines."

"I'm probably missing *Happy Days* right now."

"Eh, that show went downhill after Richie joined the army."

Moonlight spread again when the clouds passed. The girls were quiet, smoking, still thinking about how they'd rather be anywhere else but here. Then, somewhere deep within the woods, something stirred. Something shifted. Something unseen passed through the heavy amorphous shadows that strangled the land.

"Betsy… I think somebody's out there."

"I don't see anybody."

"I swear there was somebody there."

"Where?"

"I'd feel a lot safer if we were with the guys. Let's go." Jennifer stood abruptly and took big steps to the cabin.

Betsy scrambled to her feet and ran a couple steps to catch up for her. *"Wait for me."*

"Dave why don't you cut off one of his fingertips this time?"

"I don't think I have the stomach for it, Russ."

"Suit yourself."

"Hey I wanna try." Dean stuck his hand out for Russel's knife.

"Here."

Dean pressed the knife to the groundskeeper's thumb and pressed it down, bringing it halfway through and stopping. He adjusted his grip and applied more force. "You make it look so easy, dude. It's tougher than it looks. Have you had practice doing this before or something?"

"Just push harder."

Eventually half of the man's thumb was separated, and Dean set it down in the little pile of them that had been collected on one of the dusty old shelves.

The groundskeeper was leaking blood from his finger stumps, more blood than any of the boys would've guessed could come out of such small wounds. The man had lost five fingertips now, and the boys were only just getting started.

"This guy's a tough cookie." Russel pulled the tape back. "Let's see if he can answer this one for us. How did it make you feel to kill an innocent girl?"

Just then, before he could answer, there were footsteps above them. The old man screamed for help, so Dean smacked him to shut him up, then they retaped his mouth. But David could tell by how soft the sounds were that it was the girls, and they came nervously down the steps and met them.

"We got scared," Jennifer said. "We wanted to check on you—*oh my God what did you do to him?"*

"He deserves it for what he did to that girl. Whenever he doesn't answer a question we take a little piece away from him."

Jennifer and Betsy couldn't look at the mess. They turned away, keeping their arms around each other, sobbing.

"Even *he* doesn't deserve it," Betsy said.

"He's a killer, don't you understand?" Russel said. *"He hurt her. And he won't even tell us why."*

"How could you do that to somebody?" Jennifer sobbed.

"Because he deserves it, for what he did" Russel said. Then he breathed deep and addressed the groundskeeper again, removing the tape: "How did it make you feel when you kidnapped her? What did you do to her when she was here? Did you rape her?"

"No. I did not touch her."

Russel shook his head. *"There's no point in letting you speak anymore. You had your chance. Dean, do me a favor, hold his jaw open."*

Dean did so while Russel wiped his knife off on the old man's clothes again, then he reached inside and grabbed ahold of his tongue and burrowed his knife inside. David had to look away, he couldn't stand seeing the man's pain or the blood that splashed out of the wound. He joined the girls and put his arms around them.

"It'll be okay," he whispered to them.

"Look, it's still wiggling." Russel laughed.

"Hey man," Dean said, "keep that thing away from Jenny, she might put it between her legs."

8

"I WANT TO TELL you all something," Russel said.

The girls stayed turned away.

"Girls."

Jennifer and Betsy slowly turned around to face Russel. Morbidly curious, they eyed the groundskeeper momentarily.

Russel's demeanor changed. He was sullen. His voice softened. He said, "Karina was meeting me that night. We were meeting in secret because she hadn't broken things off with her boyfriend yet. That's why I have to do this to him. He took her away from me."

Suddenly David didn't feel so guilty anymore about what they had done to the old man. Suddenly it felt good to get revenge, to get justice, because Russel deserved to get even. This old man deserved everything he got.

"So this is for her. It's all for her." Russel raised his knife up above his head.

He plunged it into the groundskeeper's chest. The old man jolted forward then his head leaned back, and blood seeped from the edges of the duct tape. Tears swelled in his eyes. Everybody except Russel was still. He removed his knife, raised it again, and slammed it into the man's stomach. He did it again and again until Dean and David both grabbed his arms and pulled him away.

"Enough. He's dead. He's dead."

9

"WHAT DO WE DO with the body?" David said.

"We need to bury him," Dean said. "When the camp realizes its employee is missing, well, we can't say for certain that this wouldn't be one of the places they check."

"No. Leave him." Russel wiped his blade clean on the dead man's clothes one last time, then he put his pocketknife away. "If they find his body next to her remains I'm sure they're smart enough to get the idea."

So it was settled. They would leave the body here.

They left the forbidden cabin, everybody hoping never to return to this place of sickening horrors.

First they went to the girls' cabins. Jennifer and Betsy both were shaken by the events. David put a hand on each of their backs and said, "It's gonna be all right."

Everybody exchanged goodnights, then the girls crept into their cabin. All the lights remained off after the girls entered. David hoped that none of the other girls in that cabin were awake to question them, because chicks were notorious for not being able to keep secrets. And the last thing they needed was for any of this to slip…

Carefully they went across camp to the boys' side.

They stopped in front of Kodiak, which was Russel's cabin. Russel shook each of their hands with his bloody palm.

"It was good meeting you guys. I think this is the beginning of a beautiful friendship."

"Goodnight, Russ."

"Night man."

David and Dean's cabin was Sun, it was the second to last cabin. They had barely avoided the worst cabin, Panda.

Everybody was asleep, which was good. They were in the clear.

David's bunk was the bottom bunk because upon their arrival that morning, Dean had called dibs on the top bunk. Both of their suitcases were under David's bed, and they scrambled to silently find new clothes and towels so that they could clean themselves off from the blood.

"Where were you two faggots?"

David choked a little as he looked up at Jeremy. Jeremy was a nerdy kid with thick classes, very scrawny, and was always picked on and whipped with towels. One time, some of the other guys in their cabin had put two cockroaches in Jeremy's bed while he slept, and he woke up to find them on his face. He had trouble sleeping—or trusting anybody—after that. Right now Jeremy had been awake under the covers, reading a comic book by flashlight. *Astronaut Graveyard* on the cover.

Suddenly David felt guilty. He felt caught. Everybody would know what they had done. His mind was rushing, and he thought—

"Fuck off," Dean said.

"Goodnight." Jeremy pulled the cover back over his head and went back to reading his comic book.

"That was a close one."

10

SHE HAD SEEN THEM leave, and she wondered what they had been doing here in her home.

Once the five strangers disappeared into the night, she crept inside, anticipating the voice of her master. But he didn't say anything. The cabin was filled with uneasy silence. Steadily she moved, howling for him, but all her cries went unanswered.

And then there was the blood.

Footprints leading from deep within the cabin.

She followed them.

The door was left open, and the glimmer of lamplight climbed weakly through the opening. She crawled down carefully, her heart sinking with each movement along the steps.

He was dead.

She licked his cheek and cried. She wrapped his arms around him and cried some more.

But nothing she could do would ever bring him back.

And those strangers would pay for what they had done.

11

Everybody was on their way to the swim hole, but Jennifer ditched to meet up with Russel. She was dressed in her bathing suit and carried her beach towel with her, stopping to open her purse and check her compact mirror to be certain that not a single strand of her high ponytail was out of place, and to make sure there was nothing stuck between her teeth, and to check for any pimples that might have suddenly sprung up between the walk from her cabin and now.

And she was in the clear. She looked perfect. How could anyone resist?

They agreed to meet behind the ramada where everybody played carpetball because it was in the opposite direction of the swim hole, and nobody—most likely—would be passing through to catch them.

As she waited, she found her smokes in her purse and lit one.

A second later she saw a girl between the trees. A young blonde girl with unkempt hair. Maybe a year or two older than Jennifer. Two crestfallen green eyes that Jennifer barely had time to glimpse retreated into the woods.

"Hey, come back."

Jennifer scanned the area for Russel, but he wasn't there yet.

"Are you okay?"

She parted the thick branches and followed the girl into the dense woods. It was a lot harder to navigate through here because the trees grew closely together, and the ground was uneven and rough, and the branches scratched at her from every angle.

"Hello? Hellooooooooooooo?"

Had she been seeing things? Maybe there hadn't been a girl there at all.... But she had seemed so frightened, so lost, so scared. But why had she fled then when Jennifer noticed her? It didn't really make any sense, but Jennifer didn't want to leave the girl alone and lost and frightened here in the woods by herself.

SNAP!

A branch broke somewhere behind her. Jennifer turned around but there was nobody.

"Is anybody there? I want to help you. Hello?"

Quietness hushed over the woods for a brief second until another branch snapped and fell from somewhere above her. When she looked up she saw its vicious face.

Calling it a girl wouldn't have been quite right. It wouldn't have been right either to call it a person. It was a sickly combination of man and nature. The creature was naked except for her red Christmas hat. Her lips were pulled back to reveal chipped and blackened teeth.

It growled.

Jennifer attempted to run but the armlike branches held her back from escape as though they were purposely hellbent on keeping her within striking distance of the feral girl above her.

A quick peek above. The girl lowered herself from one branch to another.

Jennifer forced herself through the trees but her ponytail was caught on a tree branch and as she yanked it, the monstrosity leapt down with its jagged claws outstretched, and each of them sank into Jennifer's back. The force of the jump knocked them both to the ground, but Jennifer's hair was never free and was yanked from her scalp, fully separating flesh from her skull.

Desperately she reached with both of her hands for the fallen branch that had been broken under the feral girl's weight. Despite the constant pounding of the girl's fists, Jennifer was able to grab it. She swung it at the girl's face but she raised a hand to intercept it before Jennifer could succeed.

The girl tossed it away and howled.

Jennifer inched away, afraid to stand, suddenly aware of the immense pain burning in her skull and from the many wounds those darkened nails had caused along her back and torso. The girl snapped her teeth.

She jumped again, landing on top of Jennifer and jammed Jennifer's head into the base of a tree. Jennifer's vision blurred and she shut them against the pain, but they opened again when the claws struck. They slammed into her stomach above her navel.

The feral girl dragged Jennifer through the woods. Jennifer's mind was fading in and out so that she was faintly aware she was being moved. All she could really feel—all she was really aware of—was the constant pain. A pulsing and perpetual burning in her head. An oozing and gushing along her body. Breaths that wouldn't succeed. Air that wouldn't reach her lungs. Darkness that crawled over her eyes.

Then the dragging stopped.

The creature walked away.

With her consciousness fading, Jennifer prayed the girl would leave her alone.

But the girl came back carrying a rock in her hands that was the size of a puppy. Standing above Jennifer, the girl dropped the rock on her face and shattered every bone in her skull.

She dragged the body away, then found her fallen Christmas hat and put it back on.

One camper down, and four to go.

12

RUSSEL ARRIVED AT THE ramada but Jennifer never showed.

Maybe, he thought, Jennifer forgot and had gone to the swim hole.

He stayed a little bit longer just to be sure.

When she still didn't show up after another ten minutes, he left. The swim hole was down past the cabins on the boys' side. By the time he got there, about half of the other campers were on their way back.

David was laughing while Dean gave some nerdy kid with glasses holding a book in his hand a wedgie.

"Dave, Dean."

"Hey Russ."

"Where you been?"

"I was supposed to meet Jen somewhere, but I guess she forgot about me. Did you see which way she went?"

"I don't think I saw her," David said.

Dean looked at the crowd behind them then back to Russel. "I don't think I saw her either."

Russel hurried through the crowd of oncoming campers and found Betsy talking with a few other girls presumably from her cabin. He pulled her aside and all the other girls giggled and cracked jokes.

"Have you seen Jen around?"

"No, I thought she was with you? That's what she told me, anyways."

"Did she say anything else?"

"What, did she stand you up?"

"Yeah and I can't find her anywhere."

Betsy bit her lip nervously. "I'll check the cabin. Maybe she got sick or something. You know how camp food is."

Betsy walked off and rejoined her friends, who were looking back at him and still making remarks, but he didn't pay attention. He stayed in place, scanning the end of the crowd of campers, keeping an eye out for Jennifer, knowing that she wasn't among them, but searching anyways…

13

Jennifer wasn't in the cabin. Betsy checked her bed hoping to find her, but she wasn't there. She went to the back of the cabin where the showers were, but she wasn't in any of the stalls.

Betsy took a shower herself, shivering no matter how scalding the water was because she was nervous about Jennifer. If she hadn't been with her and she hadn't been with Russel, where was she? Betsy's heart was beating fast.

Maybe it was nothing. Maybe she was scared for no reason.

After her shower she went to the nurse's office, hoping and praying that Jennifer was just sick. But she had no luck finding her there. Next she went to the ramada where people were gathered around the carpetball tables. No luck finding her there either. Then she went to the cafeteria. Again no luck finding Jennifer.

Slowly the thoughts of the cabin crept into her mind. She thought about the old man tied up in the chair. What if they had been wrong? What if he hadn't died? What if he had been alive when they left him?

No, you saw what happened, Betsy thought. *That isn't possible...*

Russel checked the human foosball cage, he checked the basketball courts, he checked any of the various camp competitions and activities, but Jennifer wasn't anywhere.

He had a bad feeling about this.

From the concession stands next to the giftshop Russel bought a lemonade then sat on the bleachers watching the games that were going on. Dean was on one of the teams, and when the game finished he called Dean over.

"Hey man."

"Good job out there."

"Thanks. We won by the skin of our teeth. You want in next round?"

"Not right now. I still haven't seen Jennifer. Betsy hasn't either. Did you run into her or anything?"

"No I can't say I have. Where'd you see her last?"

"After breakfast, before she went back to her cabin."

"Huh. Yeah. I think that's the last time I saw her too."

Russel hopped off the bleachers. "Good luck with your next game."

David was playing baseball with some others, using some greasy boxes that they must have found in the mess hall's dumpster for bases. He was up at bat when the pitch came, a swing and a miss. Another pitch, another swing and a miss. A third swing, and he struck out.

"I thought you had that one, Dave."

"Hey dude."

"Look, I gotta talk to you about something in private." Russel put an arm around David. When they were out of earshot from the other players, he said, "Nobody else has seen Jennifer. If none of us can find her by supper I think we have to go back to you-know-where."

14

Suppertime.

Chili night.

But David and his friends weren't eating. They were going to figure out what happened to Jennifer.

Everybody met at the flagpole.

"Betsy," Dean said, "I think it's best you go inside and have dinner and forget about any of this. You were never there last night, and you shouldn't be there tonight."

"But Jennifer's my best friend. I—"

Russel stepped between them. "If I didn't... do it right yesterday," he said, his voice becoming more hushed with every word, "and if he got away. Well. I don't want to put you at risk. He's a sick man. We have to face the facts. It's not one missing girl now, it's two. But maybe we can get ahead of this before it begins."

Betsy frowned. "We should tell somebody."

"Oh who are we gonna tell? What are we gonna say? I stabbed a guy to death last night and now my girlfriend's missing?"

David put a hand on Betsy's shoulder. "It'll be all right. Just go have dinner, and like Dean said, forget about any of this. We'll let you know what we find. All right?"

Betsy was trembling as she left them and went into the mess hall.

From the windows David could see that everybody was happy. There were campers laughing, throwing food at each other, recounting funny stories that had happened at camp thus far and in years past. It brought about that warm feeling he had yesterday at the bonfire, thinking about the friendships that were being made and the memories that were being formed.

How different things were today from yesterday. How different things can be over the span of twenty-four hours. And, David thought, how different things might be in about another twenty-four…

They each had a flashlight this time, and Dean bought his own pocketknife from the giftshop.

"I should have made sure. I should have cut his head off his body."

"Don't beat yourself up over it," David said. "It doesn't even make sense. The more I think about it, the more it doesn't make sense. The way he was bound, and all that blood he lost, there's no possible way he could have survived…. Is there?"

"Well," Dean said, "there's a whole lot of things in this world that don't make a lick of sense. But God I hope this isn't one of those things."

"He's right," Russel said. "Y'all ever heard of those three kids in Australia that disappeared from the beach? Or that chick that went missing on a cruise with her family?"

"I think I heard of those kids," David said. "Oh, and what about JFK's assassination? I still don't buy it that Lee Harvey Oswald acted alone."

"That's because anybody with a brain knows it was the government. JFK said he'd splinter the CIA into a thousand pieces and scatter it into the wind."

"You guys ever hear the one," Dean said, "about how they altered the wound to make it look like Kennedy was only shot from behind?"

"Eh," Russel said, "not sure about that one. But me personally I blame it on the Federal Reserve."

15

THE CABIN BROODED UNDER the setting sun. It felt like a dream to be back here again. It didn't feel real to step through the doorway. Last night seemed like a distant memory that was ten years gone.

Now that there was more light in the cabin—although the dwindling sunlight was quickly leaving—they could see the details better. Deteriorating walls that were torn open in scattered sections, bundles of leaves and newspapers and garbage that was gathered in every corner, and a couch that was half-covered in mold.

"Jennifer?" Russel said.

Even the silence was dreamlike and unreal.

"This way," David said, and took the first step toward the back of the cabin.

And then he was the first one down the steps.

He was frozen in terror on the final few steps. Terror wrapped tightly around his heart and squeezed it. The others stopped on the steps behind him in disbelief as well.

The ropes had been cut.

The body was gone.

"But—but—" Russel couldn't finish his sentence.

"It's not possible." David came off the final steps finally, keeping his light extended and his knife ready for anything. *"He died. I know he did. It isn't possible..."*

Russel kicked the chair over, and couple of the splintery legs broke off of it. *"Fuck. Fuck. Fuck."*

Dean stood on the final step and scanned his light across the narrow cellar. "Jennifer isn't down here. We shouldn't assume the worst."

"Ahhhhhhhhhhhhhh! Help me! Somebody help!"

16

THE GUYS RAN AS quick as they could.

"I'm coming, Jen!"

But it wasn't Jennifer who had screamed for help, it was Betsy. About fifteen feet down from the cabin, directly under a beam of moonlight, she was face to face with a naked blonde girl whose blonde hair was riddled with twigs and leaves and stretched down to her thighs. The strange girl's lips were pulled back and she growled.

The feral girl staggered on two feet as if it were an alien concept to her, then she lowered herself to all fours and leapt for Betsy. David wasn't sure when he and the others began running, but they were at the center of the chaos within a moment and the beast hardly laid a finger on Betsy by the time the boys were there.

The girl rammed her head into Russel's gut and he fell over with the wind knocked out of him. Betsy checked on him, bringing herself dangerously close to the action, while David and Dean each grabbed one of the wild girl's arms. She fought against them with unnatural strength, gnashing her teeth and growling endlessly.

David caught a glance of her eyes. There was something *other* behind them. Something animal. She had no humanity in her. Nothing at all.

Dean swung his knife but the girl pulled her arm free of his grip and knocked the knife away. It was lost somewhere on the black ground of the woods. She swung her claws in his direction, and the only reason they didn't meet his flesh was because David still had a hold on her and tugged on her arm with all the strength he could find in his body.

Then she turned her attention to David.

In that moment of pure terror, faced with this monstrosity, he let go of her and stepped backwards.

The feral girl raised her sharp claws and brought them down upon him. With a split second to think, and even less time to act, David raised his pocketknife and it went clean through her hand. The girl recoiled in pain then howled, and while she was distracted David acted again—he cut her across the face. A gash that began below her left eye and crookedly lowered to her chin.

Animalistic cries of pain.

The girl retreated into the woods, running on all fours and quickly becoming unseen.

David joined Betsy and Dean in making sure Russel was okay. He sat up when David came by, then stood up and patted him on the back.

"Dave you've got balls."

David wanted to laugh but had a lump in his throat.

Dean grabbed Betsy's hands. "Are you hurt?"

"Nuh-no. I'm—I'm sorry." She cried into his shoulder. "I'm sorry I didn't listen."

"It's okay. It's all right."

The boys escorted Betsy back to her cabin. A few of her bunkmates were already there. Supper was still going on, but none of the guys were hungry. They went back to David and Dean's cabin. Nobody was there yet because guys always waited until the very last moment necessary to return to their cabins for the night, they were too busy pulling pranks, flirting with girls, and fighting with counselors.

David washed off from the specks of blood that had gotten on him from that girl.

"I know none of us want to say it," David said.

The others were quiet.

"Remember what the old man said when he entered the cabin? He was calling for somebody. Calling her 'darling.'"

Dean frowned. "And he said he didn't do it. He said he didn't kill Karina."

Russel punched the wall. "That… *thing* killed them both. It killed Karina and it killed Jennifer."

David wanted to tell him no, maybe Jennifer wasn't dead, but he had to face the facts. Instead he said, "One thing's for sure, that old man deserved it anyways. He knew what his… 'darling' did and he kept it his secret. He deserved everything he got in my opinion."

"I'm gonna kill her," Russel said. "I'm gonna kill her. Nice and slow. Whatever we did to the old man, she's gonna get it a whole helluva lot worse."

17

David couldn't sleep that night.

Everything about the incident kept playing over in his head. They had all been seconds from death. When he thought about it, it made him shiver. And that *thing* was still out there. She could have been outside of this cabin right now.

And where had she come from? What was she?

He thought about Jennifer and how scared she must have been, and how she had to face it all alone. Poor and defenseless Jennifer. He wanted to imagine that she was still alive, just hurt somewhere, but there was no rational way that could be. Even though he hadn't seen a body, he knew she was dead.

It should have been me. Jennifer never did anything to anybody.

Whenever he tried to clear his mind and sleep, a certain image kept forming in his mind: Jennifer in a white dress that was now predominantly red. Her throat was torn open from end to end, and blood gushed with each beat of her heart. She raised one desperate hand for David—or for anybody—to help her, but it was too late.

18

The girls in Betsy's cabin that night:

"Hey Betsy, have you seen Jen?"

"Yeah, where is she? You two are like usually attached at the hip."

Betsy said, "She had to leave early. Um, family emergency."

"Really? But like her things are still here under the bunk."

"Did she really leave without taking any of her things? And without saying goodbye?"

"Uh-huh," Betsy said. "She, well, it was urgent."

"Wasn't she seeing that guy you were talking to at the pool?"

"What, now that she's gone did you steal him away from her?"

"Geez Betsy you couldn't even let them have a whole week together. I thought you were already seeing somebody."

"No it's not like that. He's—Russel's just a friend."

"Have you kissed him yet?"

"I said it was nothing like that."

"I think she likes him."

"Oh my God, Betsy, here," one girl said as she dug through her purse then threw a handful of condoms at Betsy. *"Take these, I packed extra. Don't say I never did anything for you."*

"No, you guys, I don't need any condoms, I'm not—"

"If you were planning to sneak out tonight and see him, you should remember what happened to the last girl who snuck out to meet a guy. She never came back."

"I'm not sneaking out to meet anyone. Can we just drop it?"

"Awe she's so shy! Betsy don't worry, your secret's safe with us."

"I think you're a much better match for him than Jen anyways."

"But I don't even like him," Betsy said. "You guys don't understand, I don't—"

"Well Betsy if you really *don't like him then I'll snatch him up. Why don't you introduce us?"*

"Hey, no way. I saw him first."

"What do you say, Betsy? What did you say his name was? Russel? Oh he's so dreamy."

"I'm not introducing any of you."

"See? She totally wants him for herself."

"Will you guys just knock it off already? I don't want to talk about him or Jen or anything."

"Whatever. But you can't fool us. We can see it all over your face."

19

THE GIRL LICKED HER wounds.

She laid behind a gigantic boulder in the woods and shuddered against the cold. After she rested she crawled to a stream of water. It was ice cold, but she dipped her hand in it anyways and washed the cut that was below her eye. It stung.

She returned to the cabin, approaching cautiously in case those kids were back. Anger burned inside of her when she thought about what they had done to her master. She wanted to see them dead. She wanted to see them ripped apart.

Back home, she crept up the stairs.

His body was propped against the wall, and she had nudged the heater closer to him to keep him warm. She licked his cheek then curled up next to him to sleep.

She did dream. She saw each of her enemies torn open and eviscerated. Each of them destroyed.

I'll avenge you.

And then she had another dream: lost in the woods. A lifetime ago. Things had been so different then. She was riding on the back of a wolf, her arms around its neck to hold herself steady. She could feel it as if it were happening *now* instead of a past life.

The wolf set her down so she could feast with the pack as they ripped apart a deer.

Then the pack swarmed away at the sound of the booming gunshot.

One of the wolves had been stricken with a bullet through its back and toppled over dead. She reached to climb on top of the nearest wolf but they left without her. And then the man's shadow fell across her.

He picked her up. "Oh you poor child."

He was her new master.

20

Wednesday morning.

Breakfast.

David still couldn't eat. He drank chocolate milk instead, sitting in the corner of the mess hall leaning forward over the table. Dean carried a tray over, it was full of pancakes and cereal boxes and plain milk cartons.

"Eat something."

"I can't."

Dean shrugged. "More for me."

"I couldn't sleep. I kept thinking about Jen."

Dean stuck a fork in his pancakes. "Me too."

"That thing is gonna come back for us," David whispered, "so we have to be prepared. We got lucky last time."

"Yeah you really bailed us out last night. Betsy owes you her life."

"No, she doesn't owe me anything." David frowned. "She would've done the same for me."

"What do you suggest we do?"

David's whisper was so low that Dean struggled to hear him: "We killed the wrong person. Now we know who the right one is."

Dean looked over his shoulder into the packed mess hall. "You seen Russel this morning?"

"Nah."

"You sure you don't wanna eat something?"

"The chocolate milk's enough."

"All right, Dave."

David couldn't get last night's nightmare out of his mind: Jennifer in the white dress that was stained with blood. He wished he could have been there for her. Wished he could have stopped it. But how were any of them supposed to know?

"Do you think it's our fault?" David said.

"You want me to be honest?"

David nodded.

"Yeah it was," Dean said. "We shouldn't have taken any of that into our own hands. We should've split after I knocked him out."

"I was thinking that too. Then maybe Jen would still be here…"

21

RUSSEL CALLED FOR A meeting at the flagpole.

David, Dean, and Betsy sat on the bricks surrounding the base while Russel addressed them.

"It's Wednesday. We're out of here Friday morning. That means we don't have much time to take care of business. We're gonna hunt her down. No, I don't know exactly how this is all gonna work, but I know we outnumber her. I'm gonna need something from each of you. Betsy—"

"Wait a second," Dean said, "she almost died. She's not gonna go near that—"

"Will you let me speak, dumbfuck? Betsy, I need you to get us some nail polish remover from the giftshop. After that, you're out. All right?"

"Uh, okay."

Russel reached into his pocket for a pack of cigarettes and lit one, then offered the others. They all declined.

"We strike tonight. We're gonna trap it in there and burn the cabin down."

"What do you need from me?" David said.

"I just need you to do what you did during yesterday's altercation. Stay sharp. Stay on your toes. Yeah, maybe you couldn't win an arm wrestling competition to save your life, but you saved all of us last night.

"And you, Dean… waitasecond. Dean?"

"Yeah, Russ?"

"Don't you still have our money?"

"Well you didn't ask me for it."

"I wasn't supposed to ask. I won the bet."

Dean opened his wallet and gave Russel the money. "Here. Anything else?"

"Yeah. Can you find us any other weapons around this dump?"

"Weapons? I'm not sure where you think we are dude, but this is a summer camp. This isn't some military base where there might be grenades and guns and whatever. What do you think I'll bring us, a tank?"

"It's for your sake, not mine. You held onto your knife like it was a bar of soap. My baby sister could've knocked it outta your hands."

22

Betsy bought two bottles of nail polish remover and gave them to Russel at the bleachers by the basketball courts.

"Here you go."

"Keep the change."

"No, that's all right."

"You're an angel," he said, taking the money from her outstretched hand. "Now forget about tonight, okay?"

Dean walked around camp trying to figure out ideas for weapons, and when he saw the baseball game finishing up he had an idea. He jogged up behind the players and when the winning team was celebrating, he snatched the bat and ran away with it.

The groundskeeper's shed was locked with a small padlock, but Dean used the bat to break it open. Inside, there were the things he needed: a box of six inch nails. A hammer. A drill. A vice. He shut the door, pulled the chain on the single lightbulb, and got to work.

He secured the bat with the vice grip and drilled holes through it, then he hammered in the nails until they were flush against the bat's surface. The nails poked through in every direction so that no matter which way he swung, he would make contact with the feral girl.

Later he found Russel around the ramada where Jennifer stood him up.

“Russ, I think I got something you might like.”

Russel didn’t acknowledge him. He was staring down at the trees. Perhaps trying, Dean thought, picturing Jennifer here alone while everybody else was away at the swim hole. Perhaps trying to imagine any other way it could have ended besides death. But there was no denying it now. Jennifer had been gone too long without a trace. There was only one answer…

“Hey, Russ.” Dean shook him. “I got the thing you wanted. Come and see it.”

“Yeah. Okay.”

They sneaked into the shed. Dean had left the light on. He held up the bat for Russel to inspect. Russel grabbed it and turned it over, giving it a couple test swings and admiring it.

“You do good work.”

“This enough?”

“You can never be too careful. Think you can make a second one?”

“Of course I can.”

23

NIGHT WAS FALLING QUICKLY.

Bonfires were burning.

It was time to kill the feral girl.

Dean concealed the bats and walked through shadows, avoiding any speck of light as he journeyed to the flagpole.

David and Russel beat him there. They were smoking cigarettes by the time he showed and gave Russel the second spiked bat, keeping the inaugural creation for himself. Russel swung a couple times, rolling it over in his hands. There had been many more nails added to make it even more dangerous.

"You outdid yourself, dude." Russel tossed his pocketknife to David. "Catch. I won't need it with this around."

"Where's mine?"

"I only made two. You didn't ask for one."

"I didn't know you were making these."

"You were there when Russ told me to make something."

"Yeah but I didn't know you could make something this cool."

"Forget about it, Dave," Russel said. "You've got two knives. That's enough. Now you two can do whatever you want to her, but I want to finish the job. I'm gonna douse her in nail polish remover then light her on fire."

Russel was so calm, so cool about what he intended to it, that it disturbed the others. They exchanged a glance then returned their attention to him.

"Well what are we waiting for? Let's go."

Each boy waited until they were far enough from camp to put on their flashlights without being spotted. The last thing they needed was for a counselor to see them and stop them with all these weapons.

They were in the woods undetected, their lights flashing over the ground to guide them through to their nightmarish destination, the cabin of unending horrors.

24

David wondered what other terrors the cabin could speak about if it could talk. He wondered what horrors happened between its walls. Karina's death, and the feral child, and what they had done to the groundskeeper. David wondered if that was only the beginning of the cabin's past.

As they entered, a chill smeared over him, and he had a feeling that everything was going to go wrong.

The floorboards moaned their familiar noises as the boys stepped over them, scanning the darkness to reveal little hints of the filthy surroundings. It was dead quiet in the cabin. Too quiet. David didn't like it.

"Let's split up," Russel said. "Me, I'm going down to the cellar. David you take upstairs. Dean you watch the main floor."

David and Dean nodded in response.

Upstairs the door that ended the hallway was partway open. David kicked it open with his foot then stepped inside with his knife raised and ready.

Then he saw the body. The groundskeeper had been brought up from the cellar and placed under the window which let in moonlight that spread across the room. The bedsheets had been washed recently, there were clothes in a hamper, a box of chocolate bars on the dresser, a transistor radio on the nightstand.

He gagged from the smell of the rotting body. It had gone stiff, and one of the eyes was still open. The duct tape had been removed from the groundskeeper's mouth and wasn't anywhere in the room that David could see. Threads of long blonde hair were attached by dried blood to his clothes.

David backed out of the room and into the hallway. There were two other rooms up here. One was an old bathroom. The other was a void room, perhaps it had been a small bedroom, but nothing was in there besides collective filth, leaves and garbage which must have been blown in through the broken windows.

"Dean? Anything?" He said from the stairway.

"Nothing," Dean said. Almost a whisper. "Maybe she doesn't live here."

David came off the final steps. "His body's upstairs. She must have moved him there."

"Then I guess we wait it out."

Russel was coming back up the stairs, they heard the steps creak. They met him in the hallway.

"You two find anything?"

"The old man's upstairs now. She put him in his bedroom. That's all so far."

"Nothing new downstairs. Just Karina's bones…"

David patted Russel's back. "I'm sorry, brother."

"When she comes back, we'll be ready for her. I'll wait here all night if we have to."

25

Warmth of flames stretched tight around Betsy's body. She could feel them but they had no effect. She was still frozen inside and couldn't stop thinking about Jennifer, and couldn't stop thinking about the boys and what they were doing. Were they safe? Were they hurt? Any of them could have been dead right now and she wouldn't have known. She felt sick, as though she were cheating death. Jennifer was her friend too—shouldn't she have helped? Shouldn't she have done something?

Her bunkmates around the fire:

"So why aren't you sitting with 'Russel?'"

"Did he find somebody else already?"

"Poor Betsy got her heart broken. Well she works quick, don't you know that? I'm sure she'll find another boy in a few minutes. She just has to put herself out there."

"There's so many boys around here that would be chomping at the bit to get with any *girl, all she has to do is take two steps in any direction and she'll find a dozen."*

"You guys, enough. Okay? I don't want to hear it."

"Don't cry over some boy you just met at camp, Betsy. It's embarrassing."

"I'm not crying."

"You know, Betsy, it's no secret where all the single guys and girls go to meet up around bonfire time for a little fun. Do you want me to take you there? God knows you need a little excitement in your life."

Betsy stood up and walked away.

From behind her:

"Where are you going?"

"Are you gonna meet with Russel?"

"I'm going to the washroom. I'll be right back."

She had had enough of them, and was gonna go to the cabins to be alone, but on her walk back there, shining her flashlight ahead of her, she saw Jennifer. It was unmistakably her from the brief glimpse she had of her friend. She was lurking between the cabins then took a step out of view.

"Jen! Hey! Jen it's me! It's Betsy!"

Stepping behind the very first cabin, there was nobody there. Was she just seeing things?

"Jen...? Jen...? Anybody?"

A hushed stillness.

Then, leaving, she saw Jennifer's face again. Thin branches were propping it up through the eyeholes. Jen's torn skin shuddered with the sudden winds that passed by.

A scream was caught in Betsy's throat. Ascream so big it couldn't escape.

One step backwards and she bumped into a girl.

The feral girl.

Betsy ran and the girl chased after her. Immediately she tried the very first cabin, and the door was unlocked. She shut it and pressed her body against it while she turned the lock. The feral girl slammed against the door from the other side trying to break it open.

Once it was locked Betsy backed away, breathing heavy, her eyes darting toward every window to make sure they were shut. She ended up in the very end of the cabin in the bathroom area. She grabbed the broom that was resting against the sink and held it for protection. A dumb weapon, but what else was there?

She hid in the bathroom stall.

Maybe it would go away.

She waited...

She'd be stuck here a while.

The window was low. With a hop she was able to grip it and pull herself up. She could sense the fear of her prey, the other girl who had been there on the night that her master died. Now this girl would be held responsible.

Slowly she lowered herself into the bathroom, but she landed with a thud.

Her prey gasped. Hearing it brought a smile to her lips.

The prey emerged from the stall holding a broom and swung as she stepped backwards. *"I'm not afraid to use this thing."*

A growl.

A step further.

Another swing.

She loved watching the fear on her prey's face, and loved the fright in her voice. The girl couldn't stop shaking. Swinging the broom back and forth as they each moved slowly down the cabin. She could have struck her prey at any time, but she was having too much fun watching the girl realize that this was the end of her life, this was it.

As Betsy backed away she couldn't take it anymore. She bolted for the front door and unlocked it, leaving the cabin a split second before the creature behind her. She ran in the direction of the woods that would bring her back to the forbidden cabin. The boys were there now and they could help her, if she could outrace the *thing* behind her that was chasing on all fours.

A glimpse over her shoulder.

The terrifying monster neared closer with each swiftly passing second.

Betsy's heart was going to explode into a hundred pieces.

Then, once Betsy was within the woods, she realized the feral girl was no longer behind her. She had disappeared. Betsy looked all around her impossibly dark surroundings searching for the girl. But she was all alone.

She ran again, needing to make it to the cabin. Needing to get to the others. Needing to get to safety. There was no time to waste.

A growl up ahead.

The girl emerged from the depths of blackness and charged at Betsy.

Betsy's legs were pierced with sharp pain as she abruptly changed directions. All of her joints ached and burned. Her shoes were so thin that the bottom of her feet felt every bump on the ground, and each pebble or unseen object sent sparks of agony up her heels and into the rest of her body. Her lungs begged her for breath—she had to stop, she couldn't keep going. She wasn't as stealthy or in shape as the feral girl.

She would have collapsed if the *freak* hadn't slammed her to the ground first.

CRACK!

An unbelievable pain in her chest. A jagged edge pressed hard against the inner walls of her flesh. But she was too full of terror to completely process it, too afraid of the creature above her and what was to come. The feral girl had turned Betsy around and was sitting on top of her, breathing heavy, smiling, and then something was in her hands.

A long tree branch. Thin. Very thin. Leafless.

The girl pried Betsy's mouth open and stuck it in. Betsy squirmed and struggled but the feral girl was stronger. Betsy tried to raise her arms but they wouldn't respond, she couldn't tell if they were pinned under her attacker, or if they were broken, if they were detached. They just wouldn't lift. Were they there at all?

The branch sank further in and she felt it in her stomach tearing up her insides.

With one desperate jolt her hands finally did respond, and they both rose to her throat in a failed attempt to hit the branch away.

The feral girl then pulled the branch out of Betsy's mouth in one motion. Betsy gagged. Vomit burned the scratched edges of her throat. Breaths were still out of reach—her lungs still begged her but she couldn't take in much air. And she couldn't scream either—the screams were buried in her throat somewhere deep inside where she couldn't unlock them.

Then the feral girl grabbed Betsy by her hair and dragged her over lumpy ground until they came to a narrow stream of water.

"Please no—" It was all that her strained throat would allow her to say, she couldn't have formed more words no matter how much she tried, but it was cut off anyways when the girl held Betsy's head into the water.

It was as though her face was buried in a glacier. Stuck inside of solid ice. Immediately her skin burned with numbness and sent shockwaves through her torso.

As her lips parted against her struggling will, the feral girl pulled Betsy above water. Her lips strained to touch and separate to form words, but the sounds couldn't come out. She could no longer speak.

Then the feral girl slammed Betsy back in again. Betsy's lungs pulsed with the desire to breathe but she denied them. And while her face was submerged she begged God to do something. She begged God to get rid of the monster.

Betsy's last thought before everything went black: *I hate summer camp.*

26

DEAN SHUFFLED A DECK of cards then distributed them into three stacks on the countertop in the forbidden cabin.

"You brought a deck of cards with you?" David said.

"In case we needed to kill time," Dean said.

Russel set down the spiked baseball bat. "Sounds like a good idea to me."

"Now are you guys familiar with the card game called *'Bullshit?'*"

"Yeah I've played it before."

"Me too."

"I'll go first." Dean set down a card. "One ace."

"Bullshit," Russel said.

Dean flipped it over to reveal an eight of hearts. "How did you know?"

AWOOOOH!

The boys scrambled for their weapons at the sound of the howl. It was coming from outside, directly in front of the cabin. They raced outside and discovered nobody and nothing. It was a quiet night. Vastly dark. But danger still lingered because the feral girl was still out there somewhere.

She was hiding. Lurking. Stalking them like prey. Using her instincts to determine the precise moment to strike.

The boys spread through the trees.

"What now, Russ?" Dean said.

"Just be ready."

"Roger that."

AWOOOOOOOOOH!

Deeper in the woods. The boys followed it away from the cabin. Each of them ready. Each ready to strike with their weapons. Each ready to draw blood. All the boys wanted to celebrate the creature's death.

Chills slithered around the woods. Where was she?

Maybe she was smart, David thought. Maybe she wouldn't attack when all three were around again after what happened last time. Maybe she was sizing them up, waiting for them to slip, waiting for one of them to be separated from the others because she must have known that there was strength in numbers.

"Show yourself." Russel swung the bat.

From the treetops she watched them. Perched with the branches grabbed tight, carefully adjusting herself and moving down to a lower branch to see them better as they proceeded to travel further away from where she was hiding.

They had new weapons now. Bigger weapons. Could she strike while outnumbered? Perhaps if one of them were on their own, like the girls had been, but the boys stuck together. She would stand no chance this way.

Russel leaned against a tree. "It won't work this way. We have to set a trap for it."

"What, a bear trap?" Dean said.

"Any trap. I don't care. Just have to be smart..."

She came off the tree and crept away.

An idea was forming in her mind…

"You two should go back to the cabins. This is all my fault. I started it. I gotta end it. Just me and her."

"Are you stupid?" David said, putting his hand on Russel's shoulder. "You can't do this by yourself. It's a wild animal."

"With one more swing of your knife yesterday you could have taken her."

"I think you're a retard if you try to do this by yourself. It's a mistake."

Russel brushed David's hand off of him. "Thanks for the help. I think I know what I have to do now."

David was going to say something else but Russel walked away. And then rain fell.

"Come on," Dean said, "where are you going? Get back here."

Russel kept going.

Dean ran a few steps to catch up with him. "You said we needed to set a trap. Come on. There's still time to plan this out. Don't run into this with that big head of yours. It's not panning out, not tonight. This was a bust."

"I'll do whatever the hell I want."

"Come on," David said. "Let's go."

She beat the storm by a fraction of a second as she entered the cabin.

She crept upstairs to her master and licked the cheek of his corpse.

In the room there was a mirror. She checked her scar. It still stung and pulsed, but it was healing.

She stared into her own eyes and wondered who she was. She wondered where she came from. She wondered what it meant to be *her.* She wondered what the difference between her and all the others was—why were they all one way, but she was another?

27

IT WAS STILL POURING by the time Russel and the others finished their run back to the cabins. He hid the spiked baseball bat behind Kodiak then went inside. One of the other boys was awake and jumped down from his bunk.

"God dude you're soaking. Where the hell were you?"

"With a chick."

"Damn, was she worth it?"

"Yeah."

The guy—and Russel wasn't even sure he knew his name—grabbed him a towel. Russel thanked him as he dried off and shivered. The bunkmate went back to his bed, and Russel took a hot shower, wondering how the hell he was gonna get payback.

It stopped raining around two in the morning.

Russel was too furious to sleep—furious at himself for failing to do anything to the feral girl, furious at not having put a solid plan into place, furious that the girl had killed Karina and Jennifer and he was still so far from avenging her.

He crept out of the cabin and found the bat.

He went through camp. He wouldn't let anything stand between him and what needed to be done. In his mind he saw the feral girl on the cabin floor whimpering and begging for mercy. In his mind tears swelled in the girl's eyes. And he wouldn't give it to her. He'd bring the bat down on her head and slam it until there was nothing left but mush.

Russel was tired of coming to the cabin. Tired of coming away empty handed. As it came into view, he hoped that this would be the very last trip.

She woke up from her dream of wolves when she heard the squeal of the door hinges. She tensed. Somebody was here.

He aimed his flashlight and tiptoed.

She wasn't down here, but he saw that he had forgotten the nail polish remover on the countertop. Russel patted his pockets and he still had his lighter. He could still light her on fire, he thought. He just had to find her first.

She was frozen as the footsteps of the stranger came up the stairs.

There was one way out, and she had to work quickly.

She opened the window behind her master and climbed out…

Russel kicked the door open. The room where David had found the groundskeeper's body. He was met with a chill, along with the stench of decomposing flesh that wafted through the doorway. He stepped inside. She could have been anywhere.

CREAK!

Behind him.

The closet door pushed open before he could completely face it and he was knocked over, and the spiked baseball bat flung out of his hands. There was a body on top of him and he punched it until he discovered that it was slack against him and wasn't fighting back because it was dead.

Its head was caved in. There would have been no way to identify it if it hadn't been for the piece of severed flesh that accompanied it. Jenny's eyeless sockets stared up at him, and the contorted lips curled into an irregular smile.

He pushed the corpse away and screamed.

It wasn't just a creature he had to kill. It was an animal. A savage animal.

28

SHE JUMPED THROUGH THE window before he could grab the baseball bat. She pinned him, raised her claws, and brought them down across his face, scarring him like his friend had scarred her. The boy pried an arm free and punched her in the gut, then punched her again, and she scurried off of him and crept to the corner of the room in pain.

The boy regained his spiked baseball bat, raised it, and charged at her. He swung and she jumped to avoid it, then she sprang at him and knocked him down, but this time his grip on the bat held, and he swung again.

She staggered back to avoid it.

While he was getting back up she hurried to escape through the open door and down the stairs. The boy, she saw as she checked over her shoulder, ran down the steps two at a time.

Worry and panic flooded her mind. Her heart beat disturbingly fast.

Out the front door, and he was catching up with her.

By instinct she reached for a low tree branch and climbed up, but not quick enough to avoid the blow to her calf. The nails on the bat scraped across her flesh, and a cold sensation squirmed spiderlike through her body. For a second she couldn't move the damaged leg, but she pulled it up with a sudden rush of desperation that pulsed through her.

Blood seeped out.

The boy remained under the tree taunting her, the baseball bat ready in his hands.

She was trapped.

Absolutely trapped.

Russel backed away from the tree and moved around it to keep track of where she was going. She was shifting locations, blood spilling from the gash on her leg. He had a taste of revenge, but he had to complete the mission.

Then he thought of something. Something he had seen in the cellar.

A way to get her out of the tree.

He laughed and went the short distance back to the abandoned cabin…

She saw him leave. Where was he going? What did he want to do? She shuddered thinking about being stranded up here all night. She was tired. She was hurt. She wanted to sleep. There were a hundred hiding places she would sleep within these familiar woods, places where she could keep warm through the cold night, but she couldn't stay in this tree. It was impossible to keep balance on a branch and rest.

She climbed down the tree, peeking in each direction to see if he was there, but she was alone.

There it was on the shelf. And it was full of gas.

He pulled on the cord. The chainsaw roared.

Perfect.

She saw him. He didn't see her. And with the screaming contraption of death in his hands, she had to avoid him at all costs. But the machine's rumbling gave her one advantage, it obscured her footsteps and muffled the sounds of crunching leaves as she fled into the night.

Russel tried to spot her again, but she wasn't visible up there in the tangle of branches. He slammed the chainsaw into the tree trunk then pulled it out and anticipated her cries. Anticipated her fear.

She didn't react. Strange.

Once again he slammed the chainsaw into the side of the tree, looked up, but there was no reaction. Had she split in the amount of time he had gone up to the cabin and come back? He reached into his pocket for his flashlight and shined it around.

A trail of blood off into the woods.

She wasn't getting away that easily.

He followed the trail of blood. It went in one direction then curved when he was far past the cabin, taking him further than he had ever traveled through the Camp Solgohachia woods before. About twenty or thirty feet down, and the trees were tightening, becoming harder to navigate, and the blood was thinning. Then it changed direction. Down to the right. Deeper into the freezing woods.

An unbelievably cold summer night, and the ground was a muddy mess from all the rain that had fallen for a few hours. His feet were freezing, his socks and shoes completely soaked. And in the end, he knew, it would all be worth it, because the pain he was going to inflict on her was going to be a beautiful thing.

A hiding place that her master had constructed for her. It was at the base of a slope where rocks and boulders were plentiful. A long time ago he had helped her shift them around to create a shelter, and above them were many sticks and branches to seal her in and keep her warm. Within were blankets he had given her. She'd be safe here.

She tried to relax but the pain was throbbing too furiously in her leg. She tried to forget about it and let her mind drift away into the infinite darkness behind her eyes, but she just couldn't shake the terrible torture that was emerging from her wound.

She wished he were here. She wished her master was here to take care of her. He'd know what to do right now. He'd have known how to help her and how to get rid of her attackers.

But for now, even without him, she was safe.

And she was drifting off to sleep. Going further through the darkness…

And further…

Until the world was collapsing in on itself, until the canopy of branches above her were bashed in. In a flash of moonlight she saw the nails of the spiked bat that her attacker used. So he had found her here. How? How had he? She didn't know.

She pushed up against the impact and forced the thickest branch, which a couple of the nails were stuck inside of, and shoved against the power of the attacker. She couldn't find her footing and slipped down back into her hiding place, but the boy went down over the boulders and when she peeked up, she saw that he was holding his ankle in pain. The bat was at his side. On his other side was the contraption he had retrieved from the cellar, that vile metal jumble of death.

Their eyes met.

It was a draw.

AWOOOOOOOOOOOOH!

She howled and retreated to another place where he would not find her tonight. This eternal night was over, or such was her hope.

Russel limped back to Kodiak.

He slept through the following morning even when the others in his cabin tried to wake him.

Thursday would be his last chance for revenge.

29

BETSY'S BUNKMATES THE NEXT morning:

"Did Betsy come back last night?"

"I dunno. I don't think so… her bed doesn't look slept in."

"Her things are still here. Just like Jen's. Weird."

"Maybe she was with Russel. I knew those extra condoms would come in handy."

"Yeah, maybe he kept her busy all night. Lucky girl."

"Did she say what Jen's emergency was?"

"No I don't think so. I still think it's so weird she like… she like just left without saying a word to any of us. I didn't even see her go."

"Yeah me neither."

"Hmmm…. I'm sure it's nothing."

"Yeah, they'll both turn up eventually, you're right."

30

DAVID BROUGHT RUSSEL HIS breakfast from the mess hall over to the flagpole where he was sitting with Dean.

"I can't believe you were there again last night and didn't bring me my cards back."

Russel hit him on the side of the head. "Get 'em yourself."

"I hope you didn't cheat and check my hand."

Russel grabbed the tray from David. "Thanks dude."

"You shouldn't have gone alone. Look what happened."

"I almost had her. I almost had her..."

Dean stood up. "Well tonight's the final night. We can't let her get away. And with Russel being a cripple now, I had an idea. Last year I won the archery competition, I think I can manage to sneak a set away and do a little modification to it."

"What modification?"

"Ah, you haven't done camp archery before. Well it ain't sharp enough to impale nobody, they don't want the campers running rampant on any killing sprees and turning this place into *Lord of the Flies* so they're babyproofed. I can probably modify them like I did with the baseball bats."

"Oh hell yeah," Russel said.

"I'll get right on it," Dean said, and walked away.

David sat next to Russel. "We'll get her. Don't worry, man. We'll get her."

"Yeah, but it won't bring back Jen. Or Karina."

A boy and a girl were at the archery station having a competition.

"Let me show you how it's done," he said, and missed the target completely then inspected the bow. "This thing must be defective."

"As defective as your brain."

"Let me give it another shot," he said and fired again, this time hitting the outer blue section of the circular target. "I can't do nothing with this faulty bow."

"Suuure it's the bow. You just stink," she said. "I'll give you a dollar if you can get a bullseye within your next ten tries."

"How about a kiss instead?"

"Fat chance."

There was a counselor who oversaw the equipment. Although the arrows were not sharp, they were still dangerous, and eyes could still be poked out. Dean didn't know how he was gonna get away with stealing this right under the counselor's nose.

"You know I won the archery competition last year?"

"Oh, did you?"

"Yeah. I think I remember you dude. Weren't you one of the judges?"

"Yes I was. You've got a good memory, kid."

"Watch this." Dean launched one of the arrows for a near bullseye.

"Good shot."

"Hey, how come you're not at the meeting?"

"What meeting?"

"Camp director Charlie was going up and down yelling that he needed every last counselor in the counselors' lunchroom for something. I think it was pretty urgent, I don't know what it was about."

"Huh. I better go see what that's all about. Thanks for the head's up, kid."

"Yeah man, no problem."

The counselor ran away. Suddenly Dean noticed that the girl was at his side fawning over him.

"You've got such a nice shot, can you teach me?"

Damnit, he thought, then said, hurrying to grab the equipment before the counselor realized the story was a lie and came back. "Sorry, I can't. Maybe next time. Trust me, it pains me to do this, you are so beautiful. My name's Dean. Maybe I'll catch you on the bus tomorrow."

"Byeee Dean."

He gave her a little wave with a look over his shoulder.

Back to the groundskeeper's shed with all the tools he would need. There were twelve arrows in all. Dean put them in the grip one at a time, removing the plastic piece that was at the point of each arrow and replacing them with a nail instead. They fit like a charm but didn't hold in place.

He walked around the shed looking the shelves up and down, moving boxes of tools, moving shovels, searching for anything that could hold them in place. Then he found the hot glue gun. He tested out the first arrow, waited until the glue dried, then he set it in the bow and fired it across the shed. The nail penetrated the flimsy door.

It would work great in flesh. It would work great to take down a feral killer.

Dean pulled it from the door then returned to the bench, working tediously on each of the arrows. It would be the perfect weapon, yes it would be. This, the spiked bats, and the pocketknives. And the chainsaw that Russel had mentioned he found in the cellar. If all of these weren't enough to stop that girl, then nothing was.

Later, when he brought by David and Russel to inspect the artillery, they were both very pleased.

31

THE BOYS PRACTICED WITH the modified bow and arrows in the woods nearest to the shed. They had a bit of an unofficial competition launching the arrows and seeing whose would not only land furthest, but also manage to impale a tree. If the arrow landed without penetrating a tree trunk, then that turn did not count.

Dean was winning. Apparently the skills necessary to win the archery competition last year hadn't left him, despite an entire year having passed between then and now without having launched an arrow once until now.

Russel shot an arrow that landed on the ground about two feet short of the tree that Dean's last shot impaled. He limped to retrieve it, but David decided to grab it for him.

"You gotta stay off that foot."

Russel ignored him.

"Want to put money on this?" Dean said. "Russ I know you've got that twenty bucks. Dave you got any money left?"

"I'm not betting with you over archery, I'm practically guaranteed to lose money."

"Russ you know one time at the mall I made a bet with Dave if we each held up a little sign that said 'FREE HUGS' in big letters that I'd get more than him. You know what happened?" Dean said, then continued the story before Russ would reply: "I got three hugs within an hour, all from chicks, and Dave's one hug was from some big smelly guy."

"Oh that's not true, that's not how it happened."

"Yeah it is, this big smelly guy with pit stains. Hugged him for a good thirty seconds."

"No, no, *you told him to hug me, I tried to avoid him—"*

"You still hugged him. Did you get his number?"

David held up one of the modified arrows. "I'll stick this up your—"

"Relax, Dave. It's just a joke."

"Yeah," Russel said, "he's just busting your balls."

Dean laughed. "David that smelly guy was your type. He might've been the one that got away. I'm sure if you hold up that 'FREE HUGS' sign again he'll come back, but you better work up the courage to flirt back this time."

"You asshole." David smacked the back of Dean's head. "Stop injecting me into your faggot fantasies."

"No, you're the faggot."

"You're both faggots."

"Next person to miss their next shot is a faggot." Dean launched an arrow. It smacked into a tree and held.

"You're up, Russ."

Russel's shot held.

So did David's.

It started over with Dean's next shot. The boys went deeper into the woods and into a clearing, picking a new tree for a target. As Dean let go of the shot, David shoved him. The arrow completely missed.

"I knew you were a faggot," David said. "But it's all right, we won't tell Betsy."

"Hey… have you guys seen Betsy today?"

But none of them had.

32

SOME OF THE GIRLS that Russel recognized as Betsy's bunkmates were playing volleyball.

"Hey, you girls seen Betsy around?"

"What? We like thought she was with you."

"You're like the second guy she's gone through this week, who could she *possibly* be seeing now?"

"Awe, what happened to your foot?"

"An accident during a football game."

"You poor thing. Do you need a little help getting around?"

"No, I got it. If you see Betsy… let her know I'm looking for her…"

"Sure will."

"You sure you don't need any help?"

"I got it. Thanks."

33

THE BOYS MET IN Kodiak while Russel's bunkmates were competing in activities around camp. Some playing basketball, some swimming, some playing human foosball, some playing carpetball. Others had gone off with the girls they had met.

When Russel broke the news that Betsy's bunkmates hadn't seen her, Dean punched the wall. David held him back.

"Acting like an idiot isn't gonna bring her back."

"Let's go over this plan one more time," Russel said. "I'm injured so I'll be bait, since she only strikes when we're alone. You two…"

After he gave the plan, David and Dean left Kodiak to prepare, then to retrieve the weapons that were all hidden in the groundskeeper's shed.

Russel was on the top bunk, braced himself, and stood up against his pained ankle to reach the rafter. He carved his name and the date with his pocketknife.

As he climbed down she was in the open window watching him with hatred. She lowered her head and leapt from the window to the bed. Russel's grip increased on the knife but once he and the girl were tangled on the floor she bit his hand, and the knife came free in the struggle.

At first he didn't scream, he was too shocked and in too much pain. All that came out of his lips were an empty gasp. A cough.

He was still stronger than her despite his ankle, and he wrestled her until he had her in a headlock while her furry arms and legs painfully beat against him.

That was when he screamed.

"Help! Help!"

He couldn't hold her much longer.

"David! Dean! Help me!"

As if Russel had summoned him into existence, David entered Kodiak.

"Your belt. Hurry."

"My what?"

"Take off your belt."

"What the hell for?"

"Goddamn you David. I can't hold her much longer."

David removed his belt then dived down alongside them.

"Hurry. Her throat. To the bed."

David slid the belt over the feral girl's throat, taking the place of Russel's headlock and strapping it to the foot of the bed as instructed. The creature clawed at it, trying to break free of it with her nails that were more like the sharp claws belonging to a wild beast.

"Where's your knife?"

David felt his pockets. "I think I forgot it in my other pants. Where's yours?"

"She knocked it away—there it is." Russel snatched it up off the floor, but by then the feral girl had broken free of the restraint and climbed back through the window, fleeing into the trees. She was agile, moving swift and quick, as if the injured calf no longer bothered her.

"Get Dean. Get the weapons. I'll follow her."

"No you idiot, you can't run. I'll follow her. Give me your knife." David took it from Russel's hands without waiting for David to hand it over.

David rushed to catch up with the animalistic girl but he couldn't see her or hear her, as if she had left the cabin and wandered out of existence. He kept going in the same general direction, looking back over his shoulder in anticipation for the others.

This section of woods was far from the forbidden cabin. That girl probably spent her whole… *existence*—he hesitated to call it a *life*—here and knew it inside out. She knew every last place to hide. She could have been lurking anywhere, stalking him from anywhere. If he relaxed for one moment thinking she was out of sight, he could die.

He followed deeper into the woods…

And deeper…

"David? Daaaaaaviiiiid?"

Dean's calls startled him.

David went the opposite way to meet up with them. "I lost her."

Russel had the bow and arrow, and Dean had both bats. He gave one to David.

Opportunity of a lifetime." David slammed the bat into a tree. "And I blew it."

They searched the cabin.

The feral girl wasn't there.

The boys took out their anger by slamming the spiked bats into the walls.

"Well now what?" Dean said.

Russel swung the bat. "We wait it out. We keep an eye on this house. We each take a side."

David swung next. "I can't believe she got away. And she ruined my belt."

Dean swung the bat after taking it from David. "I'm sure if we put out heads together we can figure it out. Why don't we check out that place where you said you found her last night?"

Russel shook his head. "She wouldn't go back there again. Too risky. That's probably why she isn't here."

"Well if she isn't gonna come here, we gotta go to her."

34

Russel stayed near the cabin, keeping an eye on its perimeter since he wasn't going to be able to chase her if he crossed her path out there in the woods. But he had the arrows ready for the exact moment that she might return.

Meanwhile David went one way, in the direction of the girl's hideout that Russel had stumbled upon last night. Dean went the other way into uncharted territory.

Dean swung the bat around practicing his swing. *"Take that! And that!"* Then he thought: *Bring it on.*

Up ahead there was an outhouse. A decrepit structure of flimsy and splintered wood. It was uneven in its construction so that one side of the pointed roof was longer than the other, and the door was crooked.

Thank God, he thought, *I had to piss.*

He set down the spiked bat against the side of the outhouse then put his hand on the door.

AWOOOOOOH!

The feral girl on all fours. Dean motioned to step around the corner to retrieve the baseball bat but she was running too fast, and in that split second all he could really do was open the door and step inside, but he was flung to the ground by the body that collapsed out of the outhouse. Betsy's stiff corpse.

He darted his eyes and saw that the feral girl was midair, so he shoved Betsy's body between them, and the girl's nails sunk into Betsy's lifeless remains. Dean pinned the girl, keeping the dead body between them.

"Russel! David! You guys!"

If they heard him, he didn't know.

The feral girl successfully overpowered Dean and then he was the one that was pinned. Her teeth gnashed but once again the corpse was between them, and Dean shoved Betsy's head with his chin to keep as much distance as he could from the attacker.

She loosened her grip so she could slide Betsy's body from between them, ready to sink her teeth into him, but Dean punched her in the nose before she could do anything. Blood burst and squirted down on him. He pulled himself out from under her and gave her a kick in the abdomen. He took his eyes off of her just for a second to run next to the outhouse and grab the bat. When he had it again, she was gone.

He looked around, ready to swing it at the slightest movement.

Gone. Gone.

He knelt over Betsy's body. "I'm so sorry."

Then there was rustling between the trees. Up ahead she was retreating.

He followed.

The boys, she thought, were going to be tougher prayer than the girls had been. They were stronger and more resourceful. And they were out for blood while the girls were not. The girls had been caught off guard, but it was hard to do the same to these boys when she was the only thing on their minds.

Where was she to go? She came near to the cabin, to her home, and the boy from last night who she had almost defeated in the cabin today was ready with his weapons. It was like the one she had seen her master use not so long ago.

Then the boy from the outhouse was at the cabin too, carrying the bat over his shoulder ready to swing. While they were distracted talking to each other out front, she climbed into the cabin through one of the back windows into the master's bedroom.

She wished he could have been around to help her…

…but she was on her own.

Dean was out of breath. “She… got away… don’t know… where she went… almost… had her…”

Russel shook his head. “Goddammit Dean.”

“I tried… my best…” Still out of breath.

“Well goddammit. Which way?”

“Hard to tell. But this general direction. Maybe I should go check on Dave…”

“Yeah. You do that. I’ll stay here. And remember, hurt her all you want. But I’m the one who’s gonna kill her.”

She watched from one of the windows then moved away quickly before either could look up and see her. The one with the baseball bat was going away. Into the other direction. Still looking for her, she assumed. Little did they know she was within reach. The cabin was the perfect hiding spot until the boys decided to come inside, then she didn’t know what she’d do.

Now that she was in here it was time to plan. Time to get ready so that when she struck she could overpower them.

For her master.

Dean found David sitting down behind a boulder near a stream of water.

“Sleepin’ on the job, buddy?”

"Nah. Just waiting it out."

"This plan is retarded."

"Yeah? If you have a better one let me know. Maybe we can convince Russel to follow through. But he's kind of the self-appointed man in charge."

Dean hung his head. "Maybe we shouldn't do anything about it. Maybe we should just give up."

"It's personal to him. He wouldn't let us get the police involved. And when Betsy suggested it, we told her no."

"Yeah and look where that got her. Dead. I… found her body out there."

David put a hand on Dean's shoulder. "Oh damn. Oh Jesus. Oh fuck. Oh fuck, fuck, fuck."

Dean wiped away a tear. "It's gonna be all right."

David nodded. "I want to get out of this. Trust me I do. But what we did to that groundskeeper… we're in trouble. We're in this too deep. If anyone finds out what we did…"

"We didn't kill him, that was Russel. We'll get off easy. We can even deny it. Russel can't prove one way or the other what we did."

"Our fingerprints are probably all over that place. I say we just get this over with. We go home and never talk about it ever again."

"Agreed. After this is over we put it all behind us."

They regrouped at the cabin.

"Russel, I'm getting hungry. Let's take a break. Come on."

"No. You two can go. I'm not gonna risk missing her."

"Look, you're out here guarding the house, she can see you a mile away. Why don't you wait for her inside?"

"Because I can shoot her a mile away. She's a dumb animal, she doesn't know any better."

"We'll bring you something back."

35

WHEN SHE PEEKED OUT the window again, two of the boys were leaving, and that gave her a sudden idea. She had to be careful not to be heard. She pressed her hands and feet softly against the stairs that were still stained with dried blood. Apparently the boy outside did not hear her, thank God, but even with the quietness from outside, she had never been more scared than she was now, making her way to the other end of the cabin so that she could get to the cellar.

She didn't know what the boy outside had done with it, but she knew that there was another one down here somewhere.

The lamps that were forgotten here by those boys were still burning bright. She picked one up and look it across the cellar. When she came across the pile of bones she remembered the girl from long ago and shuddered.

Then finally she found what she was looking for on the top shelf. The red machine of death. Just as she had seen her master do it, and the boy outside had done it, all she needed to do was pull the string to turn it on. However she waited because he would be alerted to her presence if she tested it now. So she hoped it would work in the moment that she needed it.

Slowly creeping up without a sound, it was as though the floorboards knew about her mission and were silent specifically for her. And the rest of the house obliged, keeping quiet for her short travel from the cellar to the front door.

He was still out there.

It was time.

Russel set his bow and arrow down then he stood up and stretched. His ankle pulsed with pain. He couldn't believe he had made such a stupid mistake and tumbled down like that, but thank God it was only sprained, it could have been broken, and then he would've been out of here for good.

So where was she? Where could she be? In this whole big place, where could she have—

BRUM! BRUM! BRUM! BRRRRRRRRRRRRRRRRRRRRRRRRRRRRRRRRRRRRRRRRRR!

The feral girl kicked the door open and a roaring chainsaw was raised above her head. She stepped forward and Russel fell backwards. The arrows were just out of reach but he grabbed the bow and forced it between them as she brooded over him and slammed the chainsaw down, severing the bow in half.

The metal teeth of death were inches away from him. Acting quickly he pushed his right foot—his good foot that wasn't hurt—into the girl's ankle and tripped her. The chainsaw skidded from her hands and landed a few feet away, still roaring, still ready to cause destruction.

Russel didn't waste time standing up, he stretched forward to reach the chainsaw and was an inch away when the feral girl grabbed hold of him in a tight grip and pulled him backwards. Glancing at her face he saw an evil smile full of menace. She crawled over him and punched him in the jaw. He tried to punch her but missed, and her next hit landed on his jaw again.

Finally his fist made contact against her face. Her hands shot up to her jaw where she had been struck, and in that moment Russel was free to reach the chainsaw. He picked it up and charged at her, and she was fleeing back into the cabin.

She shut the door and held it shut—the dumb girl. Russel jammed the chainsaw into the door, and it swung open with little effort. She was hurrying up the stairs. He ascended, ignoring the emerging pain in his ankle and attempting to run.

The girl backed away in the hallway, standing on her legs like a normal person, moving as though such a posture and movement were unnatural to her. She was used to moving like a beast on all fours. There was terror in her eyes. She knew that death was near.

She darted into the bedroom at the end of the hall and locked it before he could get there because his ankle was holding him back. Russel cut the doorknob off with the chainsaw and pushed the door open.

The girl was gone through the window.

She had escaped yet again.

Russel sighed. Leaning through the window, she was nowhere to be seen. The trees swayed with the touch of the continual winds, and all was quiet. Now, leaving the room, he knew he needed a new plan. Maybe Dean could reattach the bow, maybe he could fix it. Without the artillery he was practically useless—he might not get lucky again with the girl coming within striking distance.

And then he heard the noise, the squeal of the floorboards behind him. He had no chance to prepare for her attack. Her nails jammed into his back and her teeth bit into his shoulder. For a split second he almost let go of the chainsaw but he tightened his sweaty grip, turning in a muddied haziness with his weapon. Everything was moving too fast, and he was in so much pain, and he was moving by impulse.

The feral girl was too swift and retreated, dodging his swing. Another swing, and another miss. As though she were always a half an inch within reach. He swung at her all the way through the hallway which now felt more like a stretch of a labyrinth or a stretch of an endless hall in a haunted house. It seemed to go on and on forever and ever, with the girl never meeting the chainsaw's destructive teeth. Payback was lingering just out of reach.

Since he was impaired, she went down the stairs faster than he could.

She opened the door and ran into David and Dean who had returned with a tray of food for him. Everything they were serving at lunch splattered all over the feral girl as she and Dean were knocked down in each direction, but David still held his spiked bat and brought it down upon her. She was just as swift as she had been against the chainsaw, narrowly dodging it. The spikes were impaled into the floorboards and David had to tug twice to lift it out.

"No fair," Dean said. "I want a chainsaw..."

"Fuck off." Russel came off the bottom steps.

The girl ran into the cabin and darted for the fireplace poker. Between her and the boys was the couch. David went around from the left and Russel from the right, but she hopped over the moldy couch and went straight, where Dean had regained his own spiked bat and swung.

Another miss.

"Goddamn we need your arrows."

"She broke the bow. Can you fix it?"

The girl had gotten past Dean and out the front door. He and David chased after her with their adrenaline rushing and kept pace with her. With a sense of desperation and obligation Dean wound his spiked bat and threw it at her when he was well within striking distance. The spikes tore through the back of her hand removing chunks of flesh and pinning her to a tree.

She screeched.

Dean and David approached her cautiously.

Behind them, Russel said, *"Atta boy! There you go!"*

The girl grabbed the bat in agony and pulled it back to remove two of the three spikes that pierced her, but she couldn't find the strength to remove it fully, and her good hand went limp as she wailed in agony.

Dean removed the bat, and he and David dragged her back to the cabin…

36

HER CONSCIOUSNESS FADED. PERHAPS not for long. When she awoke she was in the cellar. The boys were above her. At first she thought she was restrained, but then she discovered her arms could move freely, it was only the unusual pain in her body that was tightening around her, not a rope. It was coiling through her flesh and pulling tighter, wrapping around her until she thought she would snap.

She lifted her hand to her face. There were holes in it, and blood that was still dripping. It felt as though it weighed as much as a brick. It dropped down at her side.

"Good, she's awake." Russel knelt and put his pocketknife to her throat, then addressed her directly: "I wonder if you understand a word I'm about to say. Did that groundskeeper teach you any English? Or were you just his... plaything? Yeah, I bet that was it."

The girl squirmed and inched away as best she could manage. Pain all over her face. It pleased him.

"Uh-huh, yeah, you can try and get out of this all you want. That'll only make this more fun. I enjoy a good challenge. As pissed as I was that you kept eluding us, it made it that much better when we finally caught you. What great hand-eye coordination you had, Deanie."

A faint growl. The girl shivered as she tried to speak in her savage tongue.

"Begging won't work here. You took away some people that were important to us. Now it's time I put you out of your misery. But first I'm gonna hack you to pieces. Not all at once like a madman, no, I'm going to savor this. Right up until it's time to get on the bus tomorrow I'm gonna be removing your flesh, putting you through torture like no... *creature* has ever felt before." Russel almost let the word *person* slip. Although she was born a human, she most definitely was not a person.

"Where do you guys think something like this comes from?" David asked.

Dean leaned against the shelving. "I think he abducted her. Maybe he snatched her in the middle of the night on some burglary job. Maybe he was holding her for ransom then kept her."

"That sounds like the dumbest idea I've ever heard for some dumb paperback original you'd find at the airport. Something that women in their forties read."

"Well I don't know, Dave. I'm not keeping track of missing children in the area. Hell she could have been his kid for all we know."

"Doesn't matter to me where she came from." Russel poked the tip of his knife into a wound on her hand. She writhed and let out a series of small screams.

Russel smiled.

The fun was only starting.

Russel grabbed his pack of smokes from his pocket and passed around cigarettes. "Let's celebrate. Waitasecond, Dean, can you go get me the nail polish remover? I left it on the counter by the cards."

"All my hard work and I'm still running errands? Make David do it."

"Dave?"

"Ah whatever." David went upstairs.

"Mind if I have a turn?"

"Go ahead man." Russel gave him the knife.

Dean stuck the tip of the knife into the girl's flesh by another one of her wounds. She had writhed fully into the wall by then and had no place to crawl further into. She cringed against the pain that Dean inflicted.

David returned with the nail polish remover. "What, having all the fun without me?"

"You'll get your turn, don't worry dude." Russel took the nail polish remover out of the bag and set them on a shelf. "There's enough creature to go around."

Dean gave David the knife, and David took his place. He dragged the tip of the knife along her cheek where he had given her the scar the other night. The girl's lips tightened and her body stiffened. Her fright was so heavy it radiated from her body and had texture that he could feel in the room with them.

"How about a matching scar?" David dug the tip of the knife into the skin below her eye on her other side. Then he stopped.

A silent plea.

A silent beg.

Maybe there was something human inside of her after all. Something buried deep within...

"Go ahead," Russel said.

David's hand trembled. He seared his conscious as he dragged it downwards. She swung her face away from him, breaking the scar and ending it before he could completely finish and carry it to the same length as the previous one.

"I think she likes you, Dave," Dean said. "Maybe you've got a shot with this one. I think your fat boyfriend from the mall is gonna be disappointed."

"Fuck you."

Russel grabbed the girl and dragged her over and into the chair where he had killed the groundskeeper. He admired the incision David had made. Then he searched the shelves for a box of nails and found one, a little shorter than the kind Dean had used to spike the bats. Russel worked it through the girl's wound then hammered it in place with the other end of the bat to keep her attached to the chair.

The feral girl leaned back and cried. Russel thought maybe she was ready to die.

He tapped on the end of the nail until it was flush with her skin and protruded from the bottom of the armrest.

Her screams were endless.

Russel was going to keep his promise and torture like no creature had suffered before.

Now that he had her where he wanted her, he almost wasn't sure where to begin. Most of the fun had been in the chase. Now he needed to slow down, take it easy, and think. He wanted to inflict as much pain as possible and drag this out as long as he could before getting on the bus tomorrow morning.

Pluck out her eyes? Cut out her tongue? Maybe, he thought, he'd do that before it was time to light her on fire, so she would be in a blind and confused state of torture as the flames melted her furred skin…

Russel left her and sat on the bottom steps, twirling the knife around in his hands and running over what he could do.

"What's up?" David said.

"I'm wondering how much blood she can lose and still survive the night. What time you got?"

David checked his watch. "God it's eight o'clock. Time flies when you're having fun, don't it? Russ we should get you something to eat. Since Dean couldn't hold on to the food to save his life."

"That wasn't my fault."

"Yeah. Sure. I could use a break. Could use some food. Let's tie her up and lock the cellar door so she's not missing by the time we get back. If I had to chase her down again, God help me."

They left her alone with one light burning.

Ropes kept her attached to the chair. Her arms were numb. Pain throbbed under the surface of her skin, threating to tear completely through her.

This is how I die, she thought.

She cried loudly, hoping that it was a strong enough cry to awaken her master from his grave of a bedroom that she kept him in, but he didn't come back. He was still lying up there devoid of any life. She was all alone.

Time was winding down.

The boys would be back any minute now.

37

The girls from Betsy's cabin:

"Oh Russel we haven't seen you all day."

"Do you want to come to our bonfire? You could sit by me…"

"Forget the bonfire. Why don't we go off and—and—"

"Sorry ladies, I've already got a date with somebody."

"With who?"

"Yeah, with who?"

"You wouldn't know her."

"Oh you really get around, Russel. First Jennifer then Betsy and now you're going around with every single girl in camp."

"Sorry ladies."

Russel, David, and Dean set up a bonfire far away from everybody else and celebrated with cherry colas and chocolate bars.

"The dinner of champs," Russel said.

"God I can't wait to be home." Dean chugged his second soda before either of the others were done with their first.

David burped. "I can't wait to be back home and forget about all of this."

Russel held up his can of soda for a toast. "Here's to Karina, Jennifer, and Betsy."

The boys didn't return to the forbidden cabin until everybody else was asleep.

"Look, Dean, Dave, all I'm saying is that you can't deny the documents that clearly state the government was involved with—"

"You sound like a nut," David said.

"The Montauk Project is real. Don't tell me you believe everything you hear on the news. The government owns the news. They own every journalist. The only stories that get published are what they want you to see. They want to distract you so you don't learn the truth."

"Okay," Dean said, "so what's the point of this 'Montauk Project?'"

"To control society. That's all the government is up to."

"They say that about all those nutty theories. Every single one. I've heard like forty five theories about projects to control people. Doesn't the government have enough resources to... to... to do whatever it is you think they're gonna do?"

"They're perfecting it and waiting for the precise moment to strike. Trust me, it's a slow process. They want to make us all sick first so we depend on them. Like all those doctors who cured cancer who either 'committed suicide' or 'went missing.' They were all bumped off."

"I don't know," David said, "this is a bit far-fetched for me."

"We're on our way to kill a feral girl who killed three people that we know of, but this is far fetched? Just start paying attention, man. Like all these medicine companies that manufacture herbicides among other things that cause Alzheimer's and caner, and then they manufacture the drugs that are marketed as 'the cure.'"

The conversation died down when they were back at the cabin. The cabin was silent and still. The girl was still in the cellar, Russel was sure. There was no way to escape the nail and ropes and unlock the cellar door.

The boys descended down the steps and she was still there, Russel was happy to see.

He hooked the knife into the corner of her mouth and she shut her lips around the blade, attempting to fight him away. He laughed at her and forced the blade upwards, cutting into her cheek to make an extended smile.

The girl flung her head backwards to get away from him.

"Hold her straight."

His friends did so for him.

He hooked the knife into the other corner of her mouth and repeated the process, minus her lips curling around the blade to stop him. This time she let him do it, and it was less fun that way, but it was a beautiful thing to see somebody get what they deserved.

The girl sobbed. Russel stepped back to admire his work. Since the cuts were upward, it was always a smile no matter how hard she tried to frown.

"Let's untie her."

David and Dean did it for him, and when they were done he kicked the chair over. The girl slinked out of it like a helpless bug. Russel stepped on her back as she tried to stand. The girl opened her mouth to cry or scream, but no noise came out.

She lifted her hand weakly—the one that wasn't damaged with the nail holes—then dropped it down. She was defeated. There was nothing she could do. And Russel stepped on that same hand anyways to keep it down.

"Just like her... should we call him her father? Her owner? Who wants to go first?"

"I will."

Russel gave the knife to Dean, and Dean cut off the tip of her pointer finger.

"How about you, Dave?"

Dave shook his head. "I think I gotta sit this out now. I've had my fun."

"What's with you?"

"Nothing. I just... it makes me sick."

"Oh well, more for me." Dean cut off the tip of her middle finger.

"Where did I put... there it is." Russel found the chainsaw.

BRUM! BRUM! BRUM! BRUM! BRUM! BRUM! BRRRRRRRRRRRRRRRRRRRRRRRRRRRRRRRRRRRRRRRRRRRRRRRRRRRRRRRR-RRRRRRRRRRRRRRRRRRRRRRRRRRRRRRRRRRRRRRRRRRRRRRRRRRRRRRRRRR-RRRRRRRRRRRRRRRRRRRRRRRRRRRRRRRRRRRRRRRRRRRRRRRRRRRRRRRRRR-RRRRRRRRRRRRRRRRRRRRRRRRRRR!

The sounds were amplified by the eeriness of the situation.

A gleam of lamplight reflected off the chainsaw and Russel brought it down to her. She shut her eyes and forced her hands in front of her face in self defense. He pulled it away and Dean patted him on the back.

"You scared the shit out of her."

Russel laughed.

David went over to the steps and sat facing away from his friends.

"You good?" Russel said. "Dave?"

"What? Oh yeah I'm good. Just… believe it or not, I've got a weak stomach."

"Uh-huh."

Russel swung the roaring chainsaw inches from the girl and terrified her. He and Dean were having fun. After a minute or two he set the chainsaw down on the shelves, and he and Dean looked around the shelves for new items to continue the horrors.

"I should've fixed that bow, then we could've taken turns shooting her from across the room."

"Oh fuck yeah that would've been cool. Guess we gotta settle for the next best thing. Hey take a look at this." It was a piece of splintery wood. "She could use some new shoes."

Russel held the wood under her foot while Dean nailed it in. The sounds that she was making, half-animal and half-human, David couldn't even describe how sickening it was. It made his skin crawl and sent thick chills down his spine.

How could he live with himself after what they were doing—and had already done—to this person? She was a person no matter what she had done. And she was an animal too. She didn't know any better. Should they have tortured her for it? When this all began he felt as though this were a big mistake, and he had talked himself out of it. But now he was full of regrets. They were deranged to do something like this to another person…

38

So far:

Torn lips at each end.

Nails through the hand.

Tips of fingers cut off.

A piece of splintery wood nailed into her foot.

Cuts on both sides of her face.

Cuts all over her body.

Kicked, cut in so many places that she could not keep track of them all, thrown around the room.

She was at the point where she did not look like a human or animal or anything anymore, she only looked like a bloody and ripped open mass that was clinging to life. She was balled up in defense, her face buried into her knees, shielding herself from the boys.

At this point she wanted to die.

At this point she wished they'd kill her. She wanted to be reunited with her master…

According to David's watch it was one-thirty-three in the morning.

"Let's get to bed. It's so late and I'm not even packed."

"What, you got four suitcases of toiletries to pack? What are you, a chick?"

"Knock it off Russ, I'm just done here. You got the payback you wanted. But now I wanna go. We're out of here bright and early."

"What's with that look on your face?"

"What look?"

"That one."

"I don't have a look."

"You aren't going soft on us, are you?"

David shook his head. "No. I'm tired. Is that too hard to understand?"

Russel gave David the knife. "Why don't you give it a shot? One last one for the night."

"No, I already cut her. I did enough."

Russel snatched the knife back right away. "You ain't planning on telling, right?"

"No dude. Just calm down."

"Dave's cool, don't worry," Dean said, "he's just cranky. But I can't blame him, I'm beat too, and I had more excitement down here than he did. Why don't we wrap it up? Call it a night? We did have our fun. But now it's time to get going, you know?"

"I guess I see what you guys mean..." Russel lit himself another cigarette. "Anyone want another one?"

"No thanks."

Dean picked up the nail polish remover. "We doing this now?"

"I almost want her to suffer the way she is through the night, but I don't think she's gonna make it much longer, is she? She's lost a lot of blood, she's been through a lot. But she's a fighter, she's gone through it like a champ."

"Let's light 'er up. If we wait til morning we might not be able to get away in time."

"What do you say, Dave?"

David couldn't look straight at Russel, nor Dean or the feral girl. "I say we let her be."

"And burn her in the morning?"

"No, no burning. Just leave her alone."

"Oh, I knew you went soft on us. I just knew it. What, you got the hots for her or something? That's sick, David. You know that? Real sick. You're sick in the head. That's like—that's like bestiality or something."

"I'm not going soft, just—just I don't like this idea of burning is all. We could get caught if... if..."

“A change of heart. Geez.”

Russel shifted his cigarette from one corner of his mouth to the other and opened one bottle of nail polish remover while Dean opened the other.

David came off the steps. “I just don’t wanna get caught. We’re too young to be charged with larceny and murder.”

“How would they catch us? All evidence is going up in flames. If we *don’t* light this place up then all our fingerprints and shoeprints are all around the joint.”

“Listen to him, Dave. I don’t like none of this either, believe me. This was the last way I wanted to spend my week here at summer camp. I mean, I didn’t even get to meet one chick! And the chick I liked died! This is a small price to pay to avenge everybody we lost. How many more lives would this *thing* have claimed if we didn’t step in? We’re doing a bunch of people a favor here, you know. She won’t be hurting anybody ever again.”

“Ah… I guess you guys are right. For a moment there *I* felt like the monster. But I know none of that’s true. Let’s give her what she’s got coming.”

“Atta boy.” Russel patted him on the back.

“I knew you didn’t puss out on us.” Dean gave David his bottle. “I want you to do the honors, if that’s okay with Russ.”

“Fine by me.”

David stepped across to the feral girl and was about to dump the nail polish remover on her when she sprang up and clawed his hand, knocking the bottle over and spilling out half of it. The flesh on the back of his hand was torn bad.

He stepped back and punched her, but she was in one last angry and desperate frenzy to stay alive despite all her injuries and torture. She was a wild animal who wouldn’t let go. Her claws came down on David and cut him repeatedly until the others joined the fight. Russel grabbed one of the spiked baseball bats but Dean knew there was no time to waste and pulled her off of David, wrestling her to the floor and pinning her.

“She’s got a lot of fight left in her after all.”

Dean forced her onto her stomach on the earthen floor, and held her down by the neck.

“Don’t choke her. She has to burn.”

David picked up the bottle of nail polish remover. Half of it gone. Russel still had his bottle, and when the girl calmed down beneath Dean, he turned her over and Russel soaked her. He spilled it over her face, sending her into another rage, and she knocked Dean off of her back and jumped at Russel. Despite his injured ankle he kept his own against her, slamming her into one of the shelves, but she was relentless, and pushed back, and she was broken free of him.

By then, David located the chainsaw.

BRUM! BRUM! BRUM! BRUM! BRRRRRRRRRRRRRRRRRRRRRRRRRRRR!

The feral girl inched back into a corner.

"Dean," David said, "grab that wood over there. Behind the stairs."

There was a pile of loose planks like the one he had used to knock out the groundskeeper. He grabbed two from the pile of about three dozen.

"How many?"

"Just keep grabbing."

"What for?"

"Lay them down right here."

"Yeah, what for?" Russel said.

"This'll be better than burning her alive. Let's burn the wood. This way she'll choke on them flames. She'll try and keep away from the fire but it'll grow and spread and it'll be a lot worse than burning her up outright."

"See? This is what happens you apply yourself. Let me help you with that wood, Deanie."

They transferred all the planks to the center of the cellar. The girl was backed into the corner opposite from Karina's remains. About a single bottle's worth of liquid between the two, they spread it over the wood.

Russel dropped the end of his cigarette over it and watched the flames spread, but they were minuscule.

"Hey guys. Guys." Dean emerged from under the stairs. "Look what was hiding. Lighter fluid."

"Hell yeah. Give it here."

Russel squeezed what little remained in the plastic lighter fluid bottle in both hands over the wood and the flames grew wild and prolific. Smoke quickly filled the cellar. On the other side of the flames the girl was moaning in agony.

"Let's go." David was the first one up the steps.

The others hurried behind him, and when they were out, Russel locked the cellar door.

"Just in case."

39

SHE CHOKED.

She pushed herself away from the smoke but it filled every inch of the cellar so all she could do was choke on it.

She wondered what her master would do, how he would help her in this situation. She knew that water would stop the flames but what else? What else could she do? There was no water down here. And then she remembered something he used to do when he lit up the firepit for them, and after the night wound down and he wanted to extinguish the fire. He'd pour dirt over the flames. And right now, she was entirely surrounded by dirt.

Despite her vision being murky both by the dried blood on her face and by the smoke, she detected the shovel that was adjacent to the remains of the girl. The pain in her hands was so powerful that under any other circumstance it would have been impossible to hold onto this shovel, but since it was life or death she had no choice but to force herself to ignore such unimaginable pain.

She limped forward, stabbing the shovel into the ground, then forced it up over the flames. She repeated the motion, continually throwing dirt, sometimes making contact with the fire, sometimes missing completely, all in the effort of preservation. She had to work quick because the flames could overtake the whole cabin and then there'd be no getting out alive.

Working furiously, the flames were dimming. The smoke was still abundant in the cellar and she choked on it again, but the flames were dying—the flames were dying. Thank God, they were dying.

She was exhausted and collapsed. Her body was warmed by the radiance of the remaining fire.

She laid there, everything becoming dark, and then there was a booming noise from somewhere outside.

Thunder.

Then the rain started…

…and it seeped in through the cracks in the cabin's structure.

When she woke in the morning the flames were dead, put out by a combination of her efforts and by the rain. If it had not rained, she thought, she would have died. But now she needed to get out of here, needed fresh air. Needed to heal. Needed to still get her revenge.

She climbed over the wood pile, crept up the stairs, and tried to open the cellar door but it wouldn't budge. And she was too weak to try breaking it open.

40

IN THE MORNING EVERYBODY was loading back onto the busses, but when Russel saw it had rained he wanted to go back to the cabin and check if it had burned down.

"Don't." David grabbed Russel's arm. "We don't have time. And there's just no way she survived all of that."

41

Raven Hill has always been an unlucky town.

42

Wesley Lawrence's stomach dropped as the bus descended a steep slope Monday morning.

He didn't feel like going back to Camp Solgohachia but all his friends were going so he went along.

His friend Bill sat next to him, and his friend Darren was alone in the seat behind them. Darren was so fat he took up enough room for two campers.

WELCOME TO CAMP SOLGOHACHIA, the banner over the tall wooden entrance read.

The driver parked in a big gravel parking lot, opened the door, and wished the kids fun times. Most of the luggage was piled into mountains in the back of the bus, and kids tackled each other to find their things so that they could get off and go into camp. Wesley had kept his single bag at his feet so he would be the first one off the bus. He was glad to finally stretch his legs. The ride long with no stops and he had to pee from the six pack of Jolt Cola he drank on the way over.

"Hurry up dude," Wesley said as Darren wobbled over with his bag gripped in both hands.

"I'm coming, I'm coming." Darren was out of breath from the minimal physical activity he had to do by walking the length of the bus. "Oh God I'm beat."

Wesley patted him on the back. "When we get back home I'm putting you on a strict diet and exercise regimen. No more Jolt Colas or Pop Rocks for you, buddy."

"You can take anything from me, but not my Pop Rocks, Wes."

Bill got his bag from the bus then join Wesley and Darren. "Damn it's hot out today, you guys."

The boys sped to a path on the right that went to the boys' cabins at the edge of the woods that hemmed around camp. The cabins stood on a slight rise. The girls' cabins were on the other side of camp.

The boys' cabins were named: Grizzly, Polar, Kodiak, Sun, and Panda. Grizzly was the first cabin, the most desirable one, and not technically a cabin. It was the only one with air conditioning and had nice tile floors and newly installed bathrooms.

"It must be taken already," Wesley said. "No way we made it in time."

Bill pointed his thumb. "Somebody already put a garbage can outside. Look."

Putting a garbage can outside the door was tradition amongst the boys at Camp Solgohachia to let the later arrivals know a cabin was full.

"Well kill me if we've gotta be stuck in Panda."

"Panda isn't so bad," Darren said. "It may be ugly and falling apart but it's not so bad."

"The toilets in Panda don't even flush! And look how the trees almost grow *into* it, I bet it's swarming with bugs."

Polar was next on the path of cabins and was the next most desirable, but that too had a garbage can in front of it. So did Brown, Kodiak, and Sun.

The boys stopped in front of Panda. Its name was painted in wobbly red letters, and the green paintjob on the cabin was chipping away. The branches of giant trees covered it and almost formed a second roof. Somewhere in the distance bees hummed, and Wesley hoped they wouldn't have to deal with bees or any type of bug with a stinger for the next couple weeks.

"Panda it is, I guess," Wesley reached for the knob. "I had Grizzly my first year, right after they fixed it up. Man I wish all cabins were like that. I had all sorts of bragging rights that year..."

"I remember when you showed me inside," Bill said. "Sure was nice."

"Maybe Panda won't be so bad," Darren said and pushed his crooked glasses up.

Nobody else was in Panda. They had it all to themselves.

The cabin stunk but it was unclear where the stench was coming from. The bunkbeds were high off the ground, and were old and rickety, as if they hadn't been replaced since the place opened a million years ago. At least the blue covers over the musty grey mattresses were new, but they didn't have bedsheets, and there was no way Wesley was touching that with his body. Tall dressers were set between the bunks, and there were some other dressers at one end. The floor creaked with every step.

Wesley tossed his bag atop the high bunk in the far left corner with the window facing camp. "Dibs."

He climbed the ladder then studied the beams that raced across the ceiling. Often times the boys had races with these, seeing who could climb to the other end and back first. Wesley thought that if anyone tried that in Panda, that the roof would surely collapse. Wesley put his hands to it anyways and searched around the beams for treasure but only found dust. He had been lucky once and found a silver dollar on a beam, but he hadn't been lucky since.

Bill tossed his bag on the bunk below Wesley's, and Darren took the bottom bunk next to Bill.

A whisper of cold came when Wesley opened the door to leave the cabin. He looked up to see the clouds covering the sun, then turned back to his friends who were still loading their clothes into dresser drawers.

"Come on, fags."

Clouds moved away from the sun and the temperature rose. The boys went to the flagpole at the center of camp. All the boys and girls of Camp Solgohachia were heading there for morning announcements.

The flagpole was probably twenty feet high, and the American flag danced in the wind. A man stood on the bricks that ran in circles around the pole and the flowers that grew around it.

"Goooooood morning campers! I'm your camp director Charlie and welcome to Camp Solgohachia! I know many of you have been here before and know the spiel but listen up! It's time to go over some camp rules before we get things started! Now let's see a show of hands, who has *never* been camping before?"

Plenty of campers, mostly the younger kids, raised their hands.

"And who's been camping before but never been to Camp Solgohachia before?"

Some others raised their hands, but not many.

"Well it's a pleasure to have you all here! This is going to be the best summer yet! I'll need you kids to pay attention and save all questions for the end. We have five very special rules we ask you all to follow at Camp Solgohachia." Wesley zoned out what Charlie had to say until the end of his speech: "Now, the fifth and final rule is the absolute most important. *Do. Not. Go. Out. After. Curfew.* There is absolutely no sneaking out. Every year we have kids who try to break into the boarded cabin through the east end of the woods. This is absolutely frowned upon, and that area of the woods is off limits. Any camper found going there will have to clean the latrine and have privileges taken away. Is that understood?"

Wesley pulled his buddies to the side. "Guys?"

"Yeah?"

"It's our last year here. What if we went to that cabin?"

"Go to the cabin?" Darren gulped. *"Go to the cabin!?!?"*

"Shut up, not so loud," Wesley said. "Yes, go to the cabin. It sounds like fun. What're they gonna do? Send me home? I didn't wanna come this year anyways, I only came because of you guys. Look, nothing's gonna happen, it's all just some story to scare campers with. It's our last year here, if we don't do it now we never will."

"You're not gonna do it," Bill said. "You're a pussy."

"Fuck you, Bill."

"Let's make a bet." Bill stuck out his hand.

Wesley shook it. "It's a deal."

43

When Charlie was done speaking the campers were free to wander around and do as they pleased. There were no scheduled activities on the first day. The sun was blazing and it must have been touching ninety degrees, possibly more.

There was much to do: baseball, basketball, human foosball, golf, water balloon volleyball, and carpetball. Carpetball was played under a ramada that also had vending machines and tables, and was where Wesley sat with his eyes on a blondie wearing a denim skirt and tight pink shirt.

Wesley sat crouched over the edge of the table with his hands and slingshot under it, and a stack of pebbles hidden at his side. He slipped one into the leather pad on the rubber and winded it back. It hit a boy of thirteen or fourteen in the calf. Wesley laughed watching the boy grab his leg on the brink of tears.

Wesley looked away discretely, and when nobody fessed up, the boy tried to go back to carpetball. Wesley hit him again. Everyone laughed at the kid's painful reaction. Nobody saw who had shot him. Nobody, of course, except the blondie that Wesley had his eye on.

After the third time he hit the boy, Blondie came over and said, "You're a real asshole you know."

"What?"

She crossed her arms. "I saw what you did, asshole."

Wesley laughed. He had to be precise here or he could blow everything. "Hey, it's just a little prank. That's what we do around here. It's called having fun."

"Whatever. It was mean."

"I'm Wesley, what's your name?"

"Fuck off." Blondie upturned her nose then left the ramada and went off into camp.

Wesley stood up from the bench and tripped onto the cement floor—thank God she didn't see—then he got to his feet and hurried after her. *"Hey wait up."*

She turned around confused. "You gonna shoot me with that thing too?"

"What?" He looked down at his hands then stuffed the slingshot into his pocket. "I was just joking around."

She turned and walked away.

"What's your name?"

Blondie stopped. "Wendy."

"Have you been here before?"

"No," she said.

"I'll show you around then."

"As long as you don't hit me with any rocks."

"I won't, Wendy. Just as long as you behave yourself."

He took her off the path and through the grass as a shortcut. Next to the carpetball armada was the open area behind the cafeteria and before the start of the golf fields. It was on a rise, an area not typically traveled since there was nothing there. The back of the cafeteria had a porch that nobody usually used; below it was an open hiding space that—as far as he knew—no one else knew about.

"You can hide here."

"Hide here?"

"You know, if you ever want to skip out on activities."

"Uh, okay?"

He led her back to the path. It curved into the camp. "Back around here are the basketball courts. That building right next to it has postcards and candy and stuff you can buy. And a payphone in the back."

Wendy turned towards the basketball hoops and watched some girls play.

"Are those your friends?"

"No," Wendy said in a low voice. Her face turned red. "Some of them are in my cabin, but, I don't know anybody here. I just moved to Raven Hill."

They walked around a little bit more.

"Well down that way's the swim hole, past the boys' cabins. I'm down in the last one."

"Thanks for showing me around," Wendy said then walked away. "I think I'm gonna use that payphone."

"See you around?"

"I think so. This place isn't *that* big."

A few minutes later Wesley took his slingshot out and went back to the armada, grabbed handfuls of pebbles, and sat back alone at the table.

He looked around for the boy he had hit last time, but couldn't find him. Instead, he launched his rocks at a new target: another boy in shorts watching an intense game of carpetball, cheering every time the guy in the green shirt knocked over the pool balls of the guy in the *Led Zeppelin* shirt.

Wesley fired a pebble at the boy's shoulder. The boy nearly jumped over the table when he felt it hit him. The boy turned around. His face white under freckles, and turning to anger. Wesley secretly launched another from under the table and it hit the boy in the stomach. Wesley looked away quickly, bursting out in laughter, and the boy looked around the crowded armada wondering who the hell could have been throwing rocks at him.

Camp is gonna be just fine after all, Wesley thought.

44

WESLEY KEPT AN EYE out for Wendy as he and Bill and Darren waited at the front of the mess hall line.

"Could you believe it?" Darren said. "Really, could you guys believe it? Playing baseball in this weather? I almost fainted, I tell you. *Fainted.* They laughed at me when I asked to pause for a water break."

"Calm it, tits," Wesley said. "You didn't even get on base. You struck out every time."

"I got on base once."

"Because the pitcher hit you," Bill said.

The cafeteria doors opened and the line got to moving.

The camp served pizza today as they always did on the first and last days. Technically not camp food, and it was delicious. One of the only couple days when the food they served was any good. Wesley was not looking forward to awful "Bean Surprise" for lunch tomorrow or the "Mystery Meat" the day after.

Wesley and his friends sat at the end of a crowded table near a window.

"You'll never believe what happened to me guys. I met the most beautiful girl today, her name's Wendy and she's new around here. I' gonna sit by her at the bonfire tonight."

"Oh yeah?" Darren said. "What if she already has a date?"

"That's the thing. She doesn't know anybody here. She's new."

"And she's pretty?" Bill said, leaning in.

"Yeah."

"A pretty girl with no friends?"

"Yeah, that's right."

Darren and Bill looked at each other, then back to Wesley and laughed.

"What? What are you pricks laughing at?"

"Well, Wes," Bill said, "don't you know it? If a pretty girl has no friends it's usually because she's a bitch. Everyone wants to be friends with a pretty girl."

"She's not a bitch, she's nice."

"That's the Tic Tac between your legs talking," Darren said. "You've barely met her. She *has* to be a bitch."

"You'll see tonight. Just don't embarrass me."

"We won't embarrass you," Bill said. "Maybe you should try taking her to the abandoned cabin."

"Oh yeah, are still up for our little bet, Bill?"

"Definitely. Are you? Maybe after the bonfire?"

"Yeah dude."

Darren took a bite of his pizza then spit it out. *"Too hot! Too hot!"*

Darren picked up the piece he spat out and ate it.

"Gross," Wesley said. "You're gonna make me sick."

The boys went back to Panda for their trunks. The weather had cooled by now. Soft breezes whistled through the trees and fell over Camp Solgohachia. The clouds were low and thick.

A man emerged from the cabin all ready to go to the swim hole.

"Oh hey, you guys must be the others staying in Panda," the counselor said in an overly happy voice, a voice that Wesley thought the counselors were all forced into faking. "I'm Vince, I'm your cabin's counselor. Have you guys been having a great first day?"

"Yeah," Wesley said.

"And what are your names?"

"I'm Wesley. This is Bill and Darren."

Vince said it was great to meet them, and wandered off down to the swim hole.

“He seem like a weirdo to you guys?” Wesley said.

“There’s something wrong with him,” Darren said.

“He’s a weirdo,” Bill said. “That’s for sure.

There were three other campers in bunks and filling up dresser drawers and changing into trunks.

“I don’t know about you guys,” Wesley addressed the three strangers, “but I thought that Vince dude was a fag.”

The boy in blue trunks and a blue shirt laughed. “Yeah you’re probably right.”

“Hey, let me ask you new guys a question,” Wesley said. “You meet a hot girl, she’s new here, she’s got no friends. What’s it mean?”

“Easy,” the redhead said, “she’s a bitch. Every hot girl without friends must be one or she’d have friends. Everyone wants to be friends with a hot girl.”

“Even if she’s new?”

“Especially if she’s new,” Blue Trunks said. “You kidding? She wouldn’t be alone unless she’s a bitch.”

“Well she didn’t seem like a bitch.”

“Who is she?”

“Wendy. But she isn’t a bitch.”

“Wendy... Wendy...” Redhead said. “Doesn’t ring a bell.”

“Heh, we tried to tell him,” Darren said. “We *tried* to tell him. But ole Wes here doesn’t listen. Oh boy, he wants to learn the hard way.”

“I’ve seen it before.” Redhead shook his head disappointedly. “My name is Chester, by the way.”

“Ralph,” the quiet short one mumbled. Wesley had forgotten about him for a second.

“I’m Al,” Blue Trunks said.

“You assholes will meet her at the bonfire tonight, just don’t embarrass me, okay?”

45

THE SWIM HOLE WAS a giant in-ground circle of murky green-blue water divided in half by a yellow fence.

On one side, the shallow side, which anybody could use, was a volleyball net, a small slide, and two low basketball hoops with green and white striped basketballs. On the other end, the deep end, which you'd have to pass a swimming test to use, was a bigger slide, a wooden deck, and *the blob.*

The blob was a giant yellow and blue inflatable structure that required two people to use. One person, usually the smaller of the two, would jump from the deck to the blob and sit on the far end of it. The other person, the bigger of the two, would then jump straight down from the deck, causing the smaller person to go flying through the air then landing in the water.

Wesley kicked off his flipflops and ran down to the far end, where he waited in one of two lines for his turn to take the swim test. The test was simple, and he passed every year: swimming down to the other end and back.

When his turn came he jumped in and swam. The water was lukewarm, a little on the cold side, but he hit a warm pocket and went to the other end as fast as he could. When he made it there, he touched the concrete edge, glanced quickly around to see if Wendy was there, didn't see her, turned around and swam back. Down at the end he was returning to, he saw Bill and Al and Chester in line.

Now it was time for the blob.

He raced up the wooden steps. Wesley's turn came and he jumped off the platform, which must've been about ten feet high if he had to guess, then crawled to the edge. He prepared himself for liftoff, turned around, then gave the tubby dude on the platform a thumbs up.

"Ready."

Wesley turned back and by the time he was looking forward he was already in the air. There was a loud *SMACK!* of the guy slamming into the blob then everything became a blur: the world rushed by and he had that thrill of falling, limbs flailing, mouth agape but shutting as he realized he was coming down face-first into water. He splashed under the green-blue chilly surface then rose with his hair plastered to his face and big smile running across his thin lips.

Wesley looked over and saw that the tubby man who blobbed him was about to be blobbed by an even bigger man. Wesley put his arms around the yellow fence then watched the fatty climb into the sky, panic on his face—he must not have been blobbed often—and come crashing like a cannonball not far from Wesley.

Wesley swam back to the wooden deck and went back up the dripping wet stairs, grabbing the railing tight, went back in line—longer now than it had been the first time—and waited in line behind a girl. From his place up top on the deck he could see most of the swim hole, although most people on the shallow end were just dots from up here, and tried to find Wendy.

The line moved fast and when it was Wesley's turn again he was blobbed by an even bigger guy than the first time, and was flung so far he almost became the second person in history to hit the fence that divided the deep end and the shallow end. For a moment he was suspended in air, and all he saw was yellow. Even as he shut his eyes he saw the bar coming closer and closer, tried to somehow push his body away from it, and landed on his back in the water just a foot away from the fence. When he resurfaced he heard many people laughing.

After that, he decided it was time to head over to the shallow end and see what was going on. Darren and Ralph were chilling against the fence, hardly waist-deep in the swim hole. Bill, Al, Chester, and some other boys were playing basketball on one hoop while some girls were playing basketball on the other.

Wesley snuck through the game of basketball, put Bill in a choke hold, which was difficult since Bill was much taller, then dragged him under the water and let go. Bill resurfaced, grabbed Wesley, lifted him up, then dropped him in the water with a big splash.

The game of basketball abruptly ended and suddenly everybody was dunking everybody. Chester dunked Al, Al dunked a random baldheaded boy, somebody Wesley couldn't see dunked him. When Wesley came back up he saw that Darren and Ralph hadn't seen the dunking party going on because they were watching people get blobbed.

"Hey, over there." Wesley pointed. "Let's get 'em."

Wesley and Al crept over to their unsuspecting friends, then Wesley put his arm around Darren, and Al helped grab him too.

"Oh what is this what are you guys doing don't dunk me don't dunk me please."

"Everybody gets at least one," Wesley said.

Al turned back to Ralph. "What he said. You're next, Ralphie."

Ralph was frozen with terror.

Darren tried to wiggle free. *"But I can't swim I don't know what to do what do I do? Please—"*

"Just plug your nose," Al said.

Darren slipped an arm free from Wesley. He started to ask, as he raised his hand to his face, "Like this—" but before he could reach his nose, they let go of him and he went under three feet of water. A moment later he came to the surface thrashing his arms around as if the shark from *Jaws* were after him.

"I'm drowning I'm drowning oh God this is the end! Goodbye cruel world!"

Bill grabbed him by the shoulders. "Get ahold of yourself, you're standing up dude."

"Huh? I am?"

Darren looked down and wrinkled his nose. "I swallowed some of it! Some of it went in my nose! It hurts! Oh God, you know what kind of diseases could be in this water?"

"None of us have aids," Wesley said.

Al looked back at Ralph who was climbing out of the water. "Your turn Ralphie."

"Come on, Al, no."

That was the most Wesley had heard Ralph speak yet. He was a quiet boy, short and thin. He looked like a small frightened child the way he backed away from Al. There were almost tears in his eyes.

"I hate the water. Come on please no."

Wesley laughed. He was like Darren's skinny twin.

He watched Al pull Ralph back into the water and toss him down. Ralph jerked and squirmed and reached for something to grab onto as he sank. It was funny to watch, but Wesley felt bad for him and reached down to help him up. Back on the surface,

Ralph spat out a mouthful of water and coughed uncontrollably. Al walloped his hand on Ralph's back to help him spit the water up, but very little came out.

"Sorry, buddy."

One of the basketballs drifted near Wesley. He grabbed it, looked at all the guys who had been playing a few minutes ago, then asked, "Can one of you guys show me how to throw this thing?"

Bill grabbed it from his hands then demonstrated. "Like this, Wes, rest it on the tips of your right fingers like this. Left hand on the side. Just flick your wrist."

Bill took a shot for example. It hit the backboard and went in. A stranger grabbed it from under the hoop and tossed it back to Bill. Bill handed it to Wesley, then Wesley tried to shoot. It clanged off the front of the rim and splashed five feet away.

"It'll be easier on land," Bill said.

Wesley grabbed the ball again and took a shot from the left of the hoop. Backboard. Far right rim. Then down to the end of the swim hole by the concrete edge.

"You'll get the hang of it," Chester said, grabbed it, then waddled to the hoop for a dunk. "Must be what Kareem Abdul-Jabbar feels like."

Chester reached for the ball, then Darren of all people grabbed hold of him and dunked him under water. Chester resurfaced and splashed handfuls of water at Darren. Darren flinched, turned away, and flopped face-first into the water and squirmed. The boys laughed then Ralph helped him out.

Clouds ripped away from the sun and it was bright again. The water was heating up and the occasional breeze swung by. Somebody dunked Wesley again, then Wesley dunked Al, and there was another round of dunking everybody before a shootaround on the hoops. A few shots later, Wesley finally made one. It was probably one make out of fifteen tries, but at least he made it.

Time was flying by, and he went to the blob one last time before some of the counselors announced swim time was over.

46

The sun was sinking.

Tints of orange mixed with shades of red and tones of purple across the wide fading hues of rich blue sky over Camp Solgohachia. Everyone was leaving the swim hole. Cool breezes swept over them.

Wesley yawned and dried himself with his towel and went back to Panda.

Back in the cabin, the boys showered. There were three separate showers, and Wesley, Bill, and Darren were first since they had arrived at the cabin first today and therefore had dibs on first showers. The water was hot and relaxing, and Wesley didn't want to leave.

From the stall next to him: *"Ahhhhhh!"*

"Darren?" Wesley said.

Darren screamed. *"Give me back my clothes oh God my towel too! They took my towel too! Come on guys how will I get out of here?"*

Their bunkmates were laughing, and Wesley couldn't help but join in. Bill too. When Wesley was done, he dried off in the stall then dressed up, and leaving the shower, Darren was still screaming for his clothes.

"Come on guys," Wesley said. "Let's give him back his things."

Chester grabbed his can of shaving cream from the counter. "We're just getting started. Watch this."

"Take it easy on him."

Chester didn't listen. He crept up to the stall, put his hand over the railing, then sprayed shaving cream all over Darren.

"Oh my God." Darren screamed as if he were being stabbed.

"It's just shaving cream is all," Bill said. "Chill out, man. We'll get you your clothes now."

Al tossed the towel over the railing. "Here dude."

"Thank you," Darren said on the brink of tears. "My clothes? Where are my clothes?"

Chester rolled them up then tossed them into the shower like a basketball. *"Three-eee pointerrrr."*

"They're wet! They're all wet! How am I supposed to dress in these? You ever dress in wet clothes? They don't fit right!"

Wesley brushed his teeth, then laid down on his bunk and shut his eyes for a minute.

"Don't fall asleep," Bill said.

"Just shutting my eyes until we head out. Besides, it's kinda hard to sleep with Darren over there sniffling in the corner."

"I'm not crying."

It had been a tiring and fun day.

Wesley did almost sleep. He was on the brink of passing out when Al, Ralph, and Chester were all done showering then changing into new outfits.

Bill shook him. "Wake up. Bonfire time."

Darren was complaining again: *"These guys took my towel they threw my clothes into the water, what's next? They're gonna throw me into the bonfire?"*

"Oh quit it," Al said then whipped him with a towel. "Loosen up."

"Ouch."

The food that camp served at the bonfires was garbage. But the campers would eat it anyways. Doughboys, which was dough roasted over fire on a stick, without any sauce or cheese to dip it in, smores made of chemical bomb marshmallows and generic gram crackers with Hersey bars that are already half melted, and sometimes unsalted sunflower seeds.

Several small fires set around camp. Logs burned surrounded by even bigger logs used as seats. And now that it had gotten even darker outside while the boys had showered, the lights of the distant fires were the only things to guide them off the path from Panda and the other cabins down into camp.

"How do they expect us to see without lights?" Darren said. "I could fall here and twist my ankle! This is—this is insane! Do they think I have night vision? Oh this is dangerous! Very dangerous!"

"Do you ever shut the fuck up?" Chester said.

The boys went around the camp looking for an empty fire, and found one just off the basketball courts. There were boxes of smores ingredients, dough, green sticks, packs of unsalted seeds.

"Where's that chick of yours?" Al asked.

"I don't know," Wesley said. "I haven't seen her since earlier."

"Maybe Wes made her up," Bill said.

Wesley walked away from the groups. "I'll go find her."

Wesley found her by the basketball courts then took a few shots with her in darkness, barely able to see the rim, then they threw the ball into a bin and went to the bonfire.

"So you didn't make her up?" Bill said. "I thought Wes meeting a girl was too good to be true."

"Guys this is Wendy. Wendy, this is everybody."

"Nice to meet you all," she said.

Wendy and Wesley sat next to each other in the last open spots.

Under the dark sky devoid of any clouds, and scattered with stars many lightyears away, they passed around the sticks and marshmallows and dough. Wesley roasted a doughboy while everyone else went for marshmallows.

Flames flickered and shadows moved along Al's face as he suddenly said, "The murders weren't very far from camp. I'm gonna give it to you straight: he's still out there, The Raven Hill Butcher was never found. Raven Hill is jinxed."

"Yeah right," Wendy said.

"Some folks have claimed to see him in this very camp."

"None of that is true," Wendy said.

"Didn't you know why he killed them?"

Wendy leaned forward. "You mean those girls who died like… a million years ago? And the guy dressed up like Santa Claus?"

"Right. My older brother told me all about it. You know that boarded up cabin the counselors tell you to stay away from? There's a reason it's boarded up. It belonged to that guy who killed those girls, and legend has it if you go to the cabin, he'll find you."

"Then why isn't it demolished?" Wendy asked.

"Like that would stop him," Al said. "He'd come for the campers anyways."

Everyone went silent. Embers rose from the fire then fizzled out.

Al said, "If he catches you… it's not worth thinkin about. The Butcher… he's not human. Not anymore."

"You're—you're scaring me man," Darren said.

"Shut up, Darren," Bill said.

Darren stuffed his face with a smore.

"If you think those girls were random targets, think again," Al said. "You know why he killed them?"

"I'd be much more scared," Wendy said, "if I knew it was something *real*. Not boogeymen."

"My brother told me about a girl who died here when he was a camper. Do you wanna hear it?"

"Someone died here?" Ralph said.

"Does he only kill girls? Am I safe?" Darren said.

"No," Al said. "Nobody's safe."

"I wanna hear, Al," Chester said.

"Tell us," Bill said.

Al cleared his throat. "There was a girl one night who was dared to sneak out to the cabin, so she left after the counselor fell asleep. Now her bunkmates all watched her from the windows until she was out of sight. Then after a couple minutes they heard her screaming for help. It was so loud when it woke up their counselor, the girls all acted like they didn't know what was going on… and their counselor ran outside with a flashlight. You know what she found?"

Everybody was still.

"Her head. The rest of her body was never found. It's like what happened to the girl who went missing last year."

"Hey Wes," Bill said, "you ready for the thing?"

"Oh yeah."

"What thing?" Wendy said.

"We're going to the cabin, that one off in the woods somewhere," Wesley said. "Last one back gets butchered."

47

Things change in the dark.

The fires were put out and the group walked away. What were once prolific tree branches now seemed like twisted contorted arms ready to grab them.

"You guys know where the cabin is, right?" Al pointed deep towards the woods on the right. "Over there. Down past the flagpole, just off of the girls' cabins."

"Now Wesley," Bill said, "we gotta make this interesting. What's the winner get?"

"Nothing. It's just a competition. Who can get there first then back. Friendly race."

"Well good luck you two," Wendy said, "but I need to get back to my cabin. Uh, bye, Wes. And it was nice meeting you all."

"Bye, Wendy," Wesley said.

Wesley and Wendy looked at each other for a brief second before she left.

She went through the grass and over to the path that led to the girls' cabins. Soon she disappeared into the night.

"You didn't kiss her?" Al asked.

"What? We've just met."

Bill put his arm around Wesley. "Now don't blow this. This cabin thing might impress her."

"How would that impress her?"

"So she knows you're not a wimp."

"I tell you what, Wes," Al said, "if you don't make a move I think I will."

"I can't make a move this early."

"You see how close she sat next to you dude? She was practically on your lap. She was practically asking for it."

They came to cabin Panda.

Ralph opened the door and everybody flooded in, exhausted.

"Where's Vince?" Darren said.

Everyone ignored his question. They went for their bunks and collapsed.

"I'm exhausted." Wesley kicked off his shoes then threw them off his bunk. It was nice and cool in the cabin.

A bit later, Wesley grabbed onto one of the rafters and did a pullup. "Al, Ralph, Chester, you guys ever raced on these things? See who can get to that end and back like monkey bars?"

"That looks dangerous," Ralph said.

"It's harmless. If your arms start to give you can jump to a bunk."

"Jump? And what if I miss? And fall? Split my head open? And down by the door there're no beds."

"Geez, it's like having two Darrens."

"I'll race you," Al said. "We'll get you warmed up for your race with Bill tonight."

Al climbed the ladder to the top bunk across from Wesley's and grabbed the rafter. He found his balance, then said, "Whenever you're ready."

"Ready," Wesley said. *"Go."*

Wesley pulled himself across the bar, glanced at Al, and saw he was on pace with him.

"When you get to that end you have to smack the wall," Wesley said. "And winner gets Chester's mom."

Chester ran below the race and tried to jump at Wesley's feet but missed.

"Come on Chester we're racing here." Al said. "Knock it off."

Wesley was temporarily distracted and Al took the lead. He kicked into high gear, forgetting to breathe and using all his strength to get to the end as if his life depended on it, but he was too late. Al smacked the wall first.

Wesley focused on getting to the wall and didn't pay attention to what he was hearing behind him. It sounded like an argument was brewing.

Wesley smacked the wall then turned around. Chester was on the beam.

"Really Chester? During the beam race?"

"I'm gonna get you, you faggot."

Chester raced down the beam. His face turned red, he was out of breath—for a skinny guy, he wasn't very in shape—and Wesley laughed at him.

Chester came within three feet of Wesley and kicked. Wesley realized his arms were tired but he was still near the door and there was no bed to jump to, just hardwood floors.

"Move it," Wesley said.

Chester kicked Wesley again so Wesley kicked back.

"Fight! Fight! Fight!" everyone else in the cabin chanted.

Wesley wound his legs back, jumped forward a couple inches, then went for the gut. His foot landed in Chester's stomach. Chester lost his grip momentarily around the beam then regained it. Then he climbed forward as close as he could get to Wesley and tried to hit him with his elbow, then kneed him.

At the same time, the door opened and Vince came in confused at the chanting.

"What's with all the yelling and the—" Vince looked up. "Why are you two fighting?"

Wesley said, "Well—"

"I don't wanna hear it. Get down from there immediately."

Chester climbed backwards to the nearby bunk, got off first, then Wesley.

"Now shake hands and apologize. Come on guys, that's a rule. No fighting, and if you do fight, we apologize."

Wesley and Chester sat on the edge of the bunk and shook hands.

"Sorry," Wesley said.

"I'm sorry too."

"Great," Vince said. "I hope that's the end of all our fighting in cabin Panda. I've got zero tolerance for it. Let's all focus on having a great time here. Now it's time for lights out."

48

Hypnotizing coldness slipped through the rusty hinges of the door and through hidden cracks in the structure of the cabin and twisted through Wesley's flesh like wire.

"Wes? You up? Guys?" Bill whispered from the bunk below and startled him.

Wesley turned over. "Yeah. Anyone else up?"

Wesley climbed down from his bunk. He stood frozen between bunks momentarily, double checking Vince was asleep, then Wesley made his way to the door and looked outside. Something strange about the darkness tonight, he thought.

The others crept over careful not to make noise, careful not to wake Vince, but the floorboards were creaky and they made loud noises.

Thankfully, Vince did not wake up.

The boys all looked out of the windows together, then Wesley went back towards the bunks.

"Chickening out?" Bill whispered.

"Good! Let's not do this! No good can come of this!" Darren said.

"Shut up before you wake Vince," Chester whispered.

Wesley came back with his flashlight. "You got one too?"

Bill nodded, went to his bag, and pulled out a flashlight.

Al turned the knob slowly. The hinges squealed as he pulled it open a few inches. Al then stopped, turning back to Vince. Vince turned in bed but did not wake up. Al turned his attention back to the door and opened it wider; everybody piled out, then he gently closed it behind them.

"Let's go over the rules," Al said.

"Yeah we should," Bill said. "First one there and back wins. No tripping, hitting, or any other interference."

“How’ll we know who actually got there first?” Ralph asked.

“I don’t like this one bit,” Darren said. “You’ll die out there! You’re crazy for this! The Butcher will get you!”

Al rolled his eyes. “Listen, Darren, it’s all made up.”

“How about a splinter of wood?” Wesley said. “To prove we actually got there first.”

“Sounds fair,” Bill said. “And if we aren’t back in ten minutes then come looking for us.”

“Just don’t let Butch getcha guys,” Chester said. “I hear he’s dying to add new heads to his collection.”

Al walked from the door down to the gravel path spanning next to the cabins. “Wes, Bill, come on down here. Get ready, on the count of three…”

Wesley and Bill went down in front of Al, stood in running position, and looked straight ahead. The boys wished each other luck.

“One… *three.*”

The boys were off.

Wesley took the lead with a sudden burst of speed, barefoot feet pounding against grass and soft earth as they went off the gravel path. The night smelled like bark and pine needles. Wind blew hard and knocked his hair into his eyes. Wesley brushed his hair away and looked at Bill on his left, who was catching up to him and about to pass him. All at once, Wesley’s legs felt stiff. The ground was getting hard and it was hurting to run.

The boys raced across open grass to the center of Camp Solgohachia. Wesley and Bill passed the flagpole at the same time. Wesley was losing speed and Bill was ahead of him by only a step or two or three.

His lungs burned for gasps of air. He breathed through his nose as hard as he could and kept pushing. He desperately wanted to win to impress Wendy. His heart pounded so hard he felt it in his throat. Wesley moved his heavy legs with all the strength in his body, feeling chilly air beating against him. All the day’s activities had worn him out. He wondered if Bill was as exhausted as he was.

Bill’s heavy breathing came from behind Wesley. A smile came across Wesley’s face. He was in the lead.

His feet pulsed. *Why had we done this barefoot?* Wesley wondered. They were about to enter the woods.

There was a long stretch of grass before the forest, but soon they'd be stepping over twigs and rocks. Wesley prepared himself for the pain of the hidden forest floor and for the intensity of the run back. And the flashlight wouldn't do him much good. He couldn't figure out what was on the ground in the brief seconds they were illuminated while he ran furiously.

He and Bill weaved past remains of fires from earlier, and the ground was littered with green sticks and remnants of doughboys and smores and sunflower seeds that were in the process of being devoured by ants and flies.

As they came into the woods, Wesley took the lead. The race was neck and neck. Back and forth. It would be a tight one.

Fifteen feet into the woods, the boys came upon the cabin.

Jagged and faulty, as if constructed by blind men. Splintery planks were sprawled across the windows and doors with rusty nails, nails that seemed they'd turn to dust if touched. It was nothing more than a ghostly silhouette. It shuddered in the wind, creaking in the night, home to clusters of spiders. Dust lay over the cabin like a layer of dirty snow. Nasty weeds twisted up from the ground and worked their way upon the sides of the cabin as if attracted like magnets.

Wesley and Bill looked at each other. The boys had come to a halt.

"Woah." Wesley whispered, then ran the final five feet to its front door.

"Dang it." Bill bolted after him.

Wesley fastened his hands around a loose section of wood at the very end—a splinter that was almost falling off around the nail, as if it had been crafted and waiting there for Wesley Lawrence to come and pick it off.

He ripped it free. "Bill?"

"Yeah?"

"Do you want to go inside?"

"What the hell for?"

"We came all the way here. Least we could do is check it out. It's our final year. Did we really come all this way just for a splinter?"

"Fuck it. Let's go."

As opposed to the windows, the door wasn't boarded up with planks of wood. Wesley pushed it open and stepped inside; immediately he was met with the fetid stench of decay. Any sense of death that he felt outside the cabin was amplified now that he and Bill were inside of its walls.

Then their flashlights fell upon the blood.

"What the fuck."

"Wes what happened here?"

No corpses, only blood. Blood and torn walls, broken objects. There were shoeprints too in the blood—shoeprints up and down the stairway, shoeprints in every direction across the cabin. Not just shoeprints but a *foot*print too and *handprints.* Somebody had been on their hands and knees in the blood but not to clean it. What the fuck happened here? Was somebody tortured? Were the stories true?

"We gotta get out of here," Bill said.

Wesley ignored him as he followed the tracks to where they were heaviest and most frequent, coming in and out of the cabin hallway. The blood lessened the further he went, but a trail of it came to the cellar door. It was locked.

"What do you think we'd find down there?"

"Wes don't do it. This can't end well."

"I wanna see what's there. What if there's a body down there? It looks like somebody was hacked to pieces in here."

"What if it's the killer trapped down there?"

"Who says anyone's trapped in the cellar? We gotta take a look. This could be huge, dude. This could really impress..." Wesley reached down.

"What, this could really impress Wendy? Is that what this is all about? If you die she'll be really *impressed, trust me."*

Wesley undid the lock. It opened with a loud metallic clank. "You coming with?"

"No I am not coming with y—"

Just then there was a thud in the basement. Both boys exchanged a nervous glance. Fright was so thick in the room it was tangible. Both of them ran at the same time out of the room and through the cabin and screamed all the way through the front door where they crashed into a solid mass of flesh. The boys fell down and screamed at the top of their lungs. Vince could probably hear them all the way back at Panda.

But after a second the boys realized it was their friends. Al, Darren, Ralph, and Chester.

“Fellas, what’s the matter with you?” Al said. “What, did you go in there for a romantic getaway?”

“Fuck off,” Wesley said.

“Was there… was there ghosts?” Darren backed away from the doorway. “It’s The Raven Hill Butcher isn’t it!”

“I want to go home,” Ralph cried.

Chester was the only one laughing. “What a couple of pansies. What spooked you so bad anyhow?”

Then a shape emerged from the darkness. Somebody in the distance coming closer. Wesley prepared his excuse for whichever counselor it was—probably camp director Charlie himself—that was here, but it wasn’t any of them. It was Wendy.

“Are you guys okay?” She said. “I heard screaming.”

“Wendy?” Wesley said. “What are you doing here?”

Wendy came closer before answering. “I couldn’t sleep and I remembered your little race thing. I was coming by to see if I missed it but then I heard screaming. Did something happen?”

“You guys won’t believe us. You have to see this. But… but…” Wesley didn’t know how to finish it. “Come on, just look, but don’t touch anything.”

49

THINGS *DO* ESPECIALLY CHANGE in the dark—more so than any of the kids knew.

When the noises above her vanished she crawled out of the cellar weak and hungry. She watched them leave.

Wesley walked Wendy back to her cabin. He didn't know if he should kiss her or not based on what his friends had said, so he played it safe and didn't kiss her at all. She hugged him goodnight and sneaked back into her cabin.

The boys approached the cabin, surprised that only Wendy and nobody else had come towards the screaming. But maybe nobody else heard. Maybe.

Wesley yawned. "You think we woke up Vince?"

"No," Bill said. "He would have woken up the whole camp by now looking for us. He's a hardass."

Al opened the squeaking door slowly. Inside, the boys found Vince snoring very loudly. The floor creaked under their footsteps, but they found their ways back into their beds without waking Vince. He must've been a heavy sleeper, and Wesley thought about inventing a game where they could see who could make the most noise without waking him up. He thought how funny it would be to light a firecracker and see Vince waking up from the sounds thinking they were gunshots.

Wesley curled the covers over himself, yawned, then shut his eyes. He kept the wood from the abandoned cabin on the windowsill next to his bunk.

Wesley couldn't sleep yet. He just wasn't tired anymore after all the screaming and the sudden boost of adrenaline. He laid there thinking, replaying the fun day of camp in his mind. He was actually glad he came to camp.

Somewhere along the replay, dreamless sleep found him.

50

SHE WAS WEAK AND tired, and vengeance was still on her mind. She had to kill the boys who had done this to her and her master. Were they among the group that was just here? She still had the scent of the other boys, but this scent was new.

First there were a few things she had to do.

Her master's body was still upstairs. She dragged him down and dragged him out behind the cabin. Using the same shovel she had desperately used to pile dirt on top of the flames in the cellar, she dug him a grave.

Next she put logs of wood together and started a fire. She ate chocolate bars that the master had kept in his bedroom. After not eating since her imprisonment a few days ago—or perhaps she had been there longer, it was impossible to keep track of time in her situation—it hurt to have food in her stomach.

She cried desperately by the fire for her master.

She made a wish about wanting him back. Said wished for him back and she'd give anything to have him back. If anybody were listening, wouldn't they grant her wish? She would give them anything she had to have him back.

And then that was when the flames grew higher and then ebbed back down, and night chills washed over her, and something was awakened. Somebody was with her. Somebody in the night. He crept from the dense expanse of cavernous woods and joined her at the fire.

A black goat in a white robe.

He kissed her.

He would grant her wish.

The ground of the woods trembled. Leaves drifted from the dirt over her master's shallow grave as if trying to run away. Chilling winds drilled past the grass and sank into the dirt. The crescent moon shone its light down on the resting place.

One filthy black hand broke the surface of the earth and clawed. It dug its other hand free and dredged away handfuls of dirt until its decaying head was pulled through. It dragged itself out of its tomb, coming up from one black abyss to another.

He stepped forward. It was more a wobble than a walk. He'd have to get used to walking again now that he had been reborn.

It was hard to smile, but his sore muscles found a way.

The girl. He remembered her. He loved her. They had spent so much time together. She hugged him and he hugged her back and kissed her forehead. Reunited at last. Reunited at last. And she was hurt. She was in pain. Somebody had tortured her. He'd fix her. Then he'd get his revenge for her.

51

Activities between battling camp teams were underway.

Apache, Navajo, Cherokee, and Shawnee, depending on which colors wristband you pulled from a bucket. But as for Wesley and most of the boys in Panda, they didn't care about any of the competitions and went about doing their own thing.

Wesley, Bill, and Al sneaked into the mess hall's kitchen when no one was around and raised the trash for empty glass bottles. They brought them out back into the open stretch of grass behind the mess hall and set them up for a competition.

"You two better wise up," Al said. "Here's how the government works. First they break your legs, right? Then they sell you a wheelchair at like hundred times the actual cost. Next they're gonna tax you on that same wheelchair, they're gonna regulate your use of that wheelchair, and then they have the balls to tell you that without the government you wouldn't be getting around."

"Well I never thought of it that way…" Bill said.

"There's only one solution, and this is what I'm gonna do. One day I'm gonna get out of all this. I'm gonna become sovereign. I'm gonna have my own farm and live off the grid. Grow my own plants, raise my own chickens and cows. I suggest you both do the same. Learn a skill that you could barter with, too."

"You sound like my dad," Wesley said. "He always says if you took all the frauds out of politics there'd be nothing left."

Darren huffed as he walked with the girl he met through camp. She was a pretty girl out of his league and he couldn't believe she had come along with him, but he had to use Wesley and Bill's story to impress her.

"Tell me again about how you found the cabin."

"Yeah so like was saying, I beat my friend Bill here in a race last night, and with so much time to spare, might I add, so I—" Darren caught his breath, trying to continue speaking without struggling. "I went inside and there it was. All a mess."

"Were you like, scared about a psycho killer or anything?"

"What? No, uh—no—of course not—I—I could take 'em."

She laughed and touched his arm. "You're so funny."

Keep it up, he thought, then said, "Are you sure you still want to see this? It's brutal."

"Sure."

They arrived at the cabin. It was just as hideous in daytime as it was at night.

He held the door open for her and she stepped in ahead of him. Some light seeped in through the boarded windows and revealed the horrific details, so he didn't need to use his flashlight that was in his back pocket.

She looked around with wonder more than terror. "Woah. So cool. Who do you think died here? Did you see a body?"

"Do you remember that story about the girl who went missing last year?"

"Oh, Karina? *Her?* Do you really think... I mean, I dunno, I heard all these rumors that she had run off with her secret boyfriend and was living a double life in another state or something. Oh, how romantic that must be!"

"Uh, right, romantic. Sure. Uh... who else could it be?"

"I don't know... you know somebody in my cabin was saying how there were some suitcases full of clothes that somebody forgot under one of the beds. Maybe somebody else went missing last week. Could that be it? Oh I wonder where the body is."

He was chilled at the thought of a dead body still being in this house. "Maybe it's, uh, buried out back."

"Do you wanna dig for it?"

"Uh—not, uh, not really. Um..."

"Let's check the place out first. I wonder what's upstairs. It looks like they either dragged that body up or down. I swear something crazy must have happened here. Is the camp covering it up? Why would they do that?"

"I don't think they're covering anything—"

"Somebody told me camp director Charlie was a cannibal. I wonder if it's true. Is this his mess or something? He probably lures the kids here to—"

"I've heard enough."

"Awe, are you scared, Darren? You're so cute when you're scared."

"Cute? Uh, cute? Uh—yes, yes I am very scared. Very, very scared."

She took him by the hand. "Let's go up, Darren. I want to see what's hiding up here."

"Uh, sure."

She pointed to the room at the end of the hallway. "I wonder what's in there?"

The door was partly open, and as Daren stared at the small opening he didn't notice what had happened to the girl that was accompanying him. As he passed her she made a strange noise and her tracks stopped dead.

Then he saw the horror.

The lanky old man looked as if he had crawled out of a grave. Flesh was missing in places. His skin drooped. His eyes were void of life. There was no soul behind them. He cocked his head to the side as the girl squirmed under his blade that penetrated her throat.

He pulled his knife out of her in one swift motion and she collapsed into a puddle of her own blood. Or at least that's what Darren assumed happened, because he was running away from her and his mind was filling in the blanks. And he didn't dare turn around when he heard the footsteps of the man behind him, but he didn't have time to process that much either because the world was pulled out from under him as if the stairway had collapsed. The man's kick to Darren's back sent him hurdling down the steps. Darren flung his arms to grab the railings or to stop the fall but it was all effortless, there was nothing to grab a hold of, and his head cracked open against the edge of the bottom step.

Vince, cabin Panda's counselor, had seen Darren and a girl sneak off into the woods so he followed them. He waited outside to confront them but neither had returned in a few minutes so he decided to go inside and catch them.

"All right you kids, I know what you're up to in there." He put his hand on the door and a knife impaled his hand.

He was too shocked to scream.

The knife retracted and he held his hand up to his face. Then the door opened and a man was there. Completely mutilated, his skin was greenish-gray and his black lips were curled into a wicked smile.

Vince ran for the woods to get away from him but the man was fast and moved in huge steps. He grabbed Vince's throat in both hands and pressed so tightly that Vince's squeals could not escape. The man dragged Vince into the woods, dragging him further and further until the cabin was just a memory.

The figure pushed Vince into a tree and held him with one hand by the throat. Vince tried to scream but it was locked inside of him as he looked into the eyes of a madman.

The attacker lifted his blade, and in that moment Vince remembered all the stories about The Raven Hill Butcher, but he couldn't reminisce about them for long.

The Raven Hill Butcher brought the knife halfway through Vince's skull and watched him squirm and writhe. Vince's eyes twitched, pleaded, begged. They fluttered shut then creaked open again, and his body convulsed. The Butcher removed the blade—Vince wiggled like a torn worm—then sank it into Vince's pelvis and dragged it downward.

Blood leaked out of the counselor. The Butcher used him as practice. He raised the blade up above his head and slammed it into Vince's shoulder. His arm came off in one clean swoop. If anybody found Vince, he would be unrecognizable and split into chunks scattered throughout the camp woods.

52

LATER, IN THE CABIN before dinner:

"Bill, you seen Darren?"

"No. And it isn't like him to miss lunch. And now he's cutting it close to dinnertime."

"Last I saw him he was with some girl. I didn't catch her name."

"Darren and a chick?"

"Yeah. Unbelievable, isn't it?"

"Yeah, tell me about it. How's Darren find a chick already and not me?"

"Put to shame by Darren. How's it feel, Bill?"

"Just fine. There's plenty of chicks awaiting me back home, Wes. Did you finally get Wendy's number?"

"No I haven't had the chance today. She's actually participating in the activities so I haven't seen her much."

"Wes? Let me ask you something."

"Yeah man?"

"What do you think was up with that cabin?"

Wesley took a moment to think about it. "I don't really know. I guess it could have had something to do with the missing camper from last year."

"Do you think we should tell somebody about it?"

"I don't know. I mean if they did that whole big search for her then they must have looked there, right?"

"I think I wanna tell someone."

"You heard what the camp director said though, anyone who goes there has to clean the latrine and gets their privileges taken away."

"Yeah I guess you're right. Maybe it's best we say nothing at all."

53

In the mess hall Chester was scarfing down Bean Surprise when he got a wink from the girl he met earlier that day as she was walking out. He dropped his spoon and told Al and Ralph that he'd be back later. They got the idea when they looked through the window and saw him chasing after her.

"I thought you lost interest," she said.

"Are you kidding me? I've been thinking about you since we met."

"Thinking about me or thinking about getting me into bed?"

"Both. But mostly the second one."

"God, finally. I was starting to think I'd have to beg."

"I know a place where we can be alone and nobody will find us."

"Good, because I was about to throw you onto a table and fuck you in front of the whole mess hall."

Don't ruin this don't ruin this don't ruin this, he was thinking. He had always found ways to ruin these kinds of things in record speed.

They stopped by Panda to grab a blanket. "The guys will be back soon. Lucky for us I know a cabin that's completely vacant."

"Oh yeah? Which one?"

"It's on the other side."

"You mean the girls' side? All the girl cabins are taken too."

"No, no. Behind them."

"Behind them?"

"You know, the forbidden cabin."

"Oh, that? You're taking me *there?"*

"Yeah. Me and my friends went there last night on a dare."

"Really?"

"Yeah. I had a—a race with my friend Al to see who could get there first. I beat him by a whole two minutes. He's not as tough or in shape as he thinks he is."

"So what was it like?"

"It was cool and all, a little gross like you'd think. But it's full of empty rooms and we could lay this blanket down anywhere."

She didn't say anything. She was staring off into space while he was talking.

"Babe? *Babe?"*

"Oh, sorry—yeah?"

"I was just saying.... What were you thinking about?"

"Oh," she said. "Just the violent overthrow of the government."

Finally they were at the cabin.

Chester let her in. "Ignore the blood."

"Oh God, what is all this? Did politicians sacrifice some children to Moloch for their adrenochrome or something in here?"

"Adreno... *what?"*

"You don't know how deep the rabbit hole goes, do you, Chester?"

"No but I'd like to find out tonight."

"Hurry up and lay that blanket down, all right?"

He laid it down and kicked off his shoes, pulled her down onto it and kissed her. He slid his shirt off. Then abruptly they both paused when they heard a loud creak of the floorboards above them. Immediately the sound went dead. It was very brief, perhaps it was the cabin shifting and settling on its own as old buildings tended to do when they were as rickety or decrepit as this one was.

"There's nobody else here, right?"

"No, just us. I'm pretty sure."

"Pretty sure, or you *are* sure? Maybe your friend that lost the race had the bright idea to bring somebody else here too. Why don't you go up and check for me? It would make me more comfortable."

"Okay..." Chester abandoned her and went to the stairs. On his way up he called, *"Al? That you up there, Al? Al I'm coming up, if you're naked you better say so. I don't wanna see your penis again, you sicko."*

Upstairs there was a lot more blood. Under the hints of moonlight that came through a distant window it almost looked fresh.

Chester pushed one of the doors open and there was the carcass of a girl that was half-eaten. Another girl, naked except for her Christmas hat, with long hair was hunched over the body with a chunk of the corpse's flesh in her hands and blood dripping down her mouth. Suddenly Chester was dizzy, and thought he'd collapse under sudden shock as he tiptoed backwards, his mouth open fully so that he could scream a warning to his date, but nothing escaped his lips.

Then the strange girl ran on all fours, and Chester bolted. He jumped off the final four steps of the stairway and then he found that his date was gone. All that remained on the blanket was her severed head staring up at him.

He opened the door but a man was in his way. A tall man that took up the whole frame and wore a Santa Claus coat. There was a misshapen darkness in his eyes, and his skin was torn in places where Chester saw maggots squirming within. He held a knife that dripped blood—his date's blood. The man stepped forward and Chester stepped backwards.

Then the monstrous girl was at his side and tackled him to the hardwood floor. Chester tried to fight her but she was so strong, and he was weak and unprepared and defenseless, and her claws were raised high and sank into him over and over and over...

54

Wesley and Bill and Wendy joined Al and Ralph in the mess hall.

"Yeah," Al said, "Chester ran off with some girl. I don't know her name."

"Funny," Wesley said, "because Darren went off with some girl too, and now we can't find him. Look I can't even get Darren to skip out on a snack, you should have seen him on the bus ride over here, all he did was eat and eat. But to miss two meals… I don't know about this, you guys. Something's up."

Ralph spoke up, which was a rare occasion. He said, "Chester told me something."

Everybody watched him, ready for what he had to say, but he was silent.

"Yeah?" Al said. "What did he say?"

"He said he wanted to impress her… so he was gonna…"

"Yeah? He was gonna what?"

"He was gonna tell her he went to the cabin last night. And that he won the race."

"Why would he take a girl there?" Wendy said. "All that blood—I would be freaked. I'd have run screaming if a boy tried to get me alone in there."

"Well the girl was kind of a weirdo."

"Maybe he didn't take her there," Wesley said. "Maybe he just took her back to the cabin, I walked in on my bunkmate one year who brought a girl back. You guys saw him walk off, I don't think there's anything wrong there. But Darren? Where is he? He didn't tell me anything. How about you, Bill?"

"No he didn't tell me nothing either."

"Is it The Butcher? Is he coming for us because we disturbed his—"

"No." Al hit him upside the head. "It wasn't no Butcher, that story is made up. The corporations controlling everything and the government wanting you dead, that's real. The Butcher isn't."

"Are you a flat earther or something?" Wendy said.

"No." Al shook his head. "The earth isn't flat or round. It's fucked."

There were some late-night activities going on, but the guys from Panda were ditching. They were heading up to the cabin to plan what they were gonna do.

"Let's see," Wesley said, "I've got my slingshot, water guns, I think Bill you brought the fireworks with, right?"

"Bottle rockets, a whole lot of 'em."

Al lit a cigarette. "Anyone want one?"

Wesley and Bill each took one and thanked him.

Back in the cabin Ralph downed a Coke and gave Bill the empty glass bottle. "For your bottle rockets."

"Thanks dude."

"You know," Al said, "I ain't seen Vince around either."

"Maybe the three of 'em snuck off together."

"No, I think something might be going on here..."

Bill put one of the bottle rockets in the Coke glass and touched his lighter's flame to the wick. It *WHIZZZZED!* across the room and hit Ralph in the back. Ralph dove onto the floor crying.

"Get up you big baby." Al grabbed him by the hand. "You aren't dying."

"That hurt."

"Welcome to camp. This isn't your first time here, Ralph."

"I've been hit with towels before but I've never been shot."

"Hurry up fellas," Bill said. "We can have a lot of fun with this tonight."

"And to think I was the one that gave you the bottle."

55

Wesley opened the cabin door to leave. Wendy was running up the pathway shouting for him. He ran and met her partway to the cabin while the others stood in the doorway and watched.

"What's going on?"

"Wesley—Wesley something bad is happening. There were screams coming from the woods, from the cabin. It sounded like somebody was being killed."

They went to see it. The boys and Wendy went to the other side of camp and crept between the trees. There was a fire behind the forbidden cabin. Small, but just big enough that the glimmer of light and the occasional wave of smoke were visible.

"Stay here," Wesley whispered toward her as he broke away from her touch.

Ralph and Bill stayed in place but Al followed behind Wesley.

Around back there was a man and a girl at a firepit, and meat was roasting over it. The man was tall and leaned forward with his hands warming against the radiation of the flames that Wesley felt even from the distance and behind a bush. Even from the little glimpses Wesley was taking, the man looked like a monster, something that had been constructed in hell. And the girl was not any normal either. She was a beast herself. A savage. She was naked, and her long hair covered her. Her body was furred. She was vicious—Wesley could see it in her eyes. And she was torn and cut along her face and arms. She had been through hell.

And behind the man and the girl were the spikes. On each a severed head: Darren's. Chester's. Two girls, the ones that the boys had brought here. And Vince's.

Then the man looked their way.

Wesley and Al were already out of sight but they ducked regardless and hoped to stay unseen.

After what felt like an hour passed, Wesley peeked up. The man and the girl were gone. Perhaps back inside the cabin.

"Let's go." It was hard to make the words form under the terror he was feeling.

They pulled camp director Charlie aside from the ongoing activities. Wesley did all the talking.

"Four campers and a counselor are dead. We just saw them at the forbidden cabin."

"Nice try, kids. Somebody always pulls this prank every year."

"We aren't kidding! They're all dead! We saw them! They were being eaten alive!"

"Why don't you go join the activities? There's nothing to be worried about."

It was clear that no adults were going to listen no matter what they said, so the kids held a meeting in Panda. The plan was to leave tonight around two in the morning so they could be sure they wouldn't be caught. The activities ended around eleven-thirty. That gave them enough time to get ready and sneak out of camp completely undetected.

56

Wendy showed up at Panda right on time. She didn't have a single bag with her besides her purse, and said it would've been impossible to pack two suitcases with all those other girls around.

Wesley led her and his bunkmates through the dark tangled woods. Every shadow became The Raven Hill Butcher. Every shadow was his arm, every shadow was his knife, and every shadow threatened to pull them into their death and demise.

"Is—is it far?" Ralph said.

"No, not very far," Wesley said. "We'll be there soon. Me, Bill, and Darren found this path a few summers ago."

From the right came footsteps. the group stopped. Through the night, they all looked at each other, eyes darting, wondering who the stranger with them was. The distant person was silent for a while—frozen—then the footsteps started up again. It was coming from the direction they intended to travel.

"Who—who's there?"

"Shush." Wendy whispered.

The noises stopped again.

"Must've been an animal," Al said.

"I hope you're right," Wesley said.

The group moved past low branches and swatted mosquitos. Night thickened. Night consumed them. The darkness was claustrophobic.

"Now through here," Wesley said lower than a whisper, "towards the right we'll find a path. A clearing. We—"

Ralph tripped on something, bumped into Wesley's back, and both boys crashed into a tree. Pain raced up Wesley's body. He was so angry at Ralph he could've smacked him.

"Sorry," Ralph said after catching his breath. "I slipped on something."

Wendy lent Wesley a hand. "You okay?"

"Yeah, thank you."

Al and Bill offered hands to Ralph but he didn't take them. He was staring at something between his feet.

"Ralph?" Al said. "Come on dammit let's go."

Wesley shined his light on Ralph's body then lowered it between his legs and to his feet to reveal the severed foot of a man being picked at by bugs. Veins hung over the sides and the jagged edges of bone tore through a layer of flesh.

Wesley moved the light away quickly. Ralph screamed at the top of his lungs, so Al put his hands around his mouth to mask it.

"Shut up."

"Oh God," Wendy said. "Whose foot could that be?"

Suddenly it was no longer footsteps from the distance to their right, but full-fledged running. Someone was rushing to get them.

The group scrambled away from the sound. Wesley didn't know what waited on the other side of these woods. Everybody had gone their own direction, completely avoiding whoever was running at them from their intended destination.

Wesley was all alone and pressed his body against a tree. Down below him he heard footsteps. People running and hiding in every direction.

He peeked around the tree to see a figure ten or twelve feet below him towering over Ralph. Ralph cried, threw his hands over his face, staggered backwards, then the figure—The Raven Hill Butcher, the man that was at the cabin earlier with the strange girl—put his hands around Ralph and raised him into the air. He knocked Ralph back and forth and Ralph screamed as loud as thunder. The Raven Hill Butcher raised Ralph and slammed his neck into a six-inch thick tree branch. Ralph's head split off his body.

Wesley couldn't control his own screams and dropped his flashlight in shock. He reached to pick it up then changed his mind. The Butcher was after him.

Wesley Ran.

Al shrieked somewhere far away. He screamed when he found Ralph. Wesley could hear it even over the crunching leaves below his feet and the killer's.

It took him a while to realize the killer's footsteps had stopped. Wesley flinched when he turned around to see darkness. He wondered if the killer was hidden in pure darkness, becoming one with it, and was ready to grab him and decapitate him too. He wondered if The Butcher could move through shadows, teleporting from one shadow to the next, and was going to come up from the ground and slash his legs open.

Footsteps suddenly came from behind Wesley. He turned around, ready to fight somehow.

But it wasn't The Butcher. It was Wendy.

"We're gonna die," she whispered then hugged him, her face full of tears. "I don't wanna die."

He hugged her back and ran a hand through her hair. "No, no, we are not dying. Come on. We need to find Bill and Al. We need to get out of here."

"He's gonna kill us."

"Shush. No he's not. Come on, Wendy."

He held her hand and they cautiously tiptoed back the way he was originally running from, the way that they were originally meant to go. He took deep breaths, bravely leading her, and looked furtively for the others or for The Butcher.

They hid behind a tree, looked in every direction, then paced to another one.

Al's cries started again, and with the cries came footsteps.

The Raven Hill Butcher came forward down the slope and raised his knife, then cocked his head to the side.

Wesley and Wendy held each other, looking down at him slithering closer to Al. Wesley wanted to yell, but that'd be a dead giveaway. He prayed Bill was safe somewhere, maybe he had made it back to the road, maybe he was running and running and going to make it home.

Again he felt the urge to yell. He didn't know what they could do, but they had to do something, didn't they?

"Let's run," Wendy whispered. "Let's go—ohmigod."

Wesley was fixated on Al and The Butcher. The Butcher came within five feet of Al, and Wesley finally screamed, *"Al watch out."*

Wesley was ready to run with Wendy but couldn't leave without Bill—it might've been too late for Al, but Bill was his best friend, he couldn't leave him alone in the forest to die. Maybe Bill had made it to the road already and wasn't still here, but Wesley needed to know for sure.

Al faced The Raven Hill Butcher. *"I'm gonna kill you."*

Then Al raised his knife and charged, aiming for the throat, and came within inches of it; The Butcher grabbed him at the wrist and twisted it around all the way backwards; Wesley heard it snap through Al's screams of pain. With his other hand, he tried to punch The Butcher—tried to do something, anything—then The Butcher brought his blade up from his side and severed Al's other hand.

The Butcher grabbed Al by the hair, then split his head open on a tree. Brains oozed from the crack. Blood gushed like a fountain.

Immediately, he turned straight around to face Wesley and Wendy. The pair looked at each other and screamed. Hand in hand they ran, and The Raven Hill Butcher chased. He moved with an elegance, with a knowledge of where every branch and root in the woods was. Where everything in the woods was. And when Wesley and Wendy ran, they had to dodge many crooked branches and winding roots and it slowed them down. Wesley glanced over his shoulder...

...The Butcher was near.

Wendy was tired and slowing them down, their hands were slipping away from each other.

She was two feet behind Wesley, and he tried to pull her forward when The Raven Hill Butcher grabbed her first. He yanked on her hair and pulled her body into his arms. He set his dirty blade to her throat and she wailed uncontrollably.

The first incision was small, and as he started to pull it across her squirming body, he collapsed.

Bill grabbed onto the killer's torso, brough him to the ground clutching Al's knife—Wesley couldn't imagine prying that from a dead man's hands—and buried it in The Butcher's neck. The Butcher let go of Wendy and reached for Bill.

"Go." Bill screamed. *"Go now."*

"We can't leave you."

Wendy pulled on Wesley, trying to pull him with her into the woods.

"Go."

Wesley listened to Bill. He ran away with Wendy.

They ran to the road and never stopped, even when they heard his footsteps behind them.

From the road, they ran for miles to the bus stop, and even when they arrived back to their homes...

...they still heard him running behind them.

57

Everything was going well for Dean following his return home from Camp Solgohachia. After a while he didn't look over his shoulder so often in fear of the feral girl, and after a week he stopped having nightmares about the groundskeeper.

Tonight after his shower his bedroom phone rang.

"Hello?"

"Hey Dean it's me."

"Hey gorgeous. Did you want me to sneak over tonight?"

"No. I don't know. Maybe. Last time we almost got caught, and I'm still anxious about it."

"Well my parents are out of town tonight. You should come over."

"Hmmm…"

She was over in record speed. He let her in and they made a frozen pizza, then they cuddled together on the couch watching a movie. *The Last Picture Show* was on TV.

"This is so boring Dean. How could you watch this?"

"No shit it's boring, it's in black and white. There's never been a good movie in black and white. Do you see anything better on?"

"Your parents don't get the dirty channel, do they?"

"I wish I were that lucky."

"Let's just forget about the movie." She leaned in for a kiss then pulled away. "What was that noise? I thought you said no one else was home?"

"What noise? I didn't hear any noise."

"I swear I heard somebody."

"It's just you and me."

"Dean, someone's upstairs."

"I was up there all day, nobody's in my house with us."

She crossed her arms. "Well, I would feel a whole lot better about it if you just looked."

"Are you kidding me?"

"Check it out or I'm leaving. I'm not gonna stay in here to be hacked to pieces."

"God the way you're acting it's like we were watching a horror movie instead of some dumb Texas drama about God-knows-what."

"Go check."

"I'm going. I'm going."

She came off the couch and stood at the bottom of the stairs watching him ascend.

"Hello? Is there anybody up here? Is somebody hiding in my house? My date is terrified because she thought she heard somebody. Anyone up here? Anybody? Anybody? Anybody at all? Hello? Hellllloooooo?"

He walked upstairs and checked his room and the bathroom. Nobody was there.

"The things I do to get laid..." Dean opened the hallway closet, and the feral girl was awaiting him. *"You—"*

She thrust her clawed hand forward and ripped straight through his chest, pulling out his heart from the other side. It beat in her hand as she removed her arm from his torso, and he fell over dead.

It tasted delicious.

"Dean, what's taking so long? What was that noise? Are you pranking me or something? Is somebody up there with you? Is David up there?"

Dean's date went up the stairs, but he wasn't there on the second floor.

Then her bare feet stepped in the circle of blood and she gasped. A series of screams left her lips as she hurried to run away. She lost balance and slipped because the bottoms of her feet were doused in scarlet, and she tripped down the stairs. Her neck snapped on the descent.

The feral girl looked at the body from the top of the steps while her master stood over it on the main floor.

She crawled down and took a big bite out of the girl.

58

RUSSEL LIVED IN CONSTANT fear that he would be caught for what he had done to the groundskeeper and his pet creature. On nights when he couldn't sleep he worked out at his family's home gym. He was bench pressing when the door creaked open.

He screamed as he set down the weight then turned around in defense but it was just his dad.

"I was only checking on you, buddy."

"You scared the hell out of me."

"I'm heading to bed. Goodnight."

"Night Pop."

When his father left he didn't shut the door. Russel was too lazy to go shut it himself, and he would be done in a few minutes anyways. He went back to lifting, the radio humming in the corner of the room playing Frankie Valli.

He didn't notice the new set of footsteps until it was too late, and the face of the resurrected groundskeeper was looking down on him holding a ten-pound weight in his hands. The impact shattered Russel's nose but that was the least of the pain. What hurt worse was dropping the barbell so that it crushed his throat.

The girl wandered into the room on all fours. She was covered in blood.

"Did you take care of the others?"

She nodded.

"Then there's just one more boy we need to see."

WINTER GRAVES

1

SHE WANTED TO KILL them all that night, and she had tried.

She hunted them through the dark woods and had punished two of them. But they fought back. And in the end they set fire to her and left her for dead and fled Camp Solgohachia.

But she had not died.

She sat at her master's grave and cried for him. She would have given anything to have him back. She thought it, and tried to speak it, over and over until the thing came out of the woods and joined her at the fire. A black goat in a white robe. It kissed her. It granted her wish.

The ground trembled. Her master's hand broke through the dirt and clawed upward.

Together, they searched for the boys who had been at the cabin that night. Most of them were not hard to find.

The last one was David Morrison.

And when they found him it would be a massacre…

2

THE HOUSES OF THE gated community were all of a time and style: colonial giants with copper spires that had long since turned green. Although the house was beautiful it was a tad decrepit with windows covered in dust, with Christmas lights hanging over them. Red and green bulbs fought against piling snow. The house was different: it almost had a glow.

Snow fell lightly at first then unpleasantly fast across Raven Hill.

David Morrison didn't expect to be spending his winter break here at the mansion with his sister and her friends, but his girlfriend broke up with him so all his plans were canceled. He tossed the key for the room he booked at the Asylum Resort on the mantelshelf.

When his sister Christy heard him come in she met him at the door. "What are you doing back?"

"She broke up with me."

"What?"

"Yeah. After I booked the room. After I drove all the way there to see her. Can you believe that?"

"Did she say why?"

"Who even knows. Girls change their minds every ten minutes. That's basically how every breakup works."

"Oh that's the dumbest breakup theory I've ever heard."

A little while later when Christy looked out the window she saw her friends were parking. She opened the front door and zipped up her coat as cold air drenched her. She hurried to her friends to help them with their things.

"Hey how was the trip?"

Aviana was the first one to run up to her and hug her. *"You should have heard all the screaming and bitching going on. Longest hour and a half of my fucking life. Thank God I'm out of that car before someone got murdered in there."*

Christy, Aviana, Bekah, Mary, Katie, and Julia brought everything in in two trips.

The big warm living room had Christy's friends in awe. Narrow slanting windows, dark browning carpet, a big television mounted to the wall above the fireplace, and ships in bottles and tiny statues across all the mantle shelves and tables and drawers. Beautiful paintings lined the walls. Some family portraits, some pictures of the sea and some of the desert. The walls were made of smooth stone. In the corner was a record player and two shelves of records. The living room led to three long halls.

"This place looks even bigger than the picture you showed us," Julia said. She wiped snow off her suitcase. "You won't have a problem fitting us all. We could each probably get two rooms."

David came into the living room from the hall next to the fireplace. "And there's always space in mine."

Julia gagged.

Christy rolled her eyes. "Don't be a creep, Dave. Ladies this is my brother."

David thumbed through the records on the shelf. "Anything in particular you ladies want to listen to?"

Nobody answered him, but he put on Elvis's Christmas album.

"Come on," Christy led her friends, "I'll show you to your rooms."

David pointed his thumb toward the hall he had come from. “I’m down that way if any of you need me.”

“Your house is so gorgeous,” Katie said. “Like I can’t believe how pretty it is.”

“Thanks,” Christy said, then noticed Julia, ahead of them, straightening out a picture frame and wiping off a little dust with a napkin from her pocket. “Are you cleaning up?”

Julia smiled. “You don’t know how much a crooked frame irritates me. I almost stayed behind to straighten up your whole living room.”

Christy opened a door to a bedroom. One of the rooms she’d already cleaned for her guests. This room was plain: bunkbeds with white sheets under a window, a dresser with a mirror, and a nightstand.

“There are more rooms upstairs, and one down in the basement. It’s not as nice, but you get your own bathroom—”

“I’ll take the downstairs room,” Mary said.

“Oh, of course you will,” Julia said.

“Julia, you take like an hour in there. I’m not dealing with that all weekend.”

“So who wants this room? It’s the same floor as mine.”

“I’ll take this one,” Aviana said, stepping inside. Then: “Wait, which one’s further from your brother?”

“Well he’s on this same floor.

“Never mind, I’m going upstairs.”

“Yeah, me too,” Katie said. “He gives me the creeps.”

“I’ll just stay here,” Julia said. She was straightening out the already made bed.

Bekah shrugged. “I guess I will too.”

The girls went down the spiraling stairs to the basement. The steps screamed loudly.

"Christy, I wanted to tell you something," Aviana said.

"Hmmm?"

"You remember that guy I told you about?"

"Which one?"

"Ben."

"Oh, right."

"He finally asked me out."

"Oh no," Katie said. "Not another one."

"Shut up, Katie."

"I'm serious. You cycle through them so fast I can't keep track."

The basement was big, but most of its space was taken up by junk, old dusty boxes and containers, old dressers, and anything else that her family stuffed into it over the past hundred years. Spiderwebs grew over everything, even rusty tools thrown into a corner. A hallway, also filled with junk, gave way to a dark cramped room at the very end with no doors, which was the laundry room.

"Good thing Jules is upstairs," Christy said. "She'd lose her mind down here. She'd probably spend the whole weekend cleaning."

Christy opened the door nearest the laundry room. It would be Mary's room.

"What do you think?"

Mary set her bags down just inside the door.

"It's nice."

Christy pointed to her right. "The bathroom's over there."

Mary laid down on the bed then sighed and closed her eyes. "This trip was only an hour, but can you believe how exhausted I am? I'm gonna nap, let's hope I don't get lost on the way back up."

As they ascended the twisting staircase, Christy said, "Such a workout, isn't it? Getting around in this place."

"It's brutal," Katie said.

"Well it's much needed," Aviana said. "I've been eating like shit all year."

They passed through the main floor then up another flight of stairs to the second floor.

"Being up here probably won't keep you away from David for too long. He'd walk through a bed of flames if he saw ass on the other end."

Katie looked out the window over the back yard, a blanket of untouched snow. "This view is gorgeous. I could watch snow fall all day."

Aviana came across the room to peek out the window but tripped over her duffle bag.

"Ouch. Where did that thing come from?"

"If you had your glasses on you'd have seen."

"Oh shut up."

Christy walked away, and all down the hall she could hear them going back and forth about glasses and car crashes.

A few minutes later, in the kitchen, when Christy looked through the cabinets, she noticed the door to the back yard was gaping open. She was chilled and went to the sliding door and saw that the back yard was now disturbed. A trail of footprints wandered into the house and tracked melting snow around the kitchen to the dining room.

"Huh?"

She shut the door and locked it.

3

THE FERAL GIRL AND her master spent a year and a half tracking down David.

And now they had finally found him.

He was in the mansion.

Her master crept in from the back door. And she herself climbed in through one of the windows. They met on the upper floor and lurked in the empty halls, devising their plan. They could have easily attacked while David was asleep. She and her master could have attacked all of the guests while they were sleeping. But it wouldn't be done that way because David and the others deserved to die in the same horrific way that her master had been killed, and in the same fashion that she had been tormented.

Prolonged. Slow. Pain beyond that which anybody had known before.

It would be a massacre.

4

CHRISTY WENT TO HER room and left the door cracked open. The curtains, bedspread, blankets, and pillow cases were black, her favorite color. Posters of her favorite movies were taped to the walls. She had done that six or seven years ago when she thought it was cool, now it was ugly because the posters had torn and curled and some were yellowed. Next to her door was a bookshelf of romance novels. On one of her massive dressers, she kept a single flower in a pot.

She found the ping pong balls then went downstairs.

The feral girl watched from a crack in the floor. A girl was in the living room setting up red cups on a ping pong table. She went to the contraption in the corner of the room and put a black disk on top of it. From within came soft music.

Soft footsteps in the hallway downstairs. Her master had been careless. She recognized his steps from all the way up here.

"Hello?" The girl said, dropping one of the balls. It rolled under the table and she reached to pick it back up. "Bekah? Julia? That you?"

CREEEAAAK!

"Girls?"

"Hey," David said from the other hallway. "You need any help setting up?"

"Not now, I'm almost done."

Mary woke up and had to pee.

She didn't remember which way Christy had said—if she even did say—where the bathroom was, so she tried the first door on the left of the laundry area. And to her surprise she picked the correct door.

A couple minutes later when she returned to the bedroom she noticed a set of thin icy tracks leading into her room then leaving. It wasn't all melted yet. It was fresh. Somebody had been in there with her while she had been asleep…

Maybe Christy came back to check on me.

Mary changed into a pink tank top. It was nice and toasty in the Morrison basement, and she tossed her sweater into the corner of the room. She was dripping with sweat. She stretched and yawned then she noticed the boxes in the corner of the room.

She was curious.

She opened the boxes and the contents were endless antiquarian books of varying conditions. Some were fallen apart. Others were untouched, as if they had been pulled out of time. Mary turned through the pages, but most of the books were not in English, or in any known language. Many of them contained illustrations only, or illustrations accompanied by archaic languages that had been lost to time and might have been impossible to decipher. The images within them depicted strange regions, irregular beasts, and sometimes torture.

But one book in particular caught her eye.

Its worn leather was contorted into the shape of a human face.

"Woah. It's the—"

CREEEEEEAK!

Somebody descending the stairs.

Quickly she put the book away and returned to her bed.

It was Christy. She knocked on the already open door and stepped in. Her face was bright red, like an apple in June. She moved hair out of her eyes.

"I was just about to wake you. How'd you sleep?"

"Better than I thought I would. Usually I don't sleep well far from home."

"Well I'm getting beer pong set up."

"Hey, did you come down here earlier to check on me?"

"No... why?"

"Someone did. There's snow on my floor, see? The floor's all wet."

"Maybe one of the others came by."

"Oh, Christy, before I forget, I made you something. An early Christmas gift, since I won't be seeing you again until next semester starts."

"Thank you, Mary," Christy said. "You didn't have to do that."

The girls went back into the room, and Mary grabbed her purse. "Now close your eyes."

Christy shut them and smiled.

"Hands."

Christy did so.

Mary put the gift in her hands. "Open your eyes."

Christy examined the baby blue clay cactus in her hands. "Adorable."

"It's a ring holder, but if you don't wear rings you can just put it on your dresser or something."

"I love it." Christy hugged her. "Thank you."

As Christy and Mary passed through the kitchen, Christy looked outside once more. Snow was coming down in handfuls with no sign of stopping. In fact, now it was well over a foot of snow that had accumulated, and she wondered how high it would go before it stopped.

"Do you ever remember it snowing so much?"

"Can't say I do," Mary said. "And I pray Aviana doesn't drive us in snow this bad, she'll kill us all."

The tracks that had previously been there were gone. A little chill crept up her back.

She had a bad feeling about something. But she couldn't be sure just what.

5

Bekah, Julia, and Mary were in the living room while Christy went off to get Aviana and Katie.

"Could you imagine living in a place like this?" Julia said.

Mary sat down next to Bekah and said, "Does anyone here know how to use a record player?"

"Are you serious?" Julia said. "You just drop the needle."

"Let's put something on."

Julia looked through the boxes. They were mostly jazz until she found *Christmas Hits!* and put it on the turntable, then lowered the needle to the edge of the vinyl.

A moment of static, then music blared through.

Julia winced. "Way too much crackling. These records need to be cleaned."

Christy came back with Aviana and Katie and David, who was carrying two cases of forty-eight beers.

"Let's get this started." David opened one then poured it into a cup.

He watched them.

He pressed his eye to the hole in the floor and looked at the kids in the living room and tightened his grip on the jagged blade set in aging wood. Excitement filled him. It would be fun—and soon. A wide smile crept across his face. It had been such a long time, maybe he would be rusty, but it would come back to him.

"Is this like, where you grew up, Christy?" the girl with blonde shoulder-length hair said.

"No, Jules, but it's just been in my family forever. My uncle owns it and let me borrow it this weekend." Christy threw a ping pong ball on the table and it landed in a cup. She drank it in one chug.

Christy was beautiful. Long coppery hair parted in the middle, freckles splattered on her skin, brown eyes gleaming even from the tiny hole where he watched.

Another girl bounced a ping pong ball and it hit the rim of a cup then fell to the floor. "Ah, screw it," she said then drank anyways.

"Hey, no cheating," the only boy among them said.

"You'd make it if you had your glasses on."

"Fuck you and fuck the glasses."

The resurrected groundskeeper moved away from the hole in the floor then stood up.

It was almost time.

"Mary, don't be a buzzkill," Christy handed her a ping pong ball.

Mary grabbed it. "I don't know. Last time I tried it, it was..."

"Yeah, yeah, you hated it," Aviana said. "We get it."

"It's one drink," Katie said. "You'll live."

Mary rolled her eyes and gave in. She went to the end of the table and bounced it into a cup. She took one small sip, grimaced, then forced it down. "It tastes awful."

"It's an acquired taste," David said.

Mary kept a disgusted face after a second sip. "God, you guys are the worst."

"Look at her face," Katie said.

"By the ways," Julia said, "Christy, do you have a brush for your records? Do you hear all those crackles? They're not supposed to be doing that."

"A brush?"

"Forget it."

CREAK!

A hollow prolonged creak came from up above.

Christy looked at her friends to see if they heard it too.

"There's no one upstairs, is there?" Mary said.

"No, no, the house just does that sometimes. It's old."

"It's haunted," David said. "I'll tell you all about it tonight."

6

THE RECORD HAD ENDED long ago but nobody flipped it over to the B-side. *Rudolph the Red Nosed Reindeer* was on TV. Occasionally somebody still threw a ping pong ball into a cup, but for now most were content with grabbing a cold beer and cracking it open.

"We can break out the heavy stuff later," Christy said.

"Oh I don't feel so good," Mary said, clutching her stomach. "I think I'm gonna throw up."

"You barely drank anything."

"And it still hurts. I'm dizzy."

Julia grabbed a can out of the box, leaned over the back of the couch to Mary's shoulder, and cracked it open. "We all had at least one whole can, you need one too."

Mary inched back. "Knock it off, I already had one."

Julia opened it and held it out to Mary, who pushed it away. Julia drank it herself.

"I'm hungry," Christy said. "I'm gonna throw a frozen pizza in the oven."

"Hey David," Julia said, "is it really haunted?"

"Well, I guess I could tell you about it. It happened a long time ago."

Surprisingly, the girls were eager to hear what David had to say, and they all turned to him.

"Now I don't want to scare you girls," he said, "but I'll have to be honest about The Raven Hill Butcher. They never caught him."

"That guy from what?" Mary asked. "Like, the nineteen-forties? If he's even still out there he's ancient."

"Well the truth is that The Butcher isn't human."

"You sound fucking retarded," Bekah said.

"Let me start at the beginning, then it'll make sense. The first family to live in this place, back before it belonged to our family, was murdered. Those rooms they died in are bad luck, that's why my family never uses them and left them for all of you."

Nobody said anything.

"There was one kid who didn't die. Somehow he survived his injuries and he became The Butcher."

A draft passed through the kitchen. Christy felt a cool breeze cutting through the hot air.

She turned into a hall and went upstairs, a little chilled, and found the thermostat. Somehow it was lowered from seventy-five to forty-two.

Hollow footfalls came from down the hall. She turned her head.

The footsteps ended, and for a moment, maybe less, she was terrified. But... *This house is old, it just makes noises sometimes.*

Christy twisted it back to seventy-five, then went to her bedroom for a sweater. It was red and green with reindeer lifting Santa's sleigh through the air in the dead of night, surrounded by dozens of snowflakes.

CREEEEEAK!

Christy turned her attention abruptly to the door. Chills crawled under her skin. There was somebody out there. She was sure of it.

In the hall, she looked right then left then right again. Christy was all alone in the hall. For all she knew, she was the only person in the entire house. She looked over her shoulder every few steps in the hallway.

Christy looked through one of the windows. It was the most snow she had ever seen. At three or four feet tall it was a barricade. A blockade sealing them into the house. And it was only growing bigger. She wondered what her guests would do if it were ten feet tall, which it would certainly hit at this pace, when it came time to leave after the weekend was over. But it was only Friday and it was not time to think about leaving yet.

7

Three pizzas nearly devoured.

"Should I cook a third pizza?" Christy said.

"Ugh, this is all gonna go straight to my thighs. Do not let me eat so much, do not let me have more if you make a third," Julia said. She wiped crumbs from the table onto a napkin and tossed it in the trash.

"Don't worry about it," David said. "I can help you work it off."

"Yuck. I wouldn't touch you with a thirty-nine-and-a-half-foot-pole."

"Even if my heart grows three sizes?"

"Sorry," Christy said. "If I knew my brother would be this weird I wouldn't have let him stay this weekend."

David left awkwardly. "Geez."

"He reminds me of this guy I was seeing last year," Aviana said. "I stopped taking his calls, then he keeps calling. Then at school I'd always catch him looking at me. It was so gross."

Christy opened one of the cabinets to see what else she could find. A big red and green tin of Christmas cookies.

Bekah went to the liquor cabinet and found whisky. "Do you have orange juice?"

"Leave it to Bekah to have the most basic taste," Julia said.

"Snob," Aviana said. "Orange juice and whisky is totally fine by me."

"Keep that stuff away from me, I'm still recovering from the beer."

Christy found the orange juice in the fridge as well as lemonade. "All right ladies, everyone has to have at least one shot. That includes you too, Mary."

"Kill me. Just kill me now. If any of you have a shotgun in your purse please use it on me right now."

"Uh, a shotgun?" Christy said then extended her arms. "A shotgun is like this big. Don't you mean a pistol or a Glock?"

"Whatever. I just don't want any whisky."

"Too bad."

"You guys are worse than the government forcing fluoride in our water and letting GMOs go unlabeled."

"Here we go..." Aviana said.

"Don't get her started," Bekah said.

Everyone was taking shots, laughing, having a good time. Mary hung back from the table not wanting to get anywhere near the liquor.

Christy downed a shot of tequila. "I won't lie to you girls. Sometimes the things Mary talks about makes sense. Especially after you've had a few drinks. Uh, Mary, what were you telling me about the other day? The... FDA or something's in bed with something? I don't remember what you said."

"The FDA's in bed with Big Pharma to—oh you guys are just going to make fun of me."

"No, no," Bekah said, "we want to hear it."

"All I'm gonna say is be careful when shopping and read all the labels closely and make sure you know what ingredients are in what you eat. GMOs are linked to *at least* twenty-two different diseases. But it's 'FDA' approved, yeah right. They want to make you sick so they can profit. They make you sick then sell you the 'cure' except the 'cure' is really a prescription that'll keep you alive but won't help you feel any better."

"God you're getting all jittery. Have a little tequila to calm you down."

"Christy... I don't want to..."

"Pretty please. For me. Please."

"Ah to hell with it. Give it here."

Mary downed it then slammed her glass on the table. *"PEOPLE DON'T KNOW THEY'RE BEING POISONED AND BRAINWASHED AND ENSLAVED BECAUSE THEY'RE BEING POISONED BRAINWASHED AND ENSLAVED! PEOPLE DON'T KNOW THEY'RE BEING POISONED AND BRAINWASHED AND ENSLAVED BECAUSE THEY'RE BEING POISONED BRAINWASHED AND ENSLAVED!"*

8

David dreamt he was at the cabin again, except this time he was the one bound to the chair, and Russel and Dean were cutting him up. His hands were bound by coarse rope to the armrests, and his old friends—who had been tracked down and killed now—were cutting off his fingers joint by joint, tossing them to the feral girl in the corner of the room who devoured them.

Then the groundskeeper came down the stairs holding a machete. He brought it down on David's wrists and blood squirted out in thick streams endlessly. His new wounds pulsed as though razors were being continuously shoved deeper and deeper into his open flesh.

Russel and Dean laughed at him. They patted the groundskeeper on the back.

"Can I borrow that?" Russel snatched the machete then slashed it in front of David's face less than an inch from making contact. "Haha, look at this faggot squirm."

"I want to try." Dean took it from Russel, but when Dean waved it in front of David's face it made contact with his skin and drew blood. It left a scar reminiscent of the one that David had given to the feral girl.

David wanted to scream. His lips wouldn't part.

The groundskeeper took his weapon back then jammed it into Russel's throat. Russel's eyes widened then shut, and he collapsed in front of David. Dean was running up the stairs but the groundskeeper was faster than he was and grabbed Dean by the foot and pulled him down. Dean screamed and begged but the groundskeeper didn't care. He raised his knife and brought it down, severing Dean's head in half. His exposed brain pulsed and leaked blood.

The groundskeeper returned to David. David tried to shut his eyes so he wouldn't have to see the details of the pale droopy skin or the mold and fungus that grew within the man's skin.

David squirmed against his restraints, but without hands anymore there wasn't a chance at breaking free from this imprisonment. Certainly it meant death. This was it—this was the end. Soon he'd be with Russel and Dean…

The feral girl growled from somewhere behind him. The groundskeeper nodded then kneeled and plunged the knife into David's ankles. Both feet were severed in about thirty seconds, and he held them up so David could see.

Then he used the knife to cut the ropes. He set the knife on the ground, nodded, then went up the cellar steps.

David flung himself out of the seat. The knife was the one way he could fight her, and he had no hands. He tried to will them back into existence but his stubs—that were still overflowing with sharp pain—brushed against the handle unable to grasp it. And against faint lanternlight, he saw the feral girl creeping closer.

She smiled.

Finally David's lips parted and a scream escaped.

He forced his stubs to carry his crippled body to the stairway, and with great desperation he ascended about halfway up, but all the feral girl had to do was casually climb up and she had him. Her teeth clamped into his calf and she pulled him down.

She was hungry.

9

IT WAS GETTING LATE, darkness was seeping into the Morrison mansion, and snow was tumbling down outside the window. The girls were gathered in the living room watching *It's a Wonderful Life.* Each girl was curled under heavy covers because coldness couldn't stop emanating from the three-foot obstruction of ice and sneaking through cracks in the house's structure.

"Christy?" Mary whispered, trying not to talk over the movie.

"Uh-huh?"

"Were people really, um, killed in this house?"

"What? Of course not. Is that what David was telling you earlier?"

"Yeah."

"Listen, it was just a thing our dad made up to scare him. Nobody was killed here."

"Yeah," Julia said, "but The Butcher was real. Some girls did die in this town. And their murders were never solved. What do you think happened?"

"I'm sure it was the government. They're behind everything. You know back during Prohibition, the US government purposely poisoned alcohol and killed over ten thousand Americans. There has never been any reason to trust the government. Never ever."

"I think you've had one too many drinks."

Bekah turned down the volume on the TV. "Those girls that died were killed by some sicko. They probably caught him or he died decades ago."

"If they caught him we'd have known about it," Mary said. "But whoever killed those women might still be out there. Doesn't it scare you?"

"It's hocus pocus. For all we know eight different girls had eight different killers. I don't know. I'm not gonna live my life looking over my shoulder because some psycho might be out there. They always get caught those types of people. You know how hard it is to get away with one murder, let alone eight of them?"

"Some of us just want to watch the damn movie," Aviana said, "not talk about axe murderers."

"No it wasn't an axe, it was—"

"I don't care what it was, Bekah."

"It's terrifying," Mary said. "How could you not be scared?"

"Because it's been so long that it's practically a fairytale. What, are you really scared of the 'Raven Hill Butcher?' What kind of stupid name is that anyways?"

"Eight women were killed. It's terrifying."

"Mary, what are you, like five years old?"

"Come on," Katie said, "there's no reason to be unkind. So what if she's scared?"

Bekah shrugged. "I dunno, it's funny how dumb she is."

"Really Bekah? Are you trying to make yourself feel better by bullying me?"

"I was *not* bullying you, you stupid—oh my gosh, why did we even invite you? I don't know why you're even here. God, nobody can say two words to you without you flipping out."

"Coming from the person who's only alive because she dodged a coat hanger in her mother's uterus? Your mom should've kept the afterbirth and thrown *you* away instead. Why don't you go kill yourself Bekah?"

Bekah ran out of the room without saying another word.

"Bekah." Christy stood up from the couch and yelled after her, but Bekah didn't stop. Then to Mary she said, "Come on, you didn't have to say any of that."

"Excuse me? Christy did you even hear what she said to me?"

"I'll go check on her," Julia said.

"I think I'm getting tired." Katie walked out of the room. "I'm going to bed. Goodnight."

"Same here." Aviana left with her.

"Seriously?" Christy said. "But we haven't even finished this movie or…"

Christy and Mary were the only ones left in the living room. Christy watched her friends go down the hall and disappear. Somehow, less than a minute had passed when she heard their footsteps on the second floor… shouldn't they have been on the staircase still?

It's a Wonderful Life finished thirty minutes later. After the credits rolled, they both stood up and stretched and yawned and looked at the window. Chills crawled up their spines.

"Woah." Mary traced her hand on the window.

Mary said goodnight to Christy then double checked that she was going the right way to get to the stairs.

In a distant part of her mind, she thought, *Such a storm, might it be Krampus? I wonder which of us is the naughty child he came to punish. Maybe it's me. Maybe it's all of us.*

She imagined the horns from Krampus's goat head emerging from the endless crypt of darkness and jamming into her abdomen. She imagined him waiting for her in her bedroom across the basement, hooves covered in melting snow, shedding fur on her blankets, red sack for him to stuff her in.

Quit it. There is no Krampus.

But you've been very bad, you all have. And he's gonna punish you.

It was so dark in the basement that she crossed her fingers and hoped she didn't stub a toe or knock into anything as she made her way to that soft, gentle light barely emerging from that one inch space beneath the bedroom door.

When she was inside the bedroom, Mary opened her suitcase, then stripped to her bra and underwear. As she took off one sock, she paused.

CREEEAAAK!

Somebody was coming down the steps.

Two people, actually. Two sets of heavy footsteps.

She waited for whoever it was to come near, not realizing that the crests of her nails had dug nervously into her skin. The two people came across the basement quickly.

"Christy?"

It was Julia and Katie.

“Hey ladies.”

“Are you okay?” Julia said.

“Yeah I am. Sorry I ruined the night.”

“Oh you didn’t ruin it.”

“And Bekah deserved it,” Katie said. “God you really let her have it. I thought she was gonna punch you.”

Mary laughed a little, and her nervousness slowly went away. “I was just tired of how she was treating me. I hope this blows over. I don’t want to be the reason nobody has any more fun this weekend.”

“Hey so what were you saying earlier? That you had found something down here?”

“Oh yeah. You guys will *not* believe this. Let me show you.”

10

THE BOOK WAS GLOWING red. The girls were mesmerized by it—bewitched by it. Mary opened the book and flipped through the pages. Unspeakable illustrations, images, and texts in ancient languages filled the insides.

Katie grabbed it from her hands. "Is this the Kinonomicon?"

"It's *Necronomicon,"* Julia said.

"I want to read from it."

"Don't do that Katie, you'll doom us all."

"Wait," Mary said, "you could read those archaic languages? Since when?"

Katie held up the book open to a certain section. "This part's in English."

"Oh, okay. What's it say?"

"I'm telling you don't read it."

"It says..."

The words were spoken, and evil was awoken.

On the roof of the house were the decorations of reindeer attached to the front of a big red sleigh with Santa smiling and waving to the town of Raven Hill down below. Snow still fell in clumps but then the lightning struck Santa Claus and he was alive. He lowered his hand and flexed it. Below the costume he was flesh and blood. He felt the terrible coldness and shivered against it.

Then his reindeer turned around to face him, shaking the snow off their fur. They blinked, moving forward, learning how to construct movements. Santa wobbled, understanding walking for the first time himself, then met them ahead of the sleigh. He petted their heads.

"Ho, ho, ho. We're alive."

The reindeer licked him.

"You two stay here. I'll be right back."

There was a window on the gabled side of the roof. Santa grabbed hold of the Christmas lights and lowered himself in. The room was empty, or so he thought. As he passed through a man emerged from the darkened corner. A man wearing filthy clothes that didn't properly fit the weather. Jeans and grimy white shirt.

And there was something else wrong with him too. His eyes were empty. His skin drooped and sagged and bugs were squirming within. Under the pale moonlight he saw that the man's skin was discolored.

"Excuse me, sir," Santa Claus said, "where am I?"

The man plunged his knife into Santa's stomach. Globs of red blood poured out of him. Santa staggered backwards, learning this brand-new feeling. *Pain.* An awful sharpness that vibrated through his open wound and raced through the other parts of his body. He felt as though he were going to explode, and he didn't know what could take this suffering away.

Santa parted his lips to speak but blood leaked out of the corners of his mouth. Words couldn't form.

The stranger grabbed Santa's hat off his head and put it on his own, then he pushed Santa to the floor. Santa tried to stand up again but he was soaked in blood and couldn't find his grip, couldn't stand, could only fall. Then the man's foot pressed against his side and kept him down.

He took Santa's jacket and put it on himself.

Santa raised one desperate hand then it fell back down. He was defeated.

The man crept off into the house…

"See? Nothing happened. I don't know why you flipped out. All I did was read this evil text, and tried to read some parts in Latin."

"This won't go well," Julia said. "It never does."

"If you thought the government was bad," Mary said, "just wait until you see what this book can do. It's a hundred times worse. I don't think I'm gonna get any sleep tonight. It's like when I found out the government weaponized Lyme Disease. Or like when I found out aluminum causes Alzheimer's, anemia, Parkinson's, and kidney dysfunction."

"Oh that's all just made up to scare you."

"Julia you can't tell me that with all the evidence we have now that you honestly believe the gov—"

"I don't want to hear this tonight. I'm too sober to get into it. Maybe if we had a gallon vodka in this room, maybe."

"Should I read some more passages?"

Mary ripped it from her hands. "No. You've doomed us enough for one night."

"Why do you get to hold onto the Kinonomicon? Huh?"

"Necronomicon."

"Whatever."

The feral girl thought that the scent of blood belonged to her master, but when she entered the room they used as basecamp, she found the mutilated body of another man. She sniffed him then stepped over him and to the window, where the sounds of otherworldly creatures was entering from.

She stuck her head out the window. A bucketful of snow hit her in the face. She wiped it off then saw the hind leg of an animal near the edge. It was off balance then found its footing. The feral girl climbed through the window and held onto the dangling Christmas lights, using them to scale up to the roof.

Two reindeer were on the roof each eating dead birds whose blood stained the pure white snow in vicious splatters. She crept on all fours to them, joining them, licking up the bloody snow.

Mary was left alone in the basement room. She was reading the Necronomicon when she heard heavy footsteps again and thought that her friends had come back, but there was something different about these steps.

She ran across the room and hid the book, then returned to her bed, still only wearing her bra and underwear and still only wearing one pink sock.

Then the door opened. A man dressed in a Santa Claus costume that Mary figured must have been stored away in the attic for years came into the light of the room out of the basement darkness. His face was a strange drooping mask that looked lifelike. He held a foot-long candy cane which he then extended to her.

"Awe, David, thank you. You know, *I* don't think you're creepy like the others. And I like your costume. It's cute but a little dirty. Want me to help you clean it up?"

Silence.

The black mask over his face hid him completely except for sunken eyes.

"I know you're trying to scare me but it isn't gonna work."

No reply.

"Nothing to say, huh?" She turned the candy cane around in her hands then sucked on the end of it. "I love having sweets before bed. Want some?"

He shook his head.

"Why don't you take that costume off and come over here?"

He sat down, put his hands on her legs, then grabbed the cane and jammed it down her throat so far that she couldn't scream. Her fists beat weakly against his chest. Her eyes shut as she tried to process the pain and think of a way to fight back.

His hands clamped around her throat. She wished for air—any air at all, even if it was the frozen winds separated from her by the thin walls. The room spun. Her eyes twitched then closed, stuttered open, then fluttered closed. The last thing she saw was the long blade with a faded wooden handle. She mouthed words that did not reach the air, then she was gone.

11

THE HOUSE WAS CALM with stillness through the halls.

Wind beat against the windows and screamed over the rooftop that pointed against the sky full of dark clouds massed together. Cold set in past the fading heat.

In the bottom bunk, Julia turned her pillow over to the cool side and then turned onto her left. She was drifting away, when—

"Are you awake?" Bekah asked, looking down from the top bunk.

Julia's eyes creaked open. She looked up to see her with thin moonlight filtering through the window; Bekah brushed her curly brown hair from her eyes. "Yeah. You all right?"

"I can't sleep."

For a moment the girls were silent because there was the sound of footsteps in the hallway and they thought somebody was going to enter the room, but the person did not. Whoever it was went straight past their door, through the hall, and, as they imagined, up the stairs.

"Who else is up?" Bekah said.

"I don't know."

"I know I'm a bitch," Bekah said. "I know it. And honestly I *have* thought about killing myself before. I'm not saying that for sympathy. I just. I don't know. I think about it sometimes."

They talked about it for a few more minutes then Bekah rolled back over and said she was gonna try and sleep, thanks, Jules, for letting me get it off my chest.

Julia laid on her back and stared at the white bars supporting the mattress. The room was quiet except for Bekah's tiny snores.

Julia shut her eyes, tossed and turned, but she could not return to the very edge of sleep she had previously been climbing over when Bekah had started talking to her. She had been so close to falling over the edge, but now she was wide awake.

I wish I could sleep.

She tried to fall into the blackness behind her eyes, tried to dream, tried to tell herself what to dream. It never worked, but sometimes daydreaming knocked her right out. She was comfortable, very comfortable, but sleep was avoiding her.

"Bekah?"

No response.

Some weekend this is turning out to be. Day one has majorly sucked ass. There's gotta be something fun around here.

Julia sat up, slipped out of bed, and went to the door.

After one last glance to Bekah, she went back to her bottom bunk and fixed the covers. It would irritate her so much to know that there was an unmade bed. She fixed the covers, straightened out any wrinkles, then went back to the door.

Julia stepped into the pitch black hall. There was one single light on. The lights in the hallways were divided into sections, and there were multiple switches to light up one hallway. She thought she remembered them being all the way down at the other end, and instead went the opposite way to the living room. The living room was a mess, with all the cups and beer cans scattered, and some beer spilled out on the ping pong table and dripping onto the floor. She would have made too much noise if she cleaned up everything right now.

In the morning, she thought, *I'll help clean.*

She found switches on one of the walls, but didn't turn them on. She didn't know exactly where she wanted to go or what she expected to do. She still hadn't explored the place yet, still didn't know where everyone's rooms were at. Then, as she turned around, something crunched under her foot.

An empty chocolate bar wrapper. There was another one a few feet down too.

You know, it's not that hard to find a garbage can people. But what do I expect from people who can't even clean their vinyl?

Julia laid on her stomach on the couch. *Let's see if I can sleep here.*

Minutes ticked away; she was more awake here than in her bunk. She did all she could, moved into every different position she could find, daydreamed, cleared her mind, counted sheep, but nothing could bring her sleep. So she stood up and walked around, looking at the little statues of penguins, snow globes, ships in bottles, and other little trinkets and knickknacks. Then she went to the window and looked out at the world. The snow was calming down. Instead of fistfuls of snow falling, it was now a soft trickle. But the snow was about five feet high and untouched. The streets were not cleaned and it would be impossible to go through it. Their ride was completely covered.

I wonder when they'll clean the streets. Can they clean the streets when it's like this? I've never seen anything like this. I hope we aren't here that long.

But she had to admit that the unblemished sea of white was beautiful. It *was* a White Christmas, which she had hoped for. It hadn't snowed yet a week into December, and it only started to come down once she and the others left campus for the Morrison house, an idea that had been Christy's. And it had been a fun idea, but now being here she realized it wasn't so great.

Julia yawned; maybe sleep would come now. Maybe.

She turned away from the winter wonderland and stepped on another wrapper.

"Seriously?"

Then footsteps upstairs. Somebody else was up.

"Hello?" Julia said. Then: "You idiot, they can't hear you from here."

A breeze crept up her back. She thought she heard another step being taken directly above her, and wondered what Aviana or Katie was up to.

Through a hall she had not been through yet, the one next to the fireplace, she made a left past two beautiful paintings of the ocean. A door far down on her right was cracked open and there was dull light flowing water-like into the hallway. The hallway was different in the raven darkness, even with that small smudge of light shining at the end. In total darkness it seemed like something out of *Dracula.* It seemed like a hallway in a castle, and soon Dracula's coffin would open, and he'd creep into town at night to suck blood from unsuspecting people.

Listen to them, Julia thought, *the children of the night. What music they make!*

She came to the door slowly, peeked inside, and saw David laying on his bed, looking at the ceiling, listening to Christmas music coming through the radio. *I Saw Mommy Kissing Santa Claus.*

He turned to see her as she opened the door wide.

"Julia?"

"Unless I have a twin." Julia closed his door behind herself. "I couldn't sleep."

"Me either. I napped earlier and now I'm wide awake. And bored out of my mind."

"I've been wandering around the house." Julia sat next to him on his bed. "Have you seen the snow outside?"

"It's insane how hard it's coming down. Looks like you're stuck here with us."

"That might not be a bad thing."

"Why couldn't you sleep?"

"Oh who knows. Just one of those nights."

"So out of all the places to be, you visit me?"

"Yeah, well, you were the only one awake," she said.

David stood up, went to his dresser, and grabbed a candy bar out of a box. "Want one?"

"Were you the one who threw those wrappers on the floor?"

"Wasn't me."

"Well no thanks," she said. "Maybe if you tell me another one of your stories it'll put me to sleep."

He returned to his bed and sat next to her. "What, you want me to bore you?"

Her hands were interlocked under her chin. She sat cross legged on the bed, looking at David with her pretty blue eyes. David was red. He fidgeted with a loose thread on the covers.

Julia leaned back on her hands. "What did you ask Santa for Christmas this year?"

"Nothing until about a minute ago when I wished we were standing outside the house."

"Outside the house?"

"Yep."

"Standing in snow up to here?" Julia said, raising her arm up as high as it could go.

"Of course."

"What for?"

"Because there's a mistletoe out there."

Julia rolled her eyes.

"I should've hung one in here."

Julia pulled him in with both hands for a kiss. It lasted for half a minute then she let go of him. “There you go. We didn’t have to die in the snow for it. Merry Christmas.” Then she took her shirt off and he climbed on top of her.

12

"I'M GETTING A BEER from the fridge," David said, "do you want one?"

"Please. And don't take too long." Julia winked.

"I'll be right back."

David left his bedroom. The door closed on its own behind him.

Dude how did you get so lucky? David wondered, turning the corner of the hallway. *Don't even question it just go with it. This is the best thing to ever happen to you. Snowed in for the day and she's spending all her time with you instead of her friends. This will definitely speed things up—spending a holiday together accelerates a relationship, it's like the effect of twelve months condensed into one.*

In the kitchen, David looked out the tall sliding glass doors. The snow seemed to calm down now. It was no longer falling and the sun was out and blazing. He wondered how long it would take for the ungodly amount of snow to melt; how long it would take for the cleaners to come through and make the streets drivable again.

David whistled *Carol of the Bells* as he opened the fridge, looking inside for beers, pushed past the plate of leftover pizza, and grabbed two cold ones. When he shut the fridge, the furred hand jammed a fork through his nose.

David did not feel pain at first; first it was the sensation of pouring blood like a nosebleed. Then the fork went deeper. David opened his mouth to scream but only a gasp escaped from behind his lips. The scream was too deep and too big to find its way out.

David shot his hands to the counter for support. Tried to push himself away from the man, tried to tell his body to run, and feeling a damn painful searing pain going through his face and reaching his brain.

David then desperately reached his hand towards the knife set on the counter, taking his eyes momentarily off his nightmare who raised the long blade of her knife and brought it down on David's fingers before he could reach the knife set. As the scream finally began leaving David's throat, the feral girl brought the knife across David's neck and dragged it from end to end, silencing him for good.

His past had finally caught up with him.

Julia laid on David's bed smiling. It was going to be a great weekend after all.

What's taking him so long with those drinks?

Julia took her shirt off. She stood in front of his mirror and applied lipstick and made kissing faces.

The doorknob turned and the door opened an inch. Julia watched it, expecting David to open it and walk through, but he didn't. Nobody did. The door hinges squeaked loudly. There was someone standing behind the door, she could hear the floorboards screeching below his feet as he took a step back.

"David?"

The door creaked again.

"David, you there? Are you trying to scare me again? Oh I am *so* scared."

The door shifted on its hinges; it came back to almost close but the latch didn't catch. Julia listened to the heavy breathing.

"Oh no, Mr. Butcher, don't kill me." Julia laughed. "If only David were here to protect me from the evil maniac."

Everything was still.

"Okay you can come out now. I want my drink."

The door creaked open another inch. Julia hummed with the radio playing *Do They Know It's Christmas,* and went to the door. She was prepared for David to jump out and scare her—she was prepared for some terrible joke.

"You could do something creepier than this—" she began to say, but when Julia pushed the door open and looked down the hall in either direction, she did not see David or anybody. "Hello? Who's there?"

The door slammed shut on its own and Julia jumped back. She nearly had a heart attack. "Shit."

If David wasn't here, where could he be?

She walked down the hallway and headed for the kitchen.

Christy woke up and rubbed her eyes, adjusting to the darkness. She reached for her nightstand and pulled the string on her lamp, then she reached for her cup of water and pulled her hand away when she saw the cockroach. She jumped out of bed and patted down her body as if she had been covered in them, but there was not another one anywhere around her.

She was shaking. She despised bugs, especially roaches. She stepped back from it. She needed David to come and kill it. She would have to wake him up. But then she couldn't leave her room and let it disappear. Because if the bug had a chance to disappear in her room then she couldn't sleep in it because it could be *anywhere.* It had already been so close to her, and if she had moved her hand slightly differently she would have touched it… and that thought made her squirm again.

But the sudden screaming coming from somewhere deep inside the house shocked her. Somewhere below her somebody was screaming so intensely that it put her every thought and movement on hold. Somebody—and she couldn't tell which of her friends that it was—was screaming endlessly.

Christy moved carefully out of her room, keeping her eye on the bug for as long as she could, and trembled as she came to the stairway. The screaming did not stop, but rather it blended into cries. Then she heard stampeding footsteps coming from the other regions of the house. The scream had woken everybody else up.

Suddenly Christy was running, slamming one foot in front of the other.

A hush came over the house.

Her friends entered the kitchen first, she could hear them from the stairway. Whispers and cries. Christy stood motionless on the stairway, heart thumping loudly, sweat billowing down her cold skin, knees shaking and about to give out. She felt an obscure compulsion to scream. She prepared herself for whatever horrors might be lurking in the kitchen. She prayed it was a prank, but the deathly screams were too convincing for it to be anything other than reality.

She sprinted off the final steps into the kitchen.

Christy screamed, backed into the glass doors, then covered her eyes and wailed and sniveled. Only once did she peek through her fingers just to be certain she was seeing things correctly.

And she was.

David was sprawled on the kitchen floor in front of the refrigerator, blood mixing with exploded beer cans, and his hand chopped in half and resting on the countertop. His throat was torn open from end to end and—oh God, who put that fork in his face? It might've gone far enough inside of him to reach his brain.

Julia was at the other end of the room crying. Katie and Bekah and Aviana were stunned and sickened and came over to console Christy. Aviana put her arms around her and tried to hug her, but Christy hit her away.

"Don't touch me."

"Christy I'm—"

"Ohmigod ohmigod ohmigod."

"Christy—"

"Shut up shut up shut up!"

Aviana, Katie, and Bekah looked back at Julia.

"Where's… where's Mary?" Bekah asked.

"I think—I think Mary's lost her mind," Julia said.

"Ohmigod," Katie said, looking out the glass door. "I want to go home."

Christy screamed and cried. *"Mary I'm gonna kill you I'm gonna kill you you maniac!"*

"Oh God oh God oh God," Julia shrunk into her corner. "Oh God oh God."

Aviana went to the counter, breathing heavily, staying as far away from David and the severed hand as possible, and reached for the set of knives.

"Wuh-what are you doing?" Katie asked.

"That girl is insane. If she comes near me—"

Katie cried. *"This is not what I had in mind for winter break."*

Aviana handed her a knife. "Just. Fucking. Take it."

Katie did. Then Aviana handed one to Bekah and grabbed another for Julia and another for Christy.

Katie took Julia by the hand and helped her up. Aviana came back to Christy, who was watching them with sunken watery eyes, and hugged her. Christy didn't hit her away this time—she needed it.

The girls walked closely together through the kitchen and through the hallway to the living room where they were huddled together in the tightening darkness of the house, each raising a knife. Christy set hers down on the arm of the couch and collapsed onto her seat. She couldn't bring herself to grab it in such a *nasty* situation. Coldness reasserted itself in her flesh, even if it was bright outside the windows.

Katie joined Christy and put an arm around her while Julia and Bekah stood in front of them. Christy felt like they were all sitting ducks. Aviana stood in front of the fireplace and faced them. She looked as if she had something important to say, and her mouth opened then shut. Christy studied her with weary eyes; she couldn't believe David was dead.

Just like that.

"How will I explain this to Mom and Dad?"

Tears streamed like a waterfall. Katie hugged her tighter. Everything seemed like a grey-black blur. She wiped the tears away but every single tear was replaced by another two or three or four. No matter which way she tried to process it, she just couldn't believe it. Her brother dead, by a killer she had invited into her own home.

She killed him and I'm gonna kill her.

"Listen, Ladies," Aviana said, "we've got to stick together. Let's all stick together. Nothing could happen to us if we're together. There's strength in numbers."

Santa Claus came around the corner of the hallway only two feet away from Aviana. His bloody knife was raised and he grabbed Aviana by the collar of her shirt then jammed his blade into her side and dug it across her stomach. The ball of Aviana's intestines swung against her body. She grunted. Blood spilled from her mouth. Then the man shoved her head into the fireplace and held her down while she squirmed and burned.

Christy screamed.

She hadn't realized that the others had already run away. When she ran, she didn't remember to grab her knife from the couch's armrest.

Footsteps echoed through the house. Doors slammed and bolted shut. At the end of the hallway, Christy turned around and saw the man standing near the living room staring at her with his black eyes.

Abruptly he raised the knife from his side and came for her.

Christy knocked over a little table in the hall, as if that would somehow slow him down, then turned a corner and rushed downstairs. As best she could tell he was moving at a calm pace, not running, but he had still seen where she had gone and not the others and he would surely be after her.

He would undeniably hear her footsteps. And suddenly a thought came to her as the darkness of the stairwell overtook her and she came nearer to the must basement: *He's the one who killed David. Oh God, he must've killed Mary too.*

13

Christy tried to calmly open one of the basement room doors but the rusty hinges squealed as the door unlatched and opened but she didn't think he heard it. His footsteps were still above her, he wasn't anywhere near the stairway yet, there was no way he heard her… was there? Hopelessness filled her. She felt nothing but desolation when she shut the door and entered the raven-black storage room of old junk.

A nervousness in her gut. The door didn't have a lock. None of them save for the bedroom did in the basement. She hid behind the door, her body flush against the wall, and wondered how could she get to a phone. There was a landline in the living room, there was a line upstairs, but there was no line down here. Her best chance was to make a run for the living room. Could she get back there? There was the poker adjacent to the fireplace. She could defend herself with that. But would the police ever get here in time? Were the streets cleaned at all?

Suddenly his footsteps came down the stairs.

Christy threw her hands over her mouth and tried not to scream. She listened to his knife being dragged against the walls.

The scream almost escaped. She pressed her hands tighter and reminded herself to shut up or she'd end up like the others. Suddenly the image of Aviana's guts came back to her. Christy could almost feel blood dripping from her own mouth as it had fallen from her friend's.

Her stomach clenched at the thought of grabbing the poker and dialing the police, because she realized that the smell of Aviana's melting flesh must've filled the room.

All at once the footsteps stopped and she couldn't tell which part of the basement he was in. For all she knew, he had somehow phased through the walls and was in here with her. For all she knew, he was about to strangle her in darkness without any warning. Just a mass of evil. A mass of wickedness ready to slither his hands around her like snakes and choke her. The thought was so real she could almost feel it happening. Christy searched the room with her eyes.

CREAAAK!

The steps came back, and they were coming her way.

He tried the door of the room next to her. Her heart sank. He was the reaper, and he would be here soon. Christy listened carefully. The boogeyman went into the room and stood there for about a minute before shutting the door. She hoped and prayed that he would go the other way, or go back upstairs and not open the door to the room she was in.

The knob turned. Christy almost lost it. She held her breath. Light from the hall illuminated the room. He stood in the doorway and studied the room. He did not bother going inside. There was no need to. The way the boxes were laid on the floor, there would not be a single place for her to hide, unless she was the world's most flexible woman and could hide in one of those small brown boxes.

He closed the door and moved away but was still in the basement.

THUD!

A roach landed on Christy's head. She was frozen in terror. A nasty chill raced up her spine. She cringed as its gross little legs pattered in her hair; it was stuck on its side and trying to move. Shivering, Christy hit it and almost yelled; then she gasped silently. Her foot banged into the wall and made a noise. The roach was still in her hair.

The butcher suddenly stopped moving, and she knew she blew it. She knew he was going to come back and push the door open so far that it would crush her. She could see the obituary now, and the embarrassing headlines of the newspapers: *College Student Christy Morrison Impaled by Doorknob.*

She knew he was listening.

She waited.

The final seconds of her life ticked by.

Footsteps.

Her scream was on the edge of her lips until the footsteps moved farther away and back to Mary's former room. She wondered how long she could hide here. Wondered how long he'd be spending in the basement. Would he ever leave? Did the others know where the phone was? Had they tried to call the police? Was help on its way?

Her mind couldn't stop flooding with questions.

Christy listened to him pace around the basement, drag his knife across the walls. Eventually—thankfully—he left with heavy footsteps over screaming stairs. A bit of calmness came back to her but it wasn't much. Her heavy breathing now almost masked his footsteps. He went up to the main floor, his footsteps disappearing above her.

As she cried in the dark, finally hitting away the roach in her hair, Christy wondered what she should do next.

14

Bekah and Julia shut themselves into one room. Katie had been ahead of them and ran into a room all by herself.

"We should grab the phone," Julia said, ear pressed tightly to the door. "I don't care if it's impossible to drive in these streets. We can't just sit around. We have to get help." Then she moved away from the door. "I haven't heard him come anywhere near here. I can make a run for it."

"Oh no you fucking won't."

"So we just sit here until he gets us, Bekah? Is that what you want?"

"If we open that door, we die."

"Listen to me, Bekah, listen to me. We're not gonna die. Not if we get the phone. Not if we call the police. I'll dial it and run back in here with it, okay? The cord can reach under the door."

Bekah cried uncontrollably. "That's a stupid plan and we're all gonna die."

"Calm down, it'll all be okay, it'll all be okay, calm down." Julia said. "I'm gonna dial it, okay? We're gonna call them and they'll come and everything will be okay. You and me and Katie and Christy, we're getting out of here, okay?"

Through tears, Bekah agreed.

Julia pressed her ear to the door one more time then unlocked it. Waiting for them was a strange girl with long blonde hair and a furred body. Animalistically she growled. Her teeth were sharp and jagged and her gums were black. Long scars on both sides of her face. Nails that were essentially claws.

Julia slammed the door shut, but the monster on the other side shoved the door with force and it was about a quarter of an inch open, both girls struggling against each other, fighting for control.

"Help me Bekah."

Bekah snapped out of her stunned phase and helped Julia shut the door and lock it. The girl on the other side was still shoving it with her shoulder, attempting to break down the door.

They shoved the twin bed in front of the door to barricade themselves in. Then the girl on the other side stopped. Bekah and Julia wiped sweat from their foreheads and hugged each other.

"Who was she? Who else is in here?"

"I don't know."

CRAAAK!

The window on the other side of the room had broken open and in came a reindeer covered in snow. It shook itself clean and its hair scattered around the floor. The girls stared at it dumbfounded. Its nose was actually red and glowing, like the plastic display that was on top of the house. The reindeer smiled, stepped forward, then it mutated and changed.

It stood on its hind legs and its body morphed to fit its form. In outline it became humanoid. A cross between nature and man. Its lipped curled back to reveal a full set of teeth. As it neared the girls, they rushed to move the bed out of the way from their only escape and between them and the monster.

"Why hello girls. That's no way to treat a friend. My name's Rodolpho, I'm your friend. Get over here. *Get over here now."*

Julia swung the door open and she and Bekah ran. Rodolpho jumped over the bed in a giant leap.

"Get back here bitches."

They were screaming.

"Let Rodolpho put you in the real spirit of giving. *Come back here this instant. Come on ladies."*

Julia's heart was about to explode in her chest. Her mind rushed—none of this could be real, it just could not be real. It could not be happening. She glanced over her shoulder, and the humanoid reindeer was close behind, chasing on all fours, his tongue hanging out of his mouth, his dreadful nose glowing red in the deep darkness of the hallways. His eyes were wide and the whites around his irises could be completely seen.

And he was getting closer...

And closer...

Within an arm's length of both her and Bekah, and she felt herself about to faint. Felt her knees buckling with each step. Felt herself about to collapse from both terror and exhaustion. She couldn't breathe, this was too terrifying. It was like she had been pulled into some grotesque reality, some other realm that should not exist. What other horrors were lurking within this mansion and ready to surface from the shadows? Julia didn't want to know. She had seen enough: the man in the Santa Claus costume, the vicious feral girl, and now the humanoid reindeer.

"After I unwrap ya I'm gonna stuff ya! Ha! Ha! Ha! Merry Christmas girls! This is what the holidays are all about!"

The humanoid reindeer grabbed Bekah's ponytail with his hooved hand and pulled her into his arms. "Awe yeah baby I'm gonna go down the chimney!"

"Help me."

"I'm sorry Bekah. I'm sorry."

At the end of the hall, a new one, one that Julia had not been through before, formed on the right. Julia turned the corner.

"Julia you bitch."

The reindeer dragged Bekah by her hair and pulled hard on the ponytail until it tore from her scalp. He took her to the end of the hall, raised her face to the big glass window at the intersection of the halls. The reindeer smashed Bekah's face through the window, then brought her throat down on the broken glass and cut her screaming short.

"Now time to unwrap my gift!"

Julia couldn't keep running, she was so tired, but she had to force herself, or else she would die. There was much distance between her and the humanoid reindeer, but where was the… feral girl? Where was Santa Claus? Any of the monsters could have been anywhere.

She had to get the Necronomicon. She had to undo it all.

Chills rolled up and down her spine. She had stared death in the face. She wished she had her knife still but she had forgotten it in the room she and Bekah—the mere thought of Bekah made her shudder—had hidden in, and now she was defenseless with the humanoid reindeer on her tail.

Julia raced down the stairway two steps at a time, nearly slipping to her death on occasion.

When she was halfway down, she glimpsed up. He was coming down with his bloody knife raised. Her stomach clenched and her head ached. Everything was hot. Adrenaline pumped through her body.

"Ohmigod."

15

Katie heard screams and heard her friends running and was hesitant to leave the room, but she remembered there was a phone in one of the halls on the top floor, and one in the living room. She desperately wanted to know what was happening and what all the commotion had been.

She was under a bed and burying her face and tears and screams into a pillow.

If I could just get to the phone—no, if I could just get to the Necronomicon.

She wiggled out from under the bed then stood and listened. There was silence in the hallway. Katie opened the door an inch, peeked into the empty hall with her knife held tight in a white-knuckled grip. If anybody came for her, she was prepared.

Cautiously Katie snuck out of her room. Everything was still, everything was quiet, the only sound was her footsteps.

I've got this.

Katie went down her right, turned to the next hall, then screamed. Bekah's throat was buried in jagged glass in the window at the other end, and blood ran in frozen streaks. Her clothes had been torn from her body, and she was covered in animal fur.

Now or never, Christy thought.

Christy built up the courage to leave the room and discretely headed for the stairs, walking with extra care and hoping not to make noise. But that was impossible. The whole house was old and jittery and each movement would almost surely make sounds.

Christy took her first step, putting as little weight as possible on the stairs, but it was no use, it made noise. As she took her fourth and fifth steps up, she heard commotion coming from a great distance—it must've been coming from the second floor—and hurried up the stairs, unafraid now of making noise if the killer was... *distracted.*

She forgot David's body was in the kitchen, and screamed again when she saw it—a bolt of terror ripped into her heart.

Be strong he'd want you to be strong just go get the poker and go to the phone. Just go get the poker and go to the phone.

That smell. That damn smell. David's blood combined with the stench of Aviana's burned flesh. It was sickening.

Katie and Julia entered the kitchen at the same time. As soon as all three girls saw each other they screamed.

"Bekah's dead."

"I still haven't seen Mary anywhere."

"We need the Necronomicon. It's the only way to undo this."

"What? The what?"

"It's in your basement."

"What's in my basement?"

"The Necronomicon. Mary found it and we read from it. Let's go before they get us."

"They?"

"There's more than just Santa Claus in here!"

The girls went downstairs in a hurry, making so much noise that it would be impossible not to be detected in this big quiet mansion. They ran into Mary's room and the girls were turning over boxes and emptying Mary's suitcase and purse looking for the book.

"What's it look like?"

"It's an old book."

"There's a dozen boxes of old books down here. My dad collects them."

"How did he get a copy of the damn Necronomicon?"

"I don't know, he goes to estate sales and vintage book shops."

"And they sold him the grimoire by the Mad Arab Abdul Alhazred?"

"Apparently."

"Well they shouldn't have sold it to him because now we're all gonna die."

"Oh how was he supposed to know what he was buying?"

"It's the book of the dead! How did he not *know?"*

"Well where is it?"

"Here it is!" Katie held it in both hands above her head. "I found it! I found it! Now let's burn it!"

"No you don't burn it! You have to read from it!"

"Which part do I read?"

"Read the part you read the first time, but read it backwards."

"No, that's gonna make it worse."

"No, no, no, it'll reverse it, that's how you do it."

"Oh yeah? Who made you the Necronomicon expert? How would you know how it works?"

"It's just like in the movies, just read it backwards."

"What movies?"

"I don't know."

"Katie, Julia, you two are driving me crazy! Just read from it before we're killed!"

"All right!" Katie flipped through it. "Let's see… okay this looks good…." She cleared her throat and was about to read it but she was frightened and dropped the book when two humanoid reindeer were in the doorway.

One of their noses glowed bright red, the other's did not. That was the only difference between them.

"Oh baby," the one with the red nose said directly to Julia, "it looks like you brought us a couple friends, sugar. How very sweet of you. Did you meet my friend? His name's Dasher! That buck likes to fuck fast and hard."

The girls stumbled backwards from the reindeer.

Katie picked up the book quickly.

"Read from it goddammit read! Read! Read!" Julia yelled.

"I'm trying! I'm trying!"

"You're holding it upside down!"

"No I'm not!"

“Now, now,” Dasher said, “we can’t have you ladies spoilin’ our fun. Why don’t you give that here.”

Both of them advanced on Katie. She chucked the book at the glowing red nose. It smacked the humanoid reindeer in the face and he growled.

He grabbed her by one hand, and Dasher grabbed the other. They pulled until her arms were separated from her body, and blood leaked wickedly in each direction. The reindeer licked it up off the ground, but Christy and Julia weren’t staying to see the rest.

They ran up the stairs, leaving the Necronomicon behind. They were all out of options now.

Except to fight back.

16

Christy and Julia ran to the living room for the poker and the phone.

Aviana had been pulled from the fire and she was lying on her stomach. Christy had to reach past her dead friend for the poker, afraid that Aviana would spring to life and grab her hand while she did so. Meanwhile Julia picked up the phone, but she was silent. Then she screamed.

"It's dead!"

Christy grabbed it from her and pressed the phone to her ear. It was cold enough to send a chill through her. And the phone wouldn't dial. It was completely dead. There was no way for them to call for help. They were trapped with the monsters.

"Christy we need to hide." Julia tugged on Christy's arm.

Christy clutched the poker tighter. She led Julia down the hallway that had led to David's bedroom.

"I know where we can go."

"Where?"

Then a girl appeared at the end of the hallway as if by teleportation. A naked girl crouched on all fours, her body covered by fur. She growled.

The two friends screamed and went back the other way and through the living room. The strange girl gave chase behind them. Christy and Julia beat her to the kitchen, then pushed the table into the doorway, but as they went to the stairs they realized the girl wasn't with them anymore—they couldn't even hear her.

All was still. All was silent. But they wouldn't wait there for her forever.

"Come on. Up here."

Christy kept the poker raised and Julia kept close to her, constantly looking behind themselves for the animalistic girl, the humanoid reindeer, or for Santa Claus.

"Do you... do you really think we'll be safe?"

Christy did not answer her.

On the second floor they had to pass through the hallway where Bekah had been killed in order to get to where Christy had been determined to find. She raised the poker to the latch on the ceiling and tugged. The latch didn't want to come loose on the drop down stairs.

TAP! TAP!

Hollow footfalls sounded distantly in an adjacent hallway.

"Oh no. Christy he's coming—we need to hide. Hurry Christy hurry."

"Shut up, I'm hurrying."

The stairs finally unlatched. A blue ladder came down effortlessly and with it fell Mary's body on top of Christy, knocking her to the floor and knocking the poker out of her hand. She pushed Mary's body abruptly off herself and screamed painfully.

Mary's throat was slashed horizontally, and the end of a giant candy cane stuck through. The candy cane's hook dangled in her mouth with her dried tongue glued to it. A sort of Columbian necktie with a candy cane.

Julia shouted and examined the body. Christy picked up the poker then she pulled on Julia's arm, and the girls went up.

Inside the attic was a small and dusty space with Christmas decorations flooding several shelves. A lot of the room couldn't be seen because it was drenched in darkness. Their only light source came from the hallway below them. Christy began pulling the stairs up when Santa Claus grabbed hold of the steps and climbed.

There was no closing it. He was too strong.

Christy's grip tightened around her poker and she hit it in his direction but couldn't land a hit on him. He dodged them then grabbed the poker in one hand and jerked her forward then pushed it back. Christy moved away from the entrance. She and Julia held each other and moved back into a wall and cried.

The room was warm when they entered it but his presence made it cold. Christy was chilled to the roots of her hair. She gulped. Her grip tightened around not only the poker but around Julia too.

Then she let go of her.

Christy stretched the poker out and jabbed him in the stomach.

The Butcher smacked it away with little effort. It fell from her hands and she was defenseless as he towered over her, becoming one with the shadows. She saw her own face reflected between globs of blood on the knife as he winded it back, brought it forward—

She was on the ground. Julia pulled her down. She reached for the poker that was just out of reach, then heard Julia's scream. Santa Claus yanked Julia up by her hair and was about to sink the knife into her chest when Christy moved in a haze, fumbling to hold on to the poker and swing it at the attacker. She knocked the knife from his hands and he let go of Julia momentarily.

Julia took the opportunity of freedom to grab a box of Christmas decorations and slam it on top of his head, blinding him. Christy jammed the poker into Santa Claus's back and he stumbled two steps then fell over. No blood leaked from his body but the poker had sunk so deep…

She wasn't going to leave it behind. She removed the poker from his body as Julia headed for the stairs and tugged on Christy's arm.

Nowhere was safe to hide.

They had to get the Necronomicon.

When they came to the basement stairs they heard talking.

They moved as silently as possible and came off the final steps into darkness. Rodolpho and Dasher were conversing in Mary's old bedroom. They heard the conversation clearly:

"Shiiiiiiiiiiit, Dasher, that ain't the incantation to summon us concubines of bitches, that's the incantation to raise the dead."

"No brother you don't know what you're talking about, I tell ya I know somebody who used that exact spell."

"You're gonna doom us all."

"Then what do you suggest?"

"This one right here…. See?"

"The Viagra of the underworld?"

"I'm still getting' used to this body. Sometimes I can't get it to function. I wasn't born to be a reindeer. I'm a demon in an animal's body."

"I say we're wasting our time down here Rodolpho. There's at least a couple women left in this house that could be our concubines. Let's go get 'em. Dibs on the brunette."

"I thought we'd at least take turns brother."

Christy and Julia ducked behind some garbage in the basement as the reindeer passed through to the stairway. Then they stopped momentarily and sniffed the air. They were caught. They had found them, they knew they were down here.

But then the reindeer proceeded up the stairs, and when they were officially on the second floor, Christy and Julia ran to Mary's room for the Necronomicon.

"What part did you guys read?"

"I don't know I can't read Latin."

"We're fucked."

"Let's just think for a second, Christy."

"Yeah?"

"What if we pray to the dark lord?"

"Okay let's give it a shot Jules."

"Dear Satan," Julia said. "Wait, is that how I'm supposed to start it off?"

"Who cares just try something."

"Please get rid of the reindeer and the other killers. Do I say amen at the end?"

"Forget it. This is pointless. Let's just try to get out of here."

"How can we drive with the streets like this?"

"It's better than spending the last moments of our lives racing from room to room. We have to try. I think Aviana left her keys on the hook in the living room."

17

THE KEY WAS THERE on the hook by the door.

Christy grabbed it while Julia held on tight to the Necronomicon. They were partway through the door when Christy turned back and grabbed the hotel room key from the mantle shelf while Julia screamed at her to come back. Then the girls moved impossibly forward through the immense collections of snow. The streets were not cleaned at all. It might as well have been a suicide mission.

They struggled to get the car doors open, but after desperate tugging they opened, and Christy was in the driver's seat and Julia in the passenger's seat. As Christy put the key in the ignition she thought, *They're all dead. We're the only ones left. It can't be real.*

The car wouldn't start.

She tried and tried but it wouldn't start.

"We're screwed." Julia slammed her fist on the Necronomicon. *"Aren't you good for something? Can't you get the car to start? Come on, work your magic!"*

"Be nice to it!"

"Be nice to—are you stupid, Christy?"

"Fuck off Jules, that book is capable of anything, it's the book of the dead."

Julia flipped it open. *"Well, here it goes. Maybe this can get the car started."*

The resurrected groundskeeper patted the feral girl on the head, and looked out of the upper window. The girls had gotten into the car and a moment later a beam of green light emitted from within, and the snow on top of it melted.

The car reversed onto the street and moved crookedly over the cumulating mountains of snow.

The groundskeeper whistled and his trusty reindeer Rodolpho and Dasher appeared in the room with them. He pointed a finger upwards to the roof, and they understood. They went up with him and the girl. The two reindeer attached themselves to the apparatus in front of the big red sleigh, and the groundskeeper and the feral girl buckled in.

The reindeer strained for a second to pull the sleigh free from the pieces that attached it to the roof and held it in place, then the sleigh descended into the front yard.

"Ho! Ho! Ho!"

"You got dat right," Dasher said. *"Them girls some straight hoes. They finna be my hoes!"*

"Hey I seen them first," Rodolpho said. *"Them hoes mine!"*

They were off into the night…

The car they were chasing increased its speed once the sleigh came into view behind them. The girls were driving so fast that they almost tipped the car on the sharp turn. Momentarily the reindeer lost sight of the car when it went around a huge mass of snow on the corner of the street, but after they turned the girls came back into view.

"We finna get 'em!"

"Heh, here we come, hoes!"

The reindeer hurried over the snow, pulling the sleigh behind them as fast as they could to keep up with the vehicle. The chase made their mouths water. The reindeer could almost taste the flesh of their next victims.

"Faster! Faster!"

"How fast do you think this car can go?"

"I don't know! Just step on it!"

"What do you think I'm doing you dumb bitch? I'm taking us as fast as we can go!"

"Don't call me a dumb bitch you're the dumb bitch!"

"You're the one who used the Necronomicon to ruin our weekend!"

"Katie's the one who read from it, not me! I didn't want to curse us all and doom our souls to hell!"

"Well you didn't stop her from reading it and you should have!"

"It's not my fault! Just get us far away from them!"

"I'm trying! Read from the book again, maybe it can do something else for us, like how it melted the snow from the car!"

"First reading from it cursed us, now I have to read from it to save us? Make up your mind Christy!"

"Shut up or I'll shove that book down your throat!"

"Is that a threat?"

"Just read! Read dammit!"

"Okay I'm reading! I'm reading!"

"Ohmigod!"

"What?"

"The gate!"

Christy had forgotten all about the gate that surrounded the community. There was no slowing down and stopping in time—she was going full force toward it. She shut her eyes and waited for the impact, waited for the airbags to explode and break her nose, waited for the pain and terror, waited for the sleigh behind them to stop so that the monsters within it could claim her and Julia as their victims, and eventually rule the world with the Necronomicon. Instead there was only a screeching sound, the side mirrors were broken off, and the windshield cracked. When they kept going straight, Christy opened her eyes and they were headed straight for a tree. Julia reached over and grabbed hold of the wheel and turned it for her, then Christy helped her turn it too.

They narrowly avoided hitting the tree but they were still screaming, still scared, and the sleigh was closer than ever—thank God it couldn't fly and had to move over all the snow and obstacles like the car had to—and Christy wondered what would happen first: would they be able to use the power of the Necronomicon to defeat them from inside the car, or would they run out of gas first and have to face their attackers without any defense?

Oh God, she thought. She just wanted to get to the resort. Just wanted to hide. Wanted to get the police, the army, and the air force on the phone so that they could handle the attackers. Would anybody even believe them? What would she say to whoever answered the phone? 'Hello, an undead Santa Claus and a feral girl are attacking us with humanoid reindeer. Send help please.'

Christy shivered. She knew they would never make it out of this situation.

"Slow down, girls, we just tryna have a little fun wit' y'all."

"Yeah, a 'little' fun. Speak for yourself, Dasher. I got a 'big' fun to have wit' them."

Closer and closer. Inches away from the back of the car. If they reached out they could touch it. Then the car slammed on the breaks and Rodolpho and Dasher cracked their heads on the car's bumper.

They stopped in their tracks and looked at each other.

"I think I'm dying, yo."

"Hold it together, Dasher. We gotta get 'em. I ain't letting the only tail I've seen in miles get away that easy, you feel me?"

Blood leaked from their heads, and their skulls were exposed. The car was getting further and further away. Behind them the feral girl was growling, and the resurrected groundskeeper was yelling at them.

Although pain was burning in their bodies from the collision, they pushed forward…

"Great thinking Christy!"

Christy didn't have the heart to tell her it had been an accident, and that her foot had slipped to the breaks by mistake, but it had slowed down the attackers and that was great. Christy turned one corner then another and the sleigh was out of sight.

They were on their way to the Asylum Resort. They were so close than she could already feel freedom. She could feel an escape. It would all work out. The police would get here. The police would get here *very soon.* They'd take care of the reindeer. They'd take care of Santa Claus and the girl.

"Ho! Ho! Ho!"

"We're hurrying! You try pulling a sleigh on a broken hoof!"

"Yo they don't pay us enough for this, bro."

"Them girls as our prize gonna be payment enough!"

"Brother you right about dat!"

The car had gotten out of sight, but its tracks were the only blemish in the wonderland of snow that blanketed Raven Hill.

They would be easy to find.

18

THEY PARKED IN THE Asylum Resort's parking lot.

Julia grabbed Christy's hand. "Before we die I have to confess something."

"What?"

"I always made fun of Mary but she was right about the government. The government is evil. From nineteen thirty two to nineteen seventy two they tricked black citizens into believing they were receiving free healthcare so they could study the progression of untreated syphilis."

"Oh Julia, I'm a believer too, I was just scared to admit it. Everything we know is a lie. If the news is fake just imagine how bad history is. Why is it that the 'good guys' have won every war? Nothing they've taught us can be real. Where do we really come from? What really happened in the past? Are the real records of history actually destroyed and lost to time?"

"And don't get me started on Israel."

"Anyways let's get inside before they catch up and kill us."

"If Santa Claus doesn't kill us, then I'm sure the government will."

The girls ran through the building screaming.

"Help us! Help us! They're gonna kill us all!"

The key was for room four hundred and twenty nine. They ran up to the room, unlocked the door, and hid inside.

19

EMMA AND HER SISTER Jill were in the Asylum Resort's hot tub when they heard yelling.

"Was that the others?" Emma said. "Maybe I should go get them."

"Yeah, tell them it's about time they showed up."

"They probably got stuck in the snow or something. It's what those slackers deserve for leaving so late."

"I told them there was room in the van, but they didn't want to carpool."

"Their loss."

Emma wrapped her towel around herself to keep warm.

The halls were devoid of any other guests or any of the employees.

Then she had a feeling she was being watched. Eyes were drilling into the back of her head. She glimpsed behind her shoulder but saw nothing. She went up a staircase that twisted just as tightly as it would in a medieval castle. The grey walls were black in the gloom, gently curving upward out of sight. It was a long way up.

"Hey baby."

A man was covered in shadows at the landing and she couldn't see him. The bulb above her was flickering, and light wouldn't reach that corner.

"Why hello there."

"How would you like to have some fun?"

"What did you have in mind, mister?"

He stepped into the light. A humanoid reindeer with blood trickling down a busted open forehead. His hands reached for her but she pulled away and bolted up the stairs.

"No fair you run so fast. These legs of mine ain't what they used to be. Come on, baby. This chase is no fun. Dasher doesn't normally chase bitches but I guess there's a first time for everything."

Her stomach was in a knot. She looked behind herself, saw nothing, and increased her speed, pushing her body as fast as it could humanly go, and suddenly regretting all her life choices not to work out more.

As the stairs swirled her mind did too, and she felt the monstrosity's presence catching up with her; she not only heard its heavy breathing but felt its scorching breath. She feared that at any moment its hands would reach out and tear her in two.

Emma raced harder than she had ever pushed herself before. The stairs twisted and she rushed, knowing she was almost there, and seeing the platform of the fourth floor just above her.

She almost felt hands reach up from the brewing darkness below her and pull her. Tears ran in hot slants down her cheeks. Her whole body convulsed. Her heart almost leapt from her chest.

On the fourth floor platform, she shrieked with utter terror. The door wouldn't budge.

But that was because she was trying to pull when it read push.

When she realized her mistake she pushed with as much force as was left in her small, shaking body, and the door squeaked open and she ran through the empty halls, her footsteps echoing behind her menacingly and wickedly. The lights in the hallways flickered too.

Emma unclenched her hand from the key and fumbled with it before putting it into the lock and turning it desperately.

On the other side of the door, Emma finally caught her breath.

She collapsed on the floor and shivered. She was finally safe.

TAP! TAP!

She realized that she was not alone in the room.

A red light glowed in the shadows behind the door.

"Well, well, well, what do we got here?" Another reindeer stepped into the light. This one's nose glowed red. "Your ass is mine, beautiful."

SLAM! BAM!

Angry fists on the other side of the door.

"Rodolpho let me in. Dat ass is mine."

"Fat chance at that, brother. I need to have some fun. You had dat employee I had my eye on, so now I'm taking yo girl."

"Dat ain't fair man."

Emma backed away into the wall below the window when somebody reached out from behind the curtain. Two hands with narrow unpleasantly crooked fingers gripped her throat. He pushed her onto her belly, his weight restricting her movements. She writhed and shook and tried to elbow him off her body but she was too weak to hurt him.

Then the man dressed as Santa Claus loosened one hand away from her throat, holding her tight with his other one. Suddenly she heard a swift tearing noise, a knife being dragged through the covers and tearing them. He set the knife in front of her eyes. The shine of the dull lightbulbs on the ceiling reflected off of it and Emma saw her terrified reflection in its rusty surface. It was the last thing she ever saw.

And the last thing she ever heard: *"Awe hell naw, now Santa Claus is killin' my gurl! I guess I gotta go off and find another one, and keep her far away from him."*

"See Rodolpho, dat's what you get!"

"Were you in on it with him? Plotting against me?"

"Awe keep your dumb theories to yoself. I ain't the government, I ain't up to no good."

He pushed the knife onto her scalp and sawed it through her flesh. She let out a heart-stopping shriek, and the man pulled up a handful of her hair, separating her skin away from her skull. Threads of flesh tore hideously, and one final stab of terror pumped through her heart before she was gone.

Jill swam. For another twenty or thirty minutes she enjoyed herself. The lights went out then flickered back on, flickered wildly without completely returning to normalcy, then Jill left the pool. She wrapped a towel around herself and wondered what Emma was up to.

Jill felt a cold breath of air push against her body.

She stepped into the hall. "Emma, where are you?"

She went to the elevator and hit the button, awaiting the doors to open—and when they did, two humanoid reindeer were each holding human limbs in their hands and tearing out chunks of flesh. Blood soaked their fur. Their skulls were cracked open. Both of them were hellishly mutated abominations.

"Oh hey—hey look Dasher, dere's anotha one!"

"She looks tasty! Just like her little sis!"

Jill screamed and ran for the stairway, hurrying up the steps faster than she had ever moved in her lifetime. The animals were after her and running on all fours. She had some distance between her but then screamed when a feral girl came running down the stairs headed straight for her. There was also blood smeared across her mouth, and pieces of human flesh dangling from her teeth. She had feasted with those abominations.

Jill staggered back the other way and the reindeer caught up with her and took her into their grips. Each of her arms was held tight by each of the reindeer. The feral girl growled at them. That animalistic girl wanted Jill all for her own.

"You hogged da sister, she was no good by the time I got to her."

"Nah, bro, you're da one dat's no good. You don't know how to please her."

"Nah, dis one's mine. I get to go first."

"Hell nah. Oh hell nah."

The reindeer played tug-of-war with her arms, pulling her in one direction then the other, until Rodolpho let go of her and she went flying over the railing. She landed with a loud *THUD!* as her neck snapped, her skull split, and she was dead on impact.

"Now lookit what you done, brother."

"Me? You da one dat let go. It's yo fault."

"Well I got dibs on her, dead or alive."

"No I had da dibs."

"Well you gon have to beat me there."

The reindeer raced to her dead body.

The feral girl scurried away.

Outside the Asylum Resort, the others arrived.

20

IT WAS A STRUGGLE to park the car. They parked it in the middle of the way because the world was a snow globe, and it was impossible to figure out where any parking spots were. Perhaps it would get warmer in the coming days and melt away the snow. Hopefully the streets would be cleaned by morning.

Madison, Arabella, and Brynn were so tired from the long drive and getting stuck several times in the snow on their journey here to spend the weekend getaway with their friends Jill and Emma. They left their bags in the car and went inside.

Brynn said, "In all those Christmas movies where Santa is real but the parents don't believe it, don't the parents ever question where all the gifts, you know, where all the gifts come from?"

"Who cares?" Arabella said.

Briefly, Madison thought she saw something move in a window in her peripheral. She quickly looked up the disgusting brick wall. Two curtains suddenly closed against each other. She had been sure that somebody had been up there watching them. Perhaps Emma or Jill.

Icy air traced her lungs. It was uncomfortable as hell out here in the winds of Raven Hill. Her legs felt like stilts, and she pushed as fast as she could over the parking lot of ice to get into the Asylum Resort. Madison passed through the front doors. The others followed closely behind.

Inside it was quiet—too quiet.

"Hello?" Madison said, then shouted: *"Hello? Anyone home? Hellllloooo?"*

No answer.

"Where are all the workers?" Madison said. "This is a hotel, don't they have somebody on nightshift? Or did everybody call off? Well, I guess we can just get our key. What room did we have again, four-thirty-one?"

"Yep, four-thirty-one," Arabella said. "And Jill and Emma were sharing four-thirty."

Madison looked at the long rows behind where the receptionist should have been standing. She found 430, and the slot was empty. Both keys were gone. Jill and Emma were here all right. She glanced at 431. Both of its keys still there.

"Should we grab them?" Brynn asked. "We already paid... and if nobody's around..."

Madison noticed a bell on the counter and rang it four times. Still, nobody came. She shuddered. "Are we in The Twilight Zone?"

Arabella looked down the halls again then slowly walked past the counter. She grabbed the keys from the room 431 slot then tossed one to Madison. "Let's go."

Madison twirled the key around her finger then turned towards the elevator and walked down the hall. The lights flickered. "Does something smell bad to you two? This places reeks of death."

They knocked on the door to Jill and Emma's room.

"Jiiiiiiiiiiiiiiiiiiiill? Emmmmmmaaaaaaaaaaaa?"

"Jill. Emma. Wake up sleepyheads. We're here now. Let's get this weekend started."

"Hello? Are you two there?"

"Come on let's get wasted."

"Helllooooooo?"

"Jill? Emma? Wake up already."

None of their slamming fists on the door made any difference. Their friends just weren't answering.

"Well maybe they're at the pool or something. Guess they got the weekend started without us."

“Did they go to the store or something maybe?”

“What? In this weather? And at this time of night? Who’s open now? What would they need at three AM?”

Madison crossed her arms. “Something is going on here. Let’s go back downstairs and see if we can find an employee.”

“Well I gotta pee first.” Brynn opened the door and stepped inside.

Then there were footsteps around the corner.

Madison ran into the hall and looked around. “Jill? Emma? You two there? Or… is anybody there? I’m a little freaked out here.”

Arabella joined her at her side. “Hmmm… maybe they’re at the pool. I’ll go see. And if they’re not, then I’m gonna take a dip.”

“You do that. I’m gonna go look for them. I’ll be right back.”

Madison passed through the liminal hallways of the Asylum Resort cupping her hands around her mouth and calling Jill and Emma. She was only met with the natural silence of the building. Lights flickered here and there all around her, and the darkness outside the windows made her uncomfortable. The building was freezing cold and it made her sick.

She pressed the button on the elevator and stepped in. Two decorative reindeer were inside. She pressed the button for the ground floor and the doors shut, then the reindeer came to life. They ceased being plastic and became flesh. They stood on their hind legs and morphed into humanoid beings that laughed hideously.

They licked their lips.

The one with the glowing nose said, *“Oh brother, dis night just keeps getting better and better! Look at that! Fresh meat!”*

“You could say that again!”

“Fresh meat!”

“You could say that again!”

“Fresh meat!”

“Yeah! Fresh meat!”

They cornered her. She was so frightened she couldn’t scream—then she wet herself, and the reindeer fell over laughing.

“She’s so excited she took a piss!”

“Hey she’s definitely yer type of girl, Rodolpho.”

"Nah brother that's all you!"

"Ha, yer right! Now come to Dasher!"

Madison punched him in the gut as he came back to her but he was unphased.

"Is dat the best you got, baby? Ha! You gotta be rougher than that if you want to play with Dasher!"

"Stay away from me!" She punched him again.

Rodolpho stepped between them. "Let me show you how to treat a lady. Ma'am, may I have this dance?"

He took her by the hand and she shouted at him to let go, but there was no escape from his tight grip. Rodolpho pulled her close, spun her around the elevator that had finished descending and whose door had opened, then slammed her into the wall and shattered her nose.

"Awe look at you Rodolpho, always damaging the dames we find."

"Nah, I think she looks *fineeee* in red."

She reached desperately for the door but couldn't break free from him.

"I think she's tryna leave!"

"Well that ain't no good! Why don't you come to Dasher, I'm gonna make you feel all right!"

Madison crumbled under the pain and her knees gave out. Rodolpho continued to drag her along the elevator, swinging her around, trying to make her dance, then Dasher grabbed her hand and tried to pull her away from him, but Rodolpho tugged painfully and Madison felt her shoulder straining on the verge of popping out of its joint.

"Puh-please..."

The reindeer ripped off her clothes, slamming her head into the wall in the process. Blood burst forth and soaked her eyes. She couldn't see what was happening, could only feel them as they violated her and threw her back and forth between each other.

With a sudden burst of desperation she slipped away from them and ran in the direction of the doorway, but she slipped and fell as it shut, and her head was caught between the bottom of the doors right as they shut, crushing her head and killing her.

"Awe man, anotha one gone!"

"It was yo fault, Rodolpho, just like da other one!"

"Naw man dat was all you! You killed dat other one just like you killed dis one!"

"Oh, word? Maybe I am da problem."

Rodolpho bit her arm. "Tastiest one of dem bitches yet!"

21

Arabella was determined to find her friends after Madison never returned to their room. She knocked on Jill and Emma's door one more time, hoping that they'd open up and reveal it had all been one big prank, but nobody answered her.

"Madison, are you in there too?"

Silence.

"Where can you be?"

She walked to the end of the hall and pressed the button for the elevator. When it opened up there was blood everywhere, and a half-eaten corpse that had once been Madison. Full of shock, Arabella ran back to her room, and would have gone inside if there hadn't been a man dressed like Santa Claus standing in front of it with an axe in his hands.

Her heart beat as fast as lightning. The man lifted the axe and Arabella ran away, she ran for the door to the stairway.

She slammed the door shut behind herself, glanced for a lock but there was not one, and wasted no time going down the steps.

Arabella raced like she had never done before.

She glanced behind her shoulder but did not see the man or anybody. It was as if she were only racing against herself, against her own wild imagination, against a figment of her thoughts. Something that wasn't real.

She rushed down the steps, her hands burned as she clenched them around the railings, and she wondered what she'd do when she reached the bottom, because her jacket and the car keys were in their room. Could she survive out there in this weather with just a light sweater? No. She would die from the coldness. Was there a place to hide in here? She did not know.

As Arabella went down to the third floor platform, her feet slipped on the final two steps and she faceplanted onto the cold hard metal ground. Her body was wet. She looked up to see the steps covered in blood. It was all over her clothes and hands and face.

Then, turning slowly to the corner of the platform, an employee's severed head watched her.

She clasped her hands over her mouth to hold in the hellish scream that was eager to pass her lips.

She descended to the main floor and found the employee lounge. She was not prepared for what she stumbled into. The stench of death hit her first before she saw the pile of dead employees torn open with their insides decorating the walls. They were thrown lazily into a pile, like how one would toss out garbage into an alleyway. Lackluster dead eyes from a face looked at her—their last moments of sorrow plastered into them. Arabella knew the face. It was Jill. Emma was next to her sister, missing her scalp.

Arabella dialed 9-1-1 with the employee phone.

"Hello please he's gonna kill us all—"

Then the swoop of the axe cut the phone's cord and it dangled in Arabella's hand. The vile Santa Claus towered over her laughing.

"Ho! Ho! Ho!"

"Noooooooooooooo!"

"Hold up, brother."

In the doorway were two humanoid reindeer and a feral girl.

The reindeer with the glowing red nose spoke. "Before ya chop her up I'd at least like to take the lady to dinner. Or a midnight snack, before she becomes my snack, you feel me?"

Arabella tried to run past the reindeer and the girl out the door, but the one with the glowing red nose grabbed her.

"Hey Dasher, looks like this one's eager ta play!"

"Fresh meat! Fresh meat! Fresh meat!"

"Let go of me!"

They dragged her to a table and set her in a chair, then they set everything up. From the employee sink and dishrack they found plates and cups and put them around a cramped table. Arabella wanted to run for the door but Santa Claus had a hand on her shoulder, and an axe in his other hand. One move and she was dead, if she wasn't dead already.

The reindeer were laughing loudly as they dropped chunks of flesh and guts onto the plates.

"I tell ya if I knew we were gonna have a woman over for breakfast I woulda cleaned up a little bit."

"Boy you ain't never cleaned nothing up in yo entire life."

"Dat's what you think, boy."

"The day I see you clean up is the day pigs fly."

"Boy your momma been knew how to fly."

"That joke is whack dude, I ain't even got a momma, we were both plastic reindeer displays up until a couple hours ago."

"Dat's right, I forgot. Thank you for reminding me yo."

"Yo it's cool bro."

"Now let's dig in!"

The one without the glowing nose dropped Jill's head on the plate in front of Arabella and forced a knife and fork into her hands.

"Eat up, girl. You're too skinny. Dasher likes ya nice and fat."

"No—Rodolpho wants her as skinny as she is. Don't eat too much, bitch."

"Haha, yeah, because later on she's gonna fill up on *deer*."

"Awe yeahhhhhhhhhhh."

The reindeer high fived.

Arabella stuck her knife inside of Santa Claus then ran for the door while the feral girl and reindeer were eating. They didn't notice at first that she ran, and as she made it to the door Santa threw his axe and it nearly hit her, but it missed by inches and slammed into the wall.

She was free of the employee lounge, but she needed to find another phone. Needed to get back to her room, but if they had an axe and knew where she was headed for, they could break in easily. And she was outnumbered. Maybe she needed to steal another key, get into another room where they couldn't find her.

She headed for the front desk when she bumped into Brynn.

"Oh God I'm so glad I found you!"

"Me too!"

"Let's grab a key and hide!"

Brynn grabbed one. "It's here on the first floor! Let's hurry!"

They ran to their new room, their new destination, and slammed the door shut.

"What's going on out there?" Brynn said. "I couldn't find anyone—I thought… I thought I saw a monster. This girl…"

"They've killed them all! They've killed Jill! They've killed Emma! They've killed Madison! They've killed the front doorman! They've killed the bellhop! They've killed the receptionist! They've killed the receptionist's relief! They've killed the maid! They even killed the maid who was off duty and coming by just to say hi! They've killed the manager! They've killed the assistant manager! They killed the *other* assistant manager! They've killed—"

"I get it!"

"They've killed—"

"I said I get it!"

"And now they want to kill us! We have to get out of here!"

"Call the police. I've got a way to handle them." Brynn opened her purse and pulled out a gun. "They aren't killing us tonight!"

"Why did you bring that with you!"

"Always be packing! You never know when you might need one! This is America, you should always be carrying in the land of the free and home of the brave! Criminals won't leave their guns in their cars because of a 'no guns allowed' sign on the door, so why shouldn't we carry?"

"I can't argue there."

22

"PLEASE SEND HELP. THEY'RE trying to kill us at the Asylum Resort."

"Who's trying to kill you?"

"A man dressed as Santa Claus and two men dressed as reindeer."

"Yeah right! This is a line for emergencies, young lady. You shouldn't call in pranks at three in the morning."

"No this is serious! They killed everybody! There's only two of us left!"

"Yeah? Who's 'everybody?'"

"Jill! Emma! Madison! The front doorman! The bellhop! The receptionist! The receptionist's relief! The maid! The maid who was off duty and coming by just to say hi! The manager! The assistant manager! The *other* assistant manager! The—"

"You're right. That is just about everybody. Help is on the way."

"Please hurry."

"Ma'am. You don't have to tell me to hurry. That's our job is to hurry."

"I'm sorry, it's just this is an emergency."

"They're all emergencies."

"Yes but this is life or—"

"They're just about all life or death. Don't sass me."

"I'm not sassing you I'm just telling you to hurry or else we're gonna die."

"You know what? Forget it. I'm not sending anybody. You're on your own."

"What? You can't do that."

"I can and I will! Goodbye!"

"But—but—"

"Arabella? What just happened?"

"That jerk hung up on me! They aren't sending anybody to help us!"

"What did you have to argue with him for?"

"I didn't argue I just asked him to hurry!"

"Now we're all gonna die because of you! This isn't how I wanted to spend my winter vacation! I knew I shouldn't have come!"

"Oh no you don't, this was your idea in the first place. You're the one who picked out this place."

"No it was Jill that picked it out."

"Yeah right. Sure."

"You know this is just like you to start a fight over something so trivial."

"Well you're the one who brought this up, bitch."

"And you're the one who made 9-1-1 decide that we don't need saving! I'm dead meat because of you!"

"But we have your gun!"

"What if we can't fight them?"

"Keep your voice down, they might hear us!"

"We've both been yelling for twenty minutes, if they haven't found us yet they're just deaf!"

"I don't want to die..."

"Well too bad!" The hideous reindeer voice on the other side of the door said.

Suddenly an axe was pounded through the door and Rodolpho stuck his face through.

"Here's Rudy!"

"Shoot him, Brynn!"

Brynn steadied her gun and fired a shot but the reindeer moved out of the way and the bullet didn't strike anybody.

Then the door was knocked down. Arabella grabbed Brynn extra tight. This was the end...

The reindeer, Santa Claus, and the feral girl entered.

"Now hold your fire, baby," Rodolpho said.

"Yeah, what he said," Dasher said. "Save all your anger for the sheets, baby."

"Don't come any closer or I'll shoot!!!"

"Now honey let's be rational here," Dasher said. "Put dat gun down, ain't nobody wanna fight you."

"Brynn shoot them! Shoot!"

"Awe look at her," Rodolpho said, "desperate for a little attention now dat her friend caught our eye. Don't worry, ladies, there's enough reindeer meat to go around."

"What do you want from us?" Brynn said.

"We just want a good time," Dasher said. "Tell you what, if you put a bullet in your friend's head we'll let you go."

"Yeah right, Brynn wouldn't do that."

Brynn gulped.

"Would you, Brynn?"

Brynn stepped away from Arabella and gulped again. "I… I…"

"Brynn!"

Brynn pointed the gun at Arabella. "Just shut up. Let me think."

"What's there to think about? I'm your friend! Shoot them!"

"Nah gurl you're doing the right thing, now shoot that bitch," Rodolpho said.

"Yeah gurl you can do it," Dasher said. *"Dead meat! Dead meat! Dead meat!"*

Arabella backed away into the dresser. "Please don't…"

Brynn backed away too to the other end of the room, gun still aimed at Arabella, then she turned her gun to the reindeer, Santa Claus, and the feral girl.

"Now gurl don't do nothing foolish, you hear?"

"Yeah we don't want no trouble. Like we said, shoot her and you walk. Ight?"

Brynn aimed the gun back to Arabella. "Arabella… I'm so sorry…"

"I don't want to die."

"Me neither."

"Don't shoot me."

"It's me or you."

"It doesn't have to be this way! You have a gun! You can shoot them! Don't be an idiot."

"Don't call a girl with a gun an idiot. You're the one who got 9-1-1 to change their mind about sending help!"

The reindeer were laughing.

"You gotta make a decision soon, gurl," Dasher said.

"No, no," Rodolpho said, "let them bitches play."

Arabella ran at Brynn who was frozen and couldn't bring herself to pull the trigger. Arabella punched Brynn in the face and knocked her into the wall. Brynn immediately bounced back from the hard hit and slammed Arabella, keeping the gun held far away as Arabella tried to snatch it away.

The girls were slapping each other, yanking each other's hair, and the reindeer were cheering them on. Then Arabella pulled Brynn to the ground and wrestled her, clawing at her hand that held the gun in an attempt to steal it away. But Brynn's grip on it was too strong to let go. Arabella was done—there was no getting out of this. Her own best friend was going to kill her.

"Brynn please no…"

"I'm sorry." Brynn backed away from her, both of them still on the ground, and had the gun aimed at Arabella.

"Awe yeah she gon die tonight!"

"I call dibs on the dead one!"

"Just save a piece of dat for me!"

"She look so fine and tasty I doubt there gon be no leftovers for ya but I'll try and control myself, ight?"

"Yeah bro, ight."

Arabella pleaded one last time. "I'm begging you not to kill me. I'll do anything."

"There's nothing you can do. But since I'm gonna be the one to live, I'll make sure to pass on the truth about the political system. It exists to rob, trick, and subjugate the population. The truth will live on with me. You did not die in vain."

"Brynn no!!!"

"I am so sorry. Goodbye, bestie. Goodbye."

Arabella shut her eyes and braced for the gunshot.

It passed straight through her head. She did not feel a thing.

"Ah she did it! I can't believe she did it!"

"She might got some balls in them pants! To do a thing like dat!"

"Feisty! Just how I like 'em!"

"Hey bro!"

"Yeah bro?"

"Did she know we was just fuckin with her?"

"Oops."

23

THE REINDEER SPED AT Brynn so quickly that she didn't have a chance to turn her gun on them. One of them—and she couldn't tell in the quick blur of chaos which it was—cut half of her fingers off as their razor-sharp hooves stomped on her hand and crushed her bones into tiny pieces. The gun lay in front of her on the ground.

The reindeer towered over her drooling.

"Awe yeah let's get it on."

"Didn't you call dibs on the dead one? Go get yo girl."

"Yeah but she can wait."

"Nah, nah, dis one's mine!"

"Whatever you say."

The reindeer laid on top of Brynn and she finally let out a scream.

"Hush hush now, ain't nobody coming to help ya." He put his hand over her throat and flattened it until she couldn't breathe.

She gasped.

She squirmed under his weight but there was no pushing him off, he was just too strong and she only had one hand. She attempted to grab the gun but it was just out of reach.

The lack of air was dizzying.

As his long slimy tongue licked her, her vision faded to black…

The resurrected groundskeeper and the feral girl had stayed for the show, but now it was time to go find the other two girls that they had hunted at the mansion. One was David's sister. The other was David's lover. They both needed to pay for what David had done.

Their fear was tangible that the groundskeeper and the feral girl could feel it as they passed through the darkened halls of the motel. They were hiding somewhere up above. Somewhere on the fourth and final floor.

"Ho! Ho! Ho!"

Christy and Julia sat on the bed with the Necronomicon between them.

"This was what Katie read." Julia pointed to the page. "I don't know where she learned Latin. Must have been one of those things that helped further the plot."

"No time for thinking about plot holes," Christy said, "we need to figure out how to use this book to our advantage. You were able to use it to defrost the car, now can we use it to turn the reindeer back to plastic and kill Santa and his lackey?"

"Here this one's in English. Let me try to read it." Julia traced her finger over the page. "The Old Ones were, the Old Ones are, and the Old Ones shall be. Not in the spaces we know, but between them, they walk serene and primal, undimensioned and to us unseen. Yog-Sothoth knows the gate. Yog-Sothoth is the gate. Yog-Sothoth is the key and guardian of the gate. Past, present, future, all are one in Yog-Sothoth. He knows where the Old Ones broke through of old, and where They shall break through again. He knows where—"

"What's any of this mean? Is this even a spell or just rambling?"

"Maybe rambling."

The book glowed green and from its pages uprose a thin mist of smoke, and when it cleared away there was a five inch monster between the pages. A squid monster. A little Cthulhu. He jumped on top of Julia and squeezed her breasts and tore through her clothes. Julia grabbed him and flung him across the room, splattering him against the wall and killing him. He slowly drooped down to the floor, leaving behind a trail of green slime against the white paint.

"Gross," she said.

"Julia, what if we could use an army of little guys like that against Santa Claus?"

"You know how many times we'd have to repeat those words? And look at what he did to my outfit. Ugh. You know how much this costs? I'm a waitress! I make no money! How am I gonna replace any of my clothes he just ruined?"

"It's better than being dead! Just read it! Read it and don't stop! This is the closest we have been to harnessing the power of this antiquarian tome."

"Okay... here it goes..."

The groundskeeper swung his axe ahead of him for fun. *"Ho! Ho! Ho! Ho! Ho! Ho!"*

The feral girl growled.

They peered outside. Snow still fell and covered up the sleigh.

They continued through the upstairs hallways until they noticed that one of the doors emitted a green glow from underneath. A luminescence that cut through the dreary darkness that curled around every last space in the Asylum Resort.

Together they stood in front of the door and looked at each other then nodded.

Finally, the last of their revenge. They'd have what they wanted soon, the heads of the girls impaled on spikes.

He raised the axe past his shoulder then swung it with angry force. All the memories came flooding back of finding David and the other campers in the forbidden cabin, and when they discovered all the secrets he had kept, the children bound him, tortured him, killed him. And he had been burning in the afterlife when suddenly an offer was made, and he accepted, and he crawled out of his shallow grave. The children needed to die, but not only for what he had been through, but for the torture that the feral girl had been through. She was an innocent girl he had found in the wilderness, and she had made mistakes because she hadn't known any better. Those boys cut her up. Left her for dead. But she was strong and she had survived just barely—she had survived only by accepting the same offer that the groundskeeper had accepted. By giving up their souls. Making a deal with the devil.

The door came loose and there were screams from the other side, then a little green squid crawled through the opening and jumped at him, covering his eyes and blinding him. He dropped the axe, grabbed the little squid, and threw it to the ground then stomped on it. Meanwhile the feral girl picked up the axe and finished tearing down the door.

She ran in there after David's sister and David's lover. When the groundskeeper had his vision again he joined her in the room. The girls were huddled in the corner with the Necronomicon. About twenty miniature green squids were attacking the feral girl, yanking her by the hair in every direction, biting her, wrapping their tentacles around her. The axe had fallen from her hands.

David's sister was about to grab the axe but the groundskeeper beat her to it and picked it up first. He swung it at her but she jumped back, and he missed her by a fraction of an inch. One of the squids jumped for an attack but another swing of the axe split it in half.

David's lover was repeating something from the Necronomicon. More squids spewed forth from the book's pages and attacked both of them, but the axe kept swinging and cutting them.

Then one of them went too far. They removed his Santa Claus hat.

The groundskeeper let go of the axe and in a rage twisted the hat grabber in his hands until the creature was split in two, then he swallowed up the mutilated squid monster whole. Next he pulled the squids away from the feral girl and stepped on some of them. Once a few of them were dead, she was able to fend for herself.

More squids were generating, even after the two girls ran out of the room.

The groundskeeper regained his axe and ran after them into the hall. The feral girl followed.

They looked each way. The girls weren't in sight but the trail of scurrying squids that writhed and squirmed and propelled themselves forward with their tentacles were leading in a certain direction, around a corner and to an elevator. One squid in particular was wedged between the doors and was snapped in half. He had just missed it by a split second.

But the groundskeeper now knew that his targets were on the descent.

He and the feral girl ran down the stairs to the ground floor. He had an idea that the girls were trying to get back to their car and use the power of the Necronomicon to get out of here. And he would not let that happen. He would kill them by any means necessary.

A few squids chased after him. The feral girl grabbed each of them and bit their heads off. He couldn't blame her, the one he had eaten himself was delicious. Maybe after the girls were dead he would learn the spell so that he could summon his own squids for breakfast, lunch, and dinner.

When the door opened he swung the axe.

The girls were not there but instead a gigantic squid comprised of all the miniature squid monsters. They intertwined their bodies and fused together, constructing long tentacles by merging their bodies and being controlled of one mind. One of those long tentacles wrapped around the resurrected groundskeeper and snapped the axe in half.

While he struggled against their grip, the feral girl sprung into action and sank her teeth into the constraint that was wrapped around his body. She tore chunks of the gigantic abomination and swallowed them whole.

The squid monster lifted the feral girl and swallowed her up.

"*Ho! Ho!* No!"

The squid monster raised the resurrected groundskeeper up high to swallow him whole as well, but the feral girl burst through the stomach of the monster just in time, severing the monster into a thousand chunks. Guts, brains, and goop were thrown in every direction. Sludge covered the groundskeeper and the feral girl.

He picked up the pieces of the axe, and picked up a piece of the monster, and used the sticky tentacles he found to mend the axe. It was somewhat unsteady, but it held.

Now where were the girls?

24

CHRISTY AND JULIA LUCKED out with the groundskeeper and the feral girl taking the bait and going for the monster in the elevator.

The girls summoned some more of the little Cthulhu monsters and went down the back stairway—thank God that when their attackers went down, they had used a different stairway and had avoided them—and after their descent found the back door out of this place.

"Where to now?" Julia asked.

"The police."

"They won't believe us."

"What? Why not?"

"Because how do we explain any of this? It makes no sense. We have to lie. We have to get our story straight."

"Yeah, Jules, because lying to the police has always worked out fine."

"If the government can lie to us and not get in trouble, then we can lie to the police!"

"Jules we have the Necronomicon, the police will have to believe us."

"No way! They'll just turn it in to their overlords. The CIA and FBI would be all over that thing so fast to turn it in to the illuminati. Humanity will be fucked if it gets into their hands. We can't let it happen, Christy. We have to keep this to ourselves."

"Then how do we explain all the dead bodies?"

"I don't know. We can just say we slept through the whole thing and we were spared."

"Why would a demented and bloodthirsty killer attack only some of us and leave two witnesses?"

"You have a big house. He didn't know who else was in there."

Christy shook her head. “I don’t know if they’ll believe that.”

“Well they have to, we’re the innocent victims in this whole situation.”

“Yeah, Jules, if we survive the night.”

They were halfway to the car when the groundskeeper exited the building with his repaired axe raised and the feral girl raging through the snow. The army of little Cthulhus that had followed them out into the snow stood between them and their attackers.

Then something curious happened.

The Cthulhu monsters looked at each other and whined. They frowned. They turned from green to pale to brown. Their flesh disintegrated. It happened fast. Their flesh dissolved and all that was left were little piles of bones that sank into the snow.

Christy and Julia had no defense left between them and the feral girl.

The feral girl leapt at Julia, and Julia raised the Necronomicon in defense. The girl’s clawed hand met the cover of the book and burned her flesh. She retreated a few feet from Christy and Julia and sank her hand into the snow. A little steam rose up.

The resurrected groundskeeper ran across the snow, taking as big of steps as he could through the impossible mountains of ice.

Christy and Julia ran trying to get back to the car.

“Is there another spell we can use?”

“I don’t know!”

“Try reading something!”

The car doors were stuck. They wouldn’t open.

Julia fumbled with the Necronomicon. It fell into the snow.

“Julia hurry!”

“I’m trying!” She dug it out of the snow then glanced up at the oncoming creatures. The feral girl and the groundskeeper were forcing their way over piles of ice, and now it was snowing again, and strong winds were pounding against them, slowing them down, giving Julia time to find another spell.

“Read anything!”

“Okay!”

Julia read a text that was not in English or any known language that she could detect.

The ground shook.

The snow split.

The girls were suspended in place, watching the newly formed chasm and wondered what would emerge. Had Julia brought on their own doom, or would this come in handy like the Cthulhu army had been inside the motel?

They waited for something to rise up…

…and nothing did.

Julia stepped forward and looked inside the chasm. There was nothing but the thin length of parking lot that had been revealed beneath the snow.

"That's it?"

"Good going Julia. Anyone else could've summoned Yog-Sothoth or a Mi-Go or a Shoggoth or Azathoth or Nyarlathotep, but all you did was—"

"Ugh, you try summoning the Old Ones on such short notice. They're probably busy, okay?"

"You couldn't even summon snow right now if you tried."

Julia put one hand on her hip. "Do you want to try possessing the power of the book of the dead? I'm taking a crash course! It's not as easy as it looks!"

"Yeah, like it took much to summon the Cthulhu army. Don't forget who was helping you repeat that paragraph over and over again. Julia watch out—"

The groundskeeper had climbed through the charm and swung his axe at Julia's ankles from down within the pit, but Julia backed away.

Christy was on top of the car and grabbed Julia by the hand, helping to pull her up onto the hood too. The girls climbed to the other side and huddled together, flipping through the pages. There had to be something of use in here.

"Third time's the charm, right?" Christy said.

"Uh, sure. Sure," Julia said then began to read the text but was cut short by the howl of the feral girl on top of the van.

The feral girl jumped down. Julia didn't have time to lift the book again to defend herself. The girl's claws struck Julia across the face and dragged downward to make a vicious scar that was identical to the feral girl's own scar.

Christy picked up the Necronomicon and tugged on the van door until it finally opened, but couldn't fully extend because of how much snow was in the way. She struggled to climb in. Julia was screaming at her for help as the claws were raised and brought down again.

Christy shut the door and squirmed into the driver's seat. The car wouldn't start.

Then the axe crashed into the window and broke it open.

She opened the book and read.

It was her last chance to get out of this alive.

25

The groundskeeper grabbed David's sister as the final words of the spell left her lips. She dropped the book and screamed. She was his—all his. He lifted her up by the collar as she kicked and hit him, but her touch did not phase him. Her touch did not hurt. He laughed at her. How scared she was, how dumb she was—he loved it.

"Ho! Ho! Yes!"

Her lips parted for a loud scream, then he realized she was not screaming at him but at what was behind him.

The skeletons of the dead Cthulhu monsters had reanimated and were held together at their joints by the same thick and dark goop that they became when crushed. They formed a skeletal Cthulhu that marched forward and grabbed the groundskeeper in its boney grip. The creature had no flesh for the groundskeeper or the feral girl to bite into.

He whistled for her help and she climbed over the van, leaving behind her prey, to assist him. There wasn't a stomach on the creature so she couldn't work her magic like last time and explode it from the inside, and for all he knew, they were both powerless against the creature.

The other girls had gathered together with the Necronomicon and chanted, and the boney Cthulhu monster grew larger. The feral girl leapt at it but it intercepted her attack with the swift snap of its behemoth tentacle and captured her just as it had captured the resurrected groundskeeper.

The creature raised both tentacles that held its prisoners up toward the heavens, and stretched until the tentacles towered above the Asylum Resort. Then it slammed them into the infinite snow, burying them deep within the newly formed mountains, burying them for good.

The monster waved goodbye to the girls, then it wandered away from the motel and into the night, never to be seen by them again.

"I told you it was easy!"

"Beginner's luck!"

"As if. You're just jealous I can control the book of the dead better than you can."

"If you're so good with it then get the car to start again, Christy. Get us back home."

Christy read from the book again but the car wouldn't start. They were both sitting there in the icy weather, cold sinking further into their bodies. They were getting numb, and that numbness was spreading quickly.

"Hey, I've got an idea, Jules." Christy stepped out of the car. "Follow me."

"Yeah? Where are we going?"

The sleigh was lightly covered in snow. Christy patted it down then stepped inside, and Julia sat next to her.

"Does this thing have heating?"

Christy shrugged. "No idea, but at least it runs."

"What happened to the reindeer anyways?"

Christy whistled, and the reindeer wandered out of the Asylum Resort holding globs of flesh. One of them was carrying a severed head of a girl they did not recognize. Blood prolifically spread through their fur.

"We been lookin for you bitches."

"Lookit 'em, nice and ready, they even called for us!"

"You girls ready to have the night of yo lives?"

"Heh, yeah, an early Christmas gift. I sure do love da spirit of giving!"

Christy laughed. "I've got something for you guys too."

"Awe yeah, bring it on!"

"Me first! Me first baby!"

"How about at the same time?" Christy said, then read from the book.

The reindeer ran to the sleigh and a little zap of light flashed from the Necronomicon and struck them. They were mutated again. Their bodies shifted back to plastic, but they were still alive and breathing. They tried to open their mouths but they were fused shut.

The reindeer attached themselves to the sleigh and pulled the girls back to the mansion.

The reindeer bowed to the ladies once they stepped out of the sleigh.

"Sorry guys, but back to the plastic life you go. Permanently."

"Can I do the honors please?"

"Sure Jules."

Julia read from the Necronomicon, and the reindeer were back to being plastic displays. But they still dripped with blood.

26

"I STILL DON'T KNOW what we're gonna tell the police, Christy. This is so far-fetched."

"Yeah well we'll think of something. It can't be that hard to make up a believable lie. The government does it virtually thousands of times a day and the American people eat it up."

"Yeah you're right."

"Of course I am." Christy opened the front door and let her in. "So let's see… we just tell them we were asleep. There's so many rooms that the killer didn't find us, and we locked our doors."

"And the motive? And who was he targeting?"

"I dunno. We don't have to have all the answers, that's their job, not ours. We're the innocent ones, Jules."

Julia yawned and stretched. "Just nervous this like, won't work out, you know?"

"I hear ya. Well let's just hope for the best. Want a beer?"

"Oh, totally."

They went to the kitchen. Christy flinched.

"God, I almost forgot about poor old David."

"Yeah, poor David. He didn't deserve this. None of them did."

"We avenged you, buddy." Christy stepped over him and the shards of shattered beer bottles. She grabbed a couple cold ones from the back of the fridge and handed one to Julia.

CREEEEEEEEEAK!

Somebody was upstairs.

The girls fumbled over David's corpse and the mess in the kitchen to the knife set on the counter and they each armed themselves and stood close together. Then they used the bottle opener to remove the caps on their beers.

"We've got work to do," Christy said.

Up above them, the magic spells that had gotten rid of the reindeer and turned them back to plastic had not touched the Santa Claus from the display that had become flesh and blood. The resurrected groundskeeper's dagger had cut him deep in the stomach, but he lived, and he crawled out of the room.

And he was angry.

Unnatural blood coursed through his veins. He wasn't bound by the same properties as mortal men. The stab had hurt him, had hurt him a hell of a lot, but it wasn't enough to kill him. He staggered to his feet, then crept down the stairs.

When he came into the kitchen there were two girls facing him holding knives and beers. One of them threw a beer that struck him in the head.

"Who are you?"

"I was the display on top of the house until somebody brought me to life. And now I'm gonna kill you ladies for being impolite. Didn't anyone ever teach you not to throw beer bottles at senior citizens?"

"Yeah, we'd like to see you try. You're outnumbered and outmatched. We have knives and the Necronomicon."

"To kill me would take the entire destruction of this body. Something that neither of you are capable of."

"Mister, I could kill you with the Necronomicon tied behind my back."

He charged at them. *"I'd like to see you bitches try!"*

The girls ran to meet him and sank their knives in him repeatedly, sinking them deep into his flesh, twisting them, turning them, eviscerating him, retrieving their knives just to plunge them in again. The girls hacked at him and severed his head from his body, and even after that was done they kept stabbing—they stabbed until they were too tired to stab again, and both of them were soaked in blood, completely drenched.

"I guess we know who we can pin the blame on," Julia said.

"You can say that again."

"I guess we know who we can pin the blame on," Julia said.

27

Later, at the police station:

"Christy, tell me, who would want to kill your brother and all your friends so viciously?"

"I'm telling you, I don't know, sir."

"It's amazing how he could kill so many people singlehandedly, yet with just a little effort you and your friend Julia could overpower him. Why couldn't the others do that?"

"I don't know."

"Something doesn't add up here. You were two defenseless girls. How'd you manage to take him? Where was his murder weapon?"

"I don't know."

"I'm asking you one last time if you know his name or who he is."

"No, sir."

"Well neither do we. No wallet was found. No getaway car. No evidence of any forced entry. No evidence that he was actually the killer."

"What are you saying?"

"We're saying we have no reason to believe your story."

"But it's true! I'm innocent!"

"I didn't say you weren't."

"I'm scared. All my friends are dead."

"And your brother."

"And my brother."

"Is there anybody at all who didn't like your brother? Or any of the girls?"

She shook her head. "No sir."

He slammed his fist on the table. "I'm gonna need some answers sooner or later if we're gonna get to the bottom of this. Don't you want us to get justice for your brother and your friends?"

"Yes sir."

"Then help me out here."

"But I've told you everything I can. What more do you want from me?"

"The truth."

"I've told you the truth."

"No you haven't. Not even close."

"What do you think the truth is then?"

"I don't know, but I don't trust you. When you're ready to tell me the truth I'm right here, Miss Morrison."

"Okay, I'll tell you the truth."

"I'm listening."

"My dad collects antique books. He somehow purchased the Necronomicon and my friends found it in the basement. It made the display above our house come to life and the reindeer and Santa Claus went around killing everybody. And there was a feral girl there for some reason. But that Santa is the one who did it. He killed them all."

"Fat chance that I'd believe a story like that. What do you take me for?"

"I take you for a man who's a slave to the government within the government! I know who you really work for, sir! How much do the Rothschilds have to pay you to keep the citizens of this great nation in check? What do your reptilian bosses have on you that's so bad you bow to their every command?"

"I don't know what you're talking about, weirdo."

"I am not a weirdo, good sir! I am a student of the truth!"

"What truth?"

"Open your eyes, dude! Look around!"

"Okay I've had enough of this. I'll be back later."

"Thirteen families rule the world!"

The same officer, a few minutes later, with Julia:

"Let's hope you're not as... unhinged as your friend."

"Oh no, is Christy doing okay?"

"Yeah, yeah, she's fine. She just can't shut her big mouth about the government."

"Can you blame her? They're evil."

"Oh boy. Here we go."

"We live in a society that keeps the cures secret so they can sell medication for huge profits!"

"Yeah well—"

"Seventy-five percent of the FDA's scientific review budget is paid by Big Pharma! Possibly a hundred percent is paid by Big Pharma!"

"Look I'm here to ask you questions, not to be lectured about—"

"The system wants you dumbed down so you're easier to control!"

"Enough already. I get it. I get it. Now let's talk about your murdered friends, Julia."

"Okay. Shoot."

"Who would want to kill them?"

"A Santa Claus come to life."

"Is that your story?"

"Yes sir."

"Why are you two running with such a clear fabrication?"

"It's not a fabrication sir, it's the God-honest truth."

"Prove it."

"Well the Necronomicon isn't on me, but if you retrieve it for me and bring me another Santa I could—"

"I'm not retrieving you nothing."

"Why not?"

"Let me put it to you this way. You're on the verge of being locked up behind bars, kid."

Julia frowned. "Ugh, like seriously?"

"Yes."

"Is this gonna like go on my permanent record or something?"

"I'll be frank with you. I don't even know what that is."

"Oh okay."

He nodded. "So tell me again what happened. The truth this time."

"So like we got to Christy's house and my friends were arguing the whole way. Bekah and Mary were at each other's throats, they didn't like each other and they're both dead now, which is sad, and to spend the last day or so of your life just angry and yelling and bitching and complaining and not getting along with each other and practically ruining the whole weekend getaway for the rest of us—"

"Get to the murders already!!!"

"Okay so first I guess Mary must have died but like I don't know what all happened to her, we found her body when we went running from Santa Claus and wanted to hide upstairs. She was missing and none of us knew where she was. When David died, we thought maybe she did something to him. Then we saw the killer."

"What did he look like?"

"Santa Claus. I already told you."

"I need more details than that, ma'am."

"He was dressed like Sant—"

"I get it."

"Ugh, let me finish. So rude.... He was dressed like Santa and he was ugly."

"Define 'ugly' for me."

"Like he was old, he was—"

"Define old. What are we talking here?"

"Like mega old. Like your age."

"I'm thirty-eight."

"You fossil."

"Goddamn."

"He was old, droopy skin, dark eyes, Santa hat, Santa jacket. That's about all I can tell ya, I wasn't gonna get close enough to find out more."

He nodded. "I don't like what I'm hearing from either of you girls."

"Too bad, because we can only tell you what really happened."

"You mentioned the Asylum Resort earlier. Tell me again what happened there."

"We drove there because we had David's passkey and we wanted to hide and call the police. And look how that turned out—you're holding us here like we're a couple suspects! Well I'll tell you what, I'm innocent, my record is clean, and you're violating our rights by holding us here."

He rolled his eyes. "We just want to know the truth. We want to know who killed your friends. Don't you want to help us? Now explain to me how two girls, knowing that everybody else in the house has been slaughtered, were able to overtake a killer that had five other kills under his belt? It just doesn't happen, it doesn't work that way. But maybe it did this time. And if so, I need to know all the details."

"He was coming down the stairs so we threw our beer bottles at him then we stabbed him."

"And he was unarmed?"

"Yep."

"Do you think he disposed of the murder weapon?"

"I dunno."

"You've gotta know something."

"But why?"

"Because you were there! You were in the house! You killed the killer! How do you not understand what I'm saying to you right now?"

"Because I'm tired. I had a long night. And I need my beauty sleep. And not gonna lie, I zoned out there for a sec."

"This is hopeless."

"No, I'll tell you what's hopeless. Having reptilian overlords that feed off adrenochrome."

"Okay, I'm out."

28

"OKAY… YOU'RE FREE TO go…"

Christy and Julia left the Raven Hill police station.

"I thought they'd never let us out of there, Jules."

"Yeah me neither. He really had me going there. I thought he like, suspected us or something."

"I know, right? I'm not meant to go to prison. I almost pissed myself."

Julia yawned. "Ugh, I need a nap. How long have I been up now, like thirty-six hours or something?"

"God, me too. I got no sleep last night with all the commotion and the end of the world and all."

"I'm gonna miss them, Christy. I'm gonna miss them all."

"Yeah, me too. Me too."

The officers talked:

"I don't buy any of it."

"Oh well, what can you do?"

He shook his head. "I don't know. The girls were talking nonsense."

"We've got the body of the guy they say did it. Might as well call it case closed."

"Is it?"

"Sure it is."

"Well, neither story changed. They matched up perfectly. There's just something I don't get about any of this. Why? And how? Those poor kids with their whole lives ahead of them. I just don't get it."

"Sometimes life doesn't make sense. Hell most of the time it doesn't make sense. It isn't like some book where everything's gotta add up or you get a one-star review complaining about plot holes."

"Yeah. Yeah I guess you're right. But I don't like it. I want to get to the bottom of it."

"They mentioned something or other about the Asylum Resort. Why don't you start there?"

"Hey, that's a good idea. Care to tag along?"

"No thanks, bud. I've got my hands full here with paperwork and whatnot. I've got to deal with some wacko in cellblock ninety-nine."

"Oh God. Good luck with that."

"You too, pal. Good luck at the resort."

The officer went to the Asylum Resort. He had to park outside the parking lot because there was no way in, the snow was too immense. Already he was finding plot holes in the story those two girls recited to him, there was no way they had gotten in and out of this parking lot at that late hour, the snow had already fallen.

But when he stepped across the snow he saw some evidence that maybe he was wrong. Tire tracks over the endless mountains. Broken glass, which lined up with the story he was fed about the axe-wielding maniac that had nearly killed them.

He stumbled inside of the building. It was frozen inside. No heat at all in the big ugly building. And no employees to be seen. Nobody behind the desk. No customers. What was going on in this place? Had something gone down here last night? It wreaked of death, and it was eerily quiet. Maybe those girls were telling the truth, or at least a partial truth.

He wrang the bell.

No answer.

He ran it again and again.

When nobody came he decided to draw out his gun and check behind the counter. Nobody was there either.

Just what might he find in this place?

He went wandering down the halls, chills tracing over his body, plunging deeper into his skin, and nervously he wondered if the killers were still in this building. Even after all his years on the force, he still got nervous. He couldn't deny it. It was a scary job, especially when your bosses were reptilians disguised as humans.

He knocked on doors, opened closets, called out for employees or customers, but the place was dead silent, and the fetid smell of decay was abundant.

The stench became strongest in a certain hall. The hall with the employee lounge. He kicked over the door and was completely unprepared for what he witnessed: dozens of mutilated bodies severed. Scattered pieces everywhere. Buckets of blood spilled in every corner of the room. And a table that was set up for a cannibalistic dinner.

The officer heaved. He was gonna be sick. It was the most grotesque display of evil he had ever seen.

With his gun still raised he went around checking the room for any survivors, anybody held captive, or perhaps any of the culprits hiding. And, he thought, the girls had been right. Something had happened here last night.

He grabbed his radio to call it backup. It wasn't working. No signal. The damn weather had interfered with the signal.

Again and again he tried to no avail.

He ran out of the employee lounge and slipped on a severed leg. His finger accidentally squeezed the trigger and it went off, sending a bullet flying through the room at the same time that an employee jumped up from the pile of dead bodies.

"I'm still ali—"

Dead. He had killed the last remaining employee.

The officer stood back up and ran from the building. Back into that winter wasteland. Cold clung to his body and cut through his skin. Any longer out here and he'd probably catch frostbite. He was racing to his car when a hand reached up from the snow and grabbed his ankle, causing him to fall over again, but this time the gun didn't go off—it fell from his hand and sank into a mound of snow.

Then he felt the pain of a snapped ankle. It was broken.

He tried to crawl away but a bony hand was holding on to him. He tried to kick free but the grip wouldn't loosen.

One glimpse down and he saw the maddening black eyes of the decaying hideous face that the girls had described. The maniac that had murdered all their friends. His Santa Claus hat was on crooked and he adjusted it, then he pulled the officer down below the surface of the snow, dragging him down into a frozen hell.

29

Time passed and the snow melted.

The horrors of the murders hovered around Raven Hill. The mystery man that the police found—the Santa Claus display that had come to life—was deemed the culprit, although his identity and motive remained a mystery to investigators.

Christy and Julia returned to college and continued their studies.

But things still were not right in Raven Hill.

Later on, when the last pile of snow melted, the mutilated body of the missing police officer was found. He had been hacked apart. They had to use dental records to identify him. It was a hideous ordeal.

Summer came and passed, and Christy refused to set foot in the mansion again. She and Julia kept touch through the break, calling each other every week and sometimes going out to see a movie. Neither of them talked about the events of that awful night, that horrible massacre that had claimed the lives of their friends…

…but sometimes the girls couldn't help but wonder what became of the feral girl, and the man who had taken the Santa Claus display's clothes.

When they heard about the police officer's body that had been found outside the Asylum Resort under all that snow, they couldn't help but wonder if those same creatures were the ones that were responsible.

Did they still lurk in Raven Hill?

Were they still coming for their revenge?

The girls shuddered at the thought of being stalked by those monsters. They were never safe no matter where they were. Nothing would ever keep those killers away from them.

Whispers went around the town.

People speculated what might have happened in the mansion that night.

Some suspected Christy and Julia had done something to the others, or had known something that they did not share with police. Others assumed that the killer was a madman, and that he had escaped from an insane asylum in another city. Perhaps it was a random act of murder, and perhaps the kids were at the wrong place and the wrong time, and if it had been a different set of young people in the house that night, then those others would have been victims, because the attacker was a madman.

The whispers spread so far and wide, and were so full of gossip, that certain people wondered what would happen if they did an investigation of their own...

30

ONE YEAR LATER...

Ben, who Aviana had been seeing, was determined to know what had happened. He didn't believe what Christy and Julia had told investigators about the killer and the things that happened that night. There were too many things that didn't add up.

How could the man enter the house undetected without this big group of people knowing?

How could he know the layout of the house and succinctly kill them all?

Where was the murder weapon?

Why were Christy and Julia able to overpower him so easily, after this whole entire massacre the man committed?

Ben read all the articles but couldn't fit together an answer for any of those questions, or any of the other one hundred questions burning inside of him. The only way to get answers would be to do his own investigation. Look over the house for any clues that the police might have overlooked. Try to piece together the details of that night. And, if he could, get the answers from the two survivors himself... and by any means necessary...

Ben finished his last final of the semester and then he was off to the Morrison mansion, where the hideous events had taken place. He brought with him some supplies: a notebook and pen, a tape recorder, a ka-bar knife, a video camera, a water bottle, matches, smokes, and a box of cookies.

The knife was attached by a sheath to his belt on his right side for easy access. He kept the smokes in his front pocket with the matches. He lit one up before he started his drive. Snow was falling, but thank God not as prolifically as it had fallen during the winter of horrors.

As he drove, he spoke into the recorder: "My name is Ben. I'm documenting this… expedition so that the truth may be revealed, but also I'm recording this in case I do not survive the Morrison mansion. My girlfriend died there last year, and I'm gonna get to the bottom of it. What we've been told on the news doesn't add up.

"I believe that Christy and Julia framed the old man. I believe that the real killer is still out there, perhaps even the girls themselves. But this is all speculation. In America we're all innocent until proven guilty. It was never up to them to prove their innocence, but it is up to me to prove their guilt. So while they got off scot-free for what transpired a year ago, I think that's all about to go away. I think soon we'll see those girls behind bars.

"So why did they do it? A number of reasons. Jealousy. Insanity. A fight. All of the above, I guess. I don't know. I can't rationally claim to know all the reasons why they did what they did. I just know that the little guy in my gut is telling me we don't know the truth and the whole truth yet. So that's why I'm doing this. I need answers. And God help me as I attempt to get them.

"To get answers I need to break the law myself. I'm gonna break into the mansion. That'll at least give me some idea of what the man had to go through. I've seen the pictures and the news footage. They suspect the man snuck in through the back door. That's my goal then, to enter through that back door. Let's see how easy it is a year later while nobody is inside the house. Can I break in quietly even with no witnesses? Time will tell.

"Am I expecting to find much left over after a year? No. I'm expecting to find nothing. But I can't get it off my mind. I have to see this house just once. I have to piece it together. I have to know what happened to Aviana. Poor, poor Aviana. I have to know just once and for all what truly happened to her. I miss her every day. I need answers. It's been a long, long year without her, it's been a long year not knowing the truth. She deserves to be avenged.

"They all do."

31

HE RAMBLED INTO THE tape recorder for a little while longer then shut it off. He drove past the house a couple times, circling the block slowly, scanning the mansion for anybody that might have decided to stop by. Nobody as far as he could see. No guests, no cars. Nobody was staying in this house this winter. It would be all his.

He parked in front of the house eventually then grabbed his bookbag full of supplies and went around to the back of the house. From there he removed his video camera and set it down.

"Here I am at the back of the Morrison mansion. According to police, an old man broke in through this back door undetected and murdered everybody. Supposedly he picked the lock. I've brought with me a lockpicking kit to put this theory to the test. I should also remind you about the severe weather last winter when he broke in, and the piling snow, compared to now. Now, as you can see, there's about two inches of snow on the ground, it's bright and sunny, nothing is coming down. I'm going to time myself to see how long it takes me. Here I go."

It was a long process.

Ben turned to the camera during the procedure. "This lock picking kit was about twenty dollars at the store near my college. I practiced on some dummy locks that I assumed were similar to the ones here at the mansion and in nicer neighborhoods."

He looked away from the camera and back to what he was doing. All in all it took him about forty-five minutes to unlock the door. It was a laborious and lengthy process, and noisy as well. He put the things away then picked up the camera, and walked into the house with it still recording.

"Here we are in the kitchen, which that back door brought us straight into. Some murders occurred here in the kitchen. It's also known that the girls cooked in here on their final night. They spent some time drinking in here too, according to evidence that was found and also the testimony of the survivors. So how could this man have made all that noise picking a lock, and none of them would notice? The only explanation is that the back door was unlocked. Was there even any evidence that this old man brought along with him a set of lock picking tools? Already I'm compiling more and more questions and I have no answers. This truly is a mindboggling mystery."

He turned his camera off. He needed a moment alone.

So this was where it had happened. This was where his girlfriend had died.

It didn't feel real to be here.

Ben walked from the kitchen to the living room, which was where Aviana had been slain. She had been cut open, and her face had been shoved into the fireplace. He wished he could have been there for her in her final moments—wished he could have been there to help her. If it had been such an old man who really had in fact killed her, then Ben could have taken him.

A little sunlight came in through the windows between the curtains. He could see his breath every time he exhaled. It was cold as hell in here. He looked around for a thermostat but didn't see one—there must have been one in here somewhere, he thought.

Aviana had been the first murder that the girls had witnessed after becoming aware of the killer. According to the girls, Mary had been first to die. Her room was downstairs. Ben went down there to investigate. The basement stunk. And there were bloodstains still in the old carpet down there in the room Mary had occupied.

It was even colder down here than upstairs. He wondered if it had been this cold that night and how the girls could have endured it. He looked around the room wondering what Mary could have used as a weapon to defend herself with, and wondering if the basement had been the killer's headquarters. That would explain how he had been in here so long undetected. That would also explain why Mary had been the initial victim. He knew one of the girls was down here all alone, and he waited for midnight to attack.

Ben repeated as much into his tape recording, and announced where he was standing. Then he said, "But my theory is that Christy knew every room where her friends were staying. That would explain why everybody theorized that the man had been familiar with the layout of the house. It wasn't the man, it was Christy.

"Mary's arms were severed from her body. She was torn open. That would take multiple people. Two people that were unhinged, demented, bloodthirsty. I think one of them held Mary down while the other one hacked away at her."

He was silent for a moment, reflecting on what had transpired here.

TAP! TAP! CREAAAAK!

He looked at the ceiling.

He wasn't alone. Somebody was on the main floor.

32

"WHOSE CAR IS THIS?" Julia said.

"I dunno," Christy said. "Maybe it broke down or something and they went to find help."

"Looks like a bad omen to me. I don't like it one bit."

Christy frowned. "It's better than seeing that Santa Claus again. I'm sure it's nothing."

"I hope you're right."

"I am right. It's nothing. Nobody's getting into the house without a key."

"Are you kidding me? How'd that guy get in a year ago without a key?"

Christy shrugged. "Maybe I forgot to lock the door?"

"You forgot to lock the door?"

"I don't know, maybe."

"So all of this would have been avoided if you remembered to turn the lock."

Christy unlocked the front door and they stepped inside. It was surreal to be back. It was strange to step foot into this house, even if it was so familiar to her, after everybody had been slaughtered here. But they were back to pay their respects.

It felt like a dream to move through the long dark hallways, turn their lights back on, and go about as if nothing happened. Christy felt that any second the killers would be back and she'd have to either fight or run. Thank God the snow wasn't as ungodly as it had been a year ago. It was manageable now. They wouldn't need the power of the Necronomicon to fight any intruders.

In the kitchen she boiled a pot of water to make tea. Julia was in the living room hooking up the VCR to the TV and rummaging through their bags to find the video tape.

"Which bag is it in?" Julia called. And when Christy tried to answer her, Julia replied, *"No it's not in that one. No, I checked, it isn't there."*

Christy came back to the living room and picked up the correct bag. "I'm telling you, it's in this bag."

"And I'm telling you it's not."

Christy reached in and pulled it out. "You were saying?"

"Ugh, I swear it was *not* there a minute ago. You totally just snuck that in."

"I did? When? You would've seen it in my hands. What, do you think I took it with me to the kitchen while I made tea just to confuse you?"

"Why, yes I do. I do think that."

Christy rolled her eyes. "Whatever. Just get it set up."

"Okay." Julia took it from her.

In a few minutes the tea was done, and they cozied up on the couch with two big mugs. The heat of the tea warmed up their hands. The tape played. It was various moments from their short time together at college. Mary, Katie, Aviana, Bekah—they were all in it.

Ben whispered into the tape recorder, "Somebody is in the house with me right now. I don't know who it is. If I'm never found, I want everybody to know that if the American people ever knew the truth about what politicians and the shadow government above them had done to this nation, they would all be chased down in the streets and lynched."

He crept up the stairway. From there he heard laughter. A group of girls. Then he noticed the lights were on in the kitchen and adjacent hallway. Somebody was here all right. Several people were here.

Killers, he thought, always return to the scene of the crime. Criminals, he thought, always get off on seeing the aftermath of their own demented work. Christy and Julia must have come back to celebrate. They must have come back to gloat. They must have come back to revel in the fact that they slaughtered innocent people and got away with it.

He stood in the entryway to the living room. It was them, all right. Christy and Julia were on the couch laughing hysterically, almost demented, as they watched a video tape of the girls that they had slaughtered.

Aviana's face flashed on the screen.

He was angry.

And he knew what he had to do.

Julia looked over her shoulder. "God I'm spooked. I thought somebody was watching us."

"I thought I felt eyes on me too." Christy shuddered. "I think we're just nervous."

The video tape ended after an hour. The girls stretched and yawned. Christy folded up the blankets they had been covered with, and Julia cleaned up crumbs from the boxes of cookies the girls devoured, and then she went to the kitchen to toss it out. Christy followed her with the empty mugs.

"Oh God Christy. I know what I forgot to pack. I knew it! I knew I was forgetting something."

"What is it?"

"I forgot my toothbrush. It's in the bathroom back at the dorms."

"Sucks to suck."

"I gotta make a run to the store. Do you want to go with?"

"Yeah, as if I'd let you drive my car."

"Aviana was the bad driver, not me."

"I don't care. Nobody's laying a finger on my baby but me."

Ben waited and listened. When the girls left for the store he checked the time. It was about four PM. He figured two girls on a quick run to the store would give him until about seven, because girls could never be in and out, they always had to detour, always had to walk up and down every aisle multiple times for things they did not want or need.

And now with time to plan, with time to scheme, he had an idea…

33

Ben went to the store and bought rope with cash so that it couldn't be traced back to him. That was the only thing he needed, the only thing that was missing. And when he was done with the girls he knew he'd burn the rope so that, again, there was no chance of it being traced. So many killers before him, he thought, had slipped up by leaving easily traceable evidence behind. But he knew better. He had studied criminals. He knew where they messed up and he knew what he'd do better. He'd get away with the perfect crime.

First he'd get the confession, then he'd kill them.

It would be fair and even payback.

He'd know the truth, he'd kill them, and he'd finally have avenged his dead girlfriend.

When he returned from buying the rope, he found a house in the area that was for sale. It was two blocks up from Christy's place. He parked in the driveway then walked the rest of the way back to the Morrison mansion.

The girls still hadn't returned. There weren't any cars parked there. He still had plenty of time with the girls gone.

He was hungry. The girls had left a box of cookies out and he devoured them.

His plan was a little difficult to execute without knowing exactly which room each of them were staying in, but he remembered from the police reports that Christy's room was on the second floor. He went there and opened a couple dozen doors until he found the one that belonged to her—posters taped to the walls, their edges curling over each other after the yellowed tape fell off. She had a bookshelf of romance novels and a little clay cactus on her dresser.

He checked his watch. He guessed the girls would be back in an hour. But maybe he only had minutes. There was no way to know for sure. He grabbed his tape recorder from his pocket and pressed record.

"Here I am at Christy's room. I know what I must do now. I must get the truth out of them by any means necessary. My goals have changed. Here I thought I would map out the house, get the facts, and prove their guilt. But since they're here, things have changed. God forgive me for what I'm going to do."

34

Christy and Julia came back home with the new toothbrush they had set out for, and with about thirty bags of other things that they hadn't necessarily planned on purchasing. They bought dinner. They bought new clothes. They bought perfume. They bought a whole bunch of things they didn't need.

They sat around the living room painting their nails and gossiping.

"You know," Christy said, "I found out what happened to that professor who had to quit the class midway through the semester. Apparently his like cousin's kid or something was also one of the students and he filled me in."

"Spill. I bet this is *great.*"

"Dude's going through a total crisis because his wife caught him cheating, he was like in a three-year fling with a younger lady and got caught. So the wife filed for divorce, kicked him out, you know, the usual stuff that follows breaking the sanctity of marriage."

"Geez. Well he totally deserved it. And who would want to sleep with him? He was so ugly. God that girl must have been like ten times as hideous if she found him attractive enough to get in bed with him. And for three years? Oh God I couldn't imagine touching that guy once, Christy, but for three years? Oh God that must be like a hundred times, at least."

"Don't make me gag, Jules."

"Is the… cousin's kid cute though?"

"Oh totally. I got his number. And he gave me some test answers."

"How adorable. Are you gonna see him soon?"

"Maybe. He invited me out. I dunno."

"What don't you know?"

"I don't know if I like him or not."

"Why not? You said he was cute."

"There's more to liking someone than just looks you know. Or maybe you don't know. I don't know."

Julia examined her nails. "Do you think pink is my color?"

"Yeah. Much better than the time you did green and blue."

"Did I tell you about what my dumb coworker at the restaurant did?"

"No. What? Wait is this the one that stuffed money from the register *right into her pocket under the security camera?"*

"No, no. That's just one dumb coworker on the practically endless list that I've accumulated in my time working in the fast food industry. You know what this girl did? As long as I've been working there she's asked people to switch shifts with her, right? And asked for rides or for this or that because she has kids and has to raise them as a single mom, whatever, right?"

"Yeah?"

"So the other day I was at the bar with a few friends, and this guy that's with us tries hitting on this chick and he's trying and trying, he's with her for a good twenty minutes, maybe thirty, but gets rejected. He comes back over to our table and tells us the whole story. I recognize her after a minute and I say, 'Hey, isn't that Michelle?' And he asks me how I know. And I said I work with her, I picked up her shift the other day because she had to get her kid from a soccer game. And you know what my friend tells me?"

"What?"

"That she told him—she straight up admitted this to a stranger—she said she lies to her coworkers about having kids so it could make her work life easier."

"What the hell? Did you expose her?"

"Sure did. I told management and they almost fired her."

"Oh God," Christy said. "What a dummy. Imagine making something up like that?"

"I know, right? What comes over people to do things like that?"

"I don't know, but the world could do without a few of these morons."

From a hole in the floor above the living room, Ben watched them. They were just talking, painting their nails, and he had everything ready. The knife. The rope. The duct tape. As long as they slept in separate rooms it would work, but even if they were in the same room he had a plan that would work. A risky plan, but it would work.

After dinner the girls brushed their teeth then went to bed. They were both sharing Christy's room. They stayed up for a little longer to gossip, then they went to sleep.

Ben was in the adjacent room with all of his supplies ready. And when a little while had passed he checked on them. The door was open because the girls had had no reason to shut it, being the only ones in the house. Or rather, the only ones that they knew of.

Ben smiled.

Seconds ticked by as though they were hours. He wanted to be sure they were deeply asleep, and he wanted to make sure this was perfect. His palms were sweaty and he wiped them away on his pants. There was a strange air of finality that clung to him and choked him. He knew he couldn't afford to mess up.

His mind was rushing. Suddenly the dead of winter was so burning hot it might as well have been a scorching summer day. He was so nervous about this—and he was gonna go through with it. He was gonna do it. It was happening.

Ben was in the process and it all felt like a burning haze, as though he were watching this happen omnisciently instead of being the one to carry out the acts. He had a length of rope already bound into a noose. That was in one hand. And in the other had the piece of duct tape.

Julia was on the edge of the bed, and Christy was on the other side against the wall under the window that encased a starry sky. He slipped the tape over Julia's mouth first, then slid the noose over her neck. As he tightened it her eyes opened—opened wide, and she realized it wasn't a dream.

"Don't wake her or you die."

He led her out of the bedroom and she was sobbing as hard as she could through the duct tape.

"Don't cry. Don't make any noise," Ben said when he brought her to the adjacent room.

He pushed her onto the floor and pinned her arms behind her back. He bound her with rope, then he tugged on it to make sure it wouldn't come loose. He had done a great job. She wasn't going to break free. There'd be no chance of that.

35

HOW SWEET THE TASTE of revenge, Ben thought. And with both Christy and Julia tied up and in the center of the living room, there was better feeling. He was in control. He was in power. And he would make sure that the girls didn't get away with this.

The knife in his hand was an extension of his power, and soon, he thought, it would draw blood. Its sharp edge would sever the flesh of the crazed killers that took the life of his girlfriend and several others.

They were squirming, and they were scared. That made him feel even stronger. They were red—even in the dim lighting he could see just how red they were, like bright summer roses. Fright was abundant in their eyes.

If this was how they acted now, he could tell they would have completely folded under the terror of a *real* intruder as their story went about the night a year ago. If any of those events had truly happened, the girls would have crumbled, would have run, would have been chased, would have died just like the others. They wouldn't have had it in them to attack, to fight back, and to win.

"You girls don't know me," he said, "but it's a pleasure to meet you both for the first time. My name is Ben. I'm sure you've heard of me."

The girls exchanged a look then shook their heads 'no.'

"What, really?"

They both nodded 'yes.'

"Ben. You know, Ben."

They both stared at him blankly.

"Okay. Keep the lies coming. As a taxpayer I'm used to lies. I know the dollars I pay on my income tax, property tax, tax on purchases, tax on plastic bags, tax on breathing, tax on everything, I know they all go to the pockets of politicians. Back before we had taxes they were able to create roads and school buildings and what have you. So what do they need our money for? And if they could keep printing more of it like they do every day digging us further into debt, why do they need us to hand it over? If they keep printing more at will then they don't need us to give up our money. Taxation is theft, plain and simple. If you have to pay 'or else' then the government—"

The girls groaned.

"Sorry. I get carried away sometimes. But keep the lies coming, girls, I'm used to 'em, especially from you two." He raised his knife. "Every time you lie to me I'm going to sink this knife deeper and deeper into your bodies. Now let's start over. I'm Ben. You've heard of me, haven't you?"

They both shook their heads again. They were determined to keep the lies going.

"I'm sure Aviana mentioned me. She was my girlfriend."

The girls showed no change in emotion. Their expressions did not change.

He tore the tape from their mouths and they each let out little gasps of pain.

"Hey, jerk, that hurt," Julia said.

"Yeah, what she said," Christy said.

"When will the lying stop?"

"We aren't lying to you, dude," Julia said. "We don't know you. What do you want from us?"

"I'm Aviana's boyfriend. I know she mentioned me to you. We were in love."

"Waitasec," Christy said. "Yeah, Aviana mentioned somebody, like... like once. What did you say your name was, was it Ben?"

"Yes. Ben."

"I think that was the name she mentioned.... Or maybe it was Barrett? Bryce? Bernard? Blythe? Bruno? I don't know, when you've had a friend like Aviana who's been through like a hundred guys a semester you kinda forget all the details, the guys all sort of blend together into one kind of amorphous fleshy formless blob."

"Don't you dare talk about her that way! She was the love of my life!"

"You two went on like, what, one date or something? It couldn't have been more than that, she broke up with her last boyfriend two weeks before the semester was over. I remember because she told me she already had slept with somebody else."

"You shut your lying mouth, Christy, or goddamn I'll cut out your tongue right now!"

"Yeah go ahead dude, it'll probably be the closest you've ever come to touching a woman."

"You're asking for it!"

"So what's the point in all of this again, you freak?"

"I know you two lied on the news. You lied to everybody to cover up the fact that you two went on a killing spree! The old man they found was just a cover up! You two killed them all!"

"Prove it."

"I picked the lock on your back door! You know how long that took me! If somebody else picked that lock you would have heard them! Nothing about the timeline makes sense! Look how easy I rounded you two up—you expect me to believe that you two—"

"Ugh," Julia said, "we had the power of the Necronomicon on our sides. That's how we survived the night. We didn't kill anybody. I'm sorry the girl you liked died, but we didn't kill her. You can let us go now."

"Yeah, like I'm supposed to believe that you two harnessed the power of the book of the dead. How did you come across such a thing anyways?"

"I'd love to chitchat with you all about it but not until you remove these restraints."

Ben shook his head. "No."

"Come on, Ben. Untie me and Christy and we'll even show you the Necronomicon, and we'll give you some girl advice. I'm sure you've had your eye on another girl since Aviana died. But you're digging yourself further into a hole you might not be able to climb out of."

"Nice try. I won't be deceived by any girl who goes around batting her eyes at me."

Julia shook her head. "You're gonna wanna get us out of here, mister, or you'll regret it."

"How would I regret it?" Ben kneeled in front of her with his ka-bar knife. "Look at this thing. It's huge and deadly. One slice and you're gone. I hardly have to put any effort into it."

"Yeah that's the only 'huge' thing you got on you."

"I don't like the way you're talking to me, Julia. Now tell me what motivated you to kill everybody." He stuck his tape recorder in her face. "Was it your idea or Christy's?"

"It was all my idea. I told Christy let's kill everybody then find a random homeless man to take the blame. It would be the perfect crime."

"Yeah, I just couldn't refuse when Julia put it that way. I wanted to pull off the perfect crime. So that's it. That's why Aviana and the others had to die."

"Really? Is that the truth?"

"Ben you idiot," Christy said, "you know how hard it is to pull off one murder, let alone like five? You think we killed all those people and didn't slip up one bit? Are you insane?"

"No, I'm not insane. I'm lonely. And you took my love away from me."

"Julia, do you want to tell him, or should I?"

"I got this," Julia said. "Ben, look out behind you."

"Nice try."

Ben didn't turn around, he didn't believe them. Then he felt the hard impact on the back of his head and fell over, his clutch on the deadly knife increasing, ready to sink it into the uninvited guest, but the guest was a difficult target because it was a miniature squid. A little Cthulhu monster. About six inches tall. Purple, somehow, instead of green.

It was far out of reach. Ben jumped at it with the knife in both hands, slamming it down into the ground, but all the monster had to do was glide across the hardwood floor on its slimy tentacles and it was out of harm's way.

The monster leapt up and onto Ben's back. He reached for it but couldn't grab it. Then its tentacles slid around both sides of his neck while the girls cheered it on. The two coiling tentacles met and condensed around him, choking him, and he let go of the knife to claw free of the purple coils. The purple Cthulhu dropped down. Ben turned to face it. Its little tentacles were bawled up and ready to strike. They were in a standoff.

"So you brought reinforcements with you."

"Like, we had to be prepared. Duh," Julia said. "You go get 'em, Lavender!"

"Go Lavender go!"

"And isn't this proof enough for you to believe us now? We created him with the Necronomicon."

"I don't believe a word either of you have said."

"That's living proof right in front of you!"

"That pipsqueak is proof of nothing!"

Suddenly Lavender jumped at Ben's head and attached itself to his face, blinding him. Ben dropped the knife and staggered forward screaming. He accidentally stepped over a fallen couch cushion and smacked his head into the floor real hard. He screamed in pain. But the girls took it as an opportunity to free themselves—his knife was theirs for the taking. It was lying on the floor since he lost his hold on it in the commotion.

Christy inched to it, wiggled her numb fingers around it into a proper position, and cut gently until her hands were loose and she was freed. Then she cut the ropes from her feet. While she helped Julia out of her own restraints, Ben had ripped Lavender off his face and thrown Lavender at the wall; but Lavender did not explode or splatter like the other Cthulhus at the Asylum Resort had done on impact. Lavender was crafted differently, and had time to grow and evolve unlike its brethren. It was much stronger than the others had been in their short lives.

Now the tables had turned. The girls had the knife, and Ben was on his knees on the floor begging.

"Please don't kill me! I'll do anything! I don't want to die! I don't want to die! Please don't kill me!"

"Don't worry." Christy touched her finger to the tip of the knife. "We won't touch a hair on your ugly little head. We aren't psychopaths like you are, Ben. But… maybe we should have some fun with you first."

"Actually, no." Julia picked up Lavender. "Before we have any fun, first thing's first. I need you to apologize to Lavender."

"What? No."

"Say sorry! Say sorry right now!" Julia kicked him in the stomach. "Say it!"

"Sorry! I'm sorry, Lavender!"

"There, that wasn't so hard, was it?" Julia said, then turned to Christy. "Now what?"

"Hmmm…. I have an idea."

36

WITH THE SPELL THAT Christy read from the Necronomicon, Ben would feel pain but wouldn't die. He'd suffer from the torture that the girls planned to inflict on him, but he would stay alive because of the enchantment.

The girls explained it to him before beginning.

They used his rope to tie him by his feet and hang him upside down by a spike in the wall. All the blood in his body was rushing to his head.

"Please I'm sorry I'm sorry don't kill me."

"We won't kill you. I just told you that, because of the spell, it'll be anything but."

"You should be a better listener, Ben. Girls love that. Isn't that how you scored some points with Aviana? Oh wait—any guy could score points with her just by existing. Haha."

"You shut up about her!!!"

"I don't think so. She was a whore. Get over it."

"No!"

Julia picked up the knife. "May I?"

Christy nodded. "Go ahead."

The inaugural incision was a poke in his abdomen. He wailed as the tip of the knife ruptured his skin. It tricked down in a very, very thin streak about the width of a hair.

"That's it?" Christy said. "Jules we could hack his leg off and he wouldn't—"

"We have to build up to it. Be gentle with him first."

"Hmmmm.... Good point. Let me try."

"Sure." Julia gave her the knife.

Christy tore a one inch gash of an extension to Julia's initial cut. Blood gulped out of his body.

“You want to see something cool?” Christy said to him. He didn’t reply so she kneeled at his side, holding the point of the knife to his nose. “I asked you a question. I asked if you wanted to see something cool. Do you? Well, do you?”

“Suh-sure.”

She grabbed his hand spread his fingers flat on the floor, then Julia turned Ben’s head and kept hold of him so he couldn’t turn away.

“Please don’t. Please—”

“Nuh-uh, no begging gets you out of this, considering what you wanted to do to us two, okay? You can’t get out of this. There’s just… no way, okay buddy?”

He said nothing.

“So look how cool—” Christy chopped off his thumb before finishing her sentence. She held up the severed thumb and said, “This is.”

A blood curdling scream.

“Oh, don’t worry. Look, see?” She put the thumb back over the stub that was left behind, and the strands of flesh merged back together. He was reunited with his thumb. “All better.”

“Woah, that was cool. We could do anything we want to him and do it a hundred times over, and he’ll feel it every time!”

Christy gave Julia the knife. “Cut something off.”

“I wanna try something without the knife.” Julia gave it back to Christy, then she stuck her finger into the wound on his stomach. She dug deep and he twitched and squirmed in agony, begging her to stop.

She didn’t listen to a word of it. Instead, she pulled on his flesh with both of her hands and ripped his skin like she was ripping through thin plastic. Christy joined her and pulled a strand of flesh straight down his belly to his chest, pulling on it until it thinned and snapped at the very end.

“Oh my God! Cut it out! Cut it out!”

“You might just get what you wished for.” Christy unzipped Ben’s pants.

“Noooooooooooo!”

“Sorry. Snip, snip.” Christy dragged the knife against Ben’s pelvis and drew blood. “It’s so tiny I can’t even find it. I’m glad you didn’t have a chance to disappoint Aviana with it.”

“Kill me just kill me!”

"Oh shut your mouth," Julia said, then she pieced his torn skin back together and it healed instantaneously. She only left out the long strand that Christy had pulled. "May I use this, Christy?"

"Of course you can!"

Julia wrapped it around Ben's face to shut his mouth. It stretched like elastic, and any noise he made was muffled. He tried to smack Julia away but Christy used the knife to chop off his hands. Blood shot up in a thick burst into Julia's face. She brushed it away.

"So gross. Watch where you aim his appendages when you cut them off."

"I'm so sorry about that. Won't happen again. I promise."

"You better promise."

"Watch this, Jules." Christy plunged the knife into Ben's groin and carved out his private area. It writhed as she clutched it. She held it up close to his face for him to see.

And he passed out.

"Reattach it. When he's awake we can cut it off again."

Christy did so.

Julia smacked Ben's cheek. "Wake up champ. Come on."

When he was conscious again, his eyes were full of tears. He shook his face back and forth, begging with his eyes for this all to end. His muffled words became louder and more frequent, so Christy undid the length of flesh that Julia had tied around his mouth to shut him up. She set it back on his body and it fit back into place. He was uncomfortable as his skin retook its natural form.

"Yes?" She said.

"I'll do… whatever… you want just… make… the… pain… stop please… make it stop please…" Ben was out of breath, and still sobbing from the immense pain that was inflicted on him. "Please stop it… please… beg… I'm begging… please… whatever you two… want… I'll give… promise…"

"What could you even give a woman who has the Necronomicon?" Julia said.

"I dunno. We could do practically anything we want with it," Christy said. "But we've been careful not to let it go to our heads. After all, power corrupts. So we only use it in important instances, such as this. I don't think there's anything you can give us, Ben."

"Sorry, Ben, but this is the way it's gots to be."

"Unless…. Nah, never mind."

"What, Christy? What were you gonna say?"

"It's nothing."

"What is it?"

"Unless he could hold his own in this house against The Raven Hill Butcher. Then we'd let him survive. But I don't think he could do that, and The Butcher and his little feral girl sidekick both disappeared after our little run in last winter."

"What a shame, Christy."

"Yeah, Jules. Truly a shame."

"You have the Necronomicon. Summon them. I'll do it. Whatever. I'll fight whoever. I want to live. Untie me."

"Let me think about it," Christy said.

Julia picked up the ka-bar knife and slammed it through Ben's forehead, submerging it deep into his brain. His mouth was agape and no screams came out, only a dry moan and an empty gasp. His body convulsed and one of his eyes twitched open and closed repeatedly. Blood poured down in heavy bursts.

"Oh God—you should see the look on your face! Well, that'll give you something to think about, Ben, while me and Christy talk things over."

37

THEY CUT DOWN THE rope and set Ben up straight.

He was leaning against the back of the couch, the knife still sticking through the other end of his head, his eyes still twitching, and his skin still pale. His other eye, the one that wasn't twitching, was drooped, and he couldn't look straight at them.

"Champ." Julia smacked him. "Hey, champ. We're talking to you. Are you listening to us?"

"Maybe we should take out the knife, Jules."

"Oh don't baby him now. You baby them at this age and they'll never learn."

"Too late for that. A guy like this has been babied his whole life probably. Well, I dunno. I don't wanna talk about his parents behind their backs, they aren't here to defend themselves. But Ben, man, you are fucked up in the head."

"Fine. Do what you want."

Christy pulled the knife from his head, and dense globs of brain were pulled out with it. She wiped the blade clean on his hair. Quickly his eyes adjusted and fixed themselves, and he was able to study them without twitching or drooping.

"Now champ," Julia said, "we're gonna play a little game. We're gonna use the Necronomicon to summon them. It's up to you to outsmart The Butcher and his sidekick, and if you win you can walk right out of here. If not, well, we aren't gonna stop them from hurting you."

"And Lord knows they're thirsty for fresh meat after we defeated them."

"I don't want to die, I want to live, please just let me—"

"Nuh-uh-uh," Christy said, "we just made a deal with you and now you want to back out?"

“We can’t let you go, Ben. After what you did to us, and had planned to do to us. Look if you had just come clean before touching us then it would be a whole different story right now, but I just can’t forgive you for what you did. I admit, I’m one to hold a grudge.”

“As am I.”

“I don’t wanna die.”

“Maybe you’ll live. Now will you let us go over the rules?”

He hung his head.

“Julia, tell him.”

“You’re gonna begin this little ‘challenge’ tied up. Good luck figuring out how to free your hands. We’ll unbind your feet in a moment, so fret not, Ben. You’ll have access to this knife, but again, with your hands tied behind your back it’ll be pretty difficult. Besides that… just try to survive. Or don’t. I don’t really care either way. I’m just here for the entertainment. Did I miss anything?”

“No Jules you’ve mentioned everything. I just want a nice, clean fight. Play fair, but God knows The Butcher and that girl won’t. I just don’t want any funny business, you understand, Ben?”

“Yuh-yes.”

“Excellent.”

Julia patted him on the head. “You’re a good sport. I’m open to giving you some girl advice if you survive, but really I can’t see any girl touching you with a sixty-nine and a half foot pole.”

“No, no, it’s thirty-nine and a half foot pole.”

“Yeah well they’re not touching him with one of those either.”

38

POPCORN WAS READY.

Christy and Julia were ready for the competition to begin.

The knife was lodged into the wall to make it difficult for Ben when the game of cat and mouse started. His hands were bound behind his back. Tears were in his eyes again. He was begging them to let him go, but they refused.

Julia read from the Necronomicon, and the door opened on its own. Darkness lingered outside, as if time were clinging to the night instead of willing to pass into day. Two figures were at a distance from the house, and as they came closer, snow spilled from the sky.

The Raven Hill Butcher, still wearing that same Santa Claus outfit from before. But now the outfit was tattered and torn. Scattered holes in random places. Stains of blood. The hat was on straight. The feral girl entered with him on all fours. Her hair was the same length as last time, and now it was dusted with snowflakes and devoid of any dirt or leaves like it had been last time. Her nails were long and dirty, forming vicious claws. Her lips were curled back and a drop of blood, perhaps from a recent victim, dripped from a corner. She was smiling, and her eyes sparkled.

The Butcher and the girl were excited for the game. Excited for the hunt.

The door shut on its own behind them.

Ben wobbled a step backwards, thrown off balance by fear and his lack of arms, and he bumped into the couch. He straightened himself and his face was reddening with each passing moment, and billows of sweat dripped from his forehead. His breaths were shallow and nervous. His eyes darted between Julia and Christy and The Butcher and the girl.

"Please…" A begging whisper.

The girls wordlessly shook their heads.

Then Ben pissed himself. A puddle of liquid at his feet.

The girls laughed at him, and Christy said, "Let the games begin."

39

Ben slipped on the piss and landed flat on his butt.

He stood up quickly as The Butcher approached from one side and the feral girl from the other, but he reached the ka-bar knife in the wall before either of his opponents could reach him. Before removing it, he used its edge to cut the rope, cutting his wrist in the process and drawing blood, but he didn't worry because—as far as he knew—he was still under the enchantment of the Necronomicon, and nothing could kill him, it would only hurt him.

Ben pulled the knife from the wall and backed into a corner. He held it in a shaky hand as The Butcher and the feral girl closed in on him.

"Please don't kill me! It's those girls you want! Kill them and take the Necronomicon! Leave me alone! For the love of God, please! Please!"

Julia shrugged from across the room. "Shoulda believed us, then you wouldn't be in this mess. Sucks to suck, Ben."

"Yeah," Christy said, "shoulda listened but you didn't, now you get what you deserve. Don't pretend you'd have let us go if we begged, because you wouldn't have. You big jerk."

"I'm sorry! I'm sorry!"

The feral girl was an arm's length away, raising her paws, and she slammed them down at the moment that Ben jumped out of the way. She crashed goofily into the wall, and Ben bolted for the hallway, turning corners and getting lost in the gigantic labyrinth of a house. He heard footsteps following him—The Butcher, he was sure—but didn't know where to run or where to hide.

He had to find some place where he'd be safe, where he could get away. Or better yet, he had to find an exit—whether the back door or a window in one of these rooms where he could sneak out of. The only downside was his keys weren't with him—he didn't know where he left them, perhaps upstairs where he had tied the girls up, so he couldn't drive away. He'd have to run away on foot and pray that nobody would know he was outside so they wouldn't know to chase after him.

And if he got away from here, would he ever be safe anywhere he went?

Christy and Julia laughed listening to Ben's screams and cries as he frantically ran through the house.

"When are we gonna tell him it's all in his head, Christy?"

"I'm enjoying this too much to let him know otherwise. I wonder how far we can take it."

"Doesn't he know if we were able to summon the people who killed all our friends, we'd kill them with the Necronomicon? What idiot would believe any of this is real?"

"You've become pretty skilled at that magic stuff, Jules. There's got to be some good use for that in the world somewhere someplace."

"What do you think happened to them? To the killers?"

"I dunno. Maybe they're still out there somewhere."

Ben tried to close the door quietly but he accidentally slammed it behind himself. Was that too loud? Would they hear? He didn't know, but he was panicked, and there was a window in the room. He could get out of this. He was barefoot, he wasn't in much besides his jeans and t-shirt, but he didn't care. He could worry about freezing to death later, when he was safely far away from the feral girl's claws and teeth and The Butcher's deadly dagger.

Quickly he locked the door. There was a bed in the room. He pushed it below the window to reach up to it.

As it opened, there was a loud rasping on the door. Slamming. Furious beating. Ben looked furtively over his shoulder to find that it was cracked partway open, and breaking further open by the second.

Not much time.

He crawled through, and freedom was ahead of him. That huge stretch of lawn, the street, the block across from the Morrison house, and everything that stretched far beyond it. An endless escape from this madhouse. Furiously he crawled with one hand in front of the other, and he was a free man until the hand clutched his ankle and dragged him back into the house. The knife nearly fell from his hands but he kept his hold.

It was The Butcher. He pulled Ben over the broken wood and back through the house to the living room. The feral girl was there with a box of matches. She lit one and threw it into the fireplace. Immediately it was overflowing with flames.

"No! No! No! Please help me! No!"

"Sorry." Christy called with her hands around her mouth like a megaphone. "No can do."

"Yeah, what she said." Julia laughed. "No can do."

The Butcher grabbed Ben with both hands and lifted him, and in sudden desperation Ben found it in himself to ram the ka-bar through his attacker and sink it deep inside of him. He twisted the knife and the man let go. Ben slashed the knife through the attacker another time and nearly severed his arm, then the feral girl jumped into action.

She sank her claws into Ben's back. With one swift turn he knocked her off and into the wall near the fireplace. Moving purely by savage instinct alone he plunged the knife into her stomach and pulled it upward. Blood spewed forth from her mouth.

She coughed, stepped forward, her claws raised, then she eyed The Butcher, her hands suddenly dropped, and she collapsed at Ben's feet.

The Butcher reached for the girl, but Ben pulled her away from him before he could reach her. Then he pushed her face into the fire, and she screeched like a wounded animal. The flames devoured her flesh and ran down her long stretches of hair.

Ben raised the knife. The Butcher staggered to his feet. He charged at Ben with his own knife but Ben moved quicker than his wounded attacker, and he swung the knife and decapitated him. The Butcher's head rolled around on the ground, then the body went slack and tumbled.

Ben let out a huge sigh of relief. He stepped forward and faced the girls who were still eating popcorn.

"I'm free to go, right?"

"What do you think, Jules?"

"Hmmm.... I dunno."

"I dunno either."

"But I killed them both! I won! Fair and square! So you have to let me go!"

Julia shook her head. "Ben. You are so gullible."

"Huh?"

Christy rolled her eyes. "Behind you, idiot."

Behind him the feral girl crawled out of the fireplace. Her skin was completely melted but beneath it she was laughing with a demented and sardonic smile. The Butcher picked up his head and the Santa Claus hat that had fallen off. He fixed the hat so it was nice and straight, brushed off a bit of dust, then set it back on his neck.

It healed.

And the girl's skin was in the process of healing too.

"But—but—"

"Ben, the odds were against you this whole time. You think you were dealing with a Necronomicon amateur or something? I've been practicing with this thing for a whole year between classes. I could do things with this book that you couldn't even dream of."

"So what's gonna happen to me now?"

"Christy, what do you think happens to poor Ben here?"

"Have mercy on me Christy please for the love of God, those killers are the ones you want, that guy killed your brother and your friends, not me!"

"Yeah, well, I'll deal with them later. Here's what's gonna happen. I'm gonna let them chase you around the house a thousand times more. The pain will never cease, will never go away. They'll torture you and you'll heal back up. But... there is one loophole. Should I tell him about it, Jules?"

"Sure, go ahead. It's the least we can do for him."

"Tell me! Tell me!"

"Geez, calm down," Christy said. "So… since we've enchanted you, there's only one way to make your death permanent, kay? And that's if you die by your hand."

Ben raised the ka-bar to his throat.

"Look at that, Jules! He's gonna do it!"

"Are you two just fucking with me still?"

"Not at all," Julia said. "Be a man for once and just do it already."

Ben gulped.

He pressed the blade deep into his flesh and sliced.

The girls laughed.

Christy picked up the phone. "The cops are so gonna flip when they find out there was another death in this house a year later, with us as the only survivors."

"Yeah, well, thank God you had the genius idea to set up his camera to record the suicide."

"And you had an even better idea to enchant your voice so you could sound just like him when you recorded the confession on the tape recorder. Now he's gonna take the blame for what happened last year. He couldn't live with what he did, the guilt was too much for him, so he came here to kill himself."

After Christy was off the phone, Julia said, "Do you think we'll see that cute officer again? I swear I think last time he winked at me. You better not get in my way!"

"Hey, I saw him first."

"Don't make me use the Necronomicon to give you a zit!"

"You wouldn't dare!"

"You're right, I'm not that cruel, but desperate times call for desperate measures."

40

Snow spilled across Raven Hill.

Somewhere in the shadows The Raven Hill Butcher was lurking, seeking his next victim.

RAVEN HILL COLLECTED EDITION BONUS CONTENT

Contents

BONUS CONTENT!

THE FOLLOWING ARE ALTERNATIVE scenes and deleted scenes and some of my thoughts on this series. This content is only available as a special thank you for those who purchased the collected edition, and are not available in the individual editions.

WHY DID I REBOOT THE SERIES?

I TRIED THINKING OF other authors who rebooted a book. Movies are rebooted all the time, and Michael Mann and Alfred Hitchcock both each remade one of their own movies. Especially in recent times, movies have gotten many reboots, remakes, whatever. But never really books. I suppose something kind of close is William Peter Blatty did another draft of The Exorcist for the 40th anniversary edition, where he cleaned up a few lines of prose.

I suppose since most writers are better than me, they have no need to revisit the material and redo it. But I wrote these first five books at 22. I was 25 when I decided to reboot it. I had the idea of a reboot as a joke after I finished book five, just as a joke. But the more I thought about it, the more I liked the idea. I liked the books as they were, but some things always bugged me since I never had much of the books thought out. I had this menacing killer, a strange origin, and some things that just didn't feel like they connected.

At the same time, I had an idea for a different book. A boy would see the "missing camper from last year" and try and solve the vanishing. But the more I thought about it, the more I thought I could work it into Camp Solgohachia. And I kept thinking about the cabin, and why was it off limits, and why did I never utilize it?

So I decided to reboot it. And while Camp Solgohachia was the second book in the series, I decided to reboot it as the first of the two reboots.

I did not work with an outline. I usually don't. Sometimes I have an outline. Sometimes the outline is light, sometimes it's heavy. Sometimes I get halfway through a book and outline the end. Sometimes I'll outline certain sections of books. I usually deviate so much from outlines that I end up throwing them all away. The same is said for writing a book without an outline—I often end up throwing the whole thing away.

I think when I revisited these books I wanted to prove that I could be a better writer than what I had turned out previously.

I have about 9,500 words of an alternate direction for A New Beginning. Originally I had Russell being evil, I had the kids killing the feral child, I had plans for the groundskeeper to make a deal with the devil to get supernatural abilities to be able to kill the kids. But my friend who just goes by "Hotdog" told me that the idea was dumb. It would be much more interesting if the killer was the feral child. "We've seen so many slasher movies where it's just a groundskeeper or something. You have the chance to do something different."

So I took his advice. I scrapped what I had written. But I've saved it and here it is for you to all see, just for fun.

BOOK 6, SCRAPPED ATTEMPT, CHAPTER ONE

THE HORRORS THAT BEFELL Camp Solgohachia all began on the first day of camp when David Morrison and his friends decided that they would go to the forbidden cabin deep in the woods that coiled tightly around the campgrounds.

The sun was setting, and all the little campfires were burning, casting amorphous shadows. New friendships were being made, laughs were being shared, secrets were being whispered. There was something about this feeling that David hoped would never go away.

He was sitting with Jennifer, Betsy, and Dean. They were passing around doughboys. He grabbed one from Dean, told him thanks, then held it into the fire.

"What's he look like?" Betsy asked Jennifer.

"Tall with blonde hair," Jennifer said. "I don't see him anywhere. Just my luck. I meet a guy and then he forgets about me."

"What are you chicks talking about?" David turned over his doughboy.

"Jenny met a guy, she told him to meet her by the water fountain but he completely stood her up."

"Cut the guy a break," Dean said, "it's the first day of camp."

"Jenny's already planned out her whole future with him. She told me she already picked out baby names."

"Oh God, maybe that's why he stood you up," Dean said.

“Well I didn’t tell him that. I only told Betsy, and she can’t keep her mouth shut. Just like her legs.”

“Hey.” Betsy playfully punched Jennifer.

“Well,” David said, tracing her body with his eyes, “if he doesn’t show he doesn’t know what he’s missing.”

“Oh, there you are.” A guy exactly like the one Jennifer described sat next to her on the log. He put his arm around her. “Sorry I missed you. I got in a little trouble.”

“What trouble.”

“I beat a couple guys up.”

“Woah, are you okay?”

David laughed. “You don’t look so tough dude.”

The new guy looked at David as though he were about to punch him. “I sure as hell could take you.”

David forgot about his doughboy. When he pulled it out of the fire it was completely burned. “You expect me to believe a guy like you got in trouble for beating up two other guys?”

“Yeah, what about it?”

“For one, they must have been kids left over from Junior Camp last week. For two, you—”

“The mouth on this guy,” he said to Jennifer. Then to David: “You better watch yourself.”

“What, you can’t take a little ball busting?”

Jennifer’s friend stood up and moved a step toward David. Jennifer grabbed his hand and pulled him back. *“Russel, don’t hurt him. He’s my friend too you know.”*

Russel slipped out of her grip. “Tough talk coming from you, porker.”

“Yeah? What are you gonna do about it?”

Russel sat next to David and held up his right hand. “Arm wrestle me.”

“You’re on.” David tossed the uneaten doughboy back into the pit, then grabbed Russel’s hand.

“Awe David,” Dean said, “you don’t know what you got yourself into. I’m not gonna help you out when he beats your ass.”

“Thanks Dean.”

David's arm strained under Russel's strength. Russel seemed to effortlessly overpower David, and while David held on as best he could, Russel pinned David in about ten seconds. David wiped away sweat from his forehead then challenged him to a rematch.

"Two outta three."

"Then you'll say three outta five."

"You backin' out?"

"No way." Russel shook his head. "Let's go. Just promise me you aren't gonna take a bite outta my hand."

"No guarantees."

David tried again to hold on for longer than ten seconds but it was no use. He wasn't strong enough. Russel pinned him almost instantly.

"You're all right, Russel. Jenny, I like this guy."

The boys shook hands.

"You're a good sport, David."

"Thanks. But you know, I still don't think you're so tough."

Russel laughed, rejoining Jennifer and grabbing a doughboy of his own from their little box to roast over the fire.

"Anyone could beat up a couple Junior Campers or win a couple arm wrestling matches against a guy like me. I wanna make a bet with you." David grabbed his wallet from his pocket. "Ten bucks, how about it?"

"Ten bucks for what?"

"I bet you ten bucks you won't spend a whole minute in the cabin. That one way out there, the one that the counselors always tell us is off limits."

"Ten bucks for one minute? That's it? Hell for ten bucks I'd stay in there for ten minutes." Russel pulled out his own wallet, and pulled out two five dollar bills. "You're on."

"You guys can't do that," Jennifer said. Everyone ignored her.

"Witness?" Dean said.

"Sure."

They each gave Dean their money.

"Do I keep a percentage?"

"No," both Russel and David said at the same time.

“You guys, this is a bad idea,” Betsy said. “I really don’t think we should get kicked out of camp on the first day.”

“Oh, they’re not kicking us out,” David said.

“Let’s quit wasting time,” Russel said, pulling his doughboy from the fire. It had just finished. “Let’s head there now.”

BOOK 6, SCRAPPED ATTEMPT, CHAPTER TWO

THE CONTORTED BRANCHES REACHED for everybody like crooked fingers. The cavernous darkness swallowed David and his friends up. The last remnants of the fire's lingering warmth on their skin was quickly fading, and the chill of night washed over them.

Betsy had a flashlight in her purse that she used to light the way.

"It's not too late to turn back, you guys," she said.

"Yeah." Jennifer put her arm around Betsy. "I really want to go back to the fire."

"We can't do that, sweet cheeks. Me and your friend have twenty bucks riding on this. It's easy money."

"I think we need to set up some rules," David said.

"Ah ha, here we go with the rules," Russel said. "You wouldn't be trying to find a way to back out, would ya, David?"

"What? No."

"Russel." Jennifer pulled on his arm and pouted her lips. "Please can we go back to the fire? I'm cold."

"I'll buy ya a sweater from the gift shop with the twenty bucks."

"But I don't want a Camp Solgohachia sweater. I want a Fleetwood Mac sweater instead."

"Sure, whatever, sweet cheeks."

Betsy's light passed over the cabin.

Jagged and faulty, as if constructed by blind men. Splintery planks were sprawled across the windows and doors with rusty nails, nails that seemed they'd turn to dust if touched. It was nothing more than a ghostly silhouette—it shuddered in the wind, creaking in the night, home to clusters of spiders. Dust lay over the cabin like a layer of dirty snow. Nasty weeds twisted up from the ground and worked their way upon the sides of the cabin as if attracted like magnets.

Everybody halted. Then Russel broke away from the group and up to the front door. He grabbed the board that had been nailed into the door, and it came away easily in his hands. He looked the thing over.

"Hey, somebody's already been here."

"Get away from there," Jennifer said. "Russel come on."

"This wasn't even nailed in. Look." He opened the door. "I think somebody was already here before us." Then he tossed the board down. "You got your watch ready, David?"

"Yeah. One minute."

Russel shut the door behind himself.

Jennifer punched David. "I can't believe you made him do this."

"What? I didn't make him do nothing."

"Chicks, man," Dean said, "you can't argue with them."

"Oh what's that supposed to mean?" Jennifer put her hands on her hips.

"Whatever you want it to mean."

Betsy flashed her light against the broken windows. "I don't see him in there."

"Of course not," Dean said, "those windows are all covered up."

Betsy moved a step closer toward the cabin. "I think it's been a minute already. Where is he?"

"No, not yet. According to my watch it's been thirty-eight seconds."

"I'm going in after him. I can't believe I just met this *great* guy, he's so adorable and kind, and you force him to go into this haunted cabin. What if he gets killed?"

David laughed. "What? He's not gonna get killed. And yeah, 'great guy' didn't he get in trouble for beating up a couple kids?"

"It wasn't a couple of kids and I'm sure he had a good reason. I'm gonna check on him."

"No, you wait here. This was my bet, I'll go in. I'm sure he's just trying to scare us."

The cabin door shut on its own behind David, cutting him off from the glow of Betsy's flashlight, and trapping him in an indistinct crypt. His eyes were adjusting to the darkness as he moved careful steps forward.

"Russel? Where you at?"

No response.

David was about to rejoin his friends when a powerful scream tore through the silence had had been draped over the cabin. It was coming from the cabin's second floor, the echoes spilling down from the stairway that was barely visible with the faint traces of moonlight that penetrated the back window that was not boarded up.

He was halfway up the steps when the cabin door opened and a beam of light illuminated his path. He looked down, expecting everybody, seeing Dean by himself with Betsy's flashlight.

"What happened?"

"I don't know."

They ascended to the second floor where Russel staggered forward then slumped against a wall. Blood trickled along his right forearm in a thick streak then dripped to the floor. He reached into his right pocket using his left hand, struggling until he came away with something. A pocket knife.

"What happened to you?" David said.

"There's a monster in that room." He pointed his thumb, pointing along with the tip of the knife that was spring activated. "I trapped it in there. Now I'm gonna kill it."

BOOK 6, SCRAPPED ATTEMPT, CHAPTER THREE

DAVID PRESSED THE BUTTON on his own pocketknife and had it ready for whatever was behind the door. Dean stood behind him and Russel with the flashlight held steady in both hands. Russel kicked the door open and nothing happened.

"What gives?" Dean said.

Neither David nor Russel said anything. First Russel stepped inside, then David, and in the hallway Dean inched closer with his light spreading across the floor. The room was a bedroom. It wasn't old and junky, it was fresh and new. The bedsheets were new, there were clothes in a hamper, chocolate bars on the dresser, a transistor radio on the nightstand.

And a monster in the corner below the window.

It wouldn't have been quite right to call it a girl. It wouldn't have been quite right to call it a person. It was a sickly combination of man and nature. The creature was naked, almost aware of its nakedness, crossing her arms so that she wouldn't be looked upon. She was perhaps a couple years older than David and his friends. Her green eyes were sparkling with terror. Her lips were pulled back to reveal chipped and blackened teeth.

The monstrosity couldn't form words. It growled.

"Holy shit." Dean dropped the flashlight when he saw what Russel and David were looking at.

The strange *thing* across from them lowered her head, adjusted herself, and leapt from the corner to the bed, and from the bed she leapt at Russel whose knife was held forward in his strong grip, anticipating sinking it through the abomination's flesh.

But the monstrosity avoided it completely, and knocked Russel on his back. By instinct David helped wrestle the creature off of him, putting the girl in a headlock while its furred arms and legs painfully beat against him.

"Your belt." Russel screamed. *"Hurry."*

"My what?" Dean said.

"Take off your belt."

"What the hell for?"

Russel reached for the buckle and unclasped it. He didn't have to do much else because Dean backed a step away from him and pulled it the rest of the way off.

"I can't hold her much longer."

"I'm coming, I'm coming."

Russel slid the belt over the girl's throat, taking the place of David's headlock and strapping it to the foot of the bed. The creature clawed at it, trying to break free of it with her nails that were more like the sharp claws belonging to a wild beast.

"Yours too Dave."

David pulled his own belt off, and Russel snatched it away. He used it to bound the creature's hands behind its back.

Dean picked up the flashlight again and pointed it directly at her face. She shut her eyes against the sudden brightness and turned her face away. There had been many legends around Camp Solgohachia in all of David's years coming here—this being his final year—about the forbidden cabin, but never before had there been legends about a feral child.

Her hair was long and blonde. Besides her black teeth and a stray leaf or two in her hair, she wasn't very dirty. She looked... she looked almost *clean.* For the most part, it seemed, this girl had been taken care of.

But she was something *other.* She was completely lacking the spark of humanity behind her eyes.

Russel picked up his pocket knife. "Payback's a bitch."

"Russel? David? Dean? Where are you guys?"

"Is anybody in here? Hullo?"

“We’re up here,” Dean said, leaving the room and meeting the girls on the stairway. He was eager to get out of the room.

“Don’t hurt her.”

Russel couldn’t believe what David had said. “Did you see what she did to my arm?”

“Do you see what she is?” David looked at the struggling, crying girl then back up to Russel. “She’s feral. She doesn’t know what she was doing.”

“Yeah well if a dog did that to somebody you’d have to put him down.”

“She isn’t a dog, she’s a human.”

“That don’t look like any human I know.”

David shook his head. “I think somebody lives here. I think she might be somebody’s kid.”

“What the fuck are you smoking?”

“Look around. This room’s clean. These sheets smell like they were just washed. And that radio on the nightstand’s brand new. I say we release her before whoever stays here comes back and catches us red-handed.”

“No can do, Davey boy.”

“What would Jennifer think?”

From the hallway: *“Russel?”*

“Speak of the devil.”

Jennifer ran into the room. Dean and Betsy were right behind her.

“I told her not to come up, but she wouldn’t listen to me.”

“Russel are you okay Dean said you were—you were—oh my God.”

Jennifer put the back of her hand to her forehead and fainted—Dean sprinted three steps to catch her before she hit the ground. Then Betsy caught a glimpse of the feral girl desperately pulling against the belt that attached her to the bedframe and she screamed so loudly that it felt like glass cutting up the inside of David’s ears.

“Get these chicks out of here, guys. Davey, Dean, come on.”

David was gonna help pick up Jennifer when her eyes snapped open and she jolted away from him, backing into a wall.

“What is that thing?”

Russel lifted his arm out. “It bit me.”

She crawled to his side and kissed his cheek. “Are you okay? Do you need a doctor?”

“I’m sure I’ll be fine. Jen, you shouldn’t be here for this.”

"Well we heard all these noises and I was so scared for you…"

"That's not when I meant. What I meant," Russel held up the knife, "is you shouldn't be here to see what I'm gonna do to her."

"Russel." She took the pocketknife from his hands. "Don't joke like that."

"Does it look like I'm joking? I'm getting even with it."

"Getting even… she's a defenseless girl."

"You ever seen a girl that looks like that?"

"I don't care, you're not hurting her or we're through."

David finally put his own pocketknife away, forgetting he had taken it out. "You're outvoted here. None of us want to hurt her but you. This situation's too weird. Let's all go back to our cabins and forget any of this ever happened, all right? It's best we split before somebody finds us."

"Ah, fuck you."

As the group was making their way back to camp, Dean asked: "Who do you think lives in there anyways?"

BOOK 6, SCRAPPED ATTEMPT, CHAPTER FOUR

HE WATCHED THE KIDS leave the cabin.

When they were gone he went inside he set down his lantern and whistled for her. She limped down the steps whining. He traced over her body inspecting her while she licked him and gave him kisses.

"I'll make sure they never hurt you again."

BOOK 6, SCRAPPED ATTEMPT, CHAPTER FIVE

AT BREAKFAST THE NEXT morning, Jennifer and Betsy left almost as soon as they filled their plates, and they hurried out before anybody could stop them. They returned to the forbidden cabin. Now that it was daytime they were less afraid to be in the woods, but the cabin was still as eerie as it had been last night.

Cautiously they cracked the door open and peeked inside. Nobody was there. They stepped inside and the girl was there, drinking water out of a dog bowl. When the feral child saw them she whined and backed away, but the girls softly whispered to her and calmed her down, and the girl seemed to understand them.

They sat with her on the floor and fed her.

"I need your advice Betsy."

Betsy shrugged. "I dunno, your guess is as good as mine how she got here. Do we tell a counselor or something?"

"No, not about that. What do I wear tonight? I can't let Russel see me in anything but my best."

"You'll look fine in whatever you wear."

"Quit being nice. I want to impress him."

"I think he's already impressed."

"When I sit next to him at the bonfire again, should I sit on his right so he can see the left side of my face, or on his left side so he can see my right side? Which side do you think is my good side?"

"I think you're sitting on it."

When the boys were leaving their cabin that morning, Dean stopped his bunkmate Jeremy. Jeremy was a nerdy kid with thick glasses, very scrawny, and was always picked on a whipped with towels. One time, some of the other guys in their cabin had put two cockroaches in Jeremy's bed while he slept, and he woke up to find them on his face. He had trouble sleeping—or trusting anybody—after that.

"Hey Jer, I have a question for you."

Jeremy was the last one out and shut the door behind himself. "Yeah?"

"Last year at the bonfire you told me some story about the forbidden cabin."

Jeremy nodded. "Yeah I remember that, because you gave me a wedgie afterward."

"Geez, I'm sorry bud."

"I accept your apology, good sir."

"Do you happen to remember anything about that story? Can you tell it to me again?" Dean asked. They were heading to breakfast, and Dean made sure to keep his pace slow so that they'd lag behind the others and nobody would overhear what he was asking about.

"Sure. Legend has it a couple kids went missing there."

"No but there was more to it than that."

"Well somebody told me that the remains of the kids were found years, and that their bones had been picked clean by wildlife. Somebody else said the kids ran away together. I don't really know one way or the other.

David, Dean, and Russel ended up on the same basketball team during a pickup game. It was back and forth, both teams keeping the game to twenty-one—each basket worth either one or two points instead of two or three—close. The lead was never higher than three points either way.

Deadlocked at nineteen, David passed the ball to Dean. Dean dribbled along the baseline to the basket—a dumb mistake—and picked up the ball before his defender could steal it. He kept his elbows up to create space, searching for a teammate to pass it to. Russel, standing at the top of the key, cheated a few steps left then ran right along the perimeter, losing his defender and becoming wide open for the bounce pass.

SWISH!

Nothing but net.

"Great shot." David patted Russel on the back.

"I thought it was gonna come up short. Those dumb rubber balls have no grip, I don't blame Dean for having five or six turnovers."

"One. One turnover," Dean said. Another ball skidded their way from the game going on at the neighboring hoops. Dean tossed it back then said to Russel, "And let's not forget when we were down three and you threw it out of bounds."

"What, that? That was because that black kid couldn't catch the pass. It wasn't my fault."

"Don't make it obvious," David pointed his thumb discretely, "but I think you've got a fan, Russel."

Russel turned his head fully around, completely ignoring David's request to be discrete. "Where'd she go? All I see's the groundskeeper."

"Yeah, he was practically watching you all game. Didn't you see him Dean?"

Dean nodded. "I think he was standing there a while."

"What, were you fags checking him out? Yeah, that must be why you had six turnovers."

"I didn't have six turnovers."

Jennifer tried on her tight black skirt and a white top. She walked up and down the cabin as if modeling it off for a fashion show instead of just Betsy, who was laying on her bunk with her face resting in her hands, and a magazine open in front of her.

"Do you think he'd like this outfit?"

"You've tried on half of the clothes you've brought with you. Why don't you pick one already?"

"I dunno. Do you think I look good?"

"Jen, every time you ask me that, what do I say?"

"'Yes Jen, you look fabulous. Absolutely fabulous. Can we go now?'"

"So what do you think I'm gonna say to the fortieth outfit you've tried on?"

"Well... I dunno maybe you don't like this one."

"I've liked all of them, and I'm sure Russel will too."

Jennifer looked in her bag and found a green top that she changed into while keeping the same black skirt on. "How about this shirt instead?"

"Yes Jen, you look fabulous. Absolutely fabulous. Can we go—*oh my God. Oh my God.*" Betsy screamed. She was so startled she fell backwards off the bottom bunk. While she was on the ground she peeked over the edge of the bed, grasping it tight. *"Where did he go?"*

"Where'd who go?"

"Lock the door."

"You lock the door."

Betsy ran to the front door and made sure it was locked. "I don't see him."

"What are you talking about? God Betsy is this your way of getting me to stop trying on—"

"He was right there." Betsy kept her finger pointed at the window as she walked backwards through the cabin back to Jennifer, then grabbed her hand. "There was a man in the window. He was staring at us."

Jennifer shivered. "Did you recognize him? Maybe the guys are trying to prank us."

"This man was like sixty years old. It wasn't one of the guys."

"Do we have any weapons, Betsy?" Jennifer let go of her hand and grabbed the broom that was resting against the back wall. "I'll fight him off with this."

"Yeah, you be sure to give him a good cleaning with that thing."

"Let's get out of here."

Still holding the broom, the girls tiptoed across the cabin, keeping an eye on every window. They peeked outside and there was no man to be seen. Some girls were walking in and out of neighboring cabins, coming and going to and from the campgrounds and various activities.

"Are you sure you saw somebody?"

"Yes," Betsy said as she cautiously opened the door and quickly darted her head in each direction, having to be absolutely certain that no man was waiting out here for them. She took two steps over to the front window. "He was standing right here."

A little while later, the girls were in line at the mess hall. The line spanned around the side of the building, and after ten minutes of waiting they were close to the front. Jennifer's arm was locked with Russel's, and Betsy was reading her magazine to pass the time.

"Are you feeling better?" Jennifer traced the cuts on Russel's arm.

"'Course I am, sweet cheeks. Even when… *it* cut me it hadn't hurt much."

"Well your scream sure made it sound like it hurt."

"All right," Russel laughed, "even I can get scared sometimes. It caught me off guard. I hadn't expected anyone—any*thing* to be in the cabin with me."

"I still think we should tell someone," Jennifer said in a hushed voice so that nobody around them could hear her, but they were all so caught up in their own conversations that she doubted anybody was eavesdropping. "It isn't right."

"Well I think—"

"There he is." Betsy grabbed Jennifer with both of her hands.

Jennifer turned her face where here terrified friend was staring at. A man in dark jeans and a filthy white t-shirt was holding a shovel at a distance from the mess hall. He was walking away in the complete other direction, going further into camp.

"What, that guy give you a problem or something, Jen?"

"Betsy saw him looking in at us in our cabin."

"I'll go beat his ass."

Jennifer grabbed his wrist before he could get too far and pulled him back. "Stop, I don't want him to hurt you."

"Hurt me? The dude probably can't throw one punch without throwing a muscle."

"He didn't even do anything to me."

"But he was spying on us," Betsy said. "He was—"

"I didn't even see him. I don't know if he was looking in at us or not."

"Are you joking with me right now? I saw—"

"But Betsy—"

"I saw him looking at us. That was him. That has to be him."

"I don't feel right about this."

"You know, it's funny," Russel said, eyeing the disappearing groundskeeper then turning his attention back to the girls, "David and Dean said something about the groundskeeper earlier. That he was watching us during our pickup game..."

David and Dean filled up their water guns in the bathroom of their cabin, and when they left Dean picked up a couple rocks to loan into his slingshot. They waited outside of the mess hall on the side that faced away from camp, where they attached a rope to the bottommost step so whoever came down would trip. This side of the mess hall was the counselors-only section, and the counselors came in and out through the back door. There were a few camp counselors that the boys did not like, but there was no better opportunity than when the camp director himself walked out with two plates of food.

Camp director Charlie walked down the steps whistling.

"I can't believe our luck," David whispered.

"Oh hell yeah," Dean said.

It was a thing of beauty to see Charlie slip, his foot tangled in the rope, and to hear the girlish scream he let out. The food landed in the dirt and the boys go to work right away—there wasn't a moment to spare. David kept shooting water on Charlie's head while Dean drenched the rest of him. As Charlie squirmed on the ground and the boys ran away, Dean turned back just for a second, remembering his slingshot, and launched a rock that hit Charlie on his butt—and he let out another scream.

The boys ran off between the trees to avoid being caught—but then when they were met with the groundskeeper it was their turn to scream. The smarmy man watched them with hatred in his eyes. He breaths were deep and gruff.

The boys didn't linger around longer than necessary. They exited the woods, dropping the water guns, and fled to safety.

BOOK 6, SCRAPPED ATTEMPT, CHAPTER SIX

THAT NIGHT AT CAMP Solgohachia, there was a camp-wide activity at the basketball courts. Teams of boys were trying to play basketball while groups of girls were given free reign to interfere any way possible—such as brooms to swat the ball away while it was midair, and pool noodles to smack the boys with, among other things.

Jennifer didn't care about participating because she was sneaking away with Russel. He was in the inaugural game, but after that, when he was switched out, they would sneak off together. She waited for them in their agreed upon meeting place, the flagpole.

It was terribly dark tonight, and the sun had set early, but she had the faint glow of the lights that feebly stretched to her from all the way down at the courts. She'd wait for him no matter how long he needed, but she didn't like being alone.

CRACK!

A branch that was stepped over.

Chills crept up her spine.

Jennifer turned around. "Hello? Russel?"

No answer.

"Anybody there?"

No. No response. And no other sounds. She was completely alone, waiting for him at the flagpole. The game he had been in was over, he should have been here by now. Did he forget about her? Did he end up playing in a second game?

She waited for a few more minutes, but then she was worried. Had something happened to her? She thought about the groundskeeper, who, for some reason, she and her friends had kept seeing around camp today when they had never really seen him much previously.

Suddenly something clicked. She thought, *Was that his cabin? Does he know we were there? Does he know we know about…*

Jennifer felt sick.

She left the flagpole in a hurry and went back to the basketball courts. Russel wasn't playing in the current game, which was the second or third of the night, and she went through the thick crowd searching for him. She didn't see him anywhere but did find David lingering in the back of the crowd, talking to a girl that Jennifer didn't recognize.

She pulled David away. "Sorry I need to borrow him."

"What did you do that for?"

"I can't find Russel. Have you seen him?"

"Not since the first game ended."

"I think… I think he went back to the cabin."

BOOK 6, SCRAPPED ATTEMPT, CHAPTER SEVEN

RUSSEL WASN'T GOING TO let anything stop him from doing what needed to be done.

The pocketknife was warm in his hand. His flashlight separated the darkness in front of him and guided him between the trees on this starless night. When he came to the forbidden cabin its front door swayed open and shut with each touch of the wind, then it fully extended open as if it had been awaiting his arrival.

The cabin was even colder tonight than it had been last night. Goosepimples rose on Russel's arms while he scanned his light against the interior of the cabin, anticipating the creature's growl and for her to attack once more, but he didn't find her.

He tiptoed through the place, whistling, searching. His light revealed deteriorating walls that were open in scattered sections, bundles of leaves and newspapers and garbage that was gathered in every corner of the cabin, and a couch that was half-covered in mold.

The first time Russel had been here, he had done nothing for the feral girl to attack him. Now he was here with the intent to find her and she eluded him. Perhaps, he thought, she was upstairs, so he retraced his steps and came back to the room.

She wasn't there, but David had been right. This room belonged to somebody. They had left the radio on and its thin hum filled the room. There were fewer chocolate bars than yesterday. Stretches of moonlight poured into the bedroom and dispersed the swaying shadow of trees across the floor and walls.

Russel unwrapped one of the chocolate bars from the box then ate it as he leaned against the wall, looking outside to the night. Poor Jennifer, he thought, waiting out there all alone for him at the flagpole. But this was the only way he could get away from her—and the entirety of the camp—and kill the creature.

CREEEEAK!

AWOOOH!

Russel smiled.

She was here.

It was time.

He tossed the remainder of the candy bar on the bed then put two of his fingers in his mouth and whistled as loud as she could.

The stairway screeched under each step of the creature that moved along them on all fours. Russel hid behind the door and anticipated her entrance, playing over the fantasy in his mind, picturing the knife deep inside of her throat, her blood squirting out of the gaping hole that would be left behind once he pulled his knife out of the abomination.

BOOK 6, SCRAPPED ATTEMPT, CHAPTER EIGHT

SHE FOLLOWED THE CALL of her master, but when she passed through the door into his bedroom, it was completely void of any sign of life. Instinctively she turned around to leave, and a flash of moonlight exposed the face of her attacker—the strange man from last night.

He pinned her before she could raise her claws and impale him. The impact of his jump knocked her head into the nearby dresser, and her vision blurred into a haze. All she could do was flail her arms in defense and hope that she hurt him or that he would retreat. Her body was pulsing with pain and she wished her master were here to take care of her.

She was turned onto her stomach, her vision still blurry, and apparently none of the cuts she was making when her nails met his flesh had any impact on him. The attacker felt no pain. She strained under his tight grip but he was much, much stronger than she was, and he was bigger than her, and there was nothing she could do but take the pain and try to survive it.

Something slipped around her neck. Something tight. She coughed as she attempted to take in air. But her throat was tightening further still, and air wouldn't fill her lungs.

Another cough.

She choked.

Her arm reached desperately to scratch her attacker. He dodged it by pulling away from her, and because she was so restrained by her throat—and so weak from the attack—she couldn't do anything more.

He grabbed her by the wrist and pinned it to the floor. Her other arm was too far to reach over to him, but she worked it under the contraption he had attached her to the bedframe with and penetrated the material with her nails.

Then the attacker lifted his knife in the air, and her vision was unblurred. She saw her own frightened reflection in the weapon of death as it was brought down swiftly into her wrist. The demented attacker twisted it within her flesh, and uncontrollable pain traced her wound.

With sudden desperation she clawed at the fabric around her neck once more, and completely separated it.

Painful breaths as she inhaled air in big gulps.

The attacker hacked his knife at her wrist again and pinned it to the floor. She jolted her arm forcefully and abruptly back, and the last strands of skin that connected her hand to her wrist snapped. It was completely severed.

She skidded away in an hopeless attempt to escape. She couldn't move straight. She couldn't move fast. She beat him to the steps but crawling down was an impossible task from the lack of a right hand, and the slickness of the steps that were now streaked with her blood.

Everything swirled. Newfound torture burned her body. The sharp edges of the steps cut her body in the tumble.

The demented monster descended the steps, and she backed away, eyeing the door in darkness, wishing that her master would walk in and the familiar echo of his boots would fill the cabin. She wished to see the light of his lantern again. She wished to hear his calming voice again. She wished her master would take a weapon of his own and do away with the sick beast that now lurked on the ground floor with her in the dreadful blackness.

Inching backwards. Her heart beating disturbingly fast. Gasping again for breaths as if that restraint were still fastening shut around her throat. As the enemy came closer she screamed and pushed her arms above her in defense.

The knife slashed into her chest. A cold sensation squirmed spiderlike over her body, sinking under her skin, and she was paralyzed. She couldn't fight him. The knife was raised again and plunged into her torso. Blood collected in the back of her throat and dripped over the edge of her lips.

She slumped backwards. She laid there, feeling her lifeforce ooze out of her cuts and collect in a puddle underneath her body.

Colder and colder. The room was freezing.

He was laughing.

The cabin was already so blindingly dark that she couldn't see anything, but as death washed over her eyes she was greeted with an even more demented and sickly darkness. It was less of a haze as she had sort of imagined death would be, and more of a fading. Becoming less. Drifting away, as if being carried into another realm or another place.

Something faint outside the cabin; as her consciousness left her body, she could vaguely hear it.

Her master's boots. He was home.

BOOK 6, SCRAPPED ATTEMPT, CHAPTER NINE

RUSSEL STOOD OVER THE lifeless body of the feral girl and smiled. He had done a good job.

As he turned away from her the front door opened and in stepped the groundskeeper holding a lantern that reflected some light onto his face. When the groundskeeper saw the strange girl's body he dropped his lantern and ran to her side.

Russel backed away laughed. "So you're the weirdo that lives here. Yeah, that makes sense."

"Oh no no no baby no..." The groundskeeper cried in her puddle of blood. *"No no no no no no no. Darling no."*

Russel leaned against the wall with his arms crossed, still holding the knife. "Where'd you find a thing like that?"

The groundskeeper braced his hand on the wall and stood up, staggering forward with shaking knees. *"She was a good girl. She—she wouldn't hurt a fly..."*

Russel nodded. "Yeah? She did a number on my arm yesterday."

"I'm—I'm gonna kill you for this."

"You and what army, grandpa?"

The groundskeeper threw a punch but Russel effortlessly avoided it with one step to the right, then he threw a punch of his own at the crying man and knocked him between the eyes. The groundskeeper stumbled backwards and landed on the ground.

He wasn't moving.

Russel knelt next to him. "What's wrong, old man? You can't stand up? Those legs ain't what they used to be?"

The man couldn't respond because he was knocked out cold.

"Ah, now what to do with you?"

Russel paced the cabin up and down, up and down. On a countertop there was a rope. It was flimsy and dusty in his hands, but it seemed strong enough to hold an old man. He dragged a chair over to the two bodies, set it in the blood that was hard to avoid because it kept spreading without end. He lifted the old man into the chair and tied him across his torso, then bound his hands together, and was in the process of binding the man's feet when he heard shouting.

He paused. It was his name being called. *Russel. Russellllllll.*

"Russel are you in there?"

"Ah shit."

Jennifer stood in the doorway with a flashlight. David was behind her with a flashlight of his own.

"Russel you never showed, I was so worried about you I—I thought—I—oh my God what did you do?"

Their lights had moved in unison across the floor as she had been talking to reveal the mess. Blood everywhere, the groundskeeper tied to the chair, and Russel standing in the middle of it all. He understood what it must have looked like.

Russel stepped forward but Jennifer stepped back.

"Get away from me."

"Jen you don't understand."

David stepped between them. *"You're sick. Stay away from her."*

"Woah, woah, woah, I know what it looks like but you two need to believe me. I didn't do this."

"Do I look stupid to you?"

"Dave—"

"Yesterday you were ready to sink your teeth into her, today—"

"Let me explain, I was—"

"Her corpse is at her feet and you've got blood all over you."

"David, Jen, can't I explain?"

David moved Jen further away from Russel. “Go ahead. I bet you’ve got a *great* explanation.”

“After the basketball game I was on my way to the flagpole like we agreed Jen, didn’t we?”

“Uh-huh…”

“That pervert was stalking you from across the camp. I saw him and snuck up on him. He fled through the forest but I had a hunch which way he was going. When I walked in it was already like this.”

Jen frowned. “Why would he hurt her?”

“Jen don’t tell me you believe him.”

“Maybe he saw us last night. Maybe he knew we knew his secret. He wanted to get rid of her before he was caught. I don’t know.”

“That’s bullshit and you know it.”

“David you gotta believe me. I swear to God it was already like this when I got here. That’s why I tied him up. So he wouldn’t get away. He has to answer for this.”

“You really do think I’m stupid if you think I’d believe—”

Jennifer put her hand on David’s arm. “David—”

“And you sure know how to pick ‘em. Do you want me to take you back to your cabin?”

“No.”

“What? You want to stick around here and be caught with one, possibly two dead bodies on your hands? Fine by me. I’m outta here.”

“Wait,” Russel said, “what do I gotta do to convince you I didn’t hurt that girl?”

David was in the doorway and turned back for a brief second, looking David up and down under the glow of his flashlight. “When you’re telling the truth you don’t have to do much convincing.”

Russel shook his head. “He was a crazy old man. You want logic from a crazy old man?”

“All I’m saying is you wanted her dead last night, and today we come here and she’s dead.”

“Goddamn you’re not gonna get past that are you? It’s a coincidence. Look, it’s no secret we’re in this deep. I don’t know if there’s any way to get out of this.”

“You’re in deep. Not me. There’s no blood on my hands.”

"Answer this. Do you think he's dangerous or not?" Russel pointed his thumb back at the groundskeeper.

"What's it matter what I think of him?"

"The last thing I need right now is to argue with you. I've got to figure out what's gonna happen to our new friend here. Either you can keep yelling at me and being part of the problem or you can help me be part of the solution. What do you say, kid?"

BOOK 6, SCRAPPED ATTEMPT, CHAPTER TEN

RUSSEL AND DAVID DRAGGED the groundskeeper tied up in the chair up to the second floor and into his bedroom. Russel grabbed a chocolate bar from the box on the dresser and offered David one, but David declined the offer. Jennifer lingered in the doorway with her continual frown on her face. She never looked directly at the tied up man—she hardly looked at her friends. She didn't do much besides mope and sob, and occasionally she wiped away her tears.

"What now?" David said, wiping the sticky blood from his hands onto the wall. The old man and the chair were covered in it.

"This is all too much for me," Jennifer said.

"Jen, baby." Russel joined her in the doorway.

"You know… me and Betsy visited her this morning."

"Is that so?"

"Uh-huh. We fed her. She… she was a good girl."

"I'm sorry baby."

She rested her head on his shoulder, just about the only place where there wasn't blood on him.

David paced back and forth in the bedroom. "So what's your big plan here, Russel? Since you seem to have everything figured out."

Russel ignored him and said to Jen, "You've seen too much tonight. You shouldn't have stuck around. Let's get you back to your cabin, take a shower, and pretend none of this happened, okay? By the time you wake up things will be better."

"I asked you a question."

Russel turned to David. "Can't you see I'm talking to my girl? What do you want?"

"What's your big plan now? What happens to him? What about when Charlie and the other workers realize he's missing? What if they come looking here?"

"This is the last place they'd look."

"Then we don't have much time. Camp Solgohachia isn't that a big place. And if this is the last place they look then we've got about a day to figure it out."

"Let's regroup in the morning. Let's meet back here bright and early. I'll have answers for you then."

"Okay," David said, thinking, *Hopefully the groundskeeper doesn't turn up dead by then.*

Darkness tightened in around the cabin.

The stench of death made him sick, and he choked as he woke up.

His arms were numb from being tied up. How long had he been like this? He pulled with all his strength against the rope, but his wrists couldn't break free of them. He fumbled to stand but couldn't because his ankles were bond as well.

The hum of his radio was the only thing to keep him company. It was picking up more static rather than song; indecipherable lyrics lost in the steady hiss.

He thought of the child downstairs. Whenever he shut his eyes she was all he could see—but the lifeless form she had taken on, instead of how he had known her when she was alive and happy. She hadn't deserved what she had gotten. And now those kids needed to pay.

He was going to do anything necessary to get out of here.

And he was going to do anything necessary to avenge the child's death.

Jennifer crept into her cabin. Most of the other girls had already gotten there and were in bed, and the lights were off. That was good so they couldn't see the specks of blood that accidentally stained her clothes when she leaned against Russel.

"Where've you been?"

Jennifer jumped, but it was only Betsy. "I'll tell you later."

Betsy was saying something again, but it didn't register. Jennifer grabbed the first outfit that touched her hands and brought it with her to the back section of the cabin where the showers were, and she turned the knob all the way to the left.

She stepped inside and scrubbed the blood off her cheek right away, and watched it swirl down the drain.

The events in the cabin from both nights were replaying in her head. And she wondered what was true and what was not.

She knew Russel had wanted his revenge on the feral child. She also knew that the groundskeeper was watching them based on what all the others had said about seeing him around camp—Betsy had even claimed that the groundskeeper was watching them in this very cabin. Was it possible that he wanted to kill the feral girl too? Or was Russel lying? Had Russel killed her?

She didn't know who she believed. But she wanted to believe her new boyfriend—she wanted to believe that he was telling the truth and wouldn't lie to her.

Russel and David sneaked from the girls' cabins to the other side of camp to the boys' cabins. It was lights out. David had never felt more nervous in his life than he had felt now—creeping through camp with blood smeared over his clothes. If he were caught now, then there'd be no getting out of it. Nobody would believe him that he was innocent—and he had a feeling that Russel would not back him up either.

"Why'd you do it?"

Russel didn't answer him.

"Jennifer's gone. You can tell me the truth. I won't tell her what you say."

"Not a word of my story's gonna change, pal."

David kicked a little rock across an open stretch of grass. "Nothing you've said makes sense. In my opinion you went back for 'unfinished business.'"

"I don't know why you're so eager for things to make sense. You know how many things in this world don't make sense, Dave? You ever heard of those three kids in Australia that disappeared from the beach? What about that chick that went missing on a cruise with her family? Hell what about JFK? Lee Harvey Oswald didn't act alone."

"Yeah and for every one of those there are a thousand others that make sense, plain and simple."

"If I killed her why didn't I kill the old man?"

David thought it over. "I don't know. I'm not as slick as you. I don't have a little answer for everything."

"Last night I was angry, sure. Tonight was different. I had time to think things over. I was acting irrational when I wanted to kill the girl, I know I was. I know how things look but we've got that man up there tied up and he'll probably admit to it."

They were back at the cabins now. David put one hand on the knob. "You make a good point. I don't think I'll believe you unless he says otherwise. Goodnight, Russel. Better hurry to your cabin, and better burn that outfit. There's no getting those stains out, I don't think."

David went into his cabin, and Russel walked down to his.

BOOK 6, SCRAPPED ATTEMPT, CHAPTER ELEVEN

DAVID STOOD OUTSIDE THE forbidden cabin in the dead of night, then hurried to get inside of it when he heard screams pouring out of the partly open door. He shined the light straight ahead and it temporarily blinded Russel who shielded his eyes and accidentally dropped his pocketknife.

Jennifer was on the floor in a white dress that was now predominantly scarlet. Her throat was torn open from end to end, and blood gushed with each beat of her heart. She raised one desperate hand in David's direction although it was too late for him—or anybody—to do anything about it. There was no saving her, no helping her.

Russel regained his knife. David staggered backwards through the doorway back into the chilling night, and Russel followed him. David reached into his pocket for his own knife but his pocket was endlessly deep, there was no way to find the bottom of it, and his weapon was somewhere at its very depth.

"I tried to warn you," Russel said.

David stepped backwards again and tripped over an unseen object, falling on his butt but keeping a hold on the flashlight aimed up at Russel.

"Any last words?"

David opened his mouth but he couldn't speak—words would not form. The air around him was so hot he couldn't breathe—then his eyes snapped open and he found that he had been dreaming, he was in the cabin, and he was alone, and he was safe, and Jennifer wasn't dead.

He crawled out of bed and stretched. He checked his watch; there was enough time to make it to breakfast. He put on his shoes then left the cabin, and Dean was coming his way with two cartons of milk.

Dean handed him one. "There you are."

"Plain milk? What, were they out of chocolate?"

"You're welcome, buddy."

David drank it. "Thanks."

"I had a productive morning. You wouldn't believe what I found out."

David nodded.

"The groundskeeper's name is Job. Apparently he put his resignation in yesterday."

"What kind of name is that? And how'd you find any of this out?"

"The lunch lady Bertha was the key."

"The old lady?"

"That's the one, the one that's like eighty-five," Dean said. "I went back in line for seconds then I broke down—you should have seen it, it was a thing of beauty—I told her I had a stomachache from the fish sticks they served at breakfast, and I needed to lay down and fast. I told her Charlie was my uncle and I wanted to lay down on the couch in his office, so she brought me down the employee-only hallway. But the door was locked.

"So I pretended I lost my key and then I looked under the mat and found a spare. I barged in but that sweet old lady came in with me, and I kept the charade up, laying on the couch and holding my stomach, and I asked her to get me a plastic bag so I could barf.

"She left me alone and I went to work. The resignation was on the desk, a letter in sloppy handwriting. I matched up the name to the file in the corner of the room and his picture was attached to it, along with a complete background. There isn't much in there about the guy, but he resigned. I wonder why. There's something going on here, Dave. Like what was he doing with that girl? Why did he stay in the forbidden cabin if he had a cabin of his own that the camp provided? And what's even the real story about the forbidden cabin anyways?"

BOOK 6, SCRAPPED ATTEMPT, CHAPTER TWELVE

RUSSEL RETURNED TO THE forbidden cabin bright and early, needing to make a stop here before any of the others could come by.

There was a muffled plea as he went up the stairs. The old man was awake.

Last night Russel had put duct tape over the man's mouth to keep him from making noise. When he peeled it back, the man gasped for breath.

"Good morning, sir."

The groundskeeper said nothing, still catching his breath.

"I gotta be honest with you, dude. I actually need *your* help."

The man stared at him.

"My friends are gonna be here soon. I need you to admit you were the one who killed the girl. You got me?"

Still he said nothing.

"Go ahead, say something."

"Why did you kill my darling?"

Russel pressed the button on his pocketknife and the blade sprang out. He put it under the old man's chin. "Listen to me, dude. You understand what I'm asking you? You can't tell them it was me or you're joining her. But if you play along I'll let you free. Capeesh?"

BOOK 6, SCRAPPED ATTEMPT, CHAPTER THIRTEEN

THE FLAGPOLE BECAME BASECAMP. That was where David and his friends all agreed to meet. He and Russel were the first two there.

"I guess your story checks out."

"That's a surprise. What made you change your mind, kid?"

David sat down in the shade; it was too hot today and he was sweating buckets. "Dean did a sleuthing. I don't know how he manages to get around so much. He broke into Charlie's office and found the groundskeeper's file."

"The balls on this guy to break into the camp director's office. What was in the file?"

"His resignation, apparently."

"Uh-huh."

"He must have seen us. He must have knew what we knew. Some of the stuff you were telling me and Jen yesterday's starting to make sense."

"See?"

"So he put in his resignation. I guess he wanted to sever all ties before getting rid of all the campers who knew his secret. So in a way you saved us by showing up at the cabin when you did."

"Hey, here come the others."

Jennifer was shielding her eyes from the sun. Dean and Betsy had locked arms together.

They exchanged hellos then it was time to get on with it.

Everybody entered into the woods, sneaking as carefully and conspicuously as possible to keep out of sight of any of the campers, counselors, or staff.

Although it was broad daylight, it still made David feel uneasy about coming to the forbidden cabin, especially knowing what awaited them: the sight of that body, and the smell a decomposing corpse must have made, and the vicious old man who was waiting there in the chair.

When they came to the cabin Russel turned around to address the group. Dean and Betsy hadn't been there. They hadn't known what had happened to the groundskeeper and the feral girl. He cleared his throat, then gave a speech that sounded almost rehearsed. He recounted for them the events of last night, and not a single word of his story had changed. He was right about that.

David was the last one in. Everyone gagged going up the steps to the groundskeeper's bedroom. He was exactly where they had left him, bound to the chair at the center of the room.

RAVEN HILL'S ORIGIN

THE NAME "RAVEN HILL" came from these spam emails I got in college.

Somebody kept sending me these emails, and it said it was coming from someone named "Raven Hill." And while I ignored all her emails, I kept thinking, I like that name. I didn't want to use it for a character but it sounded like a good name for a place, so when I was writing back then (I wrote a bunch of comic book scripts that'll never see the light of day, all for the best), I would set a bunch of them in Raven Hill. I have a couple cities where I want these stories of mine to take place in, all for different purposes, and all will somehow cross paths. Raven Hill, Ashfall, Moon Hook.

Raven Hill is briefly shown in book 2 of the Engstrom House series, which is primarily set in Ashfall, and will be mentioned in other books. I like having the same fictional cities because I can make everything up and don't have to be accurate to real life.

MY FAVORITE BOOK IN THE SERIES

I ALMOST GAVE YOU the fake answer of "I like them all" but my favorite has to be book 6, followed by 7. They're just such an improvement over 1-5, and I have such nostalgia for going to summer camp as a teen, and I based the camp in 2, 4, 5, and 6 on the one I went to.

Book 7 is just strange shlocky direct-to-DVD fun, so it's a runner up.

2026 update: My favorite is now 8, 9, and 10 mashed together. Seriously. I loved being unhinged with this series, and I somehow made it even crazier. I might just claim 8 as my favorite.

WHAT COULD HAVE BEEN

I DID ABOUT THREE drafts of each of the first 5 books, a draft and a quarter of book 6, and only one of book 7. I don't usually do first drafts but I knew the stories so well that it all fell into place once I figured out some of the details (like with the feral child). (2026 update: I wish I had done more drafts of book 7).

Since I was making it up as I went and didn't have a clear direction, here are some alternate things that happened previously:

-No Santa costume, the man was only dressed in black and described as a shadow, because 22 year old Nasser couldn't figure out to make him look like SANTA in a book called CHRISTMAS MORNING MASSACRE.

-Christy and Julia were the original main characters in book 3 until I replaced them. It was just lazy writing and didn't make sense.

-An entry in the series was set in 2013. I stopped setting books in modern times a long time ago, but I wanted to try writing a book set in modern day and see if I could make it good. My first few books, now out of print, were set in modern day before I decided to take cell phones and Google out of my stories and only do period pieces, or timeless pieces without years on them. But the one installment set in modern day was really awful.

-The original publication of books 1-5, with awful covers and a lot of typos, were not split up into chapters. Eventually, when I started formatting books myself, I decided to split them into chapters so I could put text on the spine. The original run of 1-5, the spines were just black.

Let's take a look at a couple of these things.

NOEL HELL DRAFT 1, ORIGINAL ENDING

CHRISTY AND JULIA RAN past the front desk into a hallway that was foreign to them, and it wasn't until they reached the end that they realized they hadn't the slightest clue where Jessie was. The end of this hallway gave way to another, shorter one, where a bright red and white exit sign glowed against darkness and spiderwebs. Jules suggested going through it and Christy agreed.

Both girls pushed on the long metal handle to open the door but it wouldn't budge most than a half an inch open, and they could see the snow outside came at least up to their bellybuttons if not higher. It would be impossible to open.

"He's almost surely got her," Christy said. "Why don't we run out the front doors?"

Julia nodded. "Yes, let's—"

The girls were hushed by sinister footsteps turning a corner, and a knife tapping along the wall.

The girls looked at each other with fright, then Julia opened the door of the storage closet in the hall and the two of them quietly hid inside.

They held each other in darkness, trying not to squeal, listening to the horrible tapping of the knife coming so close it was almost on top of them. The footfalls were louder now, coming into the very hallway the girls were hiding in.

Christy didn't think he knew about this hallway—how would he know where they were? Did he have a damn blueprint of the place? She was full of terror; the air of finality gripped them tighter now. Her stomach hurt so badly she wanted to scream, but she wouldn't let her clenched jaw budge.

The sounds stopped for a little while, as if The Raven Hill Butcher had been erased from existence.

Then the doorknob turned slowly, and Christy and Julia cried. There was no fireplace poker to help her here—and now more than ever she regretted failing; she felt like an idiot for not getting the job done, for not making sure he was dead, for not killing him. It was regret she'd feel for the rest of her life.

It flung open and diminishing light glimpsed into the supply closet. The Raven Hill Butcher raised his knife and the door slammed shut behind him. They were in pitch blackness now, and he could've been anywhere or anything. For a spit second, Christy thought she heard something like music in the distance, but didn't have time to think of it.

The girls squirmed and backed away from the monster, but the closet was tight and there wasn't much space to move. Something poked Christy in the back, and she realized it was the light switch. She flicked it on and he was above them, like he had been in the attic in her home.

He brought down his knife towards the girls but Christy broke away from Julia, both went in either direction, and the knife was stuck into the wall. He pulled it out, and Christy was frozen. But he didn't touch her—yet. Julia was closer; he grabbed her by the throat and pinned her to the wall. Julia yelled for Christy to run but she couldn't yet—she was suspended with shock.

The Raven Hill Butcher slammed his knife in one fatal swoop through Julia's face and pinned her into the wall. Her body convulsed and her hands twitched, then her feet straightened out and she was gone.

He turned to Christy.

Christy opened the door and ran.

The music was more pronounced in the hallway; it wasn't music but sirens. Somebody—and she didn't know who the fuck it could have been—must've phoned them. Was it Jessie? She wondered where Jessie was and hoped that maybe he hadn't got her, maybe he had quit looking for her and came for her and Julia instead. Julia—

Oh Julia I'm so goddamn sorry I'm sorry Julia please forgive me.

He was behind her; she heard his heavy breathing, peeked over her shoulder, and saw him with the bloody knife still full of Julia's brains. She sprinting towards the open doors which felt like they were ten—no, twenty miles away.

Her feet pushed hard on the ground and she ran with all her might, her heart thumped, her adrenaline rushed, her head pounded, she needed to breathe, needed water, but she kept pushing.

When she saw the group of officers pushing their way through the snow up to the door, she almost fainted.

Red and Z pushed through the mountains of snow; some were following, others had the building surrounding. They had tried to call the Asylum Resort when they received the calls from Mrs. Morrison, and it was impossible to get through—all the lines had been severed. If there was one silver lining to the police of Raven Hill, it was that they could finally put away the son of a bitch who was behind the massacre one year ago tomorrow.

They recognized the girl from last year—Christy Morrison—who was a few feet away from the doors, but they didn't recognize the man who was chasing her—the man who was clad-black in some sort of funny costume.

Z put two bullets in his chest; when the man fell to the ground, Red added a few.

Christy fainted, and the men knelt at her side. When Z looked back to their suspect, he was gone, without even a trail of blood. Bullet casings lined the floor. Those had been real, but the man—Z wasn't so sure.

The other officers came through the doors and asked where the man was.

Z said, "He's gone."

The entire hotel was searched head to toe twice, but The Raven Hill Butcher was not found. Julia, Jessie, Emma, and the staff of the Asylum Resort were all dead.

Hours later, Christy Morrison when Christy was laying in the hospital bed for evaluation, the clock on the wall across from her struck midnight—it all happened one year ago today, and Christy Morrison had survived the terror once again.

She wished she were dead.

EXCERPT FROM NOEL HELL DRAFT 1

"JESSIE CALLED, SHE SAID her and her little sister Emma will meet us there," Julia Holt said, zipping her bag shut. She sat down next to Christy Morrison on Christy's bed. "You okay?"

"No," Christy said. "How could I be okay?"

Christy cried again; she didn't want to but did a little anyways. Tomorrow would make one year since her brother David and her friends Mary, Aviana, Bekah, and Katie had died, and she couldn't handle it. It was a drag—that was the only way she knew how to describe it. It was shit. It was constantly on her mind. At heart, Christy felt guilty for living, and even during all the happy moments in the year since then, she still couldn't shake that awful feeling. That filthy feeling. That feeling she tried to scrub away in scalding showers but never could. That feeling she desperately wished and prayed to go away but it never wavered. It bogged down every happy moment of her life, it filled her mind during every final test of this past semester, and she wished she could get away from it for five minutes. But it was forever tattooed on her mind and her life.

"I'm sorry, Jules," she said. "I didn't mean to sound so rude."

Julia hugged her. "They're on my mind all the time too. I loved them all too."

"I was so rude to him," Christy said, hugging back. "I was so rude to David at the end. I should've been better. I should've—"

"You didn't know, Christy. There was no way you could've."

"I should've known."

"No, you shouldn't have."

"The door to the back was open, there were footprints—"

"I've heard you say this before." Julia sighed. "There's no taking it back. You're only going to drive yourself crazy."

"I might already be crazy," Christy said. " I promise you he was there. I hurt that—that maniac."

"I believe you."

"I had him… The Raven Hill Butcher…" Christy shuddered at the thought of him. "And he got away."

"He's gone," Julia said.

"I haven't stepped foot back in that place since it happened, Jules. I don't think I ever can again. I'm too scared he's waiting for me."

"You won't have to."

They were in the Morrison's usual household today and not the giant mansion they used for family gatherings and holidays. French impressionist prints lined the walls; it was a small cozy home that was welcoming, except for the void that was David's old room. Nobody entered it, and when they went past it they tried to ignore it. The house was long and narrow, two stories plus a basement. Ferns hung outside above the old crooked stone path that led to the garden and firepit and deck in the backyard.

Christy double checked that everything was packed then she grabbed her keys. "I'll get the car started."

She left with her bags, went to the driveway, and studied the falling snow as if in a trance. Christy couldn't take her eyes off of the endlessly falling flakes. Her lips pulled into a grimace. Christy knew what the avalanche of snow meant—or at least what it *felt* like. Impending doom. Fear. The chase. Feeling like a mouse in a tight space full of cats. Her stomach clenched. It took a while to shake the feeling, then she unlocked her car, tossed the bags into the trunk, slammed it shut, and started the car. After putting the heat on high she went back inside while it heated.

She tried to take her mind off of things; surprisingly it was easy today. A funny memory, perhaps her favorite with Julia, came to her. They had been walking around the college campus when she had carelessly run her hands over a bench and couldn't possible have seen the *WET PAINT* sign.

Christy had shrieked, and would never forget how badly Julia jumped in terror.

Christy looked down at her hands and laughed. “They’re blue!”

“Geez!” Julia had said. “You scared the shit out of me.”

“Gosh, I got paint all over my hands!”

“The worst part is they don’t match your outfit.”

They both laughed for a while. Whenever one of them brought it up again, they still laughed as if it *just* happened moments ago. It was a nice memory, a happy memory, one she was happy to revisit right now and be lost in instead of thinking about last year.

Back in the house she found Julia laying on the bed and shutting her eyes.

“If you fall asleep,” Christy said,” I’m leaving you here.”

Julia smiled. *“Suuure.”*

They had to shovel the driveway again, although they had already done that earlier. Snow was coming down in dreadful handfuls, and refilled the driveway. After the girls finished, they climbed into the car, and Christy turned on the windshield wipers. She pulled onto the empty street and the girls went straight down the road.

“I can feel it,” Christy said. “I’ve a really bad feeling about today.”

Julia gulped. “And so do I. But it must just be the anniversary.”

“Maybe,” Christy said. “But I don’t want to talk about this.”

“Talk about it as much as you need,” Julia said. “Holding it in does you no good.”

The girls went quiet for a while. Snow came down in clusters, and Christy realized she forgot to phone her parents to tell them goodbye before she and Julia left. It wasn’t a big deal she supposed—she’d call them from the hotel.

The hotel was the big plan. The hotel on the outskirts of Raven Hill. It was in the opposite direction from the mansion. It was in a far enough area where The Raven Hill Butcher couldn’t possibly know they were headed to. It would keep them safe; should he try to return to the mansion, he wouldn’t find anyone. But just to be safe,

Christy and Julia, the only survivors from that day, would flee for the anniversary. They booked a room for a week and would be joined by a couple of Julia's friends.

The hotel was called the Asylum Resort, it was cheap, under the radar, and the perfect place for two college women who wanted to escape.

During a long silence, Christy turned on the radio and started to flip through the channel.

"Hey, eyes on the road," Julia said. "I'll find the Christmas station."

Julia turned the dial and they caught the end of *White Christmas,* then it turned into *Have Yourself A Merry Little Christmas.* She sang along, then Christy joined her.

It was nice to get into the Christmas mood; it was nice to be happy, even for a little bit.

"It's nice to see you smiling," Julia said.

"Christmas music still finds a way to do that. God, I used to love Christmas so much." Christy sighed. "I wonder if it'll ever feel like Christmas again."

Julia turned her head to the window. "Hasn't felt like it to me in a few years."

"Really?" Christy glanced at her, then looked back to the carless streets. Snow came down in thick batches but she still managed to drive smoothly over it.

"After high school, it stopped feeling like… you know? That holiday feeling?"

"Actually yes." Christy turned the music down so she wouldn't have to talk over it. "I know exactly what you mean. It didn't feel like the holidays like it did when we were kids, I know that feeling. But it at least still brought joy. At least my brother and our friends weren't buried in the ground somewhere."

Julia started to cry. It was the first time Christy had seen her cry all day.

"I'm sorry, Jules. There's napkins in the glove compartment."

Julia opened it and found a sealed pack of tissues. She opened it and wiped away her tears. "I was just remembering something funny your brother had said. He was *such* a dork. We were asking each other what we asked for for Christmas that year, and I told him socks."

Christy laughed.

"And he said he didn't ask for anything up until now when he wished we were outside. And I said something like 'Outside the house? In snow up to here?' and he said yes, and I asked why, and he said because there was a mistletoe he had hung there."

Christy laughed until she cried. "Ah, good ole David."

"I'm glad I still have you in my life, Christy."

"And I'm glad I still have you. I don't know what I'd do without you. You're the best friend I ever had. I was just thinking earlier about the time I got the blue paint on my hands."

Julia laughed so hard that sound didn't come out. When she could finally speak, she said, "Oh gosh! Remember when we went back inside to wash your hands and I tried to make you open the doors?"

"Yeah, you bitch." Christy laughed. "That was a great day. The paint incident, our next class was canceled, we watched a movie instead and ordered pizza."

"More great days are ahead."

"You sure about that, Jules?"

"I'm positive."

Feliz Navidad came through the radio next.

Christy smiled, hummed with the music, then turned right when they came to the next light. She didn't need to use a GPS, she had looked at the directions enough times since they had settle on leaving for a hotel getaway during the anniversary.

This area of Raven Hill they passed through, still nowhere near the Asylum Resort, seemed a little different than all the rest of the town. It was only covered in a thin sheet of snow as opposed to monstrous mountains of it, and it reminded her of how things used to be. It reminded her of how little snow used to fall in Raven Hill, and made her wonder why there was such an abundance of it last year and this year.

After *Sleigh Ride* finished playing and *Santa Baby* blared through the speakers, Christy stopped at a burger joint called *Nicky's.*

"You hungry?" Christy asked. "I'm starving."

"Totally."

They went into the small brick building with a faded brown rooftop and hand-painted red and blue and yellow signs in the windows. Save for the two girls and the pictures of 1950s musicians and actors plastered on the walls, it was deserted. The silence was unsettling, and if Christy hadn't seen the two employees behind the counter she would've bolted back out the door. It was quiet—too quiet.

Christy ordered a burger, fries, and a chocolate shake, Julia had an Italian beef and a Sprite.

"Have you been here before?" Julia asked.

"No," Christy said, "but it seemed like a nice little place. And this food is good. Wonder why there aren't many people here."

"Well it's early December, and I wouldn't doubt it if most people are trying to leave Raven Hill after last year..."

"After it happened at that camp, I don't remember people leaving here for the summer."

"You didn't even hear about that until a few months ago."

Christy shrugged. "Sure. But people still aren't leaving for the summer."

"Yeah. Well who goes looking for burger joints this early on a December morning?"

"I guess you're right Jules. Might just be the time of day."

Julia reached over and stole a fry. "Delicious."

Christy emptied some of the container of fries onto Julia's tray. "Take some. They gave me so many."

"Don't mind if I do," Julia said. "Oh gosh, I'm gonna be so fat one day."

"You're a twig!"

"Oh no I'm not."

"What are you going to lose?" Christy asked. "Bone? *Grow up Heather, bulimia is* so *'87.*"

"I'll lose *anything* to keep my weight down."

"Well a couple fries won't make you obese. You're eating Italian beef anyways, that's not the healthiest thing."

"Whatever, Christy."

"If this isn't nice, Jules, I don't know what is. Aviana used to say that, whenever she was happy. It's a nice reminder that things aren't so bad."

Julia smiled. "This really is nice."

Christy reached back into her pocket and fumbled around with the change for a couple quarters. "I'm going to call my mom real quick. I forgot to before we left."

Julia took a bite and nodded.

Christy walked to the other end of Nicky's and slid her two quarters in, then dialed her mother's office number. After a few seconds of waiting, she picked up.

"Hello?"

"Hi, mom. How are you?"

"Great, Christy. Did you and Julia leave?"

"Yeah. We stopped at a place called Nicky's. They've got great burgers here. Anyways, I just wanted to call and tell you I love you, and that we were leaving."

"I love you too, honey. Maybe we'll come visit you two."

"Oh, you don't need to mom, it'll only be a week."

"Be safe."

"We will mom. We will. I'll call you from the hotel. I love you."

"I love you too. Talk to you soon. Say hi to Julia for me."

After she was done on the phone she turned back to look at Julia and thought she might've seen Julia steal a fry from her tray. Christy laughed then walked back to Julia and sat across from her again.

"My mom says hi."

"Well hello, Mrs. Morrison."

"Told her we'll call from the hotel, you can just tell her hi then. She offered to come visit us but I told her she didn't need to."

"Why would you do that? That would be sweet of her to visit."

"Just didn't seem like she needed to. It's just a hotel, it's just a little getaway from this fucked up experience."

Julia frowned. "Just be careful not to push her away. That can be easy to do when you're upset."

"I'm not pushing her away. Let's not argue about it."

"Whatever you say."

The girls fell silent while they finished up their meals. After they were done they emptied their trays into the garbage, Christy bought a refill, and they went back into her car and drove away from Nicky's.

"That was fantastic," Julia said. "Just fantastic. We should stop by on the way back from the hotel."

"Now if they had one of those by college, I *could* see you being fat." Christy laughed.

Julia frowned.

"Joking of course," Christy said. "But if they had one near us I bet we'd eat there all the time."

"No question about it."

Oh Holy Night came through the radio.

The car was heating up again, and coldness crept over the girls.

Christy yawned. "So you told David you asked for socks last year, huh? What did you ask for this year?"

"You want a lie or the truth?"

Christy laughed. "Both."

"If I had to lie, I'd say socks again. If I had to tell the truth…" she sighed. "I don't want to keep bogging you down with talk about it, but if I had to tell the truth, I wished for the pain to go away. I've been so scared for the last year."

"You aren't bogging me down, it's always on my mind," Christy said. "I don't know if I can ever get better. I'm the one that brought them all to their death. Hell, *you* even died, and that was all my fault."

"Please don't beat yourself up over it, Christy, you had no idea what was to happen."

Christy pulled over, parked the car in front of a random house, and her eyes filled with a waterfall of tears. *"I don't know if I can live with myself."*

Julia hugged her and ran her hand through her hair. "Now, now, it's okay. It'll all be okay. Just take it easy, just breathe, just—"

But Julia couldn't help it; she broke out in tears too.

For a while they sat there crying. Both of them were deeply broken.

What had happened could not be undone. Christy had apologized to all the families of her friends, and their opinions were much like Julia's—that it wasn't her fault—but she wished she could believe that. The guilt was frozen inside of her; even if it were a hundred degrees out she'd still be frozen on the inside. It wouldn't melt away like this snow would do by May or June. The guilt haunted her with every breath she took.

Christy wondered why she got to live. She wondered why it was the others instead of her. She *wished* it would've been her. The others did not deserve to die, and Christy couldn't be convinced one way or the other that she *did* deserve to live. What made it worse was that she had the opportunity to kill the sick son of a bitch, and that opportunity slipped through her hands. It all came back to her: the anger, the raw emotion, hitting him with the fire place poker, jamming it into his throat. Then the shock and pain she felt, the unsettling twisting in her guts, when she was informed by police that they did not find his body, nor was there any blood on the poker. Christy remembered screaming so loudly it hurt her throat for a week or two, and felt now like doing that again.

Deep down she didn't think guilt ever went away—it only increased as she looked back on the course of her life and remembered any time she had wronged David or one of her friends who were gone now, and it only made her feel worse. There were small times, like the time she didn't let Bekah copy her homework, or the time she wouldn't loan David $20 to cover his late fees at Blockbuster. There were also big times, the worst of which was accusing David of doing something to Mary.

Her soul grasped to keep the sound of their voices and laughs alive.

She knew how David felt about something similar, and from his own experience, she didn't think David had ever gotten better. David was not typically a bully—in fact, he was the one picked on in school. Especially elementary school. And when she was fed up with it, he picked on boy in his class named Sam. Sam was nice to him, but David knew Sam was an easy target, so he picked on him endlessly for the last two years of elementary school before they went their separate ways in junior high. It helped him feel better about himself.

But one day when they were in high school, Sam died in a car crash with another boy that David did not know, and for the first time since he was a little boy, Christy saw her brother cry.

David wrote an apology letter to Sam after he heard the news, then took it to the fire pit in the backyard and burned it. He hadn't seen Sam or said a word to him since the 6th grade, but he felt guilty for living. Sam was a nice boy, never hurt a fly, and David had picked on him and now he was dead. Although such a long time had passed, David felt endlessly guilty. Christy remembered all the times he told her about it. She hadn't known Sam personally but she thought it was a terrible that he had died. And she didn't know until now what David had felt.

Both were terribly different situations but the survivor's guilt stung just the same. Christy cried for David, Mary, Aviana, Bekah, and Katie, and soon she was crying for Sam too. She also cried as she started to remember what Julia looked like when she was stabbed. When The Butcher pulled her up by her hair, sank his knife inter her chest… Christy remembered the claret pumping out of her, watching the life slip away, watching the color drop out of her face.

A shudder twisted up Christy's back.

A WORD ON BOOK FIVE

Book 5 is so good. When I reread all 5 of the original books before republishing them without typos (2026 update: there were still typos. So many typos. I don't know how many typos could exist in such short books) and with better covers, I realized this might have been my favorite of the originals. It's such a good one, good characters, fun kills, cool ending. I can see myself getting better.

It's weird to think it almost didn't happen if I didn't scrap the original book 5 that I had. Originally book 5 was titled "DIG UP HER BONES."

It's cringe and awful but we will take a look, so you can see just how much a book can change.

EXCERPTS FROM DIG UP HER BONES, PART ONE

All was well in Raven Hill.

All was well for a while—it was so strange to say or to think, but it was well. Happiness was all the town knew for the past twenty years. The killings were over, and while what was spoken about them back then had already been more fiction than fact, the falsities grew even more plentifully now than ever. There was speculation over why this was so—over why the murders had ended—but not a soul in Raven Hill could tell. Somebody somewhere knew, but they had never come forward.

It seemed now that things would be fine forever in Raven Hill. Sure, there were still things that went wrong. Just the other day, Meredith Kircher heard in the news that somebody died in a hit and run, but that was nowhere near the level of terror that had once plagued her home town.

Meredith's blonde hair looked as if it was spun from pure sunshine; it tumbled down her shoulders and was plastered to olive skin with sweat. Burning sunlight blinded her momentarily as she looked out of the window—she had only just woken up and hadn't shut her curtains the night before. She almost never did, and it almost always resulted in her being awoken so abruptly at seven or seven-thirty when the blazing rays screamed down from the sun, past her home's rooftop, and through her window then into her eyes.

She loved to watch the stars—that was why she kept it open. She wondered what was out there—*if* there was anything out there, or if we were all alone.

Alone.

That was a funny word for a planet of billions on top of billions of people. Yet she still wondered if anything was out there, existing far away from here. Maybe they existed so far away that they'd die before they could ever make contact.

Meredith wondered if the universe expanded endlessly in every direction forever until there was no end, or if it ended somewhere. She wondered what the edge of existence—the end of the universes—might look like. She pictured a brick wall with a sign hung from a rusty nail, which would read: *Sorry, end of the line folks. No entry beyond this point.*

As she shielded her eyes from the sun, a cloud passed over it. Shade funneled into her room instantly. She looked around; her twin sister Angelica was still fast asleep. Angelica adored sleep, and it was in that way and that way only that the twins were opposites. Meredith never cared much for sleep—she was always fine in the mornings, unlike her sister who required sleeping until noon to be moderately energized and only partially groggy.

Meredith yawned; sat up; stretched.

She went down the hallway and to the kitchen and started to boil water for hardboiled eggs. As they started to boil, she fired up the coffee machine, then she found a pan and took the pack of bacon from the fridge. Mom and dad were finally taking a vacation together *alone* without the kids. Winter was underway—snow hadn't started yet, but outside was freezing—and what better time to go on a trip to Vegas than now?

They weren't gamblers—quite often, the Kirchers frowned upon it. But it was vacation, a time to have fun. And there'd be more to do in Vegas than solely gambling.

Meredith wanted to make it a perfect vacation for them, and since they'd be leaving soon, she wanted them to have a nice breakfast.

She turned on the TV, lowered the volume, and listened to the news as she finished breakfast. She poured two big cups of coffee—black, not even a spoonful of sugar or a dash of milk—peeled the eggs, and after she piled their plates with bacon, made them toast and cut it into triangles.

Lastly she set plates for herself and Angelica.

As she approached her parents' room, she heard their alarms going off. They moved around in bed and their springs made awful noises. The mattress was old and worn, and Meredith thought about buying them a new one while they were away.

"Breakfast is ready," she said. "It's on the table."

Her parents said thank you; she went down the hall back to her own room to wake her sister.

"Angie." she shook her. "Angieee wake up."

Angelica groaned, turned over, then her eyes cracked open before fluttering shut. "What do you want? What time is it?"

"I made breakfast. Come eat with mom and dad before they go."

"What time is it?"

"Just after eight."

"But it's *so* damn early!"

"You can sleep again after we take them to the airport."

Angelica wiped the crust from her eyes. "Then I'll be too awake to sleep."

"Is any of this important?" Meredith laughed. "Come on. The eggs are getting cold. Cold eggs are the worst."

Back at the kitchen table, mom and dad had already started eating before their daughters joined them.

"This breakfast is wonderful," Mom said.

"Thanks, girls," Dad said.

"Girls?" Meredith almost choked on her bacon. "I did all the work! Angelica just woke up three minutes ago."

Dad sipped his coffee. "Thanks *Meredith.*"

"Are you two excited?" Angelica asked. "Finally having a weekend without the kids since like, I don't know, you hitched."

"Are we having a weekend without you," Dad asked, "or are you having a weekend without us? No boys, no parties. I've got eyes and ears everywhere."

"No, dad," Angelica said.

"No guys allowed, got it," Meredith said. "Except for the pizza delivery man."

"And no alcohol," Mom said.

Meredith nodded. "No boys, no parties, no liquors, no crack, no meth, no mushrooms, no heroin, no weed. Is LSD fine?"

Mom held back a smile. “We’re trusting you girls.”

“Oh, mom.” Meredith picked at her toast. “You know you can trust us. We’re not even old enough to buy beer yet…”

“But give it a few months.” Angelica smiled. “Then we can.”

“My babies are almost twenty-one,” Mom said. “Where has the time gone?”

Dad grabbed her hand then kissed it. “You look exactly the same as you did back then.”

After breakfast it was time to get going.

Meredith and Angelica helped to pack their parents’ bags—which was about twenty suitcases for mom, and half of a carry-on for dad—then Meredith drove. The airport was fifteen minutes away, and despite Meredith’s love for outer space, it was one of her biggest fears. An airplane crash must’ve been, what, one in a million? But just that possibility, no matter how small, frightened her. But she had to remind herself it wasn’t as if she would be riding on an airplane every day. Her parents were just going from Raven Hill to Vegas. It wouldn’t be that long of a trip… they’d call in a few hours, letting them know they landed, and things would be fine. Then they could really get the day started.

Meredith and Angelica had plans. They weren’t huge plans, but they did intend to have some sort of party. Maybe a step down from a party—just a gathering. Shutting off all the lights in the basement and watching horror movies with friends while stuffing their faces. It would be great. It was something they didn’t have to wait for their parents to be out of town for—it was something they could do whenever they wanted—but things were always the most fun when there were no parents around. When it was just the kids, or just the kids and their friends. It was a sense of freedom.

Meredith pulled up to the curb of the building where many other cars were parked while passengers left those cars with bags. Meredith and Angelica stepped out of the car to help their parents with their bags, and after plentiful kisses goodbye, their parents hurried into the airport—triple checking their tickets were with them—and the girls went back into the car.

They couldn't have slammed the doors shut fast enough.

"They're finally gone!" Meredith smiled so wide it almost hurt.

"Time for all the meth we can handle!"

Meredith laughed so hard she didn't make a noise.

"Joking, of course," Angelica said.

"I'd hope you were joking."

Angelica shut her eyes then relaxed in her seat.

"I'm not carrying you inside if you fall asleep here."

"I can't hear you, I'm asleep."

"Oh gosh, this is so needed. Could you believe it took us this long to get them out of the house? Oh this is gonna be fun," Meredith said. "A whole week without them barging into our room without knocking."

"I'm glad, but I'm gonna miss having mom do the dishes." Angelica sighed. "I hate doing the dishes."

"We won't need dishes if we have takeout every meal."

Angelica stretched her arms and giggled. "That's true. But someone has to wash the dishes from this morning. Not it!"

"Awe man, I don't wanna be *it.* We need to flip a coin."

"In the car?"

"I asked you to flip a coin, Angie, not slaughter a pig and cook it for me. You say that like I asked you to run a marathon in here."

"I think you need better analogies, Meri." Angelica rolled her eyes. "Where'll I pull a coin from? My ass? Let me shit one out. You know me, an endless piggybank. I'll shit you a thousand silver dollars if you'd like."

Meredith made a gagging noise. "What is wrong with you?"

"We'll flip a coin when we're home. I don't bring change with me for drives to the airport."

"Whatever."

"Did something crawl up your butt today?" Angelica asked.

"What's with your obsession with butts?"

"I don't know. They're fun?"

"Okay I am *not* gonna discuss butts with you."

"Embrace the butts, Meri. Embrace the butts."

Meredith laughed, signaled, and made a left. They were almost home. It was looking like it would be an amazing week already with their parents.

She loved her twin. Angelica was the best sister and friend she could ask for. Except when she was talking about butts like she was right now.

Their winter break had started early. What was supposed to be a break from December tenth to January tenth had become a break from November fourteenth to January tenth. Their online classes they shared were scheduled to end in early December, but they were allowed to work at their own pace and had already collaborated together on answers for the finals. This semester they had both chosen to not take any classes in person at the college because they had gotten jobs together and wanted to work full time to earn extra money. They way they saw it: schoolwork in the morning, work from two o'clock to ten o'clock, then falling asleep as they ate whatever mom cooked that night. It was hectic at times but they made it work. In order to celebrate this week without their parents, they each requested the week off.

Life was great.

Meredith turned up the radio; Angelica had been talking but Meredith hadn't been paying attention. She was zoned out—so very zoned out in fact that she suddenly realized she hadn't been paying attention to the road, and wondered if she had possibly run a red light, and tried hard to remember if the light she just passed was green or not. Looking through the rearview, she could not tell at all. But they were safe and there wasn't an accident... so it probably was green.

"You know what movie we have to see?" Angelica asked.

"Which one?"

"We can probably still catch the *Carrie* remake. I'm sure it's still in theaters."

"Yeah. Doesn't look too scary."

"Horror movies are *supposed* to be scary."

Meredith nodded. "Yeah, but I don't quite like them too scary."

"I'll never forgive you for using a similar line when I wanted to see the new *Texas Chainsaw.*"

"You could've saw it on your own!" Meredith said.

"Oh, you know I hate going to the theater all alone. I feel like a loser."

"I just couldn't stomach another *Chainsaw* flick, that first one still makes my stomach hurt. Oh gosh, that hook—that movie is insane."

"That's the fun part about it," Angelica said. "I thought you liked being scared?"

"I do. It's just a love-hate thing. And I rather watch them at home than the theater. But *Carrie* should be fine. It's creepy, not scary."

"I see."

"Hey, we did go together to see *The Evil Dead* remake. What's with all these remakes though?"

"No idea, Meri."

"Now that was a fun one. I think that's my favorite franchise."

"Hmmm… *Nightmare on Elm Street.* For me." Angelica raised her fingers like claws. "One two, Freddy's coming for you!"

"More like you're coming for Freddy," Meredith said.

"Maybe I'll force you into watching that latest *Chainsaw* with me."

"Fine. I'll watch it."

"Woohoo, didn't take much convincing. If only you would've caved months ago."

"Well you really wanna watch it."

"This is nothing compared to how much I pestered you months ago."

"Yeah, you sent me the link to the trailer every day."

"It's a fun trailer."

"Totally."

Meredith parked in the garage; the garage and the car both needed a good cleaning. Maybe she'd take the car to the wash later, but she wouldn't clean the garage. It was cold out and she could barely stand the cold. Why did she live where the air hurt her face, she'd ask herself. And she had no clue.

Sunlight wormed through the slanted glass windows. The garage was old, dirty, tight. The narrow driveway leading up to it had new asphalt and was the complete and total opposite of what was inside. It felt as if parking in an abandoned building: it creaked. It almost shuddered. Bugs loved to fly around in the garage, against the ugly black ceiling and lightbulbs. Meredith wondered how long those bulbs had been there—she never recalled anyone changing them, and wondered how long they'd last. If they ever did go out, she did not want to be the one to have to get up there and change them.

"Is he outside?" Meredith asked.

"Didn't see him."

"Gosh, I hope he's not outside."

"I hope he's not either," Angelica said. "I didn't see him."

"Careful, if we don't move he can't see us."

"He isn't a T-Rex."

Meredith undid the lock on the door and stepped out with Angelica, then started to walk towards their house.

Their neighbor, Steve, waved and said, "Hey ladies!"

The girls waved back, then he started to walk over. He was raking leaves on the side of his house—they hadn't seen him from the garage but now they could see him filling up paper bags with leaves.

He came closer. "Your parents leave already?"

"Mhm," Angelica nodded.

Meredith fumbled with the key and finally got the front door open.

"Yeah they were telling me… Vegas, right?"

Meredith finally got the door open, and hurried inside as Angelica told him yes, then she hurried in after her. Steve was tall, pale, and a little too nice. He hadn't ever said anything explicitly suggestive to the girls but he always gave them the worst feeling. He was five or six years older than them, always covered in dirt, always up to something, and always eager to make some sort of conversation which always led to asking if the girls were alone. Why did he always ask that? Meredith had a bit of an idea but didn't like to think of it. She was just glad to be away from him.

"You moved."

"What?"

"I told you, Meri, he couldn't see you if you didn't move."

"Whatever."

Meredith made sure to shut the curtains tight before following her sister over to their room. When she stepped inside the room, Angelica was already flipping a quarter in the air. She caught it then flipped it again.

"What're we flipping for again, sis?" Angelica asked.

"Dishes," Meredith said. "Who gets to clean off wet food from the plates?"

"Why didn't you use paper plates?" Angelica frowned.

Meredith shrugged.

Angelica flipped the coin. As it left her fingers, she called, "Heads!"

Angelica caught the coin—it was on heads.

"I win," Angelica said. "You gotta clean 'em!"

"What? No! No! You're supposed to flip it when you catch it! You know, you catch it then flip it over. You only caught it, you didn't flip it. Redo."

"We not getting a redo!"

"Fine. Two out of three?"

"Okay. We'll let it land on the ground then, so there's no debate over flipping or whatever the hell."

Angelica tossed it in the air and called heads again. It came down, bounced off her bed, and rolled between the sisters. It was on heads again.

"There we go! Suck it!"

"Interference!" Meredith shrieked, almost laughing. "It can't hit the bed!"

"Oh geez. Luck is not on your side today, just clean them."

"Let me flip it."

"This one doesn't count if you flip it."

"Just let me do it!"

Meredith pried the coin from her sister, flipped it, and called tails. It landed on heads.

"Is this thing fucking rigged?" Meredith asked.

"Maybe it just doesn't like you." Angelica smiled. "Now go clean those eggy plates and all of that wet food."

Meredith did the walk of shame to the kitchen sink, turned on the water, and began to clean.

EXCERPTS FROM DIG UP HER BONES, PART TWO

UPSTAIRS WAS A SMALL hallway that gave way to their father's study. A room with a big oak desk in the corner, surrounded by bookshelves packed tightly with books. If Meredith had spent her entire life trying to read every book in this room, she'd never even make it a quarter of the way through. There were books he bought just to have something to read *eventually*—there was no possible way her dad would finish reading them all in his lifetime, and he was an avid reader. In addition to the books, there was a thick blue carpet that was recently installed, French impressionist paintings on the rare glimpse of wall where the bookshelves did not cover it, a fake plant next to his laptop on the desk, and two comfy couches for laying down with a good book.

Meredith perused the shelves. There was a mix of fiction and nonfiction, mostly classics like *East of Eden* by John Steinbeck. Her father was incredibly fond of Steinbeck, Hemingway, Faulkner, and Salinger.

She ran her hands along the spines—there was almost never a better feeling than running her hands along the endless spines of books. There wasn't any particular book she had in mind. The randomness was the fun part. Sometimes she would blindly grab a book off the shelf, and usually it was enjoyable. It was the nonfiction stuff that bored her, when she happened to get some lengthy book about the history of something dreadful, like Canada. There was on book she wanted to read, one her father would never let her see.

But she didn't grab a book—she was too shocked to.

Meredith gasped and stepped back after locking eyes with the creepy old man whose eyes did not blink. Then she turned away from the window and ran to the desk.

"What's all that noise?" Angelica called from the stairs.

Meredith didn't reply.

Who is that old man? she wondered. She had never seen him before, but the answer soon came to her. It was obvious: Steven's dad. Meredith had never seen Steven's parents—not that she wanted to—and had only *heard* about them despite being neighbors for so long.

She had in fact caught seen the mother once or twice but never the father. And although her eyes only held his for a moment, perhaps a moment and a half, his disgusting gaze would be etched in her mind forever like something carved on stone. His hair was almost completely white, making him look older than he might've been. He didn't look much older than fifty or fifty-one, and neither did his wife.

But there was something deeper to him, something disgusting. Something that didn't sit well with her. He seemed like… a cheap imitation of a human. As if he were an alien trying to conform to a skinsuit. Steven's dad did not smile, his lips formed into a straight line like a ruler. His back was hunched, and his wrinkles around his deeply sunken eyes made them seem like those of a monster, focused on and observing its prey.

"Jesus Christy," Meredith whispered.

When she heard the footsteps, she screamed. In that moment she pictured Steven's dad running up the stairway, but it was only Angelica storming in with worry painted on her face and half a sandwich in her hand.

"The fuck is going on?" Angelica asked.

Meredith couldn't see the window from where she sat—thank God—and didn't want to. She lifted her finger; pointed towards it. Angelica looked then screamed louder than Meredith had done, and ran to her sister.

The girls held each other at the desk.

"Is that Steven's dad?" Angelica asked.

"Well it must be!"

Angelica bit her lip. "Holy shit, he could scare the shit out of a toilet."

"Ohmigod, we need to lock all the doors. Oh God, I do *not* feel safe with that creep next door."

"That whole *family* of creeps!"

Meredith realized she had been gripping the arm of the chair rather hard, and loosened her grip. "Dad had told me... that Steven told him there was something wrong with his dad. But I've no idea what."

Angelica shivered. "I don't think it matters. Are you sure the front door is locked?"

"Yes, but I should double check. You get the back door."

Angelica nodded.

Meredith crept past the corner of the desk, made a run for the door, and after she reached it, glimpsed over at the window. The man was gone.

"He's gone," Meredith said in a shaky voice. "Come on!"

Angelica almost tripped over her own two feet; ran with Meredith out of the study.

As they went down the stairway, Meredith wondered why he had been staring in there as if he knew she was going to be in there. Was he planning on staring in there for hours until he saw somebody? It chilled her; made her sick. The way he looked into her eyes was as if he were waiting for her—it was a filthy, disgusting gaze. One that studied her sickeningly, even if it were only for a few seconds. She wondered if he had been looking through the window from the moment she stepped inside. She tried to go over in her head how long that had been from entry to realization—as she thought of this she was now in the downstairs hallway, running like the wind towards the front door—and as best she could figure, two or three minutes tops had passed from entering the room, studying the spines of books, to looking out the window.

Two or three sickly minutes of being stared at. Studied pervertedly. Being undressed with that sicko's eyes.

Her hand touched the knob; shivers crawled spider-like down her body. It was locked.

She peeked through the curtain out the window; he was not there, thankfully. Nobody was, only the sea of dead leaves that needed raking. Maybe they'd flip a coin for that later—although if they did, she was picking heads next time.

Meredith met Angelica in the kitchen.

"Was it locked?" Meredith asked.

"Yes, Meri," Angelica said, "it was."

"Holy hell..."

Angelica leaned over the skin, turned it on, and splashed water over her face. "This is gonna be a wild week, huh?"

"The wildest." Meredith took a seat at the kitchen table. "And to think, we didn't even need any horror movies to be scared."

"What else did dad tell you?" Angelica asked. "About that guy next door."

"No, nothing," Meredith replied. "Only that Steven had told him his dad had problems. But I don't know, dad didn't know much."

"Damn."

"Let's just breathe. All he did was look at us through the window."

"I can never go up there alone," Angelica said. "Never again. Oh God. Did he say anything to you before I came up?"

Meredith shivered. "I was looking at the shelves then saw him watching silently."

"I'll never understand why old men perverts watch through windows." Angelica crossed her arm. "That guys does it, everyone in movies does it. What's with old perverts and windows?"

"It's as close as they can get." Meredith laughed. "*It* probably doesn't work anymore."

"Oh geez. You'd know."

Meredith rolled her eyes. "Yeah right."

They went around the house and closed every curtain and made sure the windows were locked, even the ones upstairs. When they closed the curtains in the study, they couldn't see Steven's dad. But the curtains to the room he was in were closed too, and the girls wondered if he was secretly watching, secretly waiting, ready for them to return to the study so he could keep an eye on them.

But they wouldn't find that out. Their own curtains were shut now and neither planned on returning to the study until dad was home. And speaking of dad...

It was five o'clock and they hadn't heard from either parent yet.

Meredith said, "Mom and dad haven't texted you, right?"

They were halfway down the stairs when Angelica paused and reached into her pocket. Meredith was on the bottommost step looking up to her sister.

Angelica was pale; as pale as linen. "They haven't... they should've landed hours ago."

"We were so distracted with cleaning and with the perv next door I didn't realize..." Meredith pulled out her phone; looked through her messages. Turning back to see her sister's confused expression, "Nothing either."

"I hope you guys are just pranking me," Angelica said hopefully.

"Does it look like we're pranking you?" Meredith made one hand into a fist.

Angelica finally descended the stairs. "Let me call them."

The girls went to their room; sat on their respective beds while Angelica dialed their mother's number.

Meredith bit her nail while her sister waited on the phone.

It rang for a while; then, even from her bed, she could hear her mother's voicemail come through her sister's phone.

"That's weird... it rang... but..." Angelica said. "Mom would call, wouldn't she? She was nervous about leaving us."

"Try dad."

"Obviously."

Angelica dialed dad; same result. Voicemail.

Meredith gulped. "Are they okay?"

"How should I know?"

Before the sisters could continue arguing as they so often did, Angelica's phone rang.

She hurried to hit answer. It was mom.

"Mom!"

"Angelica! How are you and Meri?"

"Great, mom, just great!"

Meredith whispered, "Ask her why she didn't call."

"Why didn't you call mom? We were so worried about you and dad."

"Well, our luggage got lost and they had us waiting around for a while. Some way to start vacation huh? Our phones were in our bags. We just got them back and turned on when you called."

"Oh jeez."

"Are you sure you two are okay, honey?"

"Just a little jumpy. Hey, mom, can you put dad on real quick?"

While Angelica started talking to dad, Meredith bit her nail furiously until there was no more nail to bite, then she moved on to another finger.

Suddenly, she heard Angelica say, "What did you tell Meredith about Steve's dad?"

"Oh my gosh," Meredith whispered. "You did *not* just ask him that!"

"What now?" dad said.

"That creepy guy. What problems did he have?" Angelica asked.

"Why? Did he say something to you two?"

"No, no, dad. We just saw him from the window. He looks *weird!*"

"Ah, we shouldn't be gossiping about this girls. Tell Meri I'm disappointed in her."

"Oh, I will daddy."

They talked for a few more minutes but Angelica couldn't get anything out of him. Soon after they were off the phone, Meredith said, "You could've said that with a little tact."

"Sorry I didn't write it all down and run it by you first."

"Well there must not be anything that bad then, since dad didn't tell us. Guess it's nothing to worry about."

"What's for dinner, anyways." Angelica yawned.

"I feel like all you've done since they've left today is eat."

"Screw you!"

Meredith shrugged. "Yeah, I don't know what's for dinner. What do you want?"

"What do you want?"

"I hate picking, Angie."

"We both do."

"Are we flipping a coin again?"

"If you'd like."

Meredith looked around for the coin; she forgot where she left it.

Angie found a nickel and tossed it to Meredith. Meredith flipped it and called heads.

It landed on tails.

“Ha, looks like you’re picking!”

Meredith rolled her eyes. “Gosh. Well, we’re saving pizza for tomorrow, I think. Since we’re having friends over. Let’s see… Chinese?”

“We just had that last week.”

“And so we’re never gonna eat Chinese again then? Didn’t know there was a time limit between buying Chinese.”

“Okay. Let’s get Chinese.”

Meredith laughed. “Okay, sure. Let’s get ready.”

LOOSE ENDS

LOOSE ENDS

Book 4 ends with the remains of The Raven Hill Butcher being stolen. I did think about having a cult summon him again, but I felt myself straying at that part of the series and while I liked the book, I didn't want to get too crazy just yet. I felt myself losing my grasp on it with the book 5 struggles, and I decided to get back to basics with book 5. Camp slasher, straightforward, not explaining how The Butcher is back.

I don't think I'm ever gonna follow up on that idea because it's in a different timeline now. The only stuff that truly matters now is the stuff after the reboot.

THE FUTURE OF RAVEN HILL

THE FUTURE OF RAVEN HILL

As of 2026 there are ten books in this series. But I guarantee there'll be more.

I want to be taken seriously as a writer, and decided to change direction from writing goofy horror novels. But it's never something I'll abandon. And I wouldn't be surprised if one day this series has 100 books.

www.ingramcontent.com/pod-product-compliance
Lightning Source LLC
LaVergne TN
LVHW030906080826
845145LV00010B/2787

* 9 7 8 1 9 5 4 9 3 1 0 5 3 *